The Hargrave Deception

Also by E. Howard Hunt

The Berlin Ending
Undercover
Give Us This Day
A Gift for Gomala
Stranger In Town
Bimini Run
Limit of Darkness
East of Farewell

The Hargrave Deception

E. Howard Hunt

STEIN AND DAY/*Publishers*/New York

First published in 1980
Copyright © 1980 by E. Howard Hunt
All rights reserved
Designed by Louis Ditizio
Printed in the United States of America
Stein and Day/ *Publishers*/Scarborough House
Briarcliff Manor, N.Y. 10510

Library of Congress Cataloging in Publication Data
Hunt, E. Howard, 1918-
    The Hargrave deception.

    I. Title.
PZ3.H9123Har   [PS3515.I5425]   813'.54   79-3889
ISBN 0-8128-2714-7

This book is a work of fiction and the characters and events depicted in it are entirely imaginary. The author has not intended that readers infer parallels between actual persons and the characters of this book.

E. Howard Hunt
Miami, Florida

For Laura, with love.

I

Non semper ea sunt quae videntur.

Phaedrus

. . . things are not what they seem.

Longfellow

ONE

Later, Morgan remembered that it had all begun on a day that was unusually fine and promising—until the men from Washington appeared. And afterward, nothing was ever again the same.

Before dawn he dropped a six-pack into the boat's fish chest and covered it with crushed ice. Tanks filled with diesel, he cast off bow and stern lines, hauled frayed fenders aboard his forty-foot sport fisherman, and headed out of the crowded marina leaving Key West's few lights astern.

As the channel deepened Morgan climbed the tuna tower and guided the boat from duplicate controls. The sea was calm, the current only a few knots from the southwest. When he could no longer see Martello Tower astern, he climbed down, unlimbered the outrigger poles, and baited their two lines with long-beaked ballyhoos.

For a while he trolled the near edge of the Gulf Stream seeing its color deepen to indigo as the sun rose beyond the distant Keys. Then his unaided eyes made out a flock of seabirds wheeling and plunging into a patch of water foaming with the frantic churning of baitfish. Morgan turned the wheel and shoved the throttle ahead, scanning the plummeting pelicans, watching sharp-beaked gulls slash and soar until he could see the backfins of the hunter pack: kingfish feeding voraciously.

Slowing, he guided his glistening baits ahead of the ravenous kings and saw both lines snap free. Reeling first one then the other rod he horsed two good-sized kings over the transom and into the ice chest. Then he bent on shiny spoons and was rewarded with immediate strikes. After boating a dozen kings, Morgan popped open an Olympia and drank thirstily. The sun was ten degrees above the horizon and already it warmed his half-naked body. Nearly six feet and deeply tanned, he was in prime physical condition although he was nearing fifty. His salt-and-pepper hair was long, nearly reaching his shoulders, but his beard was trim.

Now he put on sunglasses and climbed the tuna tower again, hearing an occasional thump from the ice chest as a dying kingfish fought restriction and death. In the distance he could see a tanker hull-down on the horizon, heading along the sea lane to the Gulf from Vera Cruz. Less than a mile away a Russian trawler—distinguishable by its Cyrillic letters—plundered the largesse of the Stream. Morgan finished the beer and wiped his sunburned lips. Squinting, he noticed a long weed line at the edge of the Stream and smiled at this nearly infallible indication of dolphin. He shifted the engines into neutral and turned his boat alongside the drifting kelp, then lowered a spoon, free-spooling it to thirty or forty feet where it was quickly taken. Morgan reeled the fish upward until he could see it darting and trying to run, a medium-size female dolphin. Setting the drag he fitted the rod butt in a gunwale holder and watched the dolphin school gather protectively around the hooked female.

With the other rod he fished the school until he had boated two big blunt-nosed bulls and three more females, admiring as he always did—almost in awe—their gold-and-azure bodies, then hating the death that stilled and grayed the flashing colors. Finally he reeled in his first catch, killing her with a hard blow of the gaff's rounded end.

Morgan knew that he could have caught the entire school had he wanted to, but his ice chest held enough for his needs—and Marisa's— with plenty left to sell. And dolphin was the finest eating-fish in the Caribbean. So he secured the outriggers, reeled in the monofilament lines and sipped a beer as he steered *El Gallo* back toward Key West. Automatically his eyes scanned the east for the tall water tank, Martello Tower, and the other easy aids to navigation; when he saw the first, he became watchful for buoys and other boats. Barefoot, he felt the engines' smooth vibration through the deck-board, heard the rhythmic breaking of small waves at the bow, and reflected that it was now almost two years since he had left the north and wandered to the Keys after a series of personal disasters that involved his career, his marriage, his children, and his country. At first he had felt himself a refugee, alienated from everything he had known. Then he had bought the boat and soon afterward met Marisa, and gradually his empty life took on enough dimension to isolate the despair he had felt before.

12

In Key West Morgan had made few friends, eliminating at the onset all who asked about his past. Bartenders, waiters, and old Conch Town fishermen had been incurious, accepting him as part of Key West's diversity. Seasonally came the rucksack kids, hitchhiking, bicycling to the sun and unpredictable adventure; affluent tourists to fish and gourmandize on the city's distinctive cuisine. And there was the self-replenishing colony of pot-bellied males and sleek, androgynous, young consorts who paired beside resort pools and tenderly oiled each other's hairless bodies, tanning under the day-long sun.

There was bolita and cock-fighting and drug-dealing, the occasional results of which floated swollen and disfigured onto the beaches, eyes and soft flesh eaten by the crabs.

Often at sea in the late afternoon Morgan had seen old, low-flying planes drop plastic-wrapped bales of marijuana into the water for recovery by waiting boats that were fast enough to outrun the Coast Guard's heavier craft. And the prevalence of pot was another attraction to the peripatetic young. Marisa smoked it, but as a nonsmoker Morgan found the heavy, oily stench of the weed offensive and preferred a few drinks in the evening as a relaxant. Most of his life had been a model of conformity, but he declined to become morally exercised over the use of pot or other drugs by those who enjoyed them. His choice was simply to abstain.

There was treasure hunting, too, most of it surreptitious to avoid State or Federal intervention and the violence of competitors. Morgan had recovered some coral-crusted gold and silver coins from a hundred feet of water on the windward side of a coral finger beyond the Dry Tortugas. Diving for lobster with Marisa he had noticed a scatter of ballast stones on the sandy bottom and followed them to a bronze cannon, then another, both bearing the royal arms of Spain. Between them had been the little clumps of shell and coral that turned out to be Spanish coins. In Marisa's kitchen he cleaned them first with acid, then restored them in a simple electrolytic bath. Marisa sold them in Mérida and Antigua and other islands of the Caribbean where she bought fabrics and prints for her Fort Street boutique.

Returning to the site at night to avoid curious boats and aircraft, they had dived for other coins until the cache gave out. There was more down there, Morgan was sure, but currents shifted the sand, hiding and obscuring objects on the bottom, and thorough exploration would mean a barge-mounted suction hose, drawing other treasure hunters like jackals to the feast. But the cannon remained, too heavy to lift out unaided, and principally useful as a marker for some future time.

Now he could see the town's low profile, the white hulls and masts of harbor boats, and he turned *El Gallo* into the channel wondering how much of his catch he could sell. Close to the pier he backed down, easing the hull alongside, dropping over the gray canvas fenders and tossing bow and stern lines to old Pedro who worked the pier for handouts of coins, liquor, and fish. Toward the shore end of the pier Morgan could see a charter captain hauling on tackle to hoist skyward a sailfish so small it should have been released without gaffing. Shutting down the engines he snorted at the needless waste of gamefish and walked aft to the ice chest where Pedro was tossing kings and dolphin onto the pier. Morgan handed Pedro an Olympia and heard the old man say, "*Gracias. Salud*," toasting briefly with the dripping can. Then when he had gulped a mouthful, Pedro said, "Men looking for you."

Morgan glanced at the pier's far end where the brave tourist fishermen were unlimbering several thousand dollars' worth of photographic equipment to record the trophy of their epic battle.

"They ask for me—or just the boat?"

"*Ambos.*"

Both. No one had bothered him in a long time. Perhaps these men only wanted to fish.

He sat on the concrete pier, his bare feet resting on the varnished gunwale, and watched Pedro start to gut and clean the morning's catch. The foot-long curved knife was razor-honed, and it sliced cleanly through slack belly flesh, severed vertebra, and spiny fins.

"Save me some *pejerrey* steaks and two dolphin fillets," he told Pedro as buyers gathered: two from restaurants near Mallory Square, and several market-wise Conch housewives who haggled over the per-pound price. Pelicans had gathered, too, swooping onto the water for fish heads and entrails, tugging angrily over prized portions. Gulls orbited above, waiting their turn at the smaller morsels, and below, nosing the pier pilings, were psychedelic-colored parrotfish.

The sun was hot on his back but he could feel an on-shore freshening breeze. Pedro handed him sixty-three dollars and Morgan gave him seven. Wrapping Morgan's steaks and fillets in newspaper, Pedro began hosing down the cleaning stand, then the afterdeck of Morgan's boat.

From somewhere behind him came the synthetic *toot-toot* of the

Conch tour train that carried visitors to the town's few tourist sites. Morgan pulled on worn sneakers and a T-shirt, said, "Thanks, *viejo,*" and got the last Olympia from the ice chest. As he sipped he watched Pedro wander off toward a homing boat, hoping to help with its catch, too.

It was then that Morgan saw the two men coming down the pier toward him.

In a town where T-shirts were standard wear and guayabera shirts qualified as formal attire, the two men were as noticeable as whales in an aquarium. They wore suits, shirts, and ties, and one had a locally-made palm-leaf hat. Black shoes and no flare to their trousers. As they noticed Morgan watching their progress they exchanged brief words without breaking stride. White hands and faces marked them as recent arrivals.

Morgan wondered from where.

He moved into the swivel pilot chair, and heard the scrape of hard soles on the pier.

"Mr. Morgan?"

Inquiring about his treasure cache? State men? Feds?

"I'm David Morgan."

"We'd like to come aboard, talk to you."

He turned in his chair and faced them. The one with the hat was the older, maybe thirty-five. The younger man had sandy hair and a meager mustache. Instinctively Morgan disliked them, wanted them gone. He had no unfinished business with men of their sort, and their unanticipated arrival made him feel apprehensive, cautious.

"Talk about what?" he asked.

"This really ought to be done in private."

"Oh, hell, come aboard."

They stepped over the gunwale, stood in the sun of the afterdeck. From the shade of the overhead Morgan eyed them.

Palm Hat said, "You've grown a beard."

"So I have. And I need a manicure. What else?"

Palm Hat glanced at his wristwatch. "The Air Florida flight to Miami leaves in just about an hour." He stepped closer to Morgan.

"So?"

"In Miami," Palm Hat said, "you'll have a fifty-two minute layover before your Eastern flight takes off."

"To where?"

"Washington," Sandy Mustache said. He pulled a ticket envelope from an inside pocket.

Morgan ignored it. "Who's paying my fare? Somebody want my views on inflation?" Sandy Mustache laughed. "School busing?" He shook his head. "I'm a dropout, fellows, I don't even read *Time* any more, just the local for fishing news." Morgan glanced down at the envelope and said, "Put it away, kids. Not interested."

Palm Hat said, "I think you should be reasonable, Mr. Morgan." There was an edge to his voice.

"I think you're wasting my time. Bug off."

Palm Hat said, "You can travel on your own, or you can travel with us, that's our orders."

"From who?"

They exchanged glances. The younger man said, "Mr. Dobbs."

"Mmmmmm. I read he'd become Director. Risen like a Phoenix from the ashes I left behind."

"There's money in it," Palm Hat said. "From what I've seen you could use some."

"Couldn't we all? No matter how we economize there's never quite enough. You can tell Bob Dobbs I'll manage without his help."

"But you *do* take help from the lady," the younger man said softly. "So. . . ."

Morgan slapped the man's face hard, backhanding the cheeks, bringing a bright spurt of blood to the upper lip. Half-turning he glimpsed metal in the other's hand, kicked at it and a pistol clattered onto the deck. In a crouch Morgan snatched up the pistol, cocked it and covered the two men.

Palm Hat was gripping his wrist, knuckles white around it. The other man pressed a handkerchief to his face, a spray of blood on his tie and shirt.

"You assholes," Morgan grated as their eyes widened, "I'll give you ten seconds to clear the boat. Tell Dobbs I'll meet him, but not at Langley, not in Washington. Atlanta's about right. He can come alone or not at all." Morgan eyed the two emissaries. "The limp muscle you provide, he's better off without. Now fuck off."

Wordlessly they clambered onto the pier. Morgan ejected the chambered shell, slid out the magazine and dropped it into the water. "Catch," he said, and tossed the .38 at them. "I wouldn't want to be accused of keeping government property."

Sandy Mustache stooped for the pistol, pocketed it shamefacedly.

16

The two men walked quickly away. When they reached the shore end of the pier Morgan looked down at his hands; to his surprise, they were trembling slightly.

"Shit," he said and took a deep breath. So they knew about him, Marisa, where to reach out and find him.

He had always accepted that they had the capability of keeping tabs wherever he went, however he dressed, whatever he did. Total severance was unheard of.

Dobbs.

Morgan shook his head. The appointment could have been anticipated. In an era when national intelligence was being repudiated and downgraded by the administration, sallow Bob Dobbs was a natural, almost irresistible, choice. Dobbs had drifted up from minor desks in the Clandestine Services to become lackey and bag carrier for senior men now gone. Then, carefully, Dobbs had stayed aloof from operations, becoming instead an administrator, a panelist, Agency representative on countless do-nothing boards composed of equally careful, skirt-clean types from State, Defense, and Treasury. Dobbs had avoided Congressional inquiries, steered clear of nasty questions and the TV lens.

Without perjuring himself.

Because as far as Morgan knew, Dobbs had never recruited an agent, never kept surveillance on a target, never approached a Soviet diplomat.

Never exposed himself to danger.

And so in a new era when all the unpleasantness of the intelligence business was supposed to be conducted by satellite photography, a man like Dobbs had been placed in charge.

Dobbs could be counted on to slant national estimates in keeping with administration priorities, budget and policy preconceptions. Bob Dobbs would never be *vox clamantis in deserto.* For the President, the Director would be a team player.

Morgan wondered what Dobbs had to convey in a personal meeting. Their last confrontation had been brief and cold, but Dobbs had not then reached the summit. Not that total power would overcome his basic deficiencies or even permit Dobbs the luxury of occasional relaxation. The contrary seemed more logical: His craftiness would now turn to self-preservation so that he would be permitted to remain in the job by succeeding administrations, grow gray, even be revered by generations who knew not the Bob Dobbs of old.

Morgan remembered that five or six years ago Dobbs, as Executive Director, had begun cultivating powerful senior Senators and Congressmen, providing them with information tailored to their particular causes and prejudices. Nor had Dobbs been lax in socializing with newcomers to Capitol Hill who, in Dobbs's view, were likely to stay and gain seniority.

So when the Agency had its collective back to the wall, when Capitol Hill with the tacit consent of the White House began dismembering the Agency, Dobbs—by then Deputy Director—had not a word to say in its defense. In consequence, much good was said of him by Senators to the media, and by the media to the public and the politicians. At last, it was proclaimed, a *responsible* career man had been found, one who spoke out against the Agency's darker acts, who was unafraid to denounce the guilty, who called for a clean slate, a reversion to a time in America when gentlemen did not read each other's mail.

While Dobbs smiled and polished his rimless lenses, his committed colleagues went down the tube. That was how they broke my back, Morgan told himself.

Feeling pressure from the beer, Morgan went below and relieved himself in the head. Then he checked bilges, oil and fuel levels, and emerged on deck to lock the cabin door. His boat had dropped a few inches on the ebbing tide but there was ample slack in the lines. Pedro was not an educated man but he knew his job.

Unlike Bob Dobbs.

He pocketed the ignition key, picked up the package of fresh fish and stepped onto the pier. Walking along it, he nodded, waved at other captains, returned the greetings of souvenir vendors until he reached the Square. Angling across it, Morgan made for Buster's Bar with its overhead wood-blade fans, race-track shaped bar, and dim lighting. It was a cool and musty place, sawdust on the floor and bottle-rings varnished into the table tops. A place for working people to relax away from blue-jeaned freaks and prying tourists. Morgan eased onto a bar stool and passed his package to Buster who slid it into the refrigerator and, without being asked, placed a dripping schooner in front of Morgan, then a dozen shrimp steamed in beer, laurel, and peppercorns. Morgan sipped from the big glass, shelled shrimp, and deveined them with a toothpick, suppressing the memory of recent events by gazing at the broken player piano, the dusty mounted fish on the walls, old ray harpoons, and stumpy boat rods with Vom Hofe reels, the kind used fifty years ago when big marlin prowled the offshore waters and records were broken twice a year.

"What's new, David?" Buster asked. He was a short brown man whose dark eyes and utterly black hair showed his Cuban heritage.

"Caught a few this morning," Morgan replied. "Lots of kings out there if you're interested. Dolphin, too." He crunched a cool, spicy shrimp.

"Let's go this week. My boat."

Morgan nodded. Wiping foam from his lips he said, "Anyone asking about me?"

Elbows on the bar, Buster said, "Like who?"

"Couple of well-dressed palefaces."

"They didn't brace me, but why should anyone come asking about you? You're not on parole."

"No particular reason. These two came to the boat a while back. They got overly familiar and I persuaded them to leave."

Buster crossed himself. "*Ave Maria.*"

Morgan swallowed his final shrimp, washed it down with beer and laid money on the bar. As he got off the stool he said, "Okay, we'll do some fishing."

"*Estamos.* Respects to Marisa."

"*Seguro.*" He retrieved the fish package and walked slowly and thoughtfully to Fort Street where there was a big display window set into a freshly-painted store facade surmounted with the lime-green name: *Marisa's.*

He had not seen her since leaving the bed where she lay naked but for the sheet that covered her rump. Now at midday she wore a loose island-print skirt and matching halter that showed that richness of her breasts. Her dark hair was gathered behind her head with a turquoise ring. White teeth, full lips, crescent eyebrows, dark eyes, and café-au-lait skin made her seem more Hawaiian than the full-blooded Cuban she was. Seeing Morgan enter, Marisa left her customer, padded to him on leather sandals, and rose on tiptoes to kiss his cheek. "Any luck, *querido?*"

"It's not luck, skill." His nose nuzzled the top of her head.

"I missed you," she murmured. "When you leave, I always wonder will you come back. Please wake me, David. I could have made your coffee."

"Made it myself." He tapped his package. "Fish for dinner. In the mood?"

"If you'll let me fix it. *Mais oui, toujours.*"

Marisa Isabela Pardo de la Costa was not a Calle Ocho girl from Miami's Little Havana, but granddaughter of a Cuban diplomat and a graduate in romance languages of the University of Miami. She was roughly half Morgan's age, and he never ceased wondering what in him attracted her. Between them there was no contract; he shared her house and they shared each others' lives.

"Have you had lunch?" she asked.

"I stopped at Buster's."

"Just as well. I should do without. You don't want a thick-waisted Cuban broad," she said with a touch of coquetry. "Do you?"

"Hell, I take 'em as they come." He patted her hip affectionately. "Go on, make some sales, earn some money. I've been told you're keeping me."

"Am I? I thought it was the other way around."

He kissed her cheek and left the shop.

He walked away from the tourist center to a cobbled street whose root-cracked sidewalk was overhung with magnolia, tulip trees, and bearded Spanish oak. Sago and cane palms grew in profusion, thrusting branches through fence pickets, in places half-blocking the walk. A noble banyan dropped spindly roots from low, spreading branches. Flowers overflowed window boxes, surrounded the old Bahama houses with splashes of vivid color. Houses built of driftwood or ships' planking, with gingerbread cornices and elaborate, melancholy widow's walks. This was the part of town he liked, no motels or neon signs; away from noisy drunks, street kids raving on a drug high. No stench of hamburger grease or filling-station oil.

Her house was white-shuttered, the clapboards lime-green, pastel touches here and there, according to her own design. Like many transplanted Cubans Marisa had a whole galaxy of relatives, most in the Miami area, others in California, Texas, and Chicago. Some lived marginally, others were well off. A contractor uncle built expensive condominiums an architect cousin designed. In keeping with tradition the structure of her family was extensive, but Marisa had broken through the web of tradition by not attending Catholic schools, by living away from home and establishing an independent life. For that, Morgan was grateful.

As always the door was unlocked. He walked in, set the fish in the refrigerator and went upstairs. Stretched out on the balcony in a plant-shaded corner was their gray-and-white striped cat. El Tigre they called him, supposing that he was one of the Whitehead Street multitude who bestowed his regal presence on their home. El Tigre was sleeping, but his paws opened, extending the long claws, then curled again.

Morgan got into the shower. Toweled dry, he pulled down the bamboo curtains and slept until early evening when Marisa's kiss awakened him.

She had made lime rickeys, taking hers to the shower while he drank and listened to the radio news. Then she returned, body glistening with moisture, her dark delta shimmering and smooth as mink. Seating herself carefully beside Morgan she touched her glass to his. "*Nuestro amor*," she said throatily and drank.

He grinned at her. "If I ever write a book I'll call it *The Old Man and the Girl*."

She frowned. "*Prohibido*," she said. "What do I have to do to seduce you?"

"Hardly anything." He leaned forward and kissed each small nipple, her lips, and open mouth.

Later they feasted on broiled dolphin and fried *plátano*, drinking a chilled chablis-type Paternina that Morgan had come to know in Spain. Afterward he sipped Felipe II brandy while Marisa sang to her guitar, and toward ten o'clock they went to bed where they fell asleep in each other's arms, moonlight filtering through the slatted blinds across their bodies and the bed.

Morgan was deep in early sleep when the telephone rang. He answered groggily, and it was Robert Dobbs.

TWO

THE thin, contained voice of the Director said, "Sorry about the hour. I didn't get your message until a short while ago."

Morgan swallowed and blinked, trying to come fully awake. With Dobbs recording every word it was important to be precise. He sat up, keeping his voice low, hoping not to disturb Marisa's sleep.

"Your messengers were about as intimidating as Mork and Mindy. What's on your mind, Bob?"

"I want to talk to you."

"Is a plan afoot to rehabilitate me? Or do you just want a palaver?"

"Neither, actually."

"Then you must be worried about me. If a talk's in order it'll be on neutral turf."

"You mentioned Atlanta. Agreed."

"Alone."

"I agree to that, too. Shall I prepay your ticket?"

"I'll collect at your end." He took a deep breath. So far so good. Beside him Marisa stirred. One hand reached out in her sleep, touched his thigh and stayed there reassured by the contact. "In front of the Regency there's a fountain. I'll be there at four. If you stake the area I'll know."

"I'm sure you would. I appreciate this, David, and tomorrow I'll express it in concrete terms."

"Always the merchant," Morgan said and hung up.

They would be expecting him to fly to the Atlanta airport so he would go by other means. That would disconcert Dobbs, embarrass the Atlanta office. Morgan drew up his knees and rested his arms on them. Already his mind was surging ahead. He wanted to be in downtown Atlanta an hour ahead of Dobbs, and that meant an early start. Using his phone was no good, too much chance they'd already put a tap on it. Airline offices were closed in any case. But by six it would be light enough to fly non-sked from the airport. Morgan sighed: He had considerable travel ahead of him; Dobbs's Agency Lear would get him to Atlanta in an hour and a half, with a limousine to meet and whisk him into town.

Rising gently off the bed, Morgan crossed to the illuminated alarm and set it for four o'clock. Even then there would be little he could tell Marisa; that would have to wait until his return.

Assuming a return.

Morgan got back into bed, clasped the woman's hand in his, and stared at the dark ceiling until sleep came.

He choked off the alarm. Marisa stirred but did not waken. Quickly, he showered, shaved, and dressed in a business suit that smelled mildly of mildew. Nothing he could do about it. He packed a small suitcase with shaving gear and a clean shirt and took some money from a hidden hole in the frame of the wooden bed. Then he made coffee in a glass filter, sweetening it synthetically, grated cheddar across a split muffin and broiled it under the oven grill until the cheese melted.

As he breakfasted he thought of his son and daughter; they would be rising about now, but not his ex-wife. Janice had always loved her morning sleep, seldom stirred until noon. Santa Barbara was just about right for her, he reflected; affluent, good country clubs and plenty of action for the middle-aged cocktail crowd. As he rinsed his few dishes he wondered how and why they had stayed together so long. For the children's sake had been the prevailing argument, but when her chance came, the children had been the last item on Janice's mind.

Not the last, he corrected, the penultimate; I was the last, the least for whom she felt concern. If she felt anything at all.

Returning to the bedroom, Morgan sat on the edge of the bed and kissed Marisa's cheek. Her eyes fluttered open, then her body started and she sat up in alarm. "Wha . . . you're dressed. Where you going?" Her eyes sought the clock's illuminated dial.

"A man from my past wants to see me. I'm going to meet him in Atlanta."

"Planes don't leave so early." Her face was troubled.

"Pollock's going to take me," he said soothingly, "and if I have any choice I'll be back soon."

24

"When?" She gripped his hand as though to relinquish it would be to lose him.

"Tonight sometime." He glanced at the phone. "I won't call."

"It's the government, isn't it?"

"Part of it." He kissed her lips. "You know where the money is?"

"Of course."

"And the revolver."

She drew the sheet up over her breasts.

"David, you're coming back, aren't you?"

He breathed deeply; this was the hardest part. "Of course I'll come back. Don't let anyone in the house. Keep it locked day and night. No gas company men, no telephone repairmen, no cops, and especially no palefaces from the mainland."

"What am I supposed to make of all this?"

"Nothing. Yesterday two men from Washington came to the boat; I didn't want to alarm you. They know I live with you. I don't know what those people may try to get me into, but my instincts are negative and that's all I have to go on. Don't be frightened, *querida,* but be careful."

He kissed her full on the mouth, her taut fingers gripped his back. "Now the final thing: the gun. I want you to keep it beside you, here in the night table drawer." He got up, went to the old bureau and opened the top right drawer. Feeling underneath he stripped retaining tape from the revolver, felt the dry smoothness of the enveloping condom and carried the .38 back to the bed. "You don't have to peel off the rubber," he told her. "If you ever have to, just point and pull the trigger. A millimeter of rubber won't slow the bullet." He put the weapon into the night table drawer and closed it.

Soft as the sound was, it carried a harmonic of finality.

When he transferred the .38 from his boat she had laughed at the condom. Then he had explained that weapons rust and corrode in salt air, hence the application of the rubber to keep the revolver airtight. Another Agency technique.

Her voice broke the silence. "Couldn't I go with you?"

He shook his head and her lips formed a brief, nervous smile.

"A girl has to ask."

"Of course," he said.

"Love me?"

"You know I do." He kissed her forehead, then rose. "Now go back to sleep."

"Fat chance."

"Try."

Morgan left the bedroom, picked up his travel bag and turned out the kitchen lights. At the front door he set the lock, then walked down the three stone steps and passed through the front garden, air laden with jasmine. Before he opened the sidewalk gate he glanced up and down the street, saw no blacked-out cars, no surveillants, turned to his right and went four blocks before taking Eaton Street to a pink-painted house whose gate was topped with a jingling bell. Overhead the sky was beginning to lighten; the night-long breeze had fallen away. From its invisible nest a bird began its three-note morning call.

He rang the doorbell four times before Pollock's muffled voice shouted, "Awright, awright, I'm comin'."

Pollock, short, balding, heavyset, with a forest of thick chest hair, stumbled to the screen door and stared out at Morgan. A roll of flesh hung down over the drawstring of his pajama bottoms.

"David! What the hell?"

"Not so loud."

"Okay, okay, get the hell in." He stood aside to let Morgan enter, belched, and scratched his belly hair. "I was sleepin' good," he announced as they moved into the living room. "This better be important."

"Get on your flying shoes. We're taking a trip."

"Yeah? Where to?"

"Tampa. Take you what—two hours?"

"Less." He yawned and shook his head as though to snap out of his grogginess. "When you wanta go?"

"Plane gassed?"

"Sure."

"Then we'll go now."

Pollock nodded. "Gotta charge you for the gas."

Morgan took a hundred-dollar bill from his wallet and slid it under the drawstring. "One thing—don't clear for Tampa, make it Freeport or Miami or Orlando."

"You're the client. Maybe I won't clear at all." He moved into the depths of the house. Morgan heard the hiss of the gas jet, tapwater running into a pan. "Don't let this boil away," Pollock called. "I'll pull on a shirt and we'll have coffee."

Pollock hadn't turned on any lights, Morgan noticed, then heard stair risers take the pilot's weight. Floor planking creaked overhead.

26

For years Pollock had flown for the Agency: Germany, the Congo, Tibet, Turkey, the Balkans, Nicaragua, Yemen, Paraguay, Laos . . . until there was no further need for his services. Then, like other contract pilots, he had financed a plane with his termination pay and set up a one-man charter service that had everything but enough passengers.

Pollock drove his battered Land Rover to the General Aviation side of the field, parked it, and they walked to where the twin Cessna was tied down. "Nobody in the operations shack yet," Pollock said, as he unlocked the door. "Nor in the tower, for that matter. So we'll pick up the weather on the way. Good to see you, old buddy, how you been?"

"Fine."

"The missus?"

"Sensational."

Morgan buckled the safety belt across his lap. He was in the copilot's seat although the interior held six passengers. Pollock hit the starboard starting button. "Man, after what you went through you deserve her. And a hell of a lot more." He glanced at the limp windsock, said, "Let's go."

They took off over the water, climbed steadily to eight thousand and when Pollock had trimmed the tabs he locked in the auto pilot and sat back, fingers meshed over his Buddha-belly. Morgan dozed, found his chin on his chest and woke, then dozed again. Without realizing it he slept, lulled by the engines' steady throb, wakening when the wheels hit the Tampa runway.

"Since this is kind of an inconspicuous flight," Pollock said, "I'll drop you at the transient building and keep going. Hell, I'll be back before they miss me."

Morgan got out, hair blowing in the prop wash while Pollock handed down his bag. A wave of the hand and Pollock turned the Cessna back onto the runway and Morgan went into the air-conditioned corridor. He used the nearest pay phone to reserve a seat on a flight to Macon, leaving in an hour and a half. Then he lugged his bag into the terminal building and found the barber shop just opening.

From a series of wall photographs he chose a hair style to his liking. Nodding, the barber said, "A little tinting, perhaps? Take years off of you."

"Why not?" Morgan settled back.

Forty minutes later, shaved, hair styled and blow-dried, gray areas no longer noticeable, Morgan left the barber shop, went to the Southern counter and picked up the ticket he had reserved in another name. There was time for food, so he ate country ham and scrambled eggs, a hot maple Danish, juice, and coffee before riding the monorail out to the waiting plane. Two stops later he deplaned at Macon and cabbed downtown to the Trailways terminal. It was now noon and the bus would get him to Atlanta by 2:45. While he waited for the bus gate to open he thought of phoning Marisa to soothe her after what must have been his rather dramatic departure, deciding against it, passing the remaining time reading a newspaper. A Key West item caught his eye: The Coast Guard cutter *Steadfast* had intercepted a Colombian freighter at sea and confiscated fifty-seven tons of pot whose street value was estimated at forty-three million dollars.

In the 20s Key West fishermen had run rum for a few bucks a load. Now with pot at three-quarters of a million per ton it was no wonder so many boat owners took their chances. One fortunate dash from an offshore mother ship could set a man up for life.

A scratchy PA system announced the departure of Morgan's bus. He got into line, found a seat in the No Smoking area and settled down for the boring ride north on Interstate 75.

As Morgan drowsed he wondered why he was on the bus at all, why he had not simply taken a commercial flight all the way to Atlanta, tailed or not. In the latter case Dobbs would be unaware and unimpressed; but if a surveillance effort had been mounted, the Director might well be troubled and that was Morgan's hope.

His mind flashed back to the huge caucus room whose special TV lighting seared his eyes, to the Senators pompously arrayed above him, the cluster of microphones, the Agency lawyer at his side.

It was the Senate Select Committee on Intelligence, chaired by old Senator McComb of Arkansas. He had the seat of honor at the center of the raised dais, on each side of him three Senators from each party seated in order of seniority. The public hearings had been underway a week, after months of executive, closed-door sessions with Committee investigators and assistant counsels doing the questioning, amassing classified data and leaking sensational nuggets to the press.

Dick Helms had been called, along with old John McCone, Admiral Radford, Henry Kissinger, Dean Rusk, Jim Angleton, Tom Karamessines, and other officers he knew only by name. By now the Committee knew everything there was to know, had learned things Morgan was unaware of, and most of it had been aired in public. He remembered McComb's weathered face—admiring reporters had likened it to Lincoln's—the rooster wattles and the eyes like gray pebbles, magnified through thick old-fashioned lenses.

He could hear the chairman's rasping voice again:

"Mr. Morgan, the Committee has heard previous testimony on this government's role in bringing about the coup. You were there, were you not?"

"Yes, sir."

"In what capacity?"

"As the Agency's senior representative."

"And you kept the ambassador fully informed of your planning, of the events as they took place?"

"Yes, sir. However, I wouldn't want to claim entire credit for the planning."

McComb's mouth tightened, the slate eyes seemed to hood. "You would not?"

"No, sir. Most of it was done by a task force of the National Security Council." He felt Saperstein's elbow jab. "We carried out the program in the field."

The chairman said, "Ambassador Hapgood, as you may know, denies that he was ever consulted or informed."

"So I've read. Nevertheless, he was fully informed. By me and through State Department channels."

A stir in the room. Majority Counsel bent down and whispered in McComb's ear. Saperstein muttered, "Bad move, Dave."

Chairman McComb cleared his throat. "What you're saying then is that Ambassador Hapgood lied under oath."

"No, Mr. Chairman, I don't believe that was your question. The ambassador has testified under oath and so have I. Our testimony differs."

Heavily McComb said, "This Committee has no reason to doubt the ambassador's veracity."

"Respectfully, sir, I don't think the Committee has any reason to doubt *my* veracity." He heard a muffled groan from Saperstein. "In that connection," Morgan went on, "I believe it was Lord Palmerston who defined an ambassador as a gentleman sent abroad to lie for his country." Laughter and boos from the audience. Flash bulbs exploded in his face.

"Christ," Saperstein whispered, "I *told* you not to bait them."

McComb pounded his gavel and shouted, "Is the witness contemptuous of this Committee?"

"No, Mr. Chairman," Morgan said above the subsiding hubbub, "I'm very much in awe of it."

Senator Jenkins of the Minority interrupted, drawling, "If I may, Mr. Chairman, I would like to suggest that the witness be cautioned to confine his responses to those matters of which he may have personal knowledge."

"The Chair associates itself with the Senator's suggestion." McComb's eyes bored into Morgan's. "My time is up, I believe. Senator Nicoll?"

"Thank you, Mr. Chairman." Nicoll cleared his throat, consulted a paper prepared for him by his staff. "Mr. Morgan, what was your perception of the morality of attempting to topple a regime with which this country maintained diplomatic relations?"

"The morality of it?" Morgan gave Saperstein a long sideward glance. "I must preface any reply by explaining that in any clandestine program information is issued on a need-to-know basis. Other witnesses before me may have pointed this out, but for the public record it means that if an intelligence officer needs to know a particular datum, his superiors provide it. If not, then a managerial judgment has been made that the officer didn't need to know that item or area of information in order to complete his assigned task." Beside him Saperstein was fidgeting, but Morgan continued and the great caucus hall was still.

"Returning to your question, Senator, if there was a Program Annex on the directive's moral aspects it was never shown or otherwise made available to me. My superiors—and there were many— could perhaps be more responsive on that point."

The cavernous room echoed with muttered dissatisfactions, with irritable coughs and scraping shoes. Cupping his hand against Morgan's ear, Saperstein said, "I told you not to be a fucking wise-ass. The whole Agency's on trial and you're cracking wise." He was furious, the synthetic lawyer composure peeled off. Morgan ignored him. Senator Nicoll's face was dappled pink and white from suppressed anger. In a choked voice he said, "And that is your reply?"

"Yes, sir. Respectfully and to the best of my ability."

"You're portraying yourself as merely one of the troops following orders, not as one of the planners, leaders, and enthusiasts of that outlandish and criminal action?"

30

Morgan remembered wetting his lips before he spoke. "Senator, this morning I testified at length concerning my role, but in answer to your question: yes, I followed orders."

"I believe that was Eichmann's defense," Nicoll said.

When order was restored Morgan gripped the base of the microphone. "Am I on trial, Senator?" he said thinly, and Saperstein gasped, "Jesus Christ!"

"As I understand the Committee's purpose, Senator, it is fact-finding, exploratory, not judicial," Morgan continued. "And for the record I take strong exception to your linking me with Eichmann."

Bang went McComb's gavel. The Chairman ordered a twenty-minute recess and Morgan felt his arm gripped hard by Saperstein. "They won't take that shit from anybody. They'll fuckin' *murder* you."

"That's what they've been doing all day with no interference from you, pal." He shook off the lawyer's hand. "What do you do for guts?"

Saperstein swallowed. "Listen, I know Nicoll's AA, we went to law school together. Let me tell him you'll apologize, okay? Then. . . ."

"Apologize? You must be on pills. Who insulted who?"

It was only two o'clock, but already five o'clock shadow showed through the lawyer's pale-skinned face.

Controlling himself, Saperstein said, "You don't understand, do you? You really don't get it. Morgan, they're out to nail the Agency and nothing you or anyone else says or does is going to stop them. All they want from you is some yes or no replies, humbly said. You can't help the Agency, so for God's sake think of your own survival."

"As you do yours."

Saperstein regarded his client for a moment, then his milky eyes drifted away. "Yes, as a matter of fact. I wouldn't bother to tell you this but I've got a couple of friends who happen to think you're a hell of a guy, so I'll tell you what the insiders and most of the press know: This is a charade. The outcome, everything that's been revealed, was decided months ago. There was agreement among the White House, Congress, and, least importantly, the Director. This is simply the version staged for public consumption, to get the boobs in line. So this is my final advice: Go along with them, give them what they want. If they don't get it from you they'll get it from someone else." Stepping back, he gazed clinically at Morgan. "Calling Hapgood a liar was the worst. The Senators love Hapgood. His confirmation went through with paeans of praise. Either the Committee will take it out on you or

Hapgood's friends will. You'll never get another decent assignment. Who the hell would back you up? As a. . . ."

Morgan cut him off. "I got the message a long time ago, counselor. But I've been sickened by what's been going out over the air waves day after day. This is like Slansky's trial. And all the *mea magna culpa* shit. . . ." He swallowed hard. "Because you expect me to apologize for my life you're as bad as they are. Worse."

Saperstein shrugged and walked away. Reporters surrounded him but he brushed them off. Morgan sat down at the witness table and poured water from the big glass pitcher. The last of the ice had melted long ago. To his dry mouth the water tasted warm as blood.

Feeling curiously insulated from his surroundings, Morgan watched the Committee reassemble, heard the audience fall silent.

Recognized by the chairman, Senator Nicoll said, "I yield the balance of my time to the Junior Senator from California."

The TV cameras swung and focused on the modishly-styled head of Senator Haynes Eckhardt, who nodded at Nicoll before turning his gaze on Morgan.

"Mr. Morgan, I have a few questions for you that concern factual matters on which you can inform this Committee." Pausing to study his prepared question sheet he thrust out his chin. "I understand that for the purposes of your testimony you have been relieved of any secrecy obligations you might have entered into with the Agency?"

Saperstein leaned toward the table microphone. "That is correct, Senator. I believe a letter to that effect has been submitted to the Committee. In any case, representing the Director as I do I am empowered to make that undertaking."

"Thank you, Counsel." An aide whispered to Eckhardt. "Yes, that letter has been received. Consequently the witness is under no constraints of secrecy concerning his past Agency activities."

"That is the case, Senator," Saperstein agreed.

"Very well. Now, Mr. Morgan, as field chief of the program you must have had informants, agents, within the militant opposition. Through them you acquired information which you relayed to your superiors." He looked expectantly at Morgan.

"Is that a question, Senator?"

"Yes, a question." One long finger tapped his question sheet.

Morgan said, "Yes."

"You had informants, then? Agents?"

"I did."

32

"And when the coup failed, what happened to them?"

"Some were identified—the visible leaders. They were summarily executed, some quite horribly."

Eckhardt nodded. "It is not our purpose to dwell on the fate of insurgents against the government of a nation with which this country maintains friendly diplomatic and commercial ties. But you said *some* were identified, Mr. Morgan. Does that mean not all of them?"

"That was my meaning, sir."

Saperstein whispered. "Be forthcoming, pal. Last chance."

Morgan reminded himself that somewhere behind him in the vast forum was his wife, sitting anonymously among strangers, and he wondered how Janice was taking it. The children, Bill and Shelley, were in school, thank God, though they would see him on the six o'clock news, his face in the morning paper.

Eckhardt's voice ended his brief inattention. "And who were the survivors?"

"Those who were not identified."

Eckhardt set his elbows on the table surface and smiled indulgently. "Of course. To make my question more precise, Mr. Morgan, what were the *names* of those agents or informants of yours who survived?"

Morgan remembered the cold constriction of his throat. "May I consult with Counsel, Senator?"

"By all means." His smile was as pleasant as an executioner's.

To the lawyer, Morgan said, "I tell him to go fuck himself, don't I?"

"Christ, no, Dave! Give him the names."

Morgan gazed up at his interrogator. "I don't believe even the Director's letter authorizes me to reveal intelligence sources."

Quickly Saperstein spoke. "Senator, your questioning is well within the framework of the Agency-Committee understanding."

"And Mr. Morgan is free to reveal those names?"

"He is." Smugly Saperstein sat back. Morgan saw a look of triumph on the chairman's wizened face.

McComb said, "The witness will answer the question."

Morgan had been half-expecting this turn, but until now he had not decided his response. "A little while ago I was asked to comment on a question of morality," he said. "Your inquiry raises deep moral issues, Senator—at least for me—since I gave my word as a representative of the United States that their participation in an activity in which this government was a coequal conspirator would never be made public by me. These men," he went on as a wave of sound swept up around him, "were brave men, patriotic in their own view and responsive to what they felt to be the call of a higher moral duty to overthrow a strangling despotism. I've said, and the world knows, that many of them were seized and executed in the aftermath of failure. The same inhuman treatment would be the fate of those who survived, who hid or never revealed themselves as opponents of the regime. Were I to state their names in this chamber I would be condemning them, their families, and their friends to certain death."

"Surely the onus would be on their government, Mr. Morgan, not on you. And that government is not immune to world opinion."

"Senator, let me answer your suggestion in this way: were I to name these survivors—men who trusted me and the government I then represented—I would become their executioner. And that I am unwilling to do. Worse, the credibility of the United States and its representatives, covert or accredited, would instantly become worthless."

He could hardly hear his amplified words above the noise around him. But this was his only chance to define the issue, make himself finally understood: "For all the reasons I've mentioned, I respectfully decline to respond to the question."

McComb's gaze was stern. "As chairman of this Committee, sir, I must warn you that unless you reply fully and completely to the legitimate questions posed you by Senator Eckhardt, you will stand in danger of a citation for contempt of Congress."

"Morgan," Saperstein moaned, "they can send you to *jail*."

"I understand the situation, Mr. Chairman," Morgan said, suddenly feeling freed of a smothering weight. "I trust the country will understand it, too."

Slam went the gavel. "The witness is dismissed," intoned McComb. "The Committee will meet in one hour in executive session. This public hearing is adjourned until tomorrow morning at ten."

Blinded by electronic flashes, half-deafened by the turmoil around him, Morgan remembered sitting motionless while Saperstein rose, closed his briefcase, and bent down for a final word. "Sucker," he breathed, then turned to face the cameras with a troubled but compassionate mien. Wordlessly it told the world his client was hopeless, beyond help. A demented zealot.

And when Morgan stood, finally, and searched the crowd for Janice she, like other friends, had been among the missing.

The press crowded around Saperstein, and it occurred to Morgan

34

that there was a subterranean cleverness about the lawyer. Once in a house in Kolonaki outside Athens, he had become aware of a small crevice in the basement floor. From time to time a servant would bring it to his attention and he would give orders for whatever had to be done. But the crevice deepened, a rivulet appeared. In time the rivulet dug below the concrete foundation, washing out earth, causing the concrete to cave inward, crumble. This affected the walls, the support stanchions, trusses and joists, and the house became uninhabitable.

Saperstein was this year's crevice, a personified premonition of disaster. And, Morgan wondered, out of all the lawyers in the General Counsel's Office, how had Saperstein been assigned to represent him? No, represent was a parody-word for what Saperstein had done. Clearly, Saperstein was advancing the Director's interests, the Agency's interests; he was there in an adversary position that Morgan had not discerned until too late. How had he been designated? By lot? By random computer selection? By assessed suitability? Well, Saperstein was clearly a comer; he would go onward and upward, be given juicy jobs and even juicier assignments. But he would always be representing power, not justice.

Read your lawyer's Hippocratic Oath, Morgan had said silently in the direction of Saperstein's vanishing figure. And may it trouble your sleep.

Later, in Committee executive session, and once more inside the caucus room, the demand to name names had been put to Morgan. His friends within the Agency, Janice, everyone had urged him to purge himself of contempt, and when he did not, the prepared citation had been issued and he had been taken from his Alexandria home at night by federal marshals to the District jail.

And there he had stayed until the Committee's term expired, eleven months in all, during which time the names he had tried to protect were read aloud in public and reprisals taken abroad.

As he had predicted, world opinion notwithstanding.

Other things had happened as well: to him, to his country, to the outside world, but he did not want to review them now. Bury the past, the dead with it. He had tried, God knows, and gained a measure of success. Now Dobbs and the past flared up again.

Why was he being summoned? What did they want done now that they wouldn't want to dirty their official hands with?

The bus was entering the outskirts of Atlanta, the speedway on the right, farther along the stadium and off in the distance the cyclorama. The bus merged into traffic, slowed, and the rest of the way to the terminal it was stop-and-go.

He checked his bag in a locker and took a cab to the Hilton. Walking through the lobby he exited and began to reconnoiter the block occupied by the Regency. The afternoon was cool and pleasant, not too much wind.

Near the fountain a young couple were feeding sparrows, well-dressed shoppers walking by. Dobbs's people could be above, covering the site from a window. He's got to be uncertain of me, Morgan mused, so he'll take every precaution.

Ten minutes to four.

Morgan strolled past the fountain thinking that the trimmed hair and shaven face altered his recent appearance enough to give him a degree of immunity from Dobbs's watchers. Just another face in the crowd.

He turned into the hotel lobby, went to the newsstand and bought a *Journal,* stood near the house phones and scanned the front page, glancing from time to time in the direction of the fountain. Wind tipped the top of the spray, dispersing it like the needles of a pine, leaving a crescent spatter on the paving. The bird-feeding couple had moved from the dampness, discarding their paper bag. Two pigeons plucked at it while others fluttered down to dispute.

At four o'clock a black Chrysler limousine pulled up at the curb. Aside from the driver there was only one passenger. He got out from the rear door and closed it. The limousine moved away.

Director Dobbs wore a gray Glen Urquehart suit and a dark bow tie. He was hatless, and the breeze picked up his thinning hair, flaring it briefly before Dobbs patted it into place. The Director looked up and down the street then walked directly to the fountain.

For a few moments Morgan scanned the scene, folded his newspaper and stepped outside. He strolled up behind Dobbs and said, "Hello, Bob. Prompt as usual."

The Director turned quickly, face expressionless. Through rimless lenses his pale eyes surveyed Morgan. "They said you wore a beard. As usual, they were wrong."

Morgan looked up to where the sun was gilding the room windows above them. "You wanted to talk. Let's talk."

THREE

I hope," said Dobbs, "we can keep this civil."

"Why not? I passed for a gentleman once. Everyone says you're gentility itself. You loathe me as much as I detest you so we can dispense with social formalities."

"Concur." Dobbs's polished shoe tip nudged a matchstick into a crack. "I'm sorry about yesterday, David, the men involved have been reprimanded. In fact I regret a number of things that happened to you even though some of them you brought upon yourself. I believe I understand your alienation, your bitterness, but if reports are accurate you've managed to find an acceptable life for yourself."

"It suits me."

Dobbs nodded. "So I won't dwell on that aspect of the past. What brings me here is something you could not possibly either know about or imagine. Something into which you fit uniquely." He spoke with measured precision as though he were reading from, or had memorized, a legal document. His thin voice, uninflected, was irritating to Morgan. "The intelligence profession—life itself—brings many strange turns," Dobbs went on. "Of that truism you have far greater experience than most. So perhaps it will come as less of a surprise to you than it did to me that a rather famous, or notorious, figure who turned his back on the West has signaled his desire to return."

"Pontecorvo?"

"A reasonable guess, but off the mark. Besides, Pontecorvo's been traveling to Rome, Vienna, and Stockholm for over a year, to congresses of nuclear scientists. And you never knew Pontecorvo."

"I was in college when he defected. So this personage is someone I knew."

"Exactly."

Morgan swallowed. "It would have to be Roger Hargrave."

"Hargrave, yes. You must have known him very well."

"In boarding school he was my prefect. For two years we lived in the same dorm, on the same floor. . . ." He broke off thinking how long ago it had all been, how far back they went together. Roger the star athlete, top student at the Townsend School, captain of the Harvard swimming team, Rhodes scholar. . . . Morgan exhaled. "It's no secret Roger recruited me; that all came out after he defected." His face was damp. The memories were unsettling.

"True. And a very close scrutiny of you ensued."

"I was polygraphed a dozen times."

"That file has been closed. Apparently another episode is about to begin." Dobbs glanced around. "Could I persuade you to go inside? We may be at this a while. There's a pleasant lounge; we could have a drink."

They sat side by side on a curved sofa covered with nubby fabric. A waitress placed drinks on a glass-topped table, waiting stolidly until Dobbs paid and dismissed her. Morgan sipped J&B and waited for Dobbs to reopen the conversation. The Director said, "Obviously we want Hargrave back."

"To face prosecution?"

"In all candor that has not been decided. A balance will have to be struck between the evil that he did and the good he may yet do. From the few messages received we understand that he is prepared to pay his way, as it were." Dobbs examined the celery stalk in his Bloody Mary. "Have you . . . ? Do you have any reason to think we've been recognized?"

"Possibly you, not me. I'm the Forgotten Man. No, I don't think anyone's noticed us. Besides, who would believe it?"

"Agreed. It was a good idea meeting here, outside Washington. People only see what they expect to see. One of the old tradecraft maxims, isn't it?"

Morgan nodded. Now that the first impact was over, the shock of learning Hargrave wanted to return, he wanted Dobbs to get to the point. "You didn't travel here just to tell me Hargrave's had second thoughts, that he's remorseful. Besides, how did he make his wishes known?"

"Through a Western Olympic coordinator who passed the word along. After he defected, Hargrave spent a couple of years with the KGB being debriefed. Then they gave him a make-work job with the state publishing monopoly, a nice apartment, a dacha, and a month a year on the Black Sea. Then when the Olympic preliminaries were stirring up, Hargrave's athletic background was remembered, and he was ordained a Soviet adviser. That gave him his chance to send a message to the West. Evidently he's still completely trusted."

"As we trusted him."

"We decided there was enough to it to send in a direct contact, eliminate the original third-country messenger. In that way we established a dialogue."

"Securely?"

"As far as we know. To establish his bona-fides Hargrave gave us the name of the GRU *rezident* in Brussels, the one targeted at NATO headquarters. We passed it along to the Belgian service and somewhat to our surprise the information proved out."

"That alone convinced you? That could be a routine Soviet sweetener."

"We assumed that: We're not *all* fools. Hargrave capped that with two other names. An arrest was made in Capetown but the *rezident* poisoned himself before interrogation." He sighed. "In Helsinki—as Hargrave said—one of our embassy file girls turned out to be a plant for the KGB. With her we moved rather more cautiously so she is alive and well, though no longer on the embassy payroll."

"Three down," Morgan said. "A thousand more to go. What's Roger's motive? I mean, he's been gone at least eight years; his wife has been with him in Moscow all that time. It's hard to believe he suddenly got religion."

"In a sense he may have—political religion, that is—and it has to do with China. Remember, he was a Sinologist, though not a disciple of Mao. From what he's conveyed to us we believe Hargrave is apprehensive over war between China and the Soviet Union, and believes the Chinese will win."

"That makes him close to unique."

"But think of it . . . a first strike by the Chinese, then numberless hordes streaming across the Soviet heartland. . . . Hargrave's a Westerner by birth, race, and education. He seems to fear the end of Western civilization should the Chinese prevail. His motive, as far as we can determine, is his desire to prevent it."

Morgan sipped the last of his watery drink. "Grandiose," he said, "but Roger always thought in geopolitical terms." He looked up at the high domed ceiling, the twinkling suspended lights, and realized it was getting dark outside. "Had he not gone over he might have become Director, you know."

"I'm the first to admit that. Allen Dulles personally brought him in. Roger had all the credentials—more than I do. Far more." He chewed daintily on his celery. "You knew his wife."

"Alexandra. I knew her." Knew her far better than anyone but Alex would know. "She was at Farmington when I met her. We dated, saw each other summers at the shore." Then she had gone to Oxford while Morgan finished Williams. And when Roger returned, inviting Morgan to a cozy Georgetown dinner the night he recruited Morgan into the Agency, it was his bride, Alexandra, who opened the door. Morgan wondered how Alex had kept over the years, how the Moscow winters had affected her, if at all, and remembered the first night they had made love, in a sailboat tethered off the club. Fourth of July fireworks bursting overhead splashed garish color on her tanned and lovely body.

Rousing himself, Morgan said, "You've given me the *tour d'horizon,* and it brings us to what?"

"Yes, it's time we got to that." Dobbs pushed aside his emptied glass. "As you might imagine, Hargrave has established a number of terms, preconditions to his returning and cooperating. The one involving you is this: that when he steps off the plane you will be there to meet him, serve as his conducting officer back to the States."

Morgan stared at him.

"Why you? Because of your old personal relationship, I suppose. Evidently he trusts you. He spoke reverentially of your going to prison to uphold a principle. In our society that gives you an unusual credential."

For a time Morgan was silent. Then he said, "I'm not interested. I don't want to see the traitor again."

"You're too old, too experienced, too sophisticated to be simplistic, David. No one is asking you to accede to Roger's request out of affection for him or his wife or from any residual sense of duty. As much, perhaps more than anyone, I realize that you have every reason to get up now and walk away." From his coat pocket he drew out a plain envelope and laid it on the table. "A thousand dollars. You earned it by coming here, hearing me out. But you could earn much more." Behind the rimless lenses, eyes flickered. "You owe thirty-four thousand on your boat. You're eight months behind in payments to your former wife. Your son's military academy hasn't been paid for his last semester, and your daughter's institution is preparing to turn

40

her over to state care unless your indebtedness is liquidated. Against that you seem to have no significant means of support, haven't filed a tax form in three years, and. . . ."

". . . I live with a young woman who supports me."

Dobbs shook his head. "Perhaps so, perhaps not. It's not an item on my list. I was going to say that what income you seem to have comes from occasional charters and fish sales at the dock. Which is why. . . ," he took a deep breath, "I think you might be more than casually interested in what I'm prepared to offer for a service that might occupy you, at most, for two days."

Morgan sat back against the comfortable upholstery. "How much?"

"One hundred thousand dollars."

"Cash? No W-2 form?"

"However you desire it. If all goes well Hargrave will leave an Olympic conference in Vienna and board a plane to Geneva. That is where you would meet him. We would have our own plane ready to bring you back. Both of you."

"And Alexandra?"

"If he can work it she'll come out with him. If not. . . ." He spread his hands expressively.

"Two hundred thousand dollars."

"Very well." One hand extended. "We'll shake on it."

A sense of unreality fogged Morgan's brain. Automatically he returned the handshake, feeling the moisture of Dobbs's palm.

"Now that we've made our bargain," Dobbs said, "perhaps you'll tell me why you asked for another hundred thousand?"

"To keep me from killing him."

Audibly the Director sucked in a short breath, expelling it slowly. "Well, then, I don't begrudge the fee."

"Hargrave cost a lot of good men their lives; some of them I knew. Others were only names, pseudonyms. That hundred thousand will help keep me from throwing up each time I think of how well you're planning to treat the prodigal. A hero's welcome. And don't try to con me that there's even a remote possibility of prosecuting him; you'd have eliminated that with the President and the AG." Dobbs was silent. "So now that I've agreed to your proposal why not unburden yourself of the unsaid reasons you want him back so badly." Morgan straightened his legs, thrusting shoes out as far as the table. "Identifying illegal *rezidenturas* isn't all he's offered you."

"Quite true, and very astute of you to realize it. All right. Hargrave

41

claims there's a Soviet penetration in the Agency, a KGB agent in a very high and sensitive position." His tongue darted over his thin lower lip. "I like my job, David. I enjoy its prerogatives and prestige, the temporal power I can deploy. A Soviet penetration—if it became known—would discredit me, and I have every reason to want to remain where I am for a good many years."

"So Hargrave's going to identify the penetration and you'll handle it internally."

Dobbs nodded. "I naturally prefer we seal the leak ourselves. That's what the country will get for its money. So considering the dual benefit I view your fee as cheap." He smiled. "You could have asked for more . . . and gotten it."

"I'm not greedy."

"I thought you might ask for a pardon."

"The thought crossed my mind. Cash is more useful."

"Very practical. All right. It will take a day or so to contact Hargrave and finalize arrangements. Meanwhile, a new passport and alias documentation will be prepared for you. I prefer you not return to Key West before you leave."

"No. I've got goodbyes to make."

"Very well. You were booked on the Concorde out of Dulles tonight, but that can be canceled. However, you must be in Europe within forty-eight hours. If agreeable to you, you will be given the first half of your fee before you leave, the other hundred thousand to be paid when you bring back Hargrave."

"No. I don't regard you as totally reliable, Bob. Once I'm back here you might be troubled by second thoughts. So I'll take it in Swiss francs at destination."

"Paris acceptable for provisioning?"

"Is Frazer still Chief of Station?"

"There was a change. Frazer decided to retire, so it's George Baker. He or one of his men will supply your documentation."

Dobbs seemed more at ease now, comfortable with schedules and figures, the tangible minutiae of the profession.

"Let's review," Morgan said abruptly. "I'll travel to Paris under my own name and contact the Station."

"As Scott Bramwell. Documented in alias you'll travel to Geneva. You'll stay where?"

"The Richemond or the Du Rhone."

"Better not stray too far. We may get no more than an hour's notice of the flight Hargrave will be on. Now. You'll be at Key West tomorrow. A delivery will be made to you. I would prefer you not book passage to Paris from there. Because it. . . ."

"Bob, don't brief the novice on travel procedures. I've been abroad before."

"Yes, I'm afraid that did sound condescending. Withdrawn." He looked at his thin gold wristwatch. "If anything needs altering I'll reach you through Paris or Geneva. Otherwise it's firm." Dobbs got up. "You won't find it necessary to tell the girl, will you?"

"Probably not." He picked up the envelope and slid it into an inside pocket. "Tell me, whatever happened to Saperstein?"

"Saperstein?" The Director's brow wrinkled.

"Uh huh. The General Counsel supplied him when I was testifying before McComb."

"Of course. Gerald Saperstein. Well, he's no longer with us. Got a big job with the FCC about two years ago."

"Figures. Gone to his reward, you might say."

"You might say." The Director glanced at his watch again. "If I dress on the plane I can get to the Saudi reception on time. Ah, I think we ought to leave separately, don't you?"

Without replying, Morgan watched the Director's slight figure move away. Near the door it was joined by two men, Dobbs's protectors. Morgan had assumed they were not really alone but he had not taken the trouble to identify the interested parties.

For a couple of minutes he read the editorial page, then left the paper and moved through the lobby to the Delta counter where he booked a first-class seat to Miami. From a pay booth he telephoned Pollock's home and asked the pilot's wife if Pollock could meet the Delta flight. She said she was sure he could. After that, Morgan took a cab to the bus terminal where he reclaimed his unused bag, and from there taxied to the airport.

Airborne, he accepted a glass of champagne from the stewardess while he ordered from a dinner menu.

The meeting with Dobbs had been real. The money in the envelope was real. But to Morgan everything else seemed illusory. Perhaps tomorrow's delivery of a hundred thousand dollars would persuade him of reality, that the mission for Dobbs was straight-forward, authentic, as represented. His mind reviewed the tale Dobbs had told, seeking flaws, inconsistencies, illogic, and it seemed to Morgan that he was examining a pool of mercury in his palm—as he had first done at Townsend—finding that tilting or squeezing the fluid metal made it separate, come apart. Then, freed of pressure, it flowed together again in a single consistent mass that was whole and pristine as before. His expanded thoughts were not entirely reassuring.

Slicing the beef filet, he thought of Dobbs, of the false camaraderie that had sprung between them, and he liked neither. Everything the Director said was plausible, but then it would have to be; he was a man self-schooled in deviousness. Most plausible of all was Dobbs's confession of self-interest, his love of power and position, his understandable desire to preserve them against an internal menace.

But was that the whole story?

Bolstering it was the unanticipated promise of two hundred thousand dollars for a few days' work, and half of that sum was to be in his hands tomorrow. Despite himself, Morgan began planning its distribution. No traceable checks, just cash sent Registered to the debtors Dobbs had mentioned. As for the boat, he would continue to pay on it each month to avoid unwelcome inquiries about sudden affluence.

In place of cognac Morgan asked for Irish Mist and sipped it, accepting a refill as the big jet let down its wheels, locking with a shudder into place. The lights of Miami glittered below. With luck, Pollock's Cessna would have arrived. Tonight he would share illusion with Marisa. Tomorrow would be a day of truth and discovery.

FOUR

WHEN he woke her she embraced him in relief. Marisa was not given to Latin emotional extravagance but the room's dim lighting showed moistness in her eyes.

"I've made coffee," Morgan told her. "I need to tell you some things."

Silently she trailed him down the stairs, poured their coffee, and seated herself across the table. Then Morgan said, "It began with those two visitors. In Atlanta I talked with Robert Dobbs—he's the current Director." He told her of Dobbs's proposal, then of Roger Hargrave whom he had so long admired and whose defection had shocked and revolted him. "But I need the money," he said, "and I agreed to go."

She put down her cup. "So much money for so small a service? I don't know about such things, but if someone pays too much for too little, perhaps there is a catch? Perhaps there is danger in your bringing that man home? No money is worth your death, is it?"

"I'm not worth a plot of any kind."

Her hand touched his. "I don't know those people, I only know you. I remember what they did to you and it frightens me to think that something could happen again." Her voice wavered. "You mean so much to me, David."

He glanced away. "I don't think it will be dangerous at all, just a routine operation. I've conducted defectors before. Hargrave won't be any different from the others." His eyes sought hers. "You know how badly I need the money, *mi china*. And I've agreed."

For a few moments she was silent. Then she sighed, "I suppose I shouldn't be selfish. I don't have the right to keep you from your work. In your profession you were important, I know, though you've

45

never put it that way, and down here—since prison—you've been hiding from everything but me."

"Maybe at first I was hiding, but you changed all that."

"Did I? I'm glad. But now something has opened up for you, like an athlete perhaps trying an injured leg, finding out if it's mended, assuring yourself you're okay again."

"Listen," Morgan said, "you sound like a poet. This is just a game, a little exercise, okay?"

"The game—whatever game it is—I know that inside you want to be involved again. You need to show people you can do it all as well as you could before."

"Marisa, I can't go back to that kind of life again. It's. . . ."

"When you've carried out this job I want you to come back to me. You'll be the same but you won't ever again feel you need to prove yourself; to me, to you, to anyone. When you feel satisfied with yourself you'll be happier, and that will make me happy, too."

"Couldn't put it better myself. Ah, you're quite an analyst."

"Don't cut me off with a phrase, David. Don't raise barriers."

"I'm sorry, I shouldn't have said that and I apologize. You see through me so clearly, and invariably you're right. So I have your consent?"

She smiled. "Grudgingly. But please be careful. Remember the kind of people they are."

"I'll be careful." He stretched and yawned, tired from travel and the confrontation with Dobbs. "Now let's get some sleep."

In the morning he worked on the boat, rubbing down the brightwork, oiling his reels, and stripping teeth-frayed line. He aired sea-damp lures and cleaned the windbreak glass where salt had crystallized. A little before noon the pierside telephone rang and when Morgan answered it was Marisa. "Something just came for you."

"I'll be right over."

In her office at the rear of the shop Marisa closed the door, isolating them from salesgirls and customers. She opened the small safe and drew out a large package wrapped in brown paper and sealed with fiberglass tape. Morgan cut the tape with his fishknife and peeled away the wrappers until banded currency lay bare. Stacks of it in hundred-dollar bills. Atop one bundle lay a typed notice: Property of David Llewellyn Morgan.

"*Dios mío*," breathed Marisa. "I've never *seen* so much money," She clutched his arm. "Oh, count it!"

Dry-mouthed he sat at her desk and counted. Not since he had bankrolled the insurgents had Morgan handled so much money, and in those days it had run into millions. Still, this was his, all of it, to do with as he chose.

"Can we celebrate tonight?" she asked.

"Tonight I'll be over the Atlantic. But when I get back we'll have a double celebration."

"Promise?"

"*Te prometo, mi amor.* Now I've got to get busy."

When Marisa left the office, Morgan locked himself inside. By phone he made a flight reservation to Miami and from there, via National, to Paris. The night flight would put him there at daylight.

Using Marisa's business stationery he typed brief transmittal letters and addressed envelopes to Bill's military academy, Shelley's hospital, and his former wife. Morgan counted out eighteen thousand dollars and divided payments among the three envelopes, sealing them with heavy tape. For his travel needs plus an emergency fund he separated fifteen thousand dollars. Finally he set aside five thousand dollars in hundreds and slid them under the desk blotter. He would have Marisa use some of it to bring his boat payments current, the rest for household expenses, whatever.

At one level his mind told him he would be back within a few days, which meant there was no need for long-range planning. At another level, the cautious one, he felt that some provision against the unexpected was only prudent. So he typed a bill of sale for *El Gallo,* deeding the boat to Marisa Isabela Pardo de la Costa "for one dollar and other valuable considerations," dating and signing it in his own hand.

Of Dobbs's money sixty-two thousand dollars remained. Morgan rewrapped the bundles and taped to the package a note asking Marisa to use it for Bill's education, the costs of his daughter's hospital care and eventual rehabilitation. He put the package into her safe, closed the door, and spun the dial.

There was time for lunch so he led her to the Pier House and they ate on the balcony overlooking the water. A chilled bottle of Chevalier Montrachet brought out the deep sweet succulence of their *cangrejo moro* cocktails followed by a fresh Florida flounder sautéed in lemon butter. After savoring the last bit of firm white claw meat, Morgan said, "I'll tell Pollock he can use the boat while I'm gone. You might want to fish with him."

"Uh-uh. I'll wait for you."

"Buster and I were going out for dolphin. So. . . ."

"Not interested. Don't worry, I'll find things to do. Maybe I'll go to Miami. I haven't seen a play in months."

"My fault," he said wryly. "Visit your folks, too."

Her tongue dipped delicately into the almost-colorless wine. "One day . . . perhaps one day you'll go with me . . . meet them."

Morgan understood the significance of such a meeting and said only, "They must be fine people."

The waiter brought their entrées, and they talked, pointing out boats coming and going in the channel. On the nearby stretch of sand were sunburned kids; shaded under an umbrella a honeymooning couple kissed lengthily. An elderly woman in a large floppy hat strained sand through her fingers, seeking souvenir shells. Wind puffed the sails of a blue-hulled sloop. From the bar lounge drifted phrases of piano music.

In Europe he would miss all this, and Marisa, but in a few days he would return. This operation was a Quick and Dirty. He wondered if Hargrave thought redefection would make everything between them as it once had been. Surely not, Morgan mused; Roger can't be that ingenuous. Small-bore hijackers of boats and planes to Cuba were tried even when they returned voluntarily, as many did; but a man of Hargrave's stature? So far it had never happened. Roger would be the first major returnee, a government official so highly placed that his defection had cost the then Director his job and plunged the country and the Administration into a long and acrimonious debate over responsibility. Within the government, particularly the Agency, endless damage assessments, counter-intelligence reviews. What did Hargrave know? Who could he name? What national secrets had been compromised? Did he take documents with him, or had he been passing microfilms to his Soviet contacts all along?

"You're being *pesado*," she said. "If I were silent all through lunch, you'd rebuke me."

"Point well made. Key lime pie?"

"You?"

"Sure. Let's splurge."

"I'll diet while you're gone. That's a promise."

Lifting her hand, he kissed it. "Here we go, being affectionate in public. Anyone might think we were lovers."

"Only bad persons would think that . . . like northern trash on vacation. The locals don't bother with illusions."

48

Their Key lime pie was served on chilled pewter plates, and afterward they drank thick black *cafecitos* syrupy with sugar, Cuban style.

Walking back to the boutique he asked Marisa to send his three letters by registered mail, told her of the money in her safe and under the desk blotter. His hand rested easily on her hip, on the smooth Peruvian linen of her flared slacks; her shoulder brushed his upper arm. At the corner of Fort Street she stopped and turned.

"This is as good a place as any, I suppose. Have a good flight, be careful, and come back to me."

"I will." He held her tightly for a moment, then she broke away and went quickly from him. Morgan watched her go, breathed deeply, and walked to her house.

Changing planes in Miami, he bought a few items of heavier clothing in an airport store. Even this close to summer, Geneva would be cool, particularly at night; Paris, too, if there was rain. Morgan checked in at the National counter, then went through the metal detection system, strolled down the long, carpeted corridor, and waited in the lounge until his flight was called.

Before takeoff he drank from an iced split of champagne, selected magazines, and made himself comfortable in the wide, cushioned seats. The big jet rose smoothly, and as it banked out over the Atlantic he saw the long bar of lights that marked Miami Beach, the dotted running lights of boats on the darkness that was Biscayne Bay. When that was obscured by a drift of clouds he scanned *People* and *U.S. News,* feeling the plane lifting high above the ocean.

The champagne made him drowsy, so he put aside the magazines and glanced around. The first class compartment was less than half-filled: an elderly couple, a young mother and infant (probably a corporate wife, Morgan thought), two middle-aged European males arguing volubly, a man dressed in beach swinger style: open throat shirt whose collar covered the neck of his beige jacket, and the inevitable gold chain and three-inch ornament. The swinger had carefully-styled dark hair and he was coming on to a blond girl seated across the aisle. Large, violet fashion-lenses were set above her straight nose, and her hair was caught up and rolled in a bun behind her head. About twenty-five or so, Morgan estimated; modestly dressed in a pale blue suit and high-collared white blouse. Small, jeweled earrings glinted as she talked, and as her left hand lifted he saw a gold intaglio ring on the little finger, but no wedding band. It was obvious she would prefer reading to chatting with the macho male, and Morgan classed her as a young lawyer or executive trainee for the European office of a major American corporation. An oval, restrained face reflecting good breeding and intelligence. As he turned away he silently wished her luck in fending off the swinger.

From his seat he could see the magazine rack, the cover of a *Field and Stream* that showed a man and a boy with shotguns working through thick bracken. The scene reminded him of mornings in the field with his father and their pointers. From the time he was twelve and could shoulder a single-shot 16 gauge he had hunted upland game with his father: ringnecks and grouse in central Pennsylvania, quail after New Year's at the Georgia plantation. Each father-and-son day at Townsend his father joined him for the annual shoot on the school's restricted acres. He could still recall the throat-catching thrill of a cock pheasant bursting out of a corn-shock row, knocking it out of the air in a puff of small feathers that drifted in the wind long after the ringneck hit the ground; the scent of cherry and apple orchards after an early frost; the care he lavished on the Ferlach double twelve that had been his grandfather's and which his father had presented to him on his sixteenth birthday.

His mind reached back through thirty years, when after Thanksgiving vacation of his college freshman year his father died in what the insurance investigators charitably called a hunting accident even though it was known the brokerage was failing and could not have lasted through the year. The double indemnity policies enabled Morgan's mother to live the rest of her life in ease and paid the son's education and foreign travel. The remainder of the legacy freed Morgan of the imperative to enter business, gave him the option of government service with its marginal salary when Roger Hargrave made the suggestion that night so long ago.

His father he remembered as a tall and robust man who played squash and handball at the athletic club, emerging red-cheeked after steam room and massage; a man who stroked his single scull on the river in the spring and fall, bundled up in a sweat suit with a heavy towel around his neck. Morgan was grateful for the attention, warmth, and love his father gave him, for his father's interest in his studies, his willingness to explain a difficult Latin translation, discuss the economic causes of the Civil War, or analyze a point from Hegel. He remembered, too, his father telling him that it made little difference which college Morgan chose: "A college is, after all, a library; the professors are there to help you choose the books."

In turn Morgan had tried to pass on to his son and daughter the affection and intellectual inspiration that had been so freely given him. With Bill, he had gained a measure of success: with Shelley, nothing that could be observed. For she was her mother's child, self-centered, impractical, too-satisfied with marginal accomplishments; nothing really there behind the placid pretty face.

Morgan recalled the nightmare hours after Madeira's headmistress phoned to say that Shelley was nowhere at the school; two days later the Washington police brought her home, eyes glazed from drugs, reporting with embarrassment how she'd been found panhandling along Eighth Street, staggering, disoriented, anonymous until a missing persons check made identification possible. High school for a few weeks after expulsion from Madeira, then flight and hysterical phone calls from New York, Boston, or Dallas as the fugitive expanded her frantic search for drugs. Arizona at last, Indians and peyote, dilaudid and near starvation at the age of nineteen. He remembered flying out there with his wife, getting Shelley into a Tucson institution for the drug-damaged young where Shelley had been welcomed as a patient at two thousand dollars a month, payable in advance. After settling that, he flew back to Washington where he was scheduled to testify before the McComb Committee. The return flight had been nightmarish, Janice accusing him, blaming him for their daughter's instability, implying he had molested her, perhaps worse, drinking heavily on the plane, emerging red-eyed and sobbing at National airport, the drive back to their home a coda of the airborne ordeal.

That episode, he acknowledged, coming after the others with Shelley, the years of mutual marital dissatisfaction, had overloaded their marriage. His imprisonment had given Janice what little excuse she needed for divorcing him: his notoriety, the shame and humiliation his arrogant, self-immolating intransigence had brought upon her. Unbearable. That had become her favorite word. He was unbearable, their marriage unbearable, her degradation unbearable.

She never thought, he reflected, what it must have been like for me.

The stewardess brought him a pillow and a thin blanket. Cabin lights dimmed. Morgan folded back the armrests of the unoccupied seats and stretched out. Any reprise of memories tired him and so he tried to avoid them. Self-pity was negative, unproductive. No room for it in his life now that it involved Marisa Isabela. Too often when he had been alone the memories came, self-accusation riding their wake, and Marisa had been the antidote.

Through half-closed lids he saw that the blond passenger had moved over to the window seat, pillow beside her head. Sleep was her

51

refuge from the swinger who was now drinking and talking to an unoccupied stewardess. Now that the girl's glasses were removed Morgan saw she was a classical beauty. Even in the dimness her skin seemed to glow. And there was something distinctly reminiscent in the lines of her face, the set of nose and eyes. Had he seen her somewhere before, or did she merely remind him of someone he had once known long ago? His mind searched memories, discarding, selecting, rejecting, until a possibility emerged: The girl looked remarkably like someone from his past. Lynn McRae.

With a slight smile he remembered when he was a sixth former at Townsend, opening a letter from which fell a photograph of a blond lying naked on a bed. The unknown writer, Lynn McRae, was at Dobbs Ferry and had seen him playing the game against Pawling. She wanted to meet him, hoped the photo would bring him to the next Masters tea dance. The temptation had been powerful, but Morgan was cramming for college boards and resisted, sending her a note of explanation and appreciation. He was a Williams junior before he met Lynn, then a Holyoke freshman, at a fraternity dance. The following weekend she spent with him in Boston at the Copley-Plaza, and he found her as uninhibited as her boarding school photo had suggested. She was good company, too, usually available for a picnic or a beer-baseball game. And then unexpectedly she announced that she was engaged, left the Hole, and married a man she had met on a Bermuda cruise. Lynn was one of the few women in his life whom Morgan could think of without malice or longing. He had always wished her well, and now, relaxed at nearly forty thousand feet above the Atlantic, he wished her well again. We were good for each other, he thought; our timing was right. And we parted before hurt could be inflicted.

The blonde passenger, he told himself, would never send nude photos of herself to strangers.

Before sleep came, his mind returned to Hargrave, to the tremendously complex aspects of his life, career, defection, and return. Morgan would like to read the interrogation transcripts and learn the answers to questions that were pounding at his brain. But I'll never see the transcripts, he reminded himself; I'm not an Agency official any more, just a jailbird who turned out to be useful one last time. After that, *nada. Rien du tout.* Need-to-know prevails.

Something tugged at his shoulder. His eyes opened; gray light was streaming through cabin windows. The stewardess said, "Would you like breakfast?"

52

He nodded, licked his lips. His mouth tasted dry and old. Champagne had that effect on him. Cheerfully she handed him the preliminaries, orange juice and coffee. On the seat beside him was a plastic packet of shaving gear. He gulped down the juice and took coffee into the lavatory where he washed and shaved. More alert, he took his seat again and ate scrambled eggs, sausage, and hotcakes.

The blonde passenger was breakfasting Continental style: croissants, jam, and coffee. She was still in the window seat, insulated from the beach swinger whose face looked puffy after hours of drinking. Guys like that were ever-hopeful, Morgan thought as he held his cup for a refill. Distinctions of class escaped them so they blundered on, unaware, figuring the percentages to make out.

His tray removed, Morgan began filling out French customs and immigration forms. When he was finished he looked out of the window and saw land below, felt the slight sensation of altitude loss, heard it confirmed by the captain's announcement that landing preparations were being made. Paris temperature was 62° with a chance of light rain.

Deplaning was smooth, customs and immigration inspection perfunctory to the point of disdain. *La Republique* was strong once more, secure. What harm could Marianne suffer from a band of New World tourists?

As he waited at the curb for a taxi he noticed the blonde executive/ lawyer offering a dollar bill to her *porteur*. The man shook his head resolutely and their voices rose. Morgan admired her articulate French. He walked over and said, "Can I help?"

Gray eyes turned to him. "If I could borrow some francs. I was too rushed to buy any before the flight and now my porter won't take this dollar."

"Can't blame him," Morgan said, handed the man five francs and was rewarded with a tip of the hat. "Our dollar isn't the most sought-after currency in the world."

"How true," she said. "But I *will* repay you. I mean that. I'll get francs at the hotel." Abruptly she smiled, showing small even teeth. "I'm making a big deal of not being in your debt. Still, if you'll give me your name and hotel I'll send the money round."

"I'm David Morgan," he said, "and I haven't picked a hotel yet."

"Isn't that risky . . . coming without a reservation?" A taxi drew up beside them.

"Not this time of year." He opened the taxi door. "Where are you staying?"

"The Lancaster. Know it?"

"Rue de Berri. Mind if we share? The taxi, I mean."

"Please, let's. I'm Ghislaine Percival but I answer to Jill." She offered him a gloved hand, made space on the seat for Morgan. "*Equipage,*" he said to the driver who got out and surlily boosted her three bags and his one onto the roof luggage holder. "Rue de Berri," Morgan instructed. "Hotel Lancaster."

"*Bon, allons-y.*" The taxi ground away, Morgan acutely aware that he was seated beside an exceedingly attractive young woman. Her breasts seemed small, youthful, and there was nothing overtly sensual about her figure. Good legs and well-styled, practical, traveling shoes. Gloved hands crossed in her lap. She was almost prim, he thought, but there was another harmonic, a contrary one transmitting a warmer message to anyone tuned in. And Morgan was.

"Your French is excellent," he remarked, "but with the name Ghislaine it should be."

She smiled. She seemed to smile easily if somewhat apologetically. "I'm a hybrid in a sense. My grandparents were French and I went to school over here." Her head tilted. "You know Paris, then."

"I worked here for several years."

"Then you're here for pleasure?"

"And to attend to a small commission."

"How nice." She did not reciprocate his information but turned to watch the flow of traffic on the Autoroute that led into Paris. "Did you happen to notice that bejeweled oaf trying to pick me up on the plane?"

"Unavoidably."

"I finally took a sleeping pill. Usually on a flight like that I like to catch up on back reading but he was impossible. He owns a disco in Hallandale; he's traveling to audition French talent. He's got a small yacht and a condo on the water." She laughed. "I've got to *stop* making fun of unfortunates. Really. It was one of my worst faults in school."

"Well, there are those who ask for abuse, insist on it. Their existence and importunities demand a response. I say: geeve eet to them."

Traffic was slowing now as the morning rush into Paris enveloped their taxi. She said, "There's something so familiar about your name and face I can't help being curious. Forgive me for putting this so baldly, but are you someone famous whose name I should know?"

"Not at all. Morgan's a common Welsh name, and David is the patron saint of the Welsh, so it's not an unusual combination."

Her brow furrowed briefly. "I think that response, David, is somewhat lacking in candor, but I won't persist. For all I know you're traveling incognito on some Presidential mission involving the fate of nations. At one time I considered working for the government. The State Department or maybe even intelligence. It seemed adventurous. I had a couple of foreign languages, and was deciding between that and law school."

"What happened?"

"A school friend wanted to start a fashion house in Palm Beach and mentioned she needed capital. So I supplied it, the business took off, and I never looked back, till now."

"Fashion's gain was the government's loss."

She shrugged. "Perhaps."

"You wouldn't be happy working for the government, not in today's climate. I gather you like what you're doing."

"Love it. It's fun and it's profitable. My partner's made so much money she's suggested buying me out." Her eyes were impish. "Do you have *une amie* in Paris—or could we have cocktails together?"

"No, and yes. Ritz Bar at six, and your invitation's made my day."

"I'll try to be punctual. I have a midafternoon appointment at Guillaume and one never knows how it will go."

He looked at her approvingly. "With your hair it should go very well."

"*Merci pour le compliment, m'sieu.*"

He could see Villejuif in the distance. Once the Orly road went right past it, and if you wanted you could stop at the roadside Flea Market and haggle for antiques. The route had seemed slow in those times but it was at least as fast as the clogged super highway. Of course, Orly had been much smaller in those prejet days, a scatter of low buildings, not the magnificent multibalconied modern structure named in honor of Charles de Gaulle.

"I *am* on business, as a matter of fact," he said. "Not traveling in ladies' underwear, as salesmen customarily say, but coins in a small way of business. Antique coins." That was to quell her curiosity.

"Sounds interesting and profitable."

"Occasionally."

"But not infrequently."

"Often enough. It's an interesting *quartier* . . . do you know it? Ninth Arrondissement."

She shook her head. "On this excursion are you buying or selling?"

"Some of both."

55

The taxi was nearing the Champs Elysées. When it turned up the great boulevard he could see the Arc, massive and evocative centering the Étoile. Short of it the driver turned onto the Rue de Berri, passing the cafe where Morgan used to take midmorning apéritifs with scribblers from the *Herald,* two of whom had worked as parttime agents.

The Lancaster doorman opened the cab door, whistled up a *chausseur* to take the baggage, and Morgan separated his bag from hers. Jill glanced helplessly at him until he tipped the men and then she said, "I'm grateful, David. See you at six."

She extended her hand again and he took it briefly, got into the taxi and told the driver to turn down the Champs to the Meurice. It was an old hotel, unobtrusive and comfortable, where he and Janice had stayed until they moved to an apartment over on the Ile de la Cité. The clerk offered Morgan a double room with bath, windows overlooking the Tuileries gardens and the Louvre.

Opening his bag he unpacked, hung up clothing, and changed his shirt. Then he went down to the lobby, entered the pay phone booth, and called the embassy. When the operator answered he asked for George Baker, and after a few moments a female voice said, "Mr. Baker's office."

"May I speak with him?"

"May I say who is calling?"

"Bramwell. Scott Bramwell."

"One moment please." Then Baker's voice. "Hello, Scott. The items you ordered aren't on hand at the moment. Where can you be reached?"

"Haven't picked a place yet," Morgan lied. "I'll call you later. What would be a likely time?"

"One o'clock."

"I'll phone then."

Leaving the booth he walked out to the Rue de Rivoli and glanced around, feeling tense, alert. Travel and the proximity of his goal were having their Doppler effect on him, accelerating his mind, expanding his senses, but it was too early to peak. That would come later in another city. For now he could be unhurried, relax.

Morgan strolled under the arcade toward the Crillon Grill, where he turned in, took a seat at the nearly empty bar, and ordered vermouth *douce et glacé*. As he sipped the wry-sweet drink he thought how good it was to be in Paris again. The flight had been

56

pleasant enough, he had an unexpected date for cocktails, and memory plucked out the old cliché that a job well begun was already half-done.

The bartender polished goblets and cocktail crystal. Busboys began unfolding table napery for the luncheon trade, and outside in the Place de la Concorde rose a clamor of horns from the stalled and enraged traffic.

How truly it had been remarked that Paris never changed, he reflected, but he had never before come on so curious a mission, one whose roots reached so far back in time and involved him in so personal a way. He would feel better about it if Frazer were still station chief instead of George Baker, who was an unknown quantity. Geneva was his goal, and Roger Hargrave the defector his assigned target. Paris was only a way station this time, not a place for R&R, Morgan told himself, and he was anxious to leave and be on his way, to bring the operation to a head in Geneva.

As Morgan left the Grill it occurred to him that what Baker knew would reveal a good deal about the mission's integrity. If Baker knew a lot, then other Agency employees would also know, and one of them could be the Soviet penetration agent. If *he* knew, the KGB could be preparing for preemptive action right now.

FIVE

In the Crillon lobby Morgan pocketed train and air schedules to Switzerland; a Wagons-Lit compartment would allow him to sleep and arrive rested in the morning. Then he walked up the Rue Royale toward the Madeleine noticing that the fog had lifted above the city and that the flower stalls near the ancient church were busy. Angling right he went down the Rue Duphot to Prunier's, whose interior was concealed from the street by half curtains across the wide, plate-glass windows. Above them, gilt letters proclaimed the availability of oysters, crustaceans, and fish of the sea. Morgan pushed through the revolving door and found a seat at the *bar de dégustation.* On mounds of cracked ice were nestled *moules* and oysters. He ordered six of each, and a demicarafe of the house white wine. The shellfish were sweet and succulent, and when he had finished, he rinsed his mouth with wine, then dabbed the napkin at his lips French-style.

From there he walked down to the Faubourg St. Honoré and found a bench set back from the walk where he could observe affluent shoppers, some with Afghans, high-styled poodles, and carefully combed shih-tzus moving past the luxury shops. Soon he would be phoning Baker at the embassy, collecting new ID for the last phase of the mission. After what had happened to the Agency, Morgan wondered if the remaining technicians were capable of providing good alias documentation or whether everything was now hit-or-miss and hope-like-hell.

If Hargrave proved cooperative to the debriefers, his identifying the high-level penetration agent would be worth a great deal to Dobbs—and to the country. But first Hargrave had to come out and be shepherded home. Morgan hoped the Soviets were not paying special attention to Roger in Vienna. There would be KGB watchdogs in

Hargrave's Olympic committee but the defector should be capable of fooling them. After all, he had deceived the Agency for a number of years.

Had the KGB recruited him during his Rhodes years at Oxford? The most notorious of the known agents had been spotted and recruited at Cambridge. Perhaps Hargrave knew others from Oxford who had been acquired at around the same time, men now risen in private or public life, opinion-makers, persons of repute and influence. If so, their disguises would be stripped from them, their communist loyalties made known to the world, their value nullified.

But it could well be that Hargrave had little of value to trade for safe-haven in America; too many defectors inflated their knowledge during bargaining talks and could be wrung dry in a week, leaving the Agency with handling and management problems for years ahead and little or nothing to show on the ledger's plus side.

Hargrave was an exceptional man, however. If he hadn't been, Morgan reflected, I wouldn't have looked up to him those many years. He'll bring back information, but whether it's what the Director seeks remains to be determined.

He could imagine Hargrave's fears and preoccupations as he prepared his escape. For Roger it would be a time of tension and insecurity, when small and normal incidents assumed enormous and threatening proportions leading him to the brink of believing his intentions were known, the communications link discovered, his masters toying with him cruelly.

Yet, thought Morgan, those were the masters he chose, so let him sweat and suffer. Sympathy for Hargrave is beyond me.

At Townsend, Roger Hargrave had been top student in his class and the school's best athlete; grades and prizes seemed to come effortlessly to him.

The rest of us had to work like beavers for any recognition at all. And Hargrave had carried it off with flair, almost visibly exuding charisma, setting styles in conversation and dress, even in the types of girls a Townsend boy should cultivate. As prefect Roger would not tolerate bullying of smaller boys by larger students and so he had gained a circle of younger admirers who tried to ape him in every way. He had had blond hair, blue eyes, and a strong, aquiline nose; cleft chin and powerful shoulders. . . . Morgan wondered what he looked like now. Seedy? Crestfallen?

Alcoholic?

Careful, don't equate Roger with the Soviet defectors who've come over, some of them far-gone cases fit only for St. Elizabeth's.

There was a time when Morgan had wondered if Hargrave were homosexual or bisexual, but discarded the thought as unworthy, even vicious, derived from subconscious envy of Roger's personality and attainments. Final proof was Hargrave's marriage to Alex, who would not have lingered a day with a husband who was lacking.

Was Alexandra in Vienna with him now? Or in Moscow? And their children? Morgan did not need to know the answers; he was indulging mere curiosity, not thinking operationally ahead.

Leaving the bench he walked past Hermès to the nearest telephone kiosk. A woman was using the phone, gesturing with her free hand, cheeks flushed with emotion. Finally she slammed the receiver into place and hurried away.

Morgan dialed the embassy and in a few moments heard Baker's voice say "Bramwell?"

"Right."

"Let's have lunch. Quasimodo, over by Notre Dame."

"I know it."

"I'm leaving now."

To save time Morgan took a taxi the half-mile to the Hotel de Ville, where he left it and walked across the bridge onto the Ile St. Louis. He remembered the restaurant well, having lived on the adjoining island for nearly two years.

Baker was already seated at a small table at the rear of the restaurant, back to the varnished wall. They shook hands and Morgan sat beside the station chief on the cushioned bench-seat.

"Having a drink?" Baker asked. "I could use one."

"Wine when we get around to it."

"I'll go along with that." He took the wine card from the *maître* and ordered a Chambertin of recent vintage. His face, Morgan noticed, was showing capillary bursts around the cheeks and nose. High living and higher blood pressure was Morgan's diagnosis—a Paris occupational disease.

Baker said, "I won't even pretend I know what this is all about. But I've got an envelope for you that I'll slide down between us." He lit a cigarette and blew smoke toward the chandelier. "Are you one of us again, Dave?"

"Not exactly."

"Just transiting?"

"That's right. How do you like working under the current regime?"

"What can I tell you? It's a job." He took a menu from the *maître,* passed it to Morgan, and accepted one for himself. "Prison pretty bad?"

"Rotten."

"A lot of us were sorry about that, believe me. Nobody liked seeing you way out there, all alone."

"I didn't like it myself." He felt something slide down against his thigh. Baker being clandestine. "Any accompanying message?"

"None I know of."

The *sommelier* brought wine, Baker sniffed the cork, tasted the goblet sample, and nodded. To Morgan he said, "What strikes your fancy?"

"Vichyssoise, and some of the sole Marigny." He returned the menu, then tasted the wine. Baker ordered veal and a salad. Morgan hoped lunch would not take long for he did not particularly enjoy the station chief's company. Baker had come from the analysis side of the house, a Western Europe reports specialist with no operational background in the profession. Morgan could imagine current reports from the Paris station: models of form and rhetoric but so shallow as to duplicate overt embassy reporting. Which is what, apparently, was wanted.

"Most of your old crowd retired or quit," Baker remarked, crunching into a stalk of celery. "Peyton James, McDairmid, Palmer Syce, Emerson Forey. . . ." His voice trailed off as though he had begun thinking a similar fate could await him: the trash dump, elephant valley. "That's right—you knew Hargrave, too."

"So I did. I wonder what brought Roger to your mind?"

"Just the personal association." Baker shrugged. "No one ever learned why he made the jump, did they?"

"Not that I heard of." So Baker, apparently, was unaware of the reason for Morgan's presence in Europe. Good. Dobbs was keeping it close.

"What do you do now?" Baker asked.

"A little fishing, some boating. A quiet life. Adventure doesn't attract me."

"I'd think not," Baker said primly. "Still, doesn't it bug you that even after you refused to talk your agents were named anyway?"

"And killed. It grates my bowels. But at least I'm not responsible for what happened to them and their families."

"No. Though collective guilt gets thrown around pretty casually, doesn't it? I mean, who would take a chance like that again?"

Morgan sipped the wine. "They only have to summon up my example." He decided to change the conversational direction. "How long do you plan to stay here?"

"Paris? I finish my tour next year, and I've been selected for the War College." Pride tinged his voice. "If it weren't for that I'd probably get out, find a good job with one of the think tanks. But, well, War College will look good on my résumé."

"Ummm. George, do you think it's possible there's a top-level penetration in the Agency?"

The chief of station blinked. "Penetration?"

"Yeah, a spy. You know, like Maclean and Philby."

Baker frowned. "Well, I've never really thought of it . . . that's the Security side, of course. I mean, what else are they in business for?"

"One wonders. Still, it's possible, isn't it?"

"I guess so. But it isn't something I like to think about. Yes, it's possible. A mole."

"A mole is blind. An agent isn't."

Baker began cutting into his veal. "Well, we'll probably never know."

During coffee, Morgan got the envelope into his pocket hoping it contained all he would need. He said, "Thanks for the help, George. Pleasant times in Paris to you." He got up. "I'll be getting along. Things to do."

"I understand. Well, whatever you're up to I hope it turns out better than the coup, right?"

"One can hope," Morgan said with restraint and walked out. Good-bye and good luck.

It would be maddening, he told himself, to have to deal with one or more Bakers every day. George was making himself into another Dobbs: know-nothing, unimaginative. But he would have a good and rewarding career, and he could look forward to a comfortable after-life writing profound papers for Rand, Brookings, or the Hudson Institute. A life of minimal, attainable goals.

Morgan crossed the small footbridge to the cathedral cloisters. Gardeners were tilling floral beds, carefully clipping flowers for the cathedral. The sound of traffic seemed to die away, suppressed by the solemnity of the ancient place. Often in the evenings he and Janice had strolled here in the cloisters' quietness, smelling the perfume of the flowers, seeing fireflies darting in the dusk. The children were young then, going to their French school each morning in white smocks and floppy black bows. That family no longer existed; everything had changed.

He went back the way he had come, crossing to the quai, deciding to walk back to the Meurice and rid himself of the melancholy that had settled on his mind. So he interested himself in the midday strollers, the cars rocketing along the quayside, and when he was in his room he locked the door and opened the envelope. The passport was Canadian, made out in the name of Edward Bernard Johnson: POB Ste. Agathe-des-Monts, Québec; Age, 49; Profession, salesman. The embossed photograph, he realized with a start, had been taken while he was talking with Dobbs. The envelope also contained calling cards, a health insurance carnet, and other pocket litter for the worn leather wallet. At a travel agency near the Scribe he booked a compartment on the night train for Geneva, using his Johnson alias and letting the clerk examine his passport. Returning it, the clerk said, "You will need a hotel, *m'sieu?*"

"I have one," he said, and paid for the tickets at the dollar exchange rate, taking the balance in francs.

Back in his room he pulled down the blinds, stripped, and got into bed. The train left just before midnight, giving him plenty of time for cocktails and perhaps dinner with Jill Percival.

Guiltily he remembered Marisa and told himself defensively that he was not an unattached male on the prowl in Paris for a one-night conquest. Cocktails, dinner with an attractive young woman, and that was it. *Bon soir, c'est ça.* Later, a Wagon-Lit from the Gare de l'Est.

He slept, waking at five, took a cold shower to clear his mind. Shaved and dressed, he packed his bag and left it with the concierge. He paid his bill and reached the Ritz Bar by six.

She came to his table, sleek and young, beautifully coiffed hair—shoulder-length now—hiding the straps of her peach-colored satin sheath. Pointing to his champagne cocktail she said, "Wonderful idea." While he ordered she produced a cigarette and an expensive-looking lighter. "Did you have a good day, David?"

"It was successful," he said. "And you?"

"I indulged myself. Slept for hours, always vulnerable to jet-lag. Body chemistry, I'm told. Bought a few things, and turned myself over to Guillaume. *Bon Dieu,* how prices have risen in a few short months!"

64

He laughed. Her drink arrived and she touched her glass to his. "I'm somewhat in the fashion trade—the Palm Beach-Paris axis—so I've gotten to know some people in the press. Three phone calls, David, and the last was a fount of information. Antique coins, indeed. You were a headliner for days." Her eyes challenged. "You weren't entirely frank with me."

He spread his hands. "Surely you didn't expect my life story."

"No, but you were being defensive, concerned I'd become madly frightened in the taxi if you told me who you really were."

"How perceptive."

"Don't be angry. Will you let me take you to dinner?"

"And discharge the heavy debt? Of course."

"Friends again?"

"Friends."

An Arab group was entering, four men traditionally and expensively garbed, and four flashily-dressed young women of the kind delicately referred to in polite circles as *artistes*. Jill said, "You wouldn't believe the number of Arabs I encountered today along St. Honoré. They must have nothing but money."

"They manufacture it," Morgan said. "Out of the sands."

"And their ladies . . . I don't think they're really their wives."

"I'll confess: I don't either. Does it trouble you?"

"Not really, but I sometimes wonder about things like that. Shoddy relationships."

"The world's full of them. Now, where did you think we might dine?"

"Yvonne et André, a little place up that side street by the Crillon. . . ."

". . . With candy-stripe wallpaper and fresh flowers on miniature tables."

"Rats! I thought it was just possible I could introduce you to something new. Well, is it acceptable?"

"It's a charming choice."

"Good. May I have another cocktail?"

The second round arrived. By now the room was nearly filled with people. Everywhere he saw the flash of diamonds: rings, bracelets, neck-chokers, the latter on old women with young men who looked silky and attentive. Around the room a scattering of rubies and pearls; high-fashion gowns, ruffled evening shirts.

Morgan said, "Will you tell me a little more about yourself?"

She nodded. "Until I was thirteen we lived in Easthampton. Then one autumn weekend my parents and my older brother decided to sail to Boothbay Harbor. I preferred not to go so I stayed at my grandmother's house. The boat," she swallowed before going on "never arrived. There was a storm. Later the mast was found and a life preserver. In one weekend my family vanished. I wanted to die." Her voice trembled. "For a year I was under intensive psychiatric care. My grandparents—my mother's parents—were wonderful to me, but it was decided I should go abroad to school in order to avoid painful associations. So I was in Lucerne for three years. Then I came to Paris. By then my grandfather had died and grandmother McRae was incapable of living without him." Her eyes were very open, incredibly deep. "As happens, she just drifted away from reality."

Morgan's throat was dry. "Your mother was Lynn McRae?"

Her eyes widened even more. "No . . . Lynn is my aunt, my mother's sister. Did you know my mother?"

He shook his head. "What was your mother's name?"

"Carol. David, what a wild coincidence. To think you know Aunt Lynn! Where did you meet her?"

"At a college dance. We saw each other, dated for about a year, then she left Holyoke to marry."

"Exactly. But you never met my mother."

"No, and I'm sorry I didn't."

"So am I." Jill shrugged resignedly. "I had a brief hope you could tell me something about my mother . . . what she was like when she was younger."

"Wish I could. But where's Lynn now?"

"She married a Canadian, as you may know. They have a big ranch in Manitoba but the marriage has had its ups and down. Aunt Lynn's always on the brink of separation or divorce so she didn't think it would be a stable situation for me to move into, and my grandmother agreed." Jill sat back and gazed at him, her face cheerful and relaxed. "I travel a lot and I've never come across anybody who knew anyone in my family." She moved her head wonderingly. "Until now."

"Well, let's drink to coincidence and discovery."

"Cheers." Their glasses touched.

Morgan said, "When I first noticed you on the plane I thought you might resemble someone I knew. Later I began to think of Lynn for no apparent reason. But it had to be the family resemblance."

She nodded. "All McRaes look alike, and now you're not really a stranger at all. You knew Aunt Lynn so you've got instant credentials. In fact, you're probably close to a courtesy uncle, aren't you?"

"I'll accept that."

"No. You're far too attractive a coincidence to be put patly in the family circle." She sat forward. "How long will you be in Paris?"

"Only a few hours. I'm leaving for Geneva by train."

"Are you coming back?"

"Afraid not. I'll be flying home from there."

"Rats! Sure you can't stay another day?"

"Not a chance."

Her eyes narrowed in mock suspicion. "Got a gal in Geneva?"

"Uh-uh. Business trip."

"Live in Miami?"

"Key West. I have a boat there."

"I have a condo in Riviera Beach, so we're neighbors, sort of." Her eyes lowered. "After I get back would you call me?"

"Glad to."

Her eyes lifted to his. "I just hate to end things like this, David. No one knows I'm in Paris, so I could go on to Geneva with you . . . if you'd take me."

"It's a very tempting idea, but. . . ."

"So I'm impulsive. Will you?"

"Jill, I can't. Anyway, there's a pretty substantial gap in our ages." He lifted a hand, waved it helplessly.

"Oh, pooh. You're already booked, I bet. Taking *une amie,* aren't you?"

Morgan shook his head. "Traveling absolutely, totally alone."

"You must be on government business,; no, I won't press the point. But I feel I have a special claim to you. You *will* phone me in Florida?"

"It's a promise."

From her small purse she extracted another cigarette. Morgan took the lighter from her fingers and held the flame for her. After inhaling, Jill said, "This is getting to me, David. I feel undone, limp."

"Tomorrow it won't loom so large—you'll probably have second thoughts, anyway; be glad you're not in Geneva." He glanced at his wristwatch. "There's time for another round, or shall we leave now?"

"Let's leave, I could use the fresh air."

While she went to the coatroom Morgan paid the bill and met her at the outside door. Her short evening jacket was of Chinese silk embroidered in rich metallic thread, but it would not keep her warm if they were to walk to Yvonne et André. The doorman whistled up a taxi, Morgan gave the address, and they rode silently to the restaurant entrance. The doorway and curtained windows gave off a warm, inviting glow. Flower boxes added a cheerful touch, and as they entered Jill gave her name to André who bowed and showed them to a banquette table.

Morgan ordered a bottle of Taittinger '53 and said, "I've been on champagne much of this trip. Now there's a reason for it."

Moistening her lips, she leaned slightly forward. "How close were you and Lynn? Did you ever plan to marry?"

"We never discussed it," he said truthfully. "We were just good friends."

"Hmm. Lovers?"

"What a question, child. That was back in the '50s; customs were different then."

"But people made love." Her nose wrinkled. "Didn't they?"

"You mean, didn't your Aunt Lynn and I? Why all the intimate questions?"

"Because. You see, I find you an attractive person—male—so it must run in my family."

He attempted a casual smile. "You're pretty attractive yourself, but there's no need to rush things. I'll see you next week."

"I'm counting on it," she told him, "very much. And I want to know about you, many things."

"In time," he said, "but without getting morbid let me suggest that you're showing symptoms of father fixation."

"Because you're an older male?" She made a face. "I don't like immature boys, never have."

The *sommelier* was opening their chilled bottle, silver chain of office glinting around his neck, heavy links sliding against his apron. Morgan would have enjoyed the ritual but his mind was on other things.

Fortunately, he thought, I leave tonight, eliminating any later awkwardness. Their glasses touched.

"*A la rencontre,*" she said softly. "*Je ne me reconnais plus.*"

"*Ni moi non plus,*" he confessed. "But we'll sort things out."

They ordered then, ate lightly and leisurely, and with coffee there was cognac. Beyond the candlelight her gray eyes seemed palely warm, her skin luminescent, face unbelievably beautiful, far more than Lynn's had been.

"I wonder if I've always been looking for someone like you, David," she said. "Saying I found you attractive, I didn't mean it in any avuncular sense. I meant as a man, as a male, David. I needed to know if you'd been Lynn's lover."

68

He sipped the warm, heavy cognac. "And if I were?"

"There'd be a barrier." Her cheeks colored. "Something akin to incest."

She verbalized what both had been thinking and Morgan wished it had been left unsaid. There were sounds of silver cutlery, the chime of crystal glasses, the whisper of waiters' feet on lush carpeting. It seemed a moment suspended in time.

"Have I shocked you?" she asked.

"Not at all. But we barely know each other. We're taking all kinds of quantum leaps."

She smiled. "When does your train leave?"

"An hour and a half from now. Will you see me off?"

"Not if I can't go. But you can take me to the Lancaster if there's time." She sipped the last of her demitasse. "This has been an extraordinary day and I wish it didn't have to end. Partings destroy me."

"I'm sorry," he said.

"But you're like a link to my family. And that's the good part, the positive thing I'll remember."

I should tell her of Marisa, he thought in self-anger, come clean with the kid. Make her realize I have a set life, no crevices for strangers, but the chance is gone. The truth would have turned her away and I didn't want her to turn away.

It's obvious she's craving a father-substitute to anchor her emotions, and I shouldn't disturb them.

"You're uneasy, aren't you?" she said. "And I don't want you to be. I promise not to become a problem, David. I'm sure you have more than enough without me."

"Listen," he said, "everything's out of proportion, jammed together. It's the setting, the coincidence, the candlelight, the champagne. Tomorrow will shrink things into their normal perspective. Daylight always does that."

"I hope not," she said, and gathered the jacket around her shoulders. "Shall we go?"

Morgan had the taxi stop at the Meurice for his bag, and would have left Jill in the Lancaster lobby but for her insistence that he see her to her door. "Footpads abound," she said, handing him her key. "A thief might be ransacking my room."

They rode the lift to the fourth floor. She walked ahead of him, stopping at the paneled door while Morgan fitted the key and turned the lock. The dark room was silent. Her hand drew him across the threshold, then her arms lifted, circled around his neck. Their lips met, her body pressed subtly against his, and he felt a surge of desire. Then her body relaxed, her head drew back, and she murmured, "Until next week, then."

"Next week." Turning, he opened the door, stepped out and closed it behind him. Heart pounding, he got into the lift and punched the lobby button. He went out to the waiting cab, aware but not caring that the driver was taking him the long way to the Gare de l'Est. A porter carried his bag to the compartment. Without unpacking, Morgan hung up his suit, got into the berth, and switched off the light. His mind turned over events of the night until the train pulled out of the station.

Then his thoughts shifted to Marisa and her warnings of what might lie ahead. Tomorrow he would be in Geneva, closing the final gap between himself and Roger Hargrave.

SIX

Geneva was drizzly gray. When Morgan checked into the Hotel Richemond, he could see fog cloaking the length of the lake. He hoped the airport wouldn't close for long. He imagined Hargrave taking off from Vienna only to have his plane land somewhere else than Geneva. Then what would happen? They wouldn't take off from Vienna for Geneva if the airport was closed. If they didn't take off, would Hargrave get nervous? Would the delay give the Russians a chance to notice his absence and catch up with Hargrave? He was thinking like a civilian, not an agent. He should be planning for contingencies instead of worrying about them.

At the Rue des Vollandes he cut inward, away from the lakefront, until he found a *bijouterie* just opening. For a while Morgan inspected trays of watches, selecting finally a thin gold Piaget for Marisa. From a tray of gold bracelets he chose one with heavy 18-carat links that would look well circling Marisa's tan wrist. A gift of love, in contrition.

When he offered fifteen hundred-dollar bills in payment the jeweler took them to the cage and scrutinized them with an illuminated magnifier, then under a microscope. Returning, he said, "Please forgive the delay. So many counterfeits. . . ."

"I understand. May I have the change in francs?"

"Of course."

The two boxes were handsomely wrapped and handed to Morgan with a sales receipt. "For your Customs," the jeweler said. "Be sure not to abandon it." He dropped it into a small plastic bag, following it with Morgan's purchases. Then he counted out the change, three or four dollars' worth.

Retracing his steps Morgan went back to his room and sat by the window looking out over the dock that served the lake tour boats. Only a few tourists boarded the first one, and Morgan saw small whitecaps scalloping the water. Not really a great day for a lake ride, with wind whipping down from the Alps.

But the wind would not prevent a plane from Vienna landing at Cointrin airport. And if Dobbs was to be believed, only the KGB could prevent one special passenger from boarding that flight.

He ordered a pot of coffee and a paper. In an easy chair he read it, refilling his cup from time to time, reflecting that though the Swiss could make complex timepieces, they had yet to master the intricacies of a decent cup of coffee.

He finished the paper at 10:15.

At 10:30 there was a knock at the door.

Morgan sat upright, quietly left the chair, and walked toward the door. Standing next to the hinged edge of the door he said, "Who is it?"

"A friend."

"Better than that."

"A friend of a friend." The voice was gutteral but unaccented.

Morgan said, "Give me the name of a friend."

"Try Bob."

Bob Dobbs.

Morgan expelled the breath he had been holding. "Come in slowly," he told the caller. "No sudden moves."

Reaching across the door he pulled back the bolt. The door came open. It swung inward, and from behind the man Morgan saw him walk slowly to the center of the room. The man was wearing a green velour hat with a *gampsbart* whisk pinned to the side of the crown. Below it, dark curly hair, a fur collar, and a heavy cloth topcoat.

"Get your hands up," Morgan said, closed and bolted the door, crouched behind the man, and patted him down. No handgun.

"All right," Morgan said, "you can lower your arms."

He walked around the visitor, saw heavy features and a dark turtleneck, thick eyebrows, and eyes the color of anthracite. The lips were oddly pink. They moved.

"This is a grand reception, sir," he said in an unfamiliar accent.

"You weren't announced."

The man shrugged, eased onto a chair arm. "Here's the drill: The traveler may come today, or he may not. Most likely tomorrow. At the most there'll be two hours' warning, one hour at minimum. Figure

72

twenty minutes from here to Cointrin airport gives you, say, forty minutes waiting time. That means you stay close to this room."

Morgan nodded. "How many flights a day from Vienna?"

"Three. Morning, midday, and evening."

"All right. I get to Cointrin. Where do I wait?"

"By the Customs door. When traveler comes through, fall in beside him. Steer him to the exit door, no hanging around inside. Get out in a hurry."

"I've reached the outside stairs. What do I look for?"

"A black Mercedes limousine will be waiting there. Swiss plates NVA-878. Open the rear door, get in the back seat with him, and don't for Christ's sake let him get out. You got a piece?"

"No. The job didn't seem to call for one."

"It doesn't."

"Suppose he decides not to fly back to the States with me?"

"Use some muscle. Knock him out if you have to, but get him back in the limousine; that's essential. Okay?" Moisture speckled his thick upper lip. "The two of you are in the limousine. The driver will tool around the airport for a coupla minutes, start back toward Geneva, then turn around and head for Cointrin again. There's a gate that lets diplomatic cars directly onto the runway. The Mercedes won't carry CD plates, but that's not your worry, it's the driver's. He'll head for the private hangars and there'll be an executive jet cranked up and ready to go. Get your traveler on the plane, strap in, and enjoy a cocktail."

"Since when do exec jets fly the Atlantic?"

"This one won't have to, because you'll switch to bigger equipment."

"Where?"

"Why the hell do you have to know?"

"Duty-free shopping, pal. I said where?"

"Gatwick."

"Destination?"

"Dulles." His lip protruded belligerently. "Anything else?"

"A matter of some importance. The *sine qua non.*"

"Huh?"

"The payoff, pal. Money. My share."

"You'll get it on the plane."

"Uh-uh. In the Mercedes, or traveler can find his own way home."

"That wasn't in the plan."

"It's in *my* plan so make it happen. Otherwise I walk away and you can explain to Bob."

"Pretty sure of yourself."

"Why not? When you were in kindergarten I was roaming North Korea killing the bad Chinese. This isn't my deal, but the conditions are. Traveler comes COD or not at all."

The messenger got up, walked toward the door, and unbolted it. "Stay close," he said. "When the call comes you want to be here, not boozing it up in the bar with a coupla broads."

"Is that what I do?" Morgan frowned. "I'll be here. Only don't screw around with phony check-up calls. One's all that's needed."

The door closed hard behind him.

From the window Morgan saw him turn out of the hotel, go left, out of sight.

Such people, he mused. Where the hell do they come from?

Slowly he paced the room, thinking. Too late now for the morning flight. Midday would be next. He had at least an hour to take care of two things.

Because Dobb's man had asked if he were armed, Morgan decided to arm himself. The question had a false ring. Years of back-street dealings had bred caution into Morgan's marrow, and it seemed unwise that anyone—this green-hatted klutz in particular—should know everything about him. Carrying iron was a personal decision, intimate, too. No well-bred man would ask another, just met, if he was carrying condoms. So much for delicacy.

The second thing was a car. The tourist directory gave him the names of self-drive car agencies under the heading: *Voitures Sans Chauffeur.* The nearest one was Merco, behind the central station. With his Quebec driving license and a thousand-dollar deposit Morgan was able to rent a Ford Cortina in reasonably good condition. He had the tank topped off before driving south across the Rhone and into the old city, where he cruised the streets, looking for a dealer in sporting arms.

In Paris Morgan had considered acquiring a handgun but decided against it. Now he wished he had bought one in France, for the Swiss were notably reluctant to sell firearms to their own citizens, much less foreign tourists.

Presently he saw a display window showing rifles and shotguns. G. Stuck was the name of the store and, after finding a parking place, Morgan walked back to it.

The inside was poorly lighted, but he could see cabinet after locked cabinet of glinting gunmetal. The salesman approached, a portly man with an impressive gold watchchain that held the tooth of either a tiger or an elk. Morgan looked down into the glass-topped display cases. A good selection of handguns was to be seen.

"Goodday, *m'sieu.* You are interested in large-caliber rifles? We supply many safaris, many white hunters."

"I'm not planning to visit Africa," Morgan said, "if I can avoid it. So my needs are simpler. A pistol, for instance."

"We have many fine pistols, dear sir. Of what brands would you be interested?"

"That's a fine-looking Walther," Morgan remarked. "Near-mint condition. But 9 millimeter is pretty big bore for my targets. A .32 caliber would be about right."

"Targets, sir?" The salesman began unlocking the glass case.

"Roaches. Cockroaches."

"*Cockaroach?*"

"Yes. That's a good-looking Sauer double-action. Is it new?"

"Quite new, yes."

"I'd like to handle it, get the feel of it. Designed for Wehrmacht field officers, wasn't it?"

"You are knowledgeable, *m'sieu.*" He lifted the automatic by the trigger guard, placed it on a pad of quilted velvet. "Special safety feature: cannot be fired with magazine removed."

Morgan lifted the weapon, felt the cold, oiled metal, the knurled wood grip. He released the magazine and drew it out. No rust spots or striae on the sides. He looked through the short barrel; not even dusty. An unused weapon. About six inches long, the automatic would be comparatively easy to conceal. "I like it," he said, examined the price tag, and got out his wallet.

The salesman smiled apologetically. "Not so *facile,* sir. Many forms to fill out, police registration. Oh, my, not *facile* at all."

Morgan drew out several hundred-dollar bills. "How long would all that take?"

"Oh, at least a week, sir." From a rack beneath the case he drew out a sheaf of forms and began assembling a set. "Sometimes more even than two weeks."

"The difficulty," said Morgan, "is that I won't be here that long." He laid three bills on the glass top. "If I can't purchase from you, perhaps you know someone who would be willing to make a private sale."

The salesman rubbed his chin, considering. His eyes scanned the hundred-dollar bills. Morgan hoped avarice was getting the upper hand.

"It happens I have an uncle," the salesman said. "Merely to be of service to a foreign guest I could inquire. You *are* a foreigner, sir?"

Morgan's cue to produce his Canadian passport. The salesman fondled it, copied down the alias, and said, "You are residing where?"

"Hotel Richemond."

"Oh, a fine hostelry. How . . . ah . . . quickly would you require a weapon? Something similar to this Sauer?"

"No later than three o'clock. With shells. If it's too much trouble. . . ."

"Not at all, by no means, sir. I will at once telephone."

"I'll leave the money here for your uncle," Morgan said. He took another bill from his wallet. "Please accept this for your trouble. Two-thirty would be even better."

"Believe me, sir, I will take every effort to persuade my uncle expeditiously."

"I'm confident you'll succeed. Johnson, Hotel Richemond. By 2:30. And thank you for your personal interest." He left the store.

Two blocks from the hotel he found a commercial parking garage and left the Cortina there, preferring that the hotel doorman not know he had a car available. In his room he saw that the coffee pot and cup had been removed, the paper neatly folded on his desk. Morgan stretched out on the bed and stared up at the eggshell ceiling.

Now, Morgan thought, I know two things Dobbs doesn't, things Hargrave isn't likely to learn in advance: that I have my own transportation and my own gun.

For the first time since beginning the mission Morgan let himself feel optimistic about it.

Shortly before 2:30 the room telephone rang. The *concierge* informed him that a package had been received for Mr. Johnson. Did Mr. Johnson desire delivery to his room?

"By all means." He got off the bed, took francs from his pocket, and opened the door when the bellboy knocked. Package and *pourboire* exchanged hands, and Morgan locked the door.

Inside a decorated shopping bag was a heavy gift-wrapped box that could have contained a dozen bottles of perfume. Morgan unwrapped it carefully, thinking he might want to reuse the wrappings, came to a sturdy cardboard box, and opened it. Inside, wrapped in blue velvet, lay a Sauer .32 automatic pistol, beside it a box of German shells.

Pleased, Morgan held the serial number to the light; the last three figures were 581, identical with the pistol in the shop. In fact, it had to be the same pistol. Evidently the salesman had been unable to contact his uncle on such short notice, the uncle had been unwilling to sell, or the salesman had decided to part with the weapon at an irresistible profit and say nothing about it. So now he had his cockroach-killer.

Morgan cocked the pistol, pulled the trigger, and heard a sharp, metallic *snik*. The firing pin was healthy. He extracted the magazine, opened the box of shells, and fed eight cartridges into it, pressing each shell down on the prior one, feeling the increasing resistance of the feeder spring. He wrapped the shell box in a washcloth and put it in his suitcase. Then he snapped a cartridge into the pistol's firing chamber, set the safety, and slid the Sauer inside his belt. Stretched out on the bed again, he reflected on the high degree of confidence possession of a weapon could impart to the possessor.

For a while he thought of Marisa, his boat, the pleasures of basic living; then his thoughts turned to Ghislaine Percival. In daylight, away from the lilt of her voice, Morgan was grateful things had gone no further last night. They had been heady with wine, disoriented by discovery, and he imagined that she, too, was having steadying thoughts. Today, discomfort over her boldness would trouble her, and by nightfall she would be hoping never to see her aunt's old friend again.

Having disposed of the problem girl, Morgan began thinking of Dobbs's traveler who was perhaps even now striding down the Ringstrasse, glancing around for surveillants. *Come now,* he summoned. Now or never, Roger. In Vienna you're worth nothing to anyone, not even to yourself. Here you're worth another hundred thou to me. So get with it. Use that large and skillful brain, tense that muscled frame and take the jump. You did it once before, but nobody was watching. This time might be harder, but you can do it. I have faith in you.

Confidence.

And hate.

Turning on his side he gazed at the grayness outside his window. Linden branches moved back and forth, their leaves not fully mature. He thought of the money he was carrying, most of it stashed behind the lining of his suitcase, a mixture of francs and large dollar bills in his wallet, and he decided that he ought to get it into a safer place. A

Swiss bank was the natural depository and Morgan had always wanted a numbered account. Too late today, all banks were closed. But tomorrow, if he were still in Geneva, he would find one with international branches for his funds, converting American currency into Swiss francs; then he could draw at a branch without having to return to Geneva.

The account should be joint with his son; then in case of premature death . . . or confinement . . . Bill could claim the funds for school bills, living expenses. Otherwise, unclaimed moneys would revert to the Swiss government after a period of years.

Confinement.

The third-tier cell in A-block. Two metal bunks, a basin, and a toilet bowl. The stink of the place. Roaches uncountable. Toilet caked with ancient excrement; mattress stained, discolored with urine, vomit, and dried crap; above in the far corner a single low wattage bulb that went off at night. Blue battle-lamps showed the walkway rails. Sometimes through the far window he could glimpse the moon, striped and sectioned by iron bars. Then, after midnight count, the uproar began; howling from the new cold-turkey druggies; screams of a chicken-kid being raped, the hoarse panting of the kid's sodomists. All night up and down the walkway prowled transvestites whispering fellatic invitations through the bars. Groans from the next cell where a prisoner he never saw masturbated.

Shower every other day; tin tray shoved through the bar slot if he was in deadlock. Or the long, nervous line of prisoners at the mess vats below. Soup and rusted vegetables, small plastic spoons to scoop up beans or sever a rare chunk of meat. Sliced bread to eat and to wipe off greasy hands.

An old gray-haired trusty pushed a broom down the walkway once a day collecting scraps and trash thrown from the cells. He had a blind white eye, from birth a twisted back. He was the cell block messenger and smuggler.

Two visits a week of forty-five minutes duration. Show-and-tell. Show through the grimy plexiglass window, tell over the monitored, two-way telephone that prisoner and visitor were forced to use.

At first there were visits from Janice. For three months she came to sit and talk and sadly smile, leaving a few dollars for his commissary needs. She brought their daughter once, Bill frequently until his school resumed. Then came only reporters wanting interviews, the lawyer he had hired. . . .

Once each week he got to walk around the recreation yard surrounded by a ten-foot wall. Watchtowers and guards with shotguns at the corners. Except in summer the yard was always muddy, deeply puddled, the jogging path a furrow in the earth. The weeds, at least, were green. Sometimes he pulled them out to suck and chew their tender roots. From instinct? To satisfy a metabolic need?

Yard fights were ended by the guards slowly. Sometimes the winner was decided later in the dead of night: a shank in the kidney, a nail in the head. Bodies dragged off the bunks, gray blankets washed of bloodstains and returned for later use . . . he had seen it all, the gross cruelties, the barbarisms and brutalities. Some guards made it their custom to screw the wives of prisoners in payment for trivial favors done inside the wall.

There was the officer-guard who had been tried on a charge of raping his six-year-old daughter. Extensive surgery had been required to repair the tears and other damage to the child. But at his trial the mother-wife refused to testify, and so the ape went back to prison duty, boasting when high on drugs or liquor of his accomplishment. Tight-Pussy Brown they called him, and he reveled in the name.

One night, for reasons Morgan never knew, block prisoners began to burn their mattresses. The stench and smoke were frightful, and Morgan remembered pressing his face to the stinking floor, gasping for air until the prison riot squad with firemen freed the deadlocked men. By then four were dead, hands still fixed to the heated bars.

In the aftermath, a month of deadlock as reprisal; no showers, scant meals. Three men were carted off to St. Elizabeth's, mad.

The lucky ones, he thought: clean mattresses and decent food. How much he'd envied them.

Still, to his retrospective surprise Morgan survived, outliving the Committee's term, finding himself at first unused to freedom and then not caring much. For the house had been sold by Janice, panicking at the prospect of bank foreclosure, taking or selling what she chose, packing his clothes and books and sending them to warehouse storage whose charges he had never been able to pay. By now, he supposed, his things had been sold at auction, the books by their dead weight.

He slept uneasily and when he woke there was darkness beyond his window pierced by a few pinpricks of light on the far side of the lake. Hargrave, he realized, would not be coming today.

At seven Morgan went down to the grill room and had a light

dinner of lamb cutlets and salad. In the lobby he bought magazines and a paperback Agatha Christie, returned to his room, and while reading fell asleep.

In the morning he rose early, convinced that this would be the day. When he was dressed he extracted the currency from his suitcase and transferred it to the inside pocket of his suit coat. The Sauer he fitted under the back of his belt, next to his spine. A mirror view showed it was unnoticeable.

He took breakfast in the grill and afterward brought down his suitcase and carried it to where the Cortina was garaged. Locking it in the trunk he drove to the Banque Suisse pour le Commerce S.A. Behind a barred window a placard listed the bank's foreign agencies, a dozen in all. One was on Wall Street, New York. He waited until the doors opened at nine, went to the New Accounts section, and outlined his requirements. A mustached, middle-aged assistant showed Morgan to a small cubicle where, in privacy, his money became Swiss francs, the total listed on a small receipt that bore the number of his account: six digits separated by the letter D. He was to understand that no interest was payable on the deposit, rather a service charge would be deducted each month from principal. They shook hands formally, after which Morgan drove toward the Richemond, parking a block and a half away.

In his room he wrote a letter to Bill, enclosing the account number and specifying the circumstances under which it was to be used. As he sealed the envelope he hoped his son would not reveal the contents to Janice.

The *concierge* sold him a stamp and posted the letter in a lobby drop box. Morgan asked the cashier to total his bill, explaining that he might have to leave on short notice. He went back to the room, noticing that the time was 10:15, and ordered a large pot of coffee.

The waiter brought it on an alcohol warmer and Morgan drank coffee while going through French and British magazines; *L'Express* and *The Field.* The latter's advertisements for Irish and English country homes had always interested him; after today, if he chose, one would be within his means. Heating was said to be a constant problem and old wells often went dry; no air-conditioning, of course, and social life revolved around the vicarage. Even so, it. . . .

The telephone rang.

Morgan stiffened, reached for the phone.

80

He recognized the voice. "Today, on the Sabena flight. At 12:23. Please repeat."

"Sabena, 12:23. And the money?"

"Taken care of. Get going."

SEVEN

MORGAN replaced the telephone, drained his coffee cup, and stood up. He checked the location of his automatic and pulled on his topcoat. Everything else was in his suitcase in the Cortina's trunk. He left the room door open, went down to the cashier's booth, and paid his bill. Then he walked around the side of the hotel and over to where he had left the Cortina. The tank was full, the engine started on the second try, and after rounding the Place de Cornavin and the central station, he turned onto the Rue de la Servette that widened after a mile or so and became the airport autoroute.

He drove rapidly and carefully; after the days and hours of inaction and waiting Morgan wanted nothing to delay his encounter with Roger Hargrave.

Ahead an opening. His foot hit the accelerator and he pulled out and around a slower-moving airport bus, dodging back into his lane and barely avoiding collision with an oncoming car.

Adrenalin charged his blood, clearing vision, speeding his reactions. Anticipation dried his mouth, his hands felt welded to the wheel. He was ready for Hargrave.

Aeroport de Genève-Cointrin.

Morgan followed directional arrows around the glass and concrete building topped with a glass-sectioned control tower. He left the Cortina parked three rows from the terminal building, keys under the floormat, and walked casually toward the entrance steps. There was no black Mercedes limousine in view, but he supposed it would not arrive until the Sabena flight from Vienna was in. Prior positioning might attract unwelcome attention.

He went up the steps and pushed through the door into the terminal lobby. The electronic arrival-departure board showed the Sabena flight from Vienna coming in on schedule, at 12:23. The time was 11:50.

At the newstand Morgan bought a London paper and a small bar of Tobler's almond-chocolate, and found a seat near the counter where Swiss knives and cutlery were sold. He remembered buying an elaborate Swiss Army pocket knife for Bill five or six years ago. The knife was equipped with spoon, fork, and scissors in addition to three blades of different lengths, and it came in a leather belt-case. He wondered if Bill had lost it or whether it was with him at school. The adjoining counter sold European perfumes at prices higher than Paris, Morgan recalled. Even so, he had bought Chanel for Janice on that same trip to make up for his absence.

Over the unfolded *Times* he looked around the big room, satisfied himself that no obvious surveillants were posted. Still, he was reasonably sure Dobbs would have a team on hand when the flight got in. Too much was at stake to chance anything going wrong.

Twelve o'clock. He saw a policeman in dark-blue uniform strolling near the ticket counters. Morgan reacted with sudden tenseness, then relaxed. The policeman was no threat to him, but a presence in behalf of order and discipline, precisely the ambience Morgan most desired.

He finished his chocolate bar, wondering what name Hargrave was traveling under. Would he arrive with a Soviet passport or as a national of some other country? Surely Dobbs would not have provided Roger with American documentation; that should be withheld until Hargrave earned it. Otherwise Dobbs would needlessly forfeit one lever in controlling the defector.

Morgan turned a page and scanned it. He hoped someone other than the Director was handling operational details, for Dobbs lacked basic field experience while Hargrave did not. And it was likely that Roger had picked up a number of refinements from the KGB while under its care and tutelage. Against Hargrave, the Director was outmatched.

He thought of the man in the green velour hat with its tuft of goat-beard, silver ferrule holder pinned to the band, his strange accent. Morgan wondered how much he knew.

He got up and glanced down at the passenger pick-up point. No Mercedes waiting. He folded the *Times* under his left arm and walked down the inner staircase to the Customs exit. Half a dozen baggage handlers waited, smoking and chatting. One with a long mustache devoured a thick sandwich, leaning against the baggage cart. Morgan decided Hargrave would not be bringing checked baggage; it would have been too dangerous to leave his Vienna hotel with a suitcase. At most he might carry a briefcase on board. With only that to show the Customs inspectors inside the etched-glass doors Hargrave should come through quickly, perhaps first of his flight to clear. But Morgan could not even assume that Hargrave had managed to board the plane in Vienna: He might still be there, detained in the Soviet Embassy or forced on board an Aeroflot flight to Moscow for execution.

Nothing was certain.

The announcer's flat professional voice informed those interested that the Sabena flight from Vienna was about to land. Morgan's throat went dry. What would he say to Hargrave? What would Roger say to *him*? Had expectations of amity been encouraged? Or was the redefector prepared to accept dislike, resentment, and scorn?

Behind Morgan a group was forming. No more than a dozen men and women, one infant carried in a fur-trimmed robe. For them, Morgan reflected, the debarkation would be routine, unexciting, but he felt moisture on his palms. The blue-smocked baggagemen were beginning to move about; one jingled coins, mentally making change. The sandwich-eater wiped his mustache with a handkerchief.

They, at least, were ready.

Then Morgan heard a far door opening, the distant chatter of passengers entering the processing channels. Health card, passport, Customs.

Morgan's mind was focused now, free-association expelled; cleared for action.

He looked around at the expectant group, then beyond their faces to the exit doors. By now the black Mercedes should be nosing slowly toward the meeting point. Was the departure jet ready for the flight to Gatwick?

The Customs doors parted and a middle-aged *hausfrau* bustled through. An overcoated man took off his hat and hugged her sturdily. Next came a young couple. "Willy!" cried a voice, and the couple veered toward it. Morgan wiped his palms on his topcoat.

Now came a tall man, sallow-faced, wearing a well-cut black overcoat. Gray sideburns showed below the brim of his black hat. He moved haltingly, his cheeks hollowed with the effort. Pausing, he seemed to study the crowd. As his head turned, Morgan saw the unmistakable profile of Roger Hargrave.

85

God, how the man had aged!

Morgan felt incapable of movement. Then, as Hargrave shuffled forward, Morgan forced himself to move toward him. Hargrave discerned the motion, halted, and seemed to inhale deeply. Under one arm was a leather letter-case. Its gold catch glinted.

Hargrave's eyes watched him come. Recognition was in them but the face was expressionless. Morgan touched his arm.

"Do you need help?"

"No. David, how good of you to come." The colorless lips formed a slight smile. "After so many years . . . but we'll have time to talk, won't we? Catch up. . . ."

"The car's waiting," Morgan said, fighting down a surge of sympathy. "Come along."

Silently, Hargrave nodded, began slowly to walk beside Morgan. "I had to have someone I could trust," he said in dry tones. "How much do you know?"

"Very little. Where's Alexandra?"

"She'll try to come another day, by different means. I've been ill. It's been very difficult." He placed a hand on Morgan's shoulder. "It was time for me to return. I have so much to tell. Alex was willing to stay even though I haven't long to live."

Morgan pushed open the exit doors, motioned aside a baggageman.

"I've wanted so long to come, and now I'm nearly home."

Morgan stared at him.

Hargrave's gray eyebrows moved. "David," he said huskily, "*you* think I'm a traitor?"

"You deserted us."

Hargrave's bony fingers gripped Morgan's bicep.

"But you should have been *told*." He exhaled and there was a fluttering sound in his throat. "In time, then. Everything will be authenticated." Hargrave shook his head and Morgan said, "We have to keep moving, Roger."

They were at the top of the steps. Below at the curb the black Mercedes limousine was waiting, license NVA-878. "Our car," Morgan said and took Hargrave's arm to help him down the steps. His eyes made out a uniformed driver at the wheel, beside him a man in a velour hat, a fur-trimmed coat. Morgan had not expected him. Perhaps he was there to deliver the money. Or help Hargrave into the plane. The Director had failed to mention Hargrave's illness. Perhaps he didn't know. A dying defector was less valuable than a robust one. Morgan opened the rear door, and as Hargrave stooped to get in he whispered, "I was Dormouse. Always remember that."

Morgan had become increasingly confused. He waited until Hargrave drew in his long legs and closed the door. Morgan got in through the other door, closed it, and the Mercedes began to move. The letter-case was on the seat between them, and Morgan saw that Hargrave's hands were resting on his knees. Thin, bony hands. The man must have cancer, Morgan thought. He's come back to die.

"Did you have a good career, David?" Hargrave asked.

"While it lasted."

"I knew you would. I vouched for you before I brought you in. And you never betrayed. . . ." His face turned away but Morgan could see moistness in his pale eyes. "I was so proud of you." Again the bloodless lips parted. "A Townsend boy learns loyalty."

Morgan tapped the letter-case. "Is this important?"

"Indispensable." Hargrave swallowed. "A good English word. I've spoken Russian so long . . . so many years. . . . Is America changed now?"

"You'd hardly recognize it. We'll be there tomorrow."

"Good, good. We'll talk on the plane."

The Mercedes was leaving the airport area. To the man in the green velour hat Morgan said, "I'll take my package now."

The swarthy face looked back. "What's the hurry? You can count it on the plane."

"*Now.*"

The man bent forward, then passed back to Morgan a brown suede case, attaché size. Morgan set it across his thighs and opened the catch. Greenbacks, closely packed. Morgan closed the case and set it on the floor. He had stipulated Swiss francs.

"You were paid to come?" the tired voice asked. "I thought you might have come out of friendship."

"Friendship? We'll discuss friendship as we travel. Right now there's a plane to board."

The Mercedes was slowing, easing over to a wide part of the road where it was to turn and head back to the airport. So far the driver had not said a word. Morgan had not bothered to notice his face. He looked at Hargrave's profile, saw at close range the lines of age and suffering. But Roger was only a little more than fifty. Everything Hargrave had said in their few minutes together seemed incomprehensible. He was putting on the façade of a repatriated war prisoner. And what was "Dormouse" supposed to mean? What was to be authenticated? Morgan would have asked those questions but for the two men in the front seat.

The Mercedes turned off the road and onto a narrow lane leading toward the woods. This was not the plan. Suddenly Morgan understood that something was wrong. I don't like it, he thought, and then the Mercedes braked hard. Hargrave lurched forward, nearly hitting the front seat, but Morgan's muscles were tensed, resistant. As Hargrave recovered, began sitting back, Morgan saw the green-hatted man's head turn, saw the exposed teeth, the grin, the black silencer tube resting on the seat top. "The trip ends here," the man said. He turned the silencer toward the driver and shot him through the temple. Now the silencer was turning toward Hargrave, and Morgan went rigid. A second *phutt* and Hargrave's body jerked back against the seat. Morgan's horrified eyes saw a hole in Roger's forehead. The window glass behind it was starred by the exiting bullet, spattered with blood and brains. Then, as the silencer moved toward Morgan the man said, "This'll be a pleasure."

But Morgan slammed his case at the silencer, at the man's face. He ducked down, tearing at his topcoat, the suitcoat, gripping the Sauer automatic, thumbing off the safety. The killer's arm was half over the seat, his silenced revolver wavering. Morgan pressed the pistol muzzle to the seat and fired. The explosion in the confined space was deafening. The killer screamed and fell backward against the dash, but he was still alive. The silencer gave off its deadly *phutt,* the bullet going through the roof of the car. Twisting awkwardly, half rising, Morgan saw the revolver searching. The man's free hand clutched his thorax; between the fingers flowed fresh blood. Morgan pointed the automatic and shot him through the curve of throat and chin. The front window shattered. Slowly the body fell sideways, the green hat tilted askew uncovering a bald spot fringed with blood and gray matter. The head came to rest on the driver's thighs.

Dazed, Morgan forced himself up and onto the seat beside Hargrave's body. The blue eyes were open, so was his mouth. The black hat lay on the rear window ledge. Roger's gray hair seemed undisturbed. Death had smoothed the facial lines, giving his skin an almost youthful look, and as Morgan shuddered he saw again the handsome prefect he had known, as clearly as on the day of their first meeting.

His eyes moved to the pistol in his hand. The car was filled with the stench of cordite. A breeze through the broken window glass stirred tendrils of smoke. Morgan felt alien to the scene, as if watching the freeze-frame in a motion picture.

Finally he slid the Sauer on safety and put it in his topcoat pocket. Then he pushed open the door to clear the air. Four men in the car and only one living. That had been the plan all along, but Morgan was to have been one of the dead. His right hand opened and closed. He had not been commissioned to protect Roger, just conduct him home. Now his boyhood friend was dead, slumped in the far corner. Tears in his eyes, Morgan reached over and closed Roger's eyelids. Now the face seemed merely to be sleeping.

How can I explain this to Alex? he thought as he wiped his eyes. How explain to anyone?

EIGHT

Except for nearby traffic the place was utterly silent. Time seemed suspended. Morgan leaned across the seat and got the killer's wallet from his coat pocket. Then he removed Hargrave's wallet and placed both inside the letter-case. Ballistics could show the revolver had killed two men, but only if the battered bullets could be found. He tried to think of what else he ought to do, not only to insulate himself from danger but to aid in finding out the background of this slaughter, where the responsibility lay.

To do that, to do anything at all, he had first to survive, and that meant getting away before some curious motorist or police patrol noticed and investigated the half-hidden Mercedes with the shattered windows. *Il faut d'abord durer.*

He who lives and runs away will live to fight another day. Morgan caught himself thinking the absurd aphorism, choked off the thought, and got out of the rear door. The feel of turf under his feet enhanced his returning sense of reality.

He brought out the letter-case, then the attaché case, opened the latter and saw the greenbacks again. He laid Hargrave's leather envelope atop them and closed the case, wondering as he did so if the money it contained was counterfeit. If it was, that fact alone would give him a basic direction in which to move.

The engine was still running smoothly, almost silently, steam from the exhaust lifting like a gray plume in the cool air. He closed the rear door with his elbow, then wiped the handle with his handkerchief. Still holding it, he opened the driver's door, propping up the heavy body, finally pushing it half-upright. He found the gearshift and pulled the lever into first. As he closed the door, the limousine lumbered slowly ahead, Morgan following into the birch woods.

Where the trail curved, the Mercedes plowed ahead, through grass and fallen branches, nosing finally into a clump of birches and stalling out.

The woods around were silent. He stared at the mute limousine whose rear window was so oddly spattered, said, "I should have known," and turned back to the highway.

His left hand clutched the case grip as he walked, forcing his mind from the butchery behind him. Was there to have been a back-up car? One to follow the limousine and pick up the killer when his job was done? Or had green-hat planned to walk the highway as he, Morgan, was doing, and make his way from the scene of the triple murder?

Morgan looked at his overcoat for traces of blood. None. There was a slight smudge near the knee where he had knelt on the floor, and damp earth clung along his soles. He tightened his tie knot, wiped cold perspiration from his forehead, and followed the highway shoulder to the airport entrance. Passing cars and bicyclists paid no attention to him. He stayed as far as possible from the airport building as he made his way toward the Cortina. It had been his intention to leave it there for eventual claiming by the rental company, but now it was essential to him.

He was in no immediate danger. The Mercedes and its corpses had not been discovered yet, and there was nothing to link him to the scene. In time the police would find witnesses who could describe the man who had helped Hargrave through the terminal to the car. With their quiet efficiency the Swiss police would work with that description until they found the rental company and his hotel. Within two days at most they would be looking for Morgan at hotels, airports, and train stations.

It was necessary to leave the country while he could.

He laid the attaché case on the Cortina's front seat, recovered the keys from beneath the mat. Starting the engine he looked at the terminal building, his mind kaleidoscoping all that had happened in the hour since his arrival.

What to do with the money?

Large sums brought instant attention and suspicion to the holder were it to be noticed during inspection at, say, Orly airport. Italian restrictions were even more stringent. He was reluctant to lodge it all in his local bank account, fearing that if it were connected to him the account would be confiscated, the money forever lost.

There *was* a way, though. He opened the attaché case, then the letter-case, and took out the killer's thick wallet. As he hoped, it contained a passport. Turkish. The name under the killer's photo was Kistos Aristides Soffit, born at Lamaca, Cyprus, forty-six years ago. The wallet itself contained a small amount of Swiss and Italian currency, some nightclub cards from Geneva and Rome, nothing more.

Morgan wondered how many passports the killer had stashed away, how many names he traveled under. In whose employ?

He would have to use his Canadian passport to leave Switzerland and cross into France, because the car papers were made out to Johnson. But once in France, Johnson would disappear and Soffit begin a life beyond the grave. For a while, at least.

He drove out of the airport carefully, wondering if the alarm had yet been given but seeing nothing around the terminal area to suggest that anyone was being sought by the authorities. He took the highway along which he had so recently walked, down which the Mercedes had taken him. As he passed the birch woods he saw no ambulances or police cars. Wind stirred the birch branches, silvering them. He thought of Hargrave in the car, face calm as though in acceptance of death however unexpectedly it had come. I think I underestimated him, Morgan reflected, but perhaps I'll never know.

He realized that he had not even considered trying to contact Bob Dobbs, report what had happened, ask for instructions and help.

Why not?

The fact that his mind had never surfaced the thought until now must indicate subconscious rejection of the idea. Dobbs or his staff had made all reception arrangements; Soffit was Dobbs's man, his chosen instrument, so directly or indirectly Bob Dobbs was responsible.

Unless the killing was Soffit's idea alone.

Morgan couldn't, he knew, exclude that possibility, so final judgment would have to wait. In the meantime he had to find safe haven and isolate himself; only then could he start putting things together, laying the blame where it belonged.

And doing something about it.

It was hard to keep his mind on driving; so many questions were flooding through it that he nearly missed the crossroads arrow pointing to Lausanne. As he drove he got the rental company map out of the glove compartment, and when there were no cars ahead of him he glanced at it, noting the turnoff that led across the border to Divonne.

He had never visited the famous casino although it was strategically located a twenty-minutes' drive from the money markets of Geneva. There was no legal gambling in Switzerland, so the French supplied a casino as near the border as possible. Border guards were accustomed to tourists crossing into France with large sums to gamble. Now, with Geneva an Arab-and-oil headquarters, the sight of all that cash entering La Belle France could only please them.

In a quarter of an hour he reached the border and got out of the Cortina to unlock its trunk. In the Customs shed he showed the car's rental papers, opened his suitcase, and suddenly remembered the box of .32 cartridges. The guard was beginning to finger through his clothing when Morgan got out his passport. "*Canadien,*" he said, tapping the passport. "*Je suis Québecois. Je parle Français comme un Parisien.*"

The guard smiled, nodding enthusiastically. "*Vive le Québec Français. Vous êtes tres bienvenu.*" Without further search he closed the suitcase and chalked it, took the passport and stamped it with an entry cachet.

Morgan carried the suitcase back to the car and returned it to the trunk. The attaché case was still on the seat where he had left it, in plain view of the border guards.

One obstacle behind me, Morgan thought as he steered back onto the road. How many left to go?

Route signs directed him to Divonne, to the big hotel and its first-floor casino. As Kistos Aristides Soffit he would spend the night, get some rest and try to organize his thoughts. And change some dollars at the casino's foreign exchange facility.

Registering at the desk he used the Turkish passport, the killer's name, wondering whether Soffit was on Wanted lists circulated by France or Interpol. If so, he would know before morning.

The room, large and handsome, overlooked the casino gardens. In the distance he could see a riding ring, paddocks and stables, jumps and dressage posts. All for the convenience of casino guests. Morgan was reminded of The Homestead where his parents were accustomed to take him at Easter time. Long arched hallways, tables for backgammon and bridge; fine food, a gracious interlude from everyday living. His mother loved basking in the mineral springs while his father swam tirelessly in the enclosed, heated pool.

Morgan got out his wallet and pulled from it the pocket litter he had received from George Baker in Paris. It was no longer useful, and soon it would become dangerous. In the bathtub he set fire to it, tore apart the Canadian passport and added it to the flames. When the fire flickered out Morgan picked up the unburnt pieces and flushed them down the toilet. The shower washed ashes down the drain. *Adieu,* Ed Johnson, late of Ste. Agathe, province of Québec.

He badly wanted a drink, but there were practical things that needed doing before he could begin to relax.

From his suitcase he took the cartridge box, freed it of the Richemond's washcloth camouflage, and thumbed two cartridges into the Sauer magazine to replace those fired in the Mercedes. As he did so he remembered he had forgotten to search the limousine for the ejected shells. With them, Swiss police ballistics could do a good deal; as soon as he felt reasonably secure he would have to dispose of the Sauer.

On the bed he opened the attaché case and lifted out Hargrave's leather envelope. Roger's wallet was in it, along with whatever papers he had brought from Vienna. Hargrave had called them "indispensable." To whom? Morgan wondered, and carried the contents to a table where he sorted them out.

Roger's wallet held a few Russian rubles and a quantity of Austrian schillings. The Soviet internal passport was in the name of Hargrave and in Russian and French identified the holder as a member of the Olympic Consultative Committee of the U.S.S.R. Visa pages showed entry into and exit from Austria, and arrival at Genève-Cointrin.

Several sheets of stationery were covered with handwriting in Cyrillic. This must be the information Hargrave was so anxious to bring out, turn over to the West. But Morgan could not read Russian.

Translation, then, would have to wait until he could have the documents examined by someone he trusted, someone who could also evaluate their worth.

Frustrated, no better informed than before, Morgan returned the handwritten sheets, wallet, and passport, to the leather case and went back to the bed.

Soffit's attaché case held his gaze and Morgan felt that someone, somewhere, was waiting for a call from K. A. Soffit, confirming that the deed had been done. But who would the murderer have called? The money in the attaché case could help him find some answers.

Slowly he lifted the tightly-banded packages of hundred-dollar bills. Under the desk lamp he examined two of each, extracted at random, but he had no expertise with which to authenticate them.

Roger's phrase: *Everything will be explained.*

But who was left to perform that tragic office? Alexandra? Would she survive to tell him? And how could he believe her when he had no reason to believe her husband?

Except for the manner of his death.

I'll get to that, Morgan told himself, but not now. There's been too much confusion today, too much violence; it's still blocking my rational processes. It was a trap. For Roger and for me. Only Soffit was to leave the woods alive.

To cut off brooding, Morgan rang for the valet, then bundled his shirts and underwear, the suit he was wearing. When he gave the clothing to the valet Morgan said he needed everything back in the morning. Next he rang for room service and asked the waiter for a half-liter of Black Label, a bottle of Evian, and a bowl of cracked ice. The waiter left a menu in case *m'sieu* desired dinner in his room.

Morgan placed the letter-case in his travel bag, carried the attaché case into the bathroom. He was soaking in the tub when the waiter returned. Morgan called out instructions to leave the ice and liquor on the table, and, when the waiter left, wrapped a towel around his body and poured a double shot of Scotch, filling the glass with ice and spring water. Then he returned to the tub and drank, feeling the surrounding warmth relax his muscles, the liquor thaw the vitals that had been frozen ever since he saw the silencer and realized what was scheduled to occur.

Morgan stayed in his room until six, when the casino tables opened. He felt better now, shaved and clean; a fresh shirt did wonders for the spirit. That and the Black Label.

He made his way down to the gaming tables where a dozen clients were playing. As the evening lengthened, he knew the crowd would swell. Along one wall was a bar, the mahogany corbel so polished that it reflected light from the chandeliers. Morgan used Swiss francs to buy chips at the cage, played baccarat until the stake was lost, then walked around to the foreign exchange bureau and handed over one of the hundred-dollar bills from the attaché case. The cashier examined it closely, holding it under a large, illuminated magnifying glass, then nodded. An electronic calculator printed out the transaction. He gave Morgan a small sheaf of French francs and the receipt.

Morgan walked back toward the tables thoughtfully. That bill, at least, had been valid. But since the plan had been to kill Morgan, why bother with legitimate currency? Counterfeits—which were not hard to acquire—would have withstood his flash examination just as well, kept him cooperative until the killer was ready. He reached the dice table, saw the ivory cubes rebounding from the end, and as he readied his bet he understood. The money was intended for Soffit as his payoff for the murders. After killing Morgan the Cypriot had merely to remove the attaché case and walk away . . . as Morgan had done.

Someone, he mused, would be furious.

He bet a few francs on a throw, lost, lingered at the table a while, and went back to the *bureau de change* where he exchanged several bills after the customary scrutiny. Now he had enough French francs for his immediate needs. In Paris he could exchange larger quantities from time to time at banks throughout the city. Paris was large enough, sufficiently crowded to give him the protective anonymity he needed. In Paris he could buy false documentation, establish a base from which to start his inquiries. He had to begin working backward on the chain, following it link by link to its origin.

First, though, he had to reach Paris before the massive search began. By tomorrow, at the latest, the corpse-filled limousine would be discovered. Another day and they would know where he had left the country and how. They would be able to trace him through the Customs point, with a little luck find out that he had stayed overnight in Divonne.

From here, he thought, as he walked into the dining room, I have to vanish.

Completely.

That much decided, Morgan picked up the menu, forced a smile at the waiter, and ordered his evening meal.

His dreams were of blood and violence and they exhausted him. He woke at dawn to the sounds of birds, the clatter of horses' hooves below. They injected a sense of reality into Morgan's mind, accelerating his thoughts. When his clothing was returned he dressed and shoved his used suit down the hall trash chute. From the attaché case he took the bundled currency and Hargrave's wallet and transferred them to the suitcase. He disposed of the empty attaché case down the chute. In theory it was recognizable, and getting rid of it meant one less item to carry.

After breakfasting in his room he carried the suitcase down to the lobby and paid the room cashier with American money, taking francs in change.

While the Cortina's engine warmed, Morgan consulted the road map. He was about seventy miles from Dijon, a hundred from Lyon. At either city he could board a train to Paris and be there easily by nightfall. So he followed the road that led toward Besançon, noticing bus stops along the way. It was mountainous country, the foothills of the Jura range, and as he came over a rise he noticed a small lake below the curve of the road. He saw, too, that there was no guard rail.

Morgan turned the Cortina toward the road edge, stopped, and got out, leaving the engine running. He removed his suitcase and set it down on the road. Then he put the car in gear and released the brake. Slowly the car left the road, gathering speed as it crashed down the steep incline, rolling, turning over, and finally catapulting into the lake. At first it floated in the rippled water, bottom up, then a giant bubble broke the surface beside the chassis. The Cortina rolled over and sank. Bubbles stippled the water for a while, then the lake was as calm as before.

Carrying his suitcase, Morgan walked half a mile downhill to a bus stop, sat on the bench and stretched his legs, resting and dozing until an old bus rumbled up and let him aboard. It was half-filled with rural people, farm-wives, children on their way to country school. Their frocks and smocks and large black bows reminded him of his own children's Paris schooling.

At Besançon he transferred to the waiting Dijon bus that carried him down through the Saône Valley and in two hours came to a stop in front of the railroad station.

Morgan bought a third-class ticket, found a seat, and, when the vendor came through the car, selected a bread-and-cheese sandwich and a bottle of *cidre* for his lunch. The railway ran along the Bourgogne canal through some of the finest vineyards in Europe, stopping at Sens, then lurching onward past Fontainebleau, Melun, and finally into the Gare Saint-Lazare.

He walked out of the station's smoke and dirt and found a hotel nearby, of the category frequented by prostitutes and small-bore criminals. As anticipated, he was not asked for identification, merely for two nights' lodging in advance. He was then shown to a small hallway room that was only slightly larger than the sagging spring bed.

The quarter offered an assortment of working-class shops and stores, and in one of them Morgan bought an unattractive ready-made suit, a second-hand topcoat, and a dark brown hat. Across the street he haggled over a cheap suitcase, finally paying eleven francs for it. The suitcase locked with a key.

In his room Morgan changed clothing, transferred the currency and cartridges into the new suitcase, and walked it back to the Gare where he checked it in the baggage room. When it was settled safely on the shelf he took a bus to the Levallois-Perret section and found the place he was looking for, on the Rue des Chasses.

Opening the grime-caked door Morgan went into the printing shop. Beyond the counter three presses were working. Two men in ink-stained blue overalls fed the presses, and when Morgan rapped on the counter one of them came over.

He was a young man, smudges on his face, hands black with ink. "*M'sieu?*" he said politely.

"I was looking for the proprietor, Jules Frechette."

"A friend of his?"

"From some years ago."

"Then you will be sorry to learn that he is dead these three, no, four years, *m'sieu.*" He wiped his hands on a dirty towel.

"I regret, indeed."

"I am his son, *m'sieu,* and my name is Claude. Perhaps I can serve you as my father did. Tell me your needs."

Morgan hesitated. He wondered if the son was trustworthy, whether he possessed his late father's skills. "From time to time," he said, "your father was in the habit of accommodating me by way of documents." He paused.

"Go on, *m'sieu.*"

"Documents that, let us say, served to replace those missing for whatever reason."

"Documents of identity, *m'sieu?* Carnets and passports?"

"Precisely. My question is this: Are you in the same line of trade?"

The printer shrugged. "I am, and I am not, if you understand me. It comes down to a matter of price."

"And you have the capacity to produce, say, a passport for me? A *carnet d'identité?*"

"Most assuredly. Which nationality do you prefer?"

"Speed is of greater importance."

"Then I would suggest a British passport, *m'sieu.* It happens that one is immediately available."

"And the price?"

"One thousand seven hundred francs."

"Fifteen hundred."

"This way, *m'sieu.*"

Claude led Morgan through a wall door into a small side room. On a tripod was a 35 mm. camera, and around the wall shelves were trays and equipment for photographic developing and enlarging.

As he settled into the chair facing the camera, Morgan said, "I've been thinking of growing a mustache."

"Excellent. Let us advance the process of nature." Claude produced a bag filled with false beards and mustaches. Morgan selected a small mustache and pressed it along the curve of his lip. Claude made further adjustments, turned on the floodlights, and exposed several frames in rapid succession. The lights went off and Morgan said, "I'll want some business cards, too, half a dozen or so."

"Of course." Claude opened a wall panel and removed a stack of passports. He unsnapped the rubber band, riffled through them, and drew out a British passport. Originally it had been issued to one Charles Elias Chipman of Manchester. His photograph—that of a sallow, vapid-looking man—was affixed to the inner page by an embossed seal.

"Half now," Claude said. "Half on delivery."

Morgan counted out eight hundred francs. "I need it tonight."

"Come back at nine."

"Your father was highly reliable."

"As am I. *Bonjour, m'sieu.*"

"*Bonjour.*"

He left the shop and when he passed a sewer grating dropped Soffit's now dangerous Turkish passport through the grille. Until he received the new one, he was immobilized.

NINE

On Saturday evening Marisa Isabela Pardo de la Costa stayed late in the office of her shop, totaling sales and making out future orders. Having spent two days in Miami with relatives, she returned to Key West with barely enough time to calculate the salesgirls' commissions and pay them their week's earnings before closing time. She entered credits and debits in her account books, printing in her fine legible hand, then made out sales tax and utility checks, addressed and stamped their envelopes.

There was other work to be done—there always was—but she could take care of it on Monday, the slowest sales day of the week. Until then she planned to indulge herself; have a leisurely dinner and a good night's sleep.

Rising from her desk she stifled a yawn, glanced down at the safe where David's money was. Perhaps he would come back tomorrow; already he was somewhat overdue. She did not want him returning to an empty house so she decided to sun on the rooftop tomorrow, not go to the beach.

With a frown she remembered yesterday's caller—a pleasant-faced man in his early forties, a Mr. McNally—who came about David, saying he was an old friend, and a friend of David's employer as well.

"Is David all right?" she asked in sudden fear.

"As far as we know. But you could help us determine that. Did he leave on schedule?"

"Yes."

"Do you know where he was going?"

"I don't think I should say anything about that."

"Come, come, Miss Pardo. I'm asking on behalf of Mr. Dobbs, and you know who he is."

"Yes, I do. David was going to Geneva by way of Paris. But Mr. Dobbs knows all that. It's why they met in Atlanta."

McNally smiled. "Exactly. But because so much money is involved, Mr. Dobbs wanted to make sure that Mr. Morgan is carrying out the assignment instead of—how can I put it—just taking the money and doing nothing in return."

"David's an honorable man," she said. "He would always keep his part of a bargain. So tell Mr. Dobbs that David is doing everything he agreed to do. You can be sure of that."

McNally nodded. "I am. Now, have you discussed David's mission with anyone?"

"Of course not. What he told me was in confidence. Besides, it's nobody's business what he does."

"Couldn't agree more. Well, that's all I needed to ask, and I appreciate your responses. Oh, one other thing—has David called or written you from Europe?"

She shook her head. "He wouldn't call in any case."

"No? Why not?"

"Because our phones could be tapped."

"Right," said McNally. "A wise precaution." He thanked her again and left the shop.

Now, as she picked up her purse, it troubled her that she had been so open with McNally. David had cautioned her to be close-mouthed, and with anyone else she would have been. But Dobbs had hired David. And McNally knew David's plans, so all she had done was confirm that David was following instructions. No, there seemed no grounds for concern that she had talked too much, though she would mention McNally to David when he returned.

Marisa turned off the light and locked the office door. She walked through boutique aisles hung with skirts, blouses, scarves, caftans, and ruanas, set the burglar alarm, turned off the store lights, and locked the front door.

A block and a half away two men in a parked LTD saw her leave. One nudged the other who nodded. Neither man spoke.

Marisa walked toward Mallory Square, went into the Two Brothers restaurant and ordered Florida lobster tails with black beans and rice, a small salad, and a glass of white wine.

The LTD stationed itself across the street.

Marisa toyed with her salad, wondering how long she would enjoy

102

eating customary things. Because of certain indications she had consulted the family gynecologist in Miami who told her, to her joy, that she was nearly three months along. It seemed impossible, incredible, but Dr. Menendez had said there was no chance of error even though she had experienced no morning sickness or other associated discomforts.

On the street outside the doctor's office she had begun trembling, partly with happiness, partly with apprehension over David's reaction. They had not expected a child, they were not even married. Yet between them they had created one and she was going to bear it, with or without a husband. She thought that in his way David loved her, though not as deeply as she loved him, and she had taken pains to disguise her infatuation, letting him think she was a thoroughly modern woman quite willing to live with a man without the blessing of the Church.

She was afraid that David would suggest abortion when she told him the news. If he did, things between them could never be the same.

She sipped the wine slowly, savoring its taste. Full blouses, such as those she sold in her shop would conceal her condition for another two or three months, but after that everyone would know.

She began picking at the lobster tail, wondering where David was now, at this moment. Flying back across the Atlantic? Still waiting in Switzerland for the man he had known in his youth? The days were too long without him.

When she finished dinner Marisa left the restaurant and walked slowly toward her house. Behind her, at a distance, the LTD followed.

Inside the house she locked the front door, fed a clamoring El Tigre part of a kingfish steak, freshened his water, and went upstairs. As she turned on the lights she found herself half-planning which room would be the nursery. The corner room held her paints and easel, the litter of David's things. The storeroom they were always going to straighten up, bring order to, but never did. She opened the door and surveyed it. Cracked plaster and peeling paint. A day's work would change it completely. Pink or blue?

Turning off the light she closed the door. Her only concern, then, was the way David would respond. He was not an easy man to predict. His life before her had been complicated by travel, his profession, his wife, his children. Not the usual *yanqui* at all. His gentleness had drawn her to him, his consideration; things she discovered only after they became lovers.

103

She undressed slowly, touching her stomach, thinking that soon she would sense movement inside. *Oh, how I pray for that moment!*

In the bathroom she stepped close to the mirror to examine her breasts. A tracery of blue veins, never there before, was evident on the upper flesh. Her nipples had been slightly sore for at least two weeks and now they were darkening! So soon!

Tomorrow she would go to church, the ten o'clock Mass. Since David began living with her Marisa had not gone to Confession. Now, for the sake of their child, she would confess to a priest, anonymous behind the screen.

She stepped into the shower stall and turned on the water, washing her body carefully, then dried with a towel thinking: Oh, David, I hope you love me enough to marry me, to share our child.

She drew on a nightgown, reflecting that she would need an entirely different wardrobe now: elastic abdominal panels, drawstring waists to accommodate her growth. Her eyes sparkled in the mirror. I'm going to give birth!

El Tigre was lying at the foot of the bed, licking paws and rubbing them on his whiskers. A fine *gato,* she thought, and as she got into bed he moved aside protestingly, found another location, and went to sleep.

Her bedlamp was the only light in the house. The men in the LTD watched the shaded window. They smoked, seldom speaking, taking turns on watch. One of them had short black hair, the other, a blond, had a brown scar running the length of his jawbone. Both were costumed in bluejeans and short-sleeved shirts. Two nights ago the LTD had been stolen from the Jai Alai Fronton, its plates quickly changed, a false registration provided by a car-paint garage off the Tamiami Trail. The younger man, the blond, lighted a brown-papered marijuana cigarette, cupped his hands around it, and inhaled. Pot glazed over the boredom.

"Get stoned, you idiot," the older man warned, "and it's your ass."

"Plenty of time," the blond murmured dreamily. "Shit, man, we got hours to go. Hours like cherries on a tree."

"Don't screw up, that's all. Do your job and split."

"Relax. Reeee-lax. Croakin' while I'm tokin'."

The dark man looked at him in disgust, then lifted his eyes to the slight glow of the girl's window. When the hell did she go to sleep?

Marisa was filing her nails, watching Saturday Night Live on the TV in the corner of the room. She hoped David would surprise her tomorrow, perhaps when she returned from Mass. She buffed her nails through the last part of the program, and when the late news came on she padded over and turned off the set.

Suddenly she felt hungry, but decided not to eat, remembering how heavy most Latin women became during pregnancy. Barracudas at the table! No, she would deny herself and preserve her figure.

Reaching back, she turned off the bed lamp and lay on her side. *Oh, David, I love you so. I want you this moment, want to feel you with me. Please hurry back.*

In the LTD the dark man grunted. "Finally," he said. "Now we'll give her an hour."

The street was dark, silent, when they left the car, each man carrying a newsboy's canvas bag around his neck. They walked through the gate, divided to reach the far corners of the house. There they put on leather gloves and pulled out blocks of plastic explosive, molding them, putty-fashion, into shaped charges, taping them to the house corners quickly and expertly. They moved to the remaining corners and repeated what they had done at the rear.

In the dark bedroom El Tigre stirred, rose alertly and listened. He jumped from the bed to the balcony, and from there to the branch of a tree, making his way backward down the trunk. One of the men heard scratching sounds, froze, then relaxed when five feet from the ground El Tigre released his hold and turned in midair, hitting the sandy soil on all fours. He streaked away.

The dark man got out a coil of fuse and now they worked together, the blond man setting detonators into the malleable plastic, crimping them into the fuse until all four charges were connected.

Carefully the dark man walked the depth of the house and took a timer from his bag. Using a miniature flashlight he set the interval, fitted the fuse cord, and activated the device, strapping it against the drainpipe, a foot above the ground. He rose then, shed his gloves and dropped them into the shoulder bag, removed the strap from around his neck and rolled it into a small bundle. He walked the length of the house again and moved through the gate to the sidewalk, looking up at the dark window.

The blond man was already in the LTD, toking another joint. "Let's have a beer," he said. "I'm thirsty as all hell."

The driver started the engine and the LTD moved slowly ahead, lights dark. "Fuck your beer," he snarled.

"Along the way, man," the youth pleaded. "I got to have a drink."

"We'll see."

At the second bridge they dropped their bags into the water. Toward the north end of Key Largo they shoved the LTD into a deep salt pond where coral had been quarried. Hands on his hips the blond man watched small waves glow in the moonlight above where the car had settled. As he turned to his partner he said, "Wonder what she done wrong, who she musta crossed?"

"You'll never know," said the other and shot him in the face.

From under a low stand of palmettos he dragged four cinder blocks and a large coil of wire. He wrapped the body with wire after removing the billfold from the jeans hip pocket, and twisted the wire onto the cinder blocks. Then he dragged and shoved the weighted body to the water's edge, wading in until he could maneuver it all into the depth.

Returning to the palmetto cache he felt for a pair of khaki trousers, scuffed work shoes, and a denim shirt. He changed clothing, wrapping the other into a bundle as he walked back to the Overseas Highway. A quarter of a mile ahead was an all-night diner catering to truckers. Before he went in he slid the wet clothing into a trash can, entered, and took a seat at the crowded counter. "What'll it be?" asked the waitress.

"Not the meatloaf, honey. Give me the Delmonico steak, medium, hash browns, coffee, and, let's see, the lemon pie."

"Gotcha."

He ate hungrily, glad to be alive. At two o'clock he went out to the pay phone, jingling a dozen quarters in his hand. He dialed a number, fed coins into the slot one at a time, and spoke briefly to the man who answered.

At three o'clock the house imploded, detonating inward in a massive billow of flame. What was left of the roof crashed downward, igniting in the superheated air, shooting flames and glowing ash so high they were seen from six miles out at sea.

By the time the fire department got there, nothing could be done. Except to spray the walls and roofs of adjacent houses that suffered hardly any damage at all.

II

Every life is, more or less, a ruin
among whose debris we have to discover
what the person ought to have been. . . .
Perhaps the most tragic thing about
the human situation is that a man may
try . . . to falsify his life.

Ortega y Gasset

TEN

SITTING in an easy chair in the apartment he had sublet, Morgan read the story in the *Journal de Genéve*. A limousine with three male bodies had been found in a wooded area near Cointrin airport. The limousine and driver, one of the victims, had been hired for the day by one of the other two dead men, neither of whom were yet identified. All three victims had been shot. A fourth man who had been seen leaving the airport with them was being sought. The Cantonal police declined to give further details but indicated that certain clues were being followed.

Morgan glanced around the room. He'd been lucky. A notice in the English-language Paris *Herald's* classified section had announced the immediate availability of a charming apartment on Avenue Foch. By telephone Morgan had arranged an early appointment with the nervous young Dane who answered the door. He spoke English aided by flowing, dramatic gestures and his eyes were reddened from weeping. His mother in Ebeltoft had died and he must absent himself from Paris for at least two months to arrange her estate and regain his composure. Meanwhile his hairdressing salon was destined to go to the devil; his French employees were so *frightfully* irresponsible. He wrung his hands, sniffled into an initialed linen handkerchief, and settled with Morgan on the spot for two months' rental in dollars in advance. His furnishings were beyond price, unique, really invaluable, so a deposit to cover them was impracticable. He examined Morgan's new passport and pronounced his face an honest one; therefore he was willing to take a chance on the reliability of his new tenant, Charles Elias Chipman. He would leave his clothing in one closet if Mr. Chipman did not mind? No, Mr. Chipman did not mind at all.

The hairdresser, who introduced himself as Rolf Alting, went on to say that, though the advertisement had not mentioned it, use of his Volvo went with the apartment as an amenity, for a slight extra consideration, say five hundred francs? Did Mr. Chipman have a French driving carnet or triptych? Mr. Chipman did. Then his new tenant was welcome to utilize the Volvo . . . with appropriate care. It was parked in the courtyard below. Morgan thanked him.

There *was* one thing, the hairdresser confided. The care of his Yorkshire terrier. Néné was housebroken and needed little attention; the maid who came every other day would walk him. A little food, a walk for Néné on the odd days . . . would Mr. Chipman mind terribly?

Mr. Chipman was magnanimous; he would be delighted to see to the Yorkie. (In order to get the apartment he would have agreed to a gorilla.) Besides, the terrier's company would be welcome.

Please to pay for long distance telephone calls promptly, the hairdresser implored; the company could be *so* difficult, *so* unpleasant. And if friends of his called, Mr. Chipman was authorized to inform them that Rolf would be at home after July first and intended to work the entire summer without absence for the *grand vacance.* He hoped only that his business would not have vanished while he was away, but his tone was not optimistic.

The hairdresser turned over the apartment keys, produced Néné from a bathroom, kissed the terrier wetly, and departed. Within an hour, Morgan moved in.

The master bedroom had gold-antiqued mirrors on two walls and the ceiling; the bed was made up with silken sheets. The adjoining bathroom was immense and filled with an astonishing assortment of toiletries, cologne, and perfume. The other bedroom and bath were smaller and decorated *toute moderne.*

Dining room, sitting, and living room were furnished in Louis Quinze antiques or reproductions; Morgan did not really care. The liquor cabinet contained numerous bottles, but only two were cognac, the rest fruity, syrupy liquers from every imaginable region of the earth. He set the cognac bottles on the sideboard, went to the bedroom, and hung his clothing in the empty closet. He would ask the maid to put cotton sheets on the bed.

From the kitchen a service entrance gave out onto a small utility area that was little more than a platform on the stairwell. The doors of the service elevator were wide enough to accommodate a grand piano and, Morgan imagined, sometimes did.

The apartment building was in the Passy district, Sixteenth Arrondissement. From the front balcony Morgan could look west to the wooded Bois de Boulogne, east to the Arc de Triomphe.

A few minutes' walk to the Lancaster hotel.

He wondered if Jill were still in Paris, whether he should phone her. Eventually his true name would be released as the wanted fourth man, and he wanted Jill to know that he was not a multiple murderer. But would such knowledge compromise her? Endanger her life? Without knowing who his adversaries were, the menace was hard to assess.

The Soviets had an obvious interest in silencing Hargrave. Killing him in the West, letting Westerners take the blame, was consonant with KGB practice. If Soviet intelligence had penetrated Hargrave's communication channel, the KGB would have sufficient knowledge of his plans to arrange his execution before he could talk. Soffit could have been either KGB or an agent hired for the job. After killing Morgan, Hargrave, and the chauffeur, Soffit would have arranged the murder scene to frame Morgan as Hargrave's killer.

As a former friend of Hargrave's, as a onetime intelligence officer Morgan would fit the frame requirements perfectly. Having gone to prison as a matter of principle, he could be expected to bear Hargrave a deep grudge for his betrayal. The solution would suit the Cantonal police whether Morgan were dead or alive. And the Agency would hardly take issue.

If not the Soviets, then someone in the Agency had to be responsible for the sequence of events. Either Bob Dobbs or someone placed closely enough to the Director to have full knowledge of the redefection plan; a man who could handle operational details in Dobbs's name, then covertly insert Soffit at the final moment to make sure Hargrave did not survive. Outside the Agency only Morgan knew what was to have happened, the details of the authentic plan, so Morgan had to be killed as well.

The Director, Morgan reflected, must be losing some sleep wondering where Morgan was.

One particular man in the Agency would have both the means and motive for silencing Roger Hargrave, and that was the penetration agent Dobbs had mentioned, the agent Hargrave had offered to expose. With Soffit dead, Morgan reasoned, the unknown agent would have no way of knowing how much Hargrave told me. He may even believe I know his identity and so he'll act on that premise: to destroy me before I expose him.

He telephoned the Lancaster and asked for Mlle. Percival. Her room phone rang but there was no answer. Morgan hung up, planning to call again. It was midday and Jill was probably lunching with a fashion associate.

From his belt he extracted the Sauer automatic, deciding to keep it around until he could appraise his situation more fully. He went to the clothes closet, found a wire coat hanger, and bent it so that the automatic hung inside one of the Dane's suits. Then Morgan secreted the currency bundles behind a row of books on the built-in shelves. Hardly an original place to cache valuables, but Morgan was not expecting the apartment to be ransacked.

Among Alting's many bathroom bottles, jars, and flasks was a hair-bleach preparation. Morgan had not been looking for it, but the discovery gave him an idea: alter the color of his hair; make it completely gray, and the mustache, too. That would aid his physical disguise; an assortment of clothing beyond the few things he now had would also help.

He dialed the embassy and asked for George Baker's office. The embassy operator hesitated, then said, "Mr. Baker is no longer with the embassy. Mr. Arnow is taking his place. Shall I connect you?"

"No, thank you. I have some antique silver boxes Mr. Baker asked me to appraise for him. Could you tell me where I might send them?"

"All I know, sir, is that Mr. Baker has returned to the United States. You could write him a letter here, and the embassy will forward it."

"Excellent idea," Morgan said. "I'll do just that."

Frowning, he hung up. Baker had planned on another year in Paris so his recall was far from routine. With it the most accessible link in the chain had been pulled beyond his reach.

Morgan had assumed that if he were arrested, Baker could at least testify to the official nature of his mission, inform the court—if it became necessary—that he had met with Morgan on Agency instructions and delivered an envelope.

The stage was being managed very competently, Morgan reflected, actors entering and exiting on cue, settings rearranged promptly and efficiently in accordance with someone's scenario.

The idea, he told himself, is to make me the final actor on stage, naked under the spotlights. Well, I've played that role before and found it unrewarding; let someone else play it this time. Not me.

The Yorkshire terrier was curled on a chair near the balcony, warmed by the midday sun. Morgan patted it. If anyone enters at night, he thought, the dog's bark will warn me as quickly as any electronic alarm, and more reliably. He went out of his new lodgings and locked the door behind him.

A taxi took him along Boulevard Haussmann to a British clothier's where Morgan bought a ready-made tweed suit, heavy-soled brogues, an Irish wool sweater, a lined poplin raincoat, and a shapeless, tweed rain hat. Carrying his bundles he took a taxi to the Bazaar de l'Hotel de Ville and bought inexpensive men's clothing, of the kind worn by low-salaried office-workers, and taxied from there toward Clichy. He had the driver stop near a pawn shop, went in and persuaded the proprietor to show him the handguns that were not on display. Most of them were junk, but one was a Mauser .32 HSc in good condition, one that had probably been issued to a military policeman during the German occupation. Morgan bargained for it and settled on a price that included a soft leather shoulder holster and a box of cartridges. From there he directed the driver to the Gare du Nord, switched taxis, and returned to his apartment.

If he were going to see Jill he wanted the meeting to take place before he assumed his disguise. If questioned later she would be unable to provide a usable description of him. All Morgan's training and instincts weighed against his seeing her. But he needed help and he needed someone to confide in. Since that night in her room the only persons he had talked with were dead.

He considered—and instantly rejected—the notion of writing an account of events to Marisa. Where could she take such knowledge? And by writing her mightn't he in some way endanger her? So it came down to Ghislaine Percival, niece of the long-ago Lynn. Morgan felt reasonably confident that if it were within her powers and abilities, she would help him.

Besides, she was returning to the States almost at once and would be out of danger.

Morgan called the Lancaster again. Still no answer from Jill's room. By five her business day should be ended, and then he would phone again.

Meanwhile, he was hungry. There was dry bread in the kitchen, some ham on a well-carved bone. Morgan ate a sandwich and unwrapped his shopping parcels, hanging clothing in his closet and getting out the Mauser pistol.

It was smaller than the Sauer; his hand almost covered it. With a little cooking oil he lubricated the slide and magazine, then loaded it with cartridges. The magazine spring worked properly, and to verify the firing pin Morgan muffled the weapon in a blanket and fired it into the mattress edge. He replaced the spent cartridge and slid the weapon into the soft shoulder holster, adjusting its straps for a comfortable fit. Then he went back to the Dane's ornately inlaid desk.

Aside from Jill, who was there in Europe who could help him? He needed men with clandestine skills and knowledge, but men who were no longer with the Agency. Even if he could locate such archons as McDairmid and Palmer Syce, would they be willing to help? More importantly, could they be trusted not to betray him? They were retired, he knew, shaken out by the Agency as undesirable activists along with Emerson Forey, Peyton James, and Broom Ten Eyck. First line troops for decades, they were the first to go, even before Dobbs took control. A decade older than Hargrave, Peyton James had returned to Townsend as Headmaster. Broom was somewhere in Spain, Art Capella in West Germany. McDairmid, the genius who converted all Agency files into the computer system, had departed years ago, joining the giant electronic firm that had made the computer installation. Palmer Syce? Morgan seemed to remember that Palmer had gone to England ostensibly to research a lengthy book on the history of espionage, but the Oxford college where he was said to be performing his dusty labors was, Morgan knew, subsidized by British Intelligence as a think-tank. So it was very likely that Syce was under contract to MI-6, helping that organization with his encyclopedic knowledge of Soviet espionage.

To what use was Ten Eyck's knowledge of Soviet deception ops being put these days? None at all, most probably. Still, Broom should know a great deal about Hargrave's defection to the Soviets. Perhaps the old master would even know what "Dormouse" meant.

In any case, Morgan could not simply stay in Paris cooped up in an apartment on Avenue Foch; that was only another form of prison. I need names, he thought, motives, reasons; facts, not theories. Otherwise it's like tossing a jigsaw puzzle and expecting it to fall into place. Under the law of probabilities a billion throws might produce a connected picture, but I can't depend on chance. And there's the factor of time.

Before my name surfaces and my photo is published around the world I have to start. Otherwise the initiative remains with them and inevitably I'll make a mistake or be recognized.

Since visiting the Divonne casino, Morgan had wondered about his

American currency. Had the serial numbers been recorded? Were they now distributed to banks and foreign exchange bureaus around the world? Not to trace Morgan by, for he wasn't supposed to get the money and survive. But to keep a check on Soffit in case he was to be reined in or, in his turn, eliminated?

He dialed the Lancaster again and this time when the phone rang in her room, Jill answered.

Quietly he said, "Don't speak my name, please. You know who this is, don't you?"

"Of course. And I'm glad to hear from you. But. . . ."

"Are you alone?"

"Yes. *Certainly* I'm alone."

"I'm in Paris and I must see you."

"I want to see you, too. Very much."

"Just off Rond-Point there's a restaurant-bar on Matignon, facing the park. Do you know it?"

"I know I can find it."

"When could you meet me there?"

"Well, I just got in from a racking day and I'm hot and tired and disorganized. Could you give me an hour?"

"Reluctantly. Do you have a date later?"

"Not unless you invite me."

"That, too. I need to talk, Jill. There's been some unpleasantness, but I don't want to place you in danger. If you're seen with me, that could happen. I want you to understand, and. . . ."

"In an hour," she said briskly. "Tell me then."

Before leaving the apartment Morgan gave the rest of the ham to the Yorkie. Then he took the lift down to the small lobby, where the concierge lurked behind etched-glass panes, and walked out to Avenue Foch. Traffic around the Étoile was at its evening worst: the cars were close-packed as soldier ants, gears grinding, horns honking.

At some risk Morgan found his way between bumpers and fenders and breathed with relief as he gained the curb at the Champs Élysées. Almost at once whores approached him with low-voiced invitations, trying to link arms with him, slipping trade cards in his raincoat pockets. He shook them away and walked on, irritated.

At the restaurant he asked for a table away from the entrance with its steamed windows, ordered a sweet vermouth on ice, and waited for Jill, who arrived almost immediately wearing a white Russian-style coat trimmed with white fur, a matching hat, and white leather boots.

She was carrying a folded newspaper and she set it down on the empty chair. Morgan helped draw the coat from her shoulders and said, "What's your pleasure, *mademoiselle*?"

"My pleasure?" she smiled, showing perfect white teeth. "Ah, my pleasure I suspect is you, but here in public I'll settle for a champagne cocktail." Her lips brushed the side of his face, and her hands covered one of his. "So *cold.* Brrrr! Let me warm, please."

"I didn't think I'd see you again so soon."

"I know. We had a date in Florida."

Her cocktail arrived and she sipped appreciatively.

"We'll have to postpone it, Jill. Things have come up, circumstances. . . ."

"So you said. And something about danger." Her features tightened. "You came over here on some kind of mission, I know that. What went wrong?"

"Three men killed near the Geneva airport."

"In a limousine? It's in the afternoon paper. But I never thought it involved you." Her hand tightened around his. "David, did you. . ." her voice lowered ". . . *kill* them?"

He looked down at the ice melting in his vermouth. "Only the one who shot the other two. I was to be his third victim. Whoever planned the trap will use every possible resource to find and destroy me." His eyes met hers. "When do you leave Paris?"

"I was planning on the day after tomorrow—but I can stay if for once I can do something useful."

"I should tell you," he said, "that in Key West I have a woman . . . we've lived together for nearly a year. She loves me. If she were in Paris I'd seek her help, but she's not here." He breathed deeply and sipped from his glass. "Before I left on the flight I shared with you I told her everything I knew. In retrospect I shouldn't have, but at the time there seemed no danger to me and so, by extension, none to her." He shrugged. "Now I'm not sure."

The flesh of Jill's cheekbones was taut, white.

"What's the matter?" he asked.

"It's all right."

"Would you rather I hadn't told you about her?"

"That's not it," Jill said. "Go on."

"I'm not just unburdening myself. I need your help."

"I understand."

"And you'll listen, even if I've got this connection back home with another woman?"

116

"I'm listening," Jill said.

Around them glasses tinkled, people laughed, conversation buzzed. Morgan wished he had something to be light-hearted about. Her head turned, her eyes lowered to the folded paper she had brought. "There's something I think you should know about, David. Since we're going to talk, let's go outside." Her lips made a restrained smile. "I've always loved walking in Paris, but not after dark without an escort."

Morgan helped Jill into her coat and they left the café, turning to follow the border of the park, arms around each other's waists as they walked away from the traffic sounds on the Champs Elysées.

He began with the visit from Dobbs's messengers, summarized the Atlanta meeting, and told her as much of Roger Hargrave as he could remember. They sat on a sidewalk bench while he described the events of Geneva leading up to the slaughter in the car. How he had killed the assassin and run to Divonne before heading back to Paris.

"If it weren't you telling me," she said in a strained voice, "I'd find it quite beyond belief."

"I wish none of it had happened. But it did."

"What do you want me to do?"

"A few things I can't do openly. When you get home open a post office box, send me the number at Post Restante, Paris: Charles E. Chipman."

"Of course."

"Tomorrow you could change some dollars for me."

"Easiest thing in the world. Are you in a hotel now?"

"I don't want you to know where I'm staying but, yes, I have a base here and I use the Chipman alias."

Above them a lightolier glowed yellow on the wet acacia trees that lined the walk. Two blocks away couples were leaving the restaurant rendezvous.

She took out a cigarette. Morgan noticed that her fingers were trembling. "Are you cold?" he asked. "Want to. . . ?"

"No, my temperature's normal enough." She looked up at him. "David, I'll help you any way I can."

"I'm grateful."

She nodded and glanced away. "Now I'm afraid I may be a bearer of bad tidings."

"For whom?"

"Depends. Is your friend's name Marisa?"

"How did you. . . ."

"Is it?"

"Yes."

She opened her newspaper. It was yesterday's *Miami Herald*.

"Page four," she said, handing it to him.

There was a photo of the houses on either side of Marisa's. Between them, a burned-out gap.

God, I hope she wasn't home when it happened. Then he read the story. The fire chief called it arson by high explosives and said that barely enough of the victim had been found for identification.

The chief of police was quoted as saying that a man known to have been staying at the victim's house was being sought for questioning but had not been located. He suggested the killing was related to narcotics traffic but declined to say how.

Morgan felt Jill's arms circling his shaking shoulders. *It's my fault,* he thought. Then, to Jill, his mind raging, he said, "I'll get whoever did it, I swear I will if it takes the rest of my life!"

"Take it easy," Jill said, helplessly. "There's no use tearing yourself apart. If someone is out to get at you through her, you've got to protect yourself."

"I have to call a friend," he said dully. *Pollack. He'll tell me what happened.*

"Make the call from my room."

He turned to her. "After what happened to ... Marisa, I can't risk a call being traced back to you." He lifted one hand to his head, touched it vaguely. "Where's a Bureau des Postes?"

"Rue de Grenelle, I think." She took his arm. "Over by the Invalides."

At the curb she stopped a taxi, gave the driver instructions and the taxi pulled away. During the entire trip Morgan said nothing, his mind stunned, overflowing with rage and an overwhelming lust for revenge. They had killed Roger. Now Marisa. From the taxi he walked stiffly into the all-night post office, found the desk for overseas calls, and forced himself to remember Pollock's number.

Jill paced nervously outside, while he waited in the glass-windowed *cabine,* hearing the telephone ring in Pollock's house, wondering if there would be an answer. Finally a man's voice. Thank God, it was Pollock.

"No names, pilot," Morgan said. "What happened to her?"

"Where are you?"

"Never mind. What happened?"

"They're looking for you. They've even been asking me."

"What did you tell them?"

"Nothing. What the hell, I know *you* didn't do it. But, Jesus, boy, who did? It had to be a professional job. They found some fuse cord, bits of a timer." He paused to swallow. "How'd you find out?"

"The paper. Don't tell anyone about this call, but I want you to know I walked into a set-up over here. You could be in danger, so don't ever mention our trip, coming or going, to anyone. Christ, even the boat may be booby-trapped."

"Sounds like fuckin' *war*. Who? Why?"

"I'm not sure," Morgan said. "Nothing solid."

"I . . . I got your cat, the gray one. Found him over by the ruins, like a stray. . . ."

"Keep him for me, please."

"Sure. You comin' back?"

"I can't now. Listen, you have to check your plane, car, your house . . . take no chances."

"Got it. What you gonna do? You take care of yourself, hear?"

Morgan replaced the receiver and walked leadenly toward the operator. He leaned on the counter while she calculated the charges, then he paid for the call and left with Jill.

In her room she poured him a double scotch and added Perrier and ice. Morgan gulped it down.

"You need rest," she said in a low voice. She made another drink and went away. He sat there mute with suppressed grief, welcoming the anesthetic effect of the scotch. When Jill came back she was wearing a nightgown and bathrobe. She drew back the double bed's quilt, turned down the sheets. "Come to bed, David," she summoned.

He watched her slip out of the bathrobe, saw through the thin nightgown the dark nipples of her small breasts. He finished his drink, bent over and untied his shoelaces. Pulling off his coat he said, "I can't make love, Jill, understand that."

"If you wanted to I'd loathe you."

As she watched him he undressed, and when they were both under the covers she turned off the nightstand light.

Her presence beside him was comforting, and in the darkness he could almost believe her to be Marisa. She curled up beside him, molding her slim body against his as though questing for warmth. He pressed dry lips to her cheek and forehead, stroked her bare arm gently, held the curve of her waist until she slept beside him.

After an hour he got up, poured scotch into a glass and drank. His mind was beginning to function again, sift through courses of action he might conceivably take. There was a friend not far from Paris, he remembered; a Frenchman he had once worked with. René was someone he could turn to. Tomorrow he would find him, if René were still alive.

That much decided, Morgan got back into bed and, after a long while, was able to sleep.

ELEVEN

MORGAN had driven north from Paris on the road to Amiens, finding the farmhouse, finally, situated on a knoll overlooking a small vineyard and an expanse of harrowed fields. There was a barn, a milch-cow, and a scatter of chickens and geese sunning themselves around a spring-fed pond.

At the sound of Morgan's Volvo, Colonel René Arnaud came onto his porch and walked down its sagging steps. In late middle age the retired DST officer had gained bulk, but his skin was fresh and pink, black hair plastered across the top of his skull, mustache points as carefully waxed as though he were to review cadets at St. Cyr. He greeted Morgan in a two-armed embrace.

"The world has forgotten me," he said, "but not my old collaborator. *Cher ami,* it is good of you to come!" Emotionally he dabbed at his eyes and led Morgan across the porch and into his house. "Even so early in the day we must share a little wine." He called to his wife and showed Morgan into his book-lined study. There was a massive roll-top desk covered with files and papers. On the walls were photographs of Arnaud; as a young cadet; being decorated by General Leclerc; standing beside De Gaulle in Casablanca; crouched near breastworks at Dienbienphu; shaking hands with Pompidou; receiving a scroll from Giscard. . . .

"*Regardez, hein?* The story of my life reduced to a few snapshots, some bits of ribbon. . . ." He shrugged. "But unlike you, *mon ami,* I was permitted to retire *sans peur. Alors,* what hypocrisy we countenance!"

Mme. Arnaud bustled in with a carafe of wine and two goblets on a cut glass tray. When the colonel introduced Morgan she blushed as Morgan bent over formally to kiss her work-reddened hand. Then she went out, closing the study door.

121

Arnaud poured wine, tasted it, filled both glasses. "Confusion to our enemies," he toasted and when they had sipped, asked, "How do you find our humble *rouge*?"

"Superb."

He stroked his mustache tips and eased himself into an old, over-stuffed, leather chair. "You look well, David. The ordeal did not disrupt you physically at least."

Arnaud had been captured by the Germans in '43, later by the Viet Minh in Indochina. "It cannot be pleasant to be imprisoned by one's countrymen," he said.

"Very unpleasant," Morgan agreed. He sipped the wine, enjoying its unfledged flavor. "Still, one survives."

"Precisely. To grow morbid is to die while yet alive. But you did not come this distance to philosophize with an old soldier. It is my hope that I may be of service to you." His hand waved as though to dismiss the farmhouse and its land. "I need respite from this." He took a fissured briar pipe from an ashtray, filled it with tobacco from a ceramic jar. "*Au fond* I am not a farmer."

Morgan said, "Within the DST you have a few remaining contacts?"

He puffed on his pipe and a swirl of smoke screened his face. "I do, though it is not generally known. Some younger *copains* consult me here from time to time, hazardous though it might be for their own careers were such contact to be aired." He sipped his wine. "These debts I can collect."

Morgan got out Soffit's wallet, extracted the cards it contained and showed Arnaud the photograph on the driving license. "I'm interested in this man. I'd like any traces the DST has on him; who he works for."

The colonel took the photograph to his desk, turned on the goose-necked lamp and examined it through his eyeglasses. To Morgan he said slowly, "The Soffit name means nothing, but . . ." he turned from the desk, ". . . I know that face. Does the man exist?"

"I killed him."

"*Bon.*" Arnaud turned off the lamp. "He was himself a killer; first for the Nazis, then for the communists of Greece, the KYP. A professional, you understand, a man mixed in many dirty things wherever there was money to be made from death or torture. He was born, I think, as Stepavitch; Serb or Croatian. I am not clear. He could have killed this Soffitt for his papers; for him it would be a small

122

matter." He sat down again. "So now he, too, is dead. And when did he expire?"

"Some days ago, at Cointrin."

"Ah. The corpses in the limousine? And he was one. Excellent. May I know more?"

"He killed two men and would have shot me but I shot first." Morgan wet his lips with wine. "Do you remember the case of Roger Hargrave?"

"Who does not?"

"Hargrave was redefecting, René. I met him at the airport. Soffit—Stepavitch—was in the pick-up car. We were to fly back to America. But someone hired Stepavitch to kill the two of us. I want to know who."

"Then you must tell me more."

Just as Morgan had related the story to Jill the night before, he repeated it to the onetime chief of France's *Direction de Surveillance du Territoire.* Colonel Arnaud listening without verbal interruption, sipping wine from his glass, nodding from time to time, puffing thoughtfully on his pipe. Morgan's voice caught as he told of Marisa's death.

Arnaud refilled his glass and murmured, "Horrible. These beasts must be dealt with as such. Tell me: You are circulating with false identity papers?"

"Yes."

"And you have a secure place in which to stay?"

"For the present, yes."

"If not, my home is at your disposal. You are quite right to infer that Hargrave's death was to have been laid to you, and I understand your present difficulties. This Balkan renegade, Stepavitch, could have been employed by anyone; he was that sort. And anyone knowledgeable of Europe's underworld could have found and hired him. So there is nothing to be learned from his ideology, for he had none. Had you preserved his passport my friends might have been able to ascertain its origins. Still, we will inquire after K. A. Soffit and see what develops, though in my opinion this Soffit—the true one—either sold or was killed for his documents." Arnaud knocked dottle from his pipe, sucked noisily through the stem and set the pipe aside. After a swallow of wine he said, "Those who have now killed thrice—for whatever motives—will not be averse to killing again. They must dispose of you in order to tidy up the affair. So you must take extreme

123

precautions." He lifted his wineglass. "But you will have arrived at these conclusions without my aid. Specifically, how may I further your inquiries?"

Morgan unfolded a sheet of paper and handed it to his host. "I want to locate these men, the founding fathers of the Agency. Some retired and left, others were forced out in the general purge. Several are said to be living abroad. Your stations should have a line on them."

Arnaud scanned the list. "Your thought is that they might help you?"

"Each one could add something," Morgan said, "if he was willing to. From the little Hargrave said to me before Soffit killed him, there's a possibility Hargrave was a double. On the other hand, what he said was so ambiguous that he may merely have been trying to gain my sympathy. But if Hargrave went over to the Soviets as part of some sophisticated penetration operation, someone on that list ought to know. And because he was killed in a way that almost cost me my life, I want to know, too."

"The Soviets, of course, had the greatest motive for liquidating him."

"Or some highly-placed traitor within the Agency who faced exposure from Hargrave. He would have strong reasons for destroying Hargrave and framing me for the deed."

Arnaud nodded and refilled his pipe. "Strange, is it not, that the older we grow the more we turn to suspecting our own associates of treason? Yet our French experience has proved that such can be the case. And hardly a month passes without an exposure of some new penetration within West Germany's BnD. Ah, *mon ami,* we slept while our enemies were active, we permitted them uncritically to encapsulate themselves. And like trichinae they proceeded to invade and cripple our muscle." He lighted his pipe, got the mixture going with short, fierce puffs, rapped the list with his knuckles. "M. Ten Eyck was a specialist in Soviet deception, I believe; Peyton James worked with us over the years in counter-espionage; M. Forey, I think, was an authority on Soviet disinformation activities. Capella? What was his area?"

"Soviet liquidations."

"Ah, yes. McDairmid was my host when your files were undergoing computerization. Surely you can locate him in America?"

Morgan nodded. "So I need addresses for Ten Eyck, who is probably on the Costa del Sol, Capella in West Germany or Berlin, and

Forey in Mexico if recollection serves. I should be able to locate Syce in England. When I get back to the States I'll see McDairmid and Peyton James." He was planning to give those two names to Jill Percival for preliminary vetting. Running them through the credit bureau along with other names in a commercial credit check would be the quickest way of locating the two men, verifying that Peyton was still with the Townsend School.

"In a couple of days I'll cross over to England," Morgan said. "After I get back to France I'll phone you."

"By then I should have a report or two. Depending on how well *les copains* cooperate. And believe me I expect no miracles from the time-servers, the lethargic bureaucrats." He shrugged. "The old days were not so bad by comparison."

Morgan accepted his invitation to lunch: *pot au feu* seasoned with garden herbs, fresh bread, a salad, cheese, and more wine, then black, bitter coffee. The three of them sat around the table, Mme. Arnaud interjecting herself into the conversation only to inquire if the guest would care for more of this or that. One son had been killed in Algiers, it developed, the other kept shop in Perpignan; their married daughter lived outside Bordeaux. The Arnauds had three grandchildren whom they got to see only rarely. Still, Morgan felt an air of quiet contentment at the table, a sense of acceptance between them such as he had never known with Janice, and he envied their communion.

When he drove away from the farmhouse Morgan scanned the plowed fields, saw rows of green sproutings warming under the midday sun. In a few months the grapes would ripen. Here the life cycle was unobtrusively renewed, gave promise of summer bounty.

Arnaud watched from the window. When Morgan's car was out of sight he strode immediately to his telephone and placed a call to Paris.

To the answering voice, Arnaud said, "*Mon General*? This is René." He cleared his throat. "A visitor just left me, an American named David Morgan. Yes, that's the one. I will write you a full report of our conversation and deliver it to you tomorrow. In the meantime I suggest that you may want to notify Washington."

He listened to the general's expressions of appreciation, then replaced the receiver. I have done the sensible thing, he thought, I have protected myself.

The maid was still cleaning the apartment when Morgan returned. She had fed and walked the terrier, she told him, and he gave her money to ensure continuing service. While she busied herself in the kitchen Morgan got out Hargrave's leather envelope and opened it on the desk. He focused on the several sheets of stationery covered with Cyrillic writing. They must be the material Hargrave had called "indispensable."

The maid showed him where Monsieur Alting kept his Canon camera; in the drawer were several rolls of unexposed film. As soon as she left, Morgan photographed the two passports and, more importantly, both sides of the pages handwritten in Russian that had cost Roger his life. Then Morgan reassembled the originals, put them back in the letter-case, and taped the leather envelope to the underside of the dining room table. Rewinding the exposed film he emptied the camera and dropped the cassette into his bag of toilet articles.

Tomorrow Jill would be flying back to Miami. With her departure he would be free to go to England and search for Palmer Syce. A cross-Channel train would provide him with lower profile transportation than arrival by air. Morgan did not fully trust the Chipman passport, but he felt compelled to consult Palmer Syce even at the risk of using the passport to enter the British Isles.

Although he had not seen a paper, Morgan assumed that the Swiss police were releasing additional information to the press, perhaps identifying the fourth man as a Canadian named Johnson. That could be a dead end for the Swiss unless they were given Morgan's true name by whoever was behind the murders. And it was disturbing to know that even the Key West police wanted him for questioning.

He saw Marisa's face, visualized the burning house, and felt tears welling in his eyes. For himself as well as for her he had to find out who did it. Still, how much could he hope to accomplish? His unknown adversaries were well-financed and totally ruthless. Were it not for the wisdom of taking a pistol to the airport meeting, Morgan knew that he would be dead, his enemies gloating. Their killing Marisa was shocking proof of their thoroughness, the ease with which they could achieve their ends. Who was there to stand against them?

Myself, he thought; as long as I last.

In small ways Jill could be helpful to him. Veterans like Syce and Peyton James could help him develop operational theories, but they were old men for the most part, physically vitiated, morale damaged by what had happened to them and to their Agency. In a crunch, how valuable would they be?

To try to contact Dobbs would be foolhardy. By now the Director

126

knew Hargrave had been killed and Morgan was a fugitive. He had paid for a live defector, not a dead one, and would regard Morgan as expendable. So he could not approach the Director until he had something worth trading.

Where was Alexandra? By now she must know of Roger's death; the Soviets might even have told her Morgan was responsible, warned her that if she returned to the West, she too would be destroyed.

Earlier Morgan had considered trying to reach her in Vienna but now he saw the effort as hazardous for both of them. Too, she might already have been taken back to Moscow, or returned there of her own accord. After so many years in the Soviet Union Alex probably regarded it as "home." Perhaps she believed that Roger's death foretold her own fate. And why not? Those responsible for Hargrave's murder could easily contrive another.

In time he might be able to talk with Alex: tell her what had actually happened, explain that he, too, had lost a loved one, and ask Alex for answers to at least part of the riddle. But how much had Roger confided in her? Would she even know, really, whether either of her husband's defections were bona fide? And was it likely Hargrave had told his wife the identity of the high-level Agency penetration?

Not unless Hargrave had been desperate, and from their few minutes together Morgan had not viewed Roger as a desperate man. Rather, he had sensed that Hargrave was winding down, relieved that having reached Geneva things would become routine; confident of having time enough to make his revelations, time for authentication.

Of what?

The room was still; motes drifted in a shaft of golden light from the late afternoon sun. Morgan felt starkly, nakedly alone. Powerless.

Who was he kidding? He was on the run, exposing himself to detection every time he moved. The few assets he had managed to scrape together were ridiculous when ranged against those of his invisible enemies. What right did he have to endanger Jill Percival with his presence and his confidences? None at all. She had fulfilled his need for a listener. In rawer terms, he had used the girl for his own selfish purposes and now regretted it. When they met later he would have to try to repair the damage, disinvolve her one way or another.

His mind picked up his unease over the British passport, and he decided to visit Claude Frechette again before he left for England. By now the forger could have acquired others: American and foreign kids in France were the principal sources. Running out of money they sold their passports for a good price, reported them stolen at their consulates, and were issued replacements for the usual low fee. Meanwhile, serial numbers of the "stolen" passports were added to watch lists at ports of entry. Travelers whose passports were really stolen went through the same procedure, and those serials also went on watch lists throughout Europe.

But Britain was a Common Market country, and travelers within Common Market perimeters were not supposed to need the same degree of documentation as when they left it or reentered. Well, he would test that in two days when the boat train reached Dover.

That still lay ahead of him. This evening he had to undertake the disengagement of Jill.

She was waiting for him at the Berlioz when his taxi arrived, standing just inside the still-winterized entrance of the restaurant, near the dessert cart. She hugged him briefly then followed the *maître* from the porch tables to a banquette inside the restaurant proper. From there the sounds of traffic on Avenue Malakoff were only faint whispers.

"My last night in Paris," she said. "For a while. Champagne, please."

"*D'accord.*" To the *maître,* Morgan said, "Heidsieck," and turned to Jill. "How was your day?"

"Oh, I couldn't really focus on business because I kept thinking about the things that have happened to you. David, it's all so horribly *wrong.* Could I help you more if I stayed here at least a while longer?"

He shook his head. "No, go on back. We'll stay in touch."

"You'll let me help, though, won't you?"

"Sure," he lied. "I'll be calling on you for lots of things. Today I saw an old friend from the DST and he's willing to help."

"I'm glad. No one should turn you down."

Their champagne arrived in a bucket stand. The *sommelier* rotated the bottle neck between his hands to chill the wine in the surrounding crushed ice. When poured, the champagne was cold and dry enough to set Morgan's teeth on edge.

Jill was wearing a white wool turtleneck under a pale blue suede jacket with flared cuffs. Her crest ring glinted as her hand moved. "I've never had a trip that equaled this one," she said in a low voice.

"It's been an unusual one for me."

Her fingers reached out to touch his. "I know you're grieving for

Marisa and you'd be callous if you weren't. But when I'm gone I don't want you to dismiss me as just another girl you met on an airplane."

He started to speak but she said, "No, I want to finish. To guard against that, even though this is a lousy time for you emotionally, I want to make sure you know how I feel. Otherwise it might be easy for you to slough me off. The point I want to make, David, is that I'm probably in love with you. Later, when all this is behind us, I think you might find that we're compatible. That's possible, isn't it?"

"I'm complimented," he said after some thought, "and if I get out of this alive, after things settle down, we might want to give it a try. But now, even discussing it seems premature."

"You won't cut me off?"

"No."

He asked about her return flight, learned it left before noon, and said, "I'll be out of France a few days."

"When you return, my letter will be at Post Restante for you."

"That'll be my first stop." He lifted the napkin-wrapped champagne and refilled their glasses.

From the menu they chose squab stuffed with wild rice and truffles, *petit-pois,* artichokes, and endive salad. When the waiter went away Jill said, "At least we like the same things, David. And my schooling in Switzerland wasn't entirely wasted: I'm an excellent cook."

"Among other skills."

"To which I should add, in case you've wondered, that I've had two love affairs in my life. One was absolutely rotten, the other equally wonderful. It ended when the boy slammed his Corvette into a tree. Since then . . . until I met you . . . I haven't wanted anyone, couldn't respond. . . ." She looked away. "So I understand trauma, David. But I don't think you'll always feel this way."

"My predictions are pretty fallible," he told her, "so I wouldn't even try to guess where I'll be a week from now, much less a year into the future. But for however long I live I'll always remember Marisa, remember she was killed because of me. Jill, when I was destroyed, had nothing, she took me in and gave me a kind of love I'd forgotten could exist . . . the kind that asks nothing in return." His voice was tensing, but he went on. "Because we were close—lovers—someone decided she had to be killed. I can't ever forget that, it will always haunt me, even after I've avenged her."

"David, you can't blame yourself. Blame *them.*"

"I do," he said.

She put her hand on his but he drew it quickly away. "Don't, Jill," he said, voice harsher than he intended.

"Please don't pull away from me," she pleaded, and Morgan thought, I don't want to, but I have to.

Her breath drew in audibly. "I'll be in Florida tomorrow night, David. Where will you be?"

Maybe dead, he wanted to say, but instead he said, "I have to have some film developed, but it can't be done at a corner drugstore."

"Can I help?" she offered.

He didn't answer. Unable to cope with his silence, she said, "I know you have urgent things to do, but please don't just disappear completely. Do you understand?"

Again he said nothing.

"I mean," Jill said, "from my life. Please, David."

He wanted to reach out to her, but checked himself. *Disengage,* he told himself. *Do it now.*

He got up and walked away quickly, face averted so it would not betray the feelings churning inside him.

TWELVE

THE boat train from Calais reached Dover in the early dawn of a gray and drizzly day. A port slowdown was in progress, and Morgan and his suitcase were waved on without inspection. He boarded the London express, had breakfast in the dining car whose table linen was gray, dull cutlery spotted, and left without a second cup of muddy coffee to avoid the miasma of kippered herring that filled the atmosphere. In his compartment he dozed for the remaining hour of the trip, got off at Victoria Station and, with some help from the Enquiries counter, found a train for Oxford.

The route meandered northwest through the foggy Thames valley, the train moving at a leisurely pace between station stops. Morgan got off at midday and saw sunlight outlining the towers and spires of the ancient university town. Carrying his suitcase he decided to take a hotel room and chose the Mitre. After lunch, he set out for St. Mark's college.

At the registrar's office he inquired of Palmer Syce and was given directions to "the American fellow's" digs.

There were gowned students crossing the walks and greens between lecture halls as church towers chimed the hour of one. Morgan turned into a well-kept lane and moved onto the grass to avoid a procession of scholar-cyclists as they wheeled by. Roger Hargrave could have been one of them, he reflected, though Roger's Rhodes years had been spent at Balliol where he played rugger and won scholastic honors. Was it here at Oxford that Roger had been recruited by the Soviets? What enticements had they offered? The certainty of being on the winning side? A chance to be a moving force in worldwide political rearrangements? A tactical appeal to his vanity?

Morgan was within the precincts of St. Mark's now, and his eyes scanned the low-roofed entrys where faculty were lodged.

The name, Palmer Syce, was printed in Old English style above the letter-slot of a timbered door. At eye-level there was a small, leaded-glass window. Morgan pulled the call chain and waited.

A red-faced, middle-aged housekeeper opened the door and viewed him with challenging eyes.

"Mr. Syce, please," Morgan said.

"An' who will I be tellin' him you be?"

"An American friend, name of Morgan."

"We'll see." The door closed in his face.

After a while the door opened again and with flustered politeness the housekeeper said, "Do come in, sir. He'll be coming prompt now."

He went in through the dim entry way to a small waiting room furnished with a few chairs and a telephone stand. There was a scent of food recently cooked, of mildew and tobacco smoke. Just as Morgan was sitting down, a heavy door opened and Palmer Syce appeared.

He was a man of middle height whose stooped posture made him appear much shorter than he was. Thin gray hair, lined, stubbled face above a too-large collar. Thick, old-fashioned lenses in his spectacles, an unpressed suit of Donegal tweed.

"Morgan!" he exclaimed and shuffled forward, gnarled hand outstretched. "How good to see you, David! I've read of you, of course, but I never thought our paths would meet again. Come in, come in! Sherry? Whisky?"

"Sherry will be fine," Morgan said, following Syce into a darkly paneled study.

Syce sat down on an old leather sofa, indicated a nearby chair for Morgan. "So now you find me 'Calm of mind, all passion spent,' secure in Albion's arms. Do you come as a tourist, or are you involved in something more interesting?" From an end table he lifted a decanter, removed the glass stopper, and filled two small glasses.

Morgan sipped the rich, sweet wine and said, "Interesting is hardly the word for it, Palmer. Murderous would be more accurate. Have you heard anything to suggest that I'm a fugitive?"

Syce snorted. "Fugitive from what? Not prison, surely . . . I read of your release." His eyes narrowed. "*Are* you a fugitive, David?"

"Would it trouble you if I were?"

"That would depend, I suppose. Considering my position here, I might feel obligated to tell our British cousins." He gestured around the room. "This *is* Six, you know, so I'm still somewhat in business. And I've always been loyal to my employers."

132

Morgan nodded. "After you hear me out you'll be at liberty to inform MI-6—or even Special Branch—but I don't think you will because the problem seems to be peculiarly American." He tilted his glass, sipped and added, "With Soviet overtones."

"Now I begin to understand." He got up and moved slowly over to a low shelf Morgan had not noticed before. On it was a long glass terrarium, the soft glow of ultraviolet lamps. Beneath it perhaps twenty miniature trees, dwarfed and twisted into what looked like Monterrey cypress. "Bonsai," Syce remarked. "My wife was Japanese, you know. After her death I kept up her hobby. Here we have black pine, dwarf cedar, pomegranates, juniper, oakleaf aralia, and so on. There is so much of her in these little trees that as I nurture them I feel I must be communing with her—or at least carrying on an occupation she loved. Sometimes I even reflect that they represent man's manipulation of nature, symbolic dominance. My British colleagues find this hobby odd of me, but it has the advantage of adding to my lengthy reputation for eccentricity. And you know how excessively the British tolerate eccentrics." With a chuckle he turned back to Morgan, drew out a turnip watch and said, "My time is yours today. If you care to, please stay here tonight—at least let me give you dinner."

"I'd appreciate dinner," Morgan said. "Lunch wasn't an overwhelming success."

"Yes, our restaurants leave a good deal to be desired. Mediocrity prevails—at Oxford as in the world. Now. After prison, what did you do?" He seated himself and looked expectantly at Morgan.

"I was broke, cast-off, divorced. In Key West I found work at the docks, managed to buy a boat, lived with a Cuban girl who loved me." He swallowed hard. "A week ago two visitors from the Agency dropped by. Now the girl is dead, killed when her house was blown up. I was in a car near the Geneva airport, saw two men shot to death, and managed to shoot their killer." He breathed deeply to control his words. "The main points, Palmer, but perhaps if I tell it chronologically you can begin to make some sense from what happened."

Syce nodded approvingly. "The chronological approach recommends itself to me above all else." Silently a cat appeared and jumped into his lap, a slate-gray Angora. The form of El Tigre flashed in and out of Morgan's mind. Safe with Pollock, he hoped. Sole survivor of a house and home he had loved.

"The Wife of Bath," Syce said, stroking the neck of his pet. "An ancient retainer who's far more trouble than she's worth. Why, when I resettled here it took the intervention of the Home Secretary himself to get her into the country." He looked up apologetically. "If I ramble, David, it's because subliminally I sense that what you're about to tell me is going to be very important and in some way change my dull and dusty life. Pray proceed."

Morgan began at the beginning. Syce listened, eyes half-closed, glasses shoved up on his forehead, one hand absently stroking his cat.

The telling took nearly forty minutes by Morgan's watch—and when he ended he felt drained. Syce's eyes were barely open, but when Morgan stood up to stretch, his host said, "We might have a spot of tea, David; lubricates my lucubrations." He smiled apologetically at his classroom humor and left for the kitchen.

Throat dry, Morgan poured sherry for himself and wondered if he had left anything out. He stroked the gray Angora and, in a little while, Syce returned with a tea tray; good sterling, Morgan noticed, with Haviland cups and saucers. Palmer Syce was not the broken-down, alcoholic, ex-Intelligence officer of pejorative legend, but a man whose comfortable amenities complemented a keen and tranquil mind.

Stirring his tea, Syce said, "I have a number of comments, David, and I'll make them not necessarily in order. First, you killed in self-defense, with every justification. Proving it might be difficult, as you foresaw, and you reacted prudently by leaving Swiss jurisdiction. The Cantonal police can be pretty mutton-headed, as I've had cause to know.

"Before I take up other points, I'm going to ask you something that may startle you: are you positive the man was Roger Hargrave?"

"Yes."

"Why?"

"I knew him in his youth, saw him in later years around the Agency, so the physical identification was absolute. Roger mentioned things that were customary between us. And his speech pattern was the same."

"It's impossible that the traveler you met could have been Roger's well-briefed, surgically-altered double?"

"Impossible."

Syce sighed. "That disposes of one possibility, then. You said you photographed the contents of his letter-case?"

Morgan handed over the roll of undeveloped film. "As I said it's holographic Russian, but that shouldn't be a problem for you."

134

"I think I can manage. I'll have it developed and printed by tonight. If you'll excuse me, I'll call now." Syce went to his desk and dialed a number. While sipping his sherry Morgan heard him say, "Palmer Syce here. Tod, will you have someone come 'round to pick up some film for developing? No, I need it as soon as possible, no later than evening. . . Well, it's photography of some Russian-language documents a friend brought me to study. No, an American friend, former Agency type. Page-size blowups will do nicely. What? Yes, I'll turn over anything of more than passing interest, but let me be the judge."

Replacing the receiver, Syce sighed. "Questions, questions. Why can't fellers just do a job without wanting all the details?"

"That was your Six contact?"

Syce nodded. "Good types, mostly, though some of the younger ones fail to show proper respect for age and experience." He went back to the sofa.

When Syce was comfortably settled, Morgan said, "Did you ever hear of Dormouse?"

"In the Hargrave connection?"

"As a code name, cable slug, or project designation?"

He shook his head. "No, but that doesn't mean anything since I wasn't involved in launching deep-cover agents into the U.S.S.R. If Hargrave was one—and what he said to you suggests he was at least trying to pretend he was—then a few of our old colleagues should have been knowledgeable. Mind if I ask the British?"

"Use your own judgment."

"When you leave here how will I be able to contact you?"

"Post Restante, Paris. Charles Chipman."

Syce noted the accommodation address on a scratch pad. "I'll watch Geneva developments," he said, "in case the police develop any useful information." He rubbed the bridge of his nose. "I'm delighted you thought of me, David; even more pleased you took the trouble to seek me out and confide in me. You've given my mind a very substantial puzzle to analyze, and while some obvious and rather chilling thoughts occurred to me during your narration, I want to submit them to examination and analysis and try to winnow out the deception factors. The Soviets, as you doubtless realize, operate in rather predictable ways. Over the decades their techniques and methods have produced high-quality results. In World War Two the Soviets, unlike the Nazis, were exercising tremendous intelligence foresight through nonmilitary operations targeted at the Soviet Union's then-distant goals. Their prompt acquisition of our atomic secrets and missile technology are exemplary. The Soviets, as strategic planners, foresaw *une guerre apres la guerre,* something nobody on our side even wanted to hear about, much less make plans for. So after the defeat of Japan the United States dawdled and diddled, occupied itself principally in creating the United Nations organization which became our national substitute for the self-interest policy of the Soviet Union."

He cleared his throat. "As our British friends learned, power flows to those who utilize it; those who do not, undergo atrophy. So, as a nation withdraws from the international power struggle it no longer needs intelligence on its potential adversaries. Hand-in-glove with that observation goes this: Only a first-class power can afford a first-class intelligence service."

"What about Israel?"

He smiled sheepishly. "The exception proving the rule. But Israel is a pivotal force in world politics. Because of what it can do in both positive and negative ways, Israel exerts the same effect as though it were a large and densely populated country."

"I agree. But if the Brits aren't really interested in traditional intelligence any longer, what are you doing here? Why would they bother to hire you, Palmer?"

Syce stretched out his legs and gazed at the low, timbered ceiling. "They trained me in '41 and '42, so I have a bit of background with them. They're comfortable with me. And they believe in maintaining reserves, a cadre of knowledgeable people. In a way you could say I'm a keeper of the flame. Their flame, to be sure, but ours as well." His expression changed, he waved a hand in self-irritation. "I've maundered far from what I started to develop, given you the sort of *tour d'horizon* I used to give neophytes at the Farm. Apologies."

"None necessary. I can use the refresher course, Palmer. I've been away from the business a long time. Are you in touch with any of your former colleagues?"

Syce's eyes narrowed slightly. "For instance?"

"Ten Eyck, Peyton James, McDairmid?"

"In a loose way, yes."

"I need all the help I can get," Morgan said. "All of them knew the inner workings of the Agency; they were around headquarters when I was in the field and long before. One of them might be able to fill in some gaps."

"Go on."

136

"Dormouse. Who or what was Dormouse? Perhaps they remember."

"It's possible. No, it's probable. All of them ranked high enough to know part if not all." Syce stroked his upper lip. "There's Art Capella, too. Soviet liquidations were his area, you know. And Hargrave...." He left the thought unspoken.

"I see what you mean."

Syce nodded. "Art's in West Berlin, running a discotheque. Yes, he might be helpful, indeed. And you haven't forgotten Emerson Forey, have you?"

"What about him?"

"Retired in Mexico." His head tilted back and he gazed at the ceiling. "Dobbs—well, you know the story?"

Morgan shook his head.

"Hmm. Well, when Dobbs left Logistics, oh, five or six years ago, and came over into Operations, Forey was very helpful to him. Took him under his wing so to speak, tried to teach him the trade and keep him out of trouble. Thanks in part to Emerson's tutelage, Dobbs moved on and up. Then when Dobbs was Executive Director one of Forey's people absconded with some operational funds—five or six thousand dollars, I believe, not a large amount as those things go. Well, the man gambled it away in Haiti and killed himself. So what does Dobbs do by way of gratitude, but set the Inspector General on poor Emerson who barely knew the miscreant. Dobbs actually squeezed the money from Forey, then forced him to retire."

"On what grounds?"

Syce shrugged. "Dobbs and the IG agreed that as Staff Chief Emerson Forey should have known everything that went on in his office. Because he didn't know his employee was living beyond his means and so a security threat, they found Emerson derelict in his duties and responsible for the theft."

"That's insane! Why did Dobbs do it?"

"Why?" Syce shook his head slowly. "So Dobbs could balance the books, I suppose, show no losses during his reign." He sighed. "Some of us thought it was pretty shitty, David, discarding a fine man with a fine mind—disgracing him, really. And for such a trivial end. Dulles wouldn't have done it, you know, nor any decent officer, but that's our Robert Dobbs." He lowered his gaze to Morgan. "It's been the ruination of Emerson, and now he's in Mexico, drinking far too much."

"Where does he do his drinking?"

"Taxco, I believe. His wife's death was the last straw, so he's pretty far gone. I'm not sure I'd recommend your seeing him."

Morgan considered what Syce had said, then sat forward. "It's odd how few people really know Dobbs. Those still in the Agency are beholden to him and wouldn't dare talk. But Forey must have gotten to know Bob inside out. And he's alienated. With that combination, what would you do?"

"I think I would see him." He glanced over at his cat. "You're not at all sure about Robert Dobbs, are you?"

"So I need information about him, don't you think?"

"Quite so. But I shouldn't jump to conclusions, David. Get the evidence, then make your judgment."

"I intend to," Morgan said, "and so I'd like what addresses you have."

Readjusting his glasses, Syce consulted a thick address book, copied from it onto a sheet of paper. He gave it to Morgan and said, "We might take a break now, David, and resume after dinner. I'll get these films of yours printed, and I must say I'm eager to see what Roger was carrying. Meanwhile, you might enjoy walking about the university. Erasmus lectured here and so did Thomas More. Bacon, Wycliffe, and Newman were scholars here, as were at least half the British elite. Living here as I do, though in a comparatively modern college, I'm always aware of the weight of centuries about me. Six o'clock? And if you decide to stay overnight with me, just bring your bag."

Morgan folded the address sheet and slid it into his coat pocket. "I'll be back at six," he said, and found his way out.

At the hotel reception desk he left a call for 5:30, went up to his room, and stretched out on the bed. Last night in his compartment he had not slept particularly well, and the tension of being with Palmer increased his travel fatigue. He was not enamored of sight-seeing and never had he felt less in the mood for it. All he wanted from Syce was a translation of Hargrave's documents and Palmer's comments on them. After that he would have to decide what to do, where to go: Berlin, Spain, or Paris.

From Europe it would be easy to get into Mexico, and from Mexico easier to get into the States than from any place except Canada or the Bahamas. So unless Forey's brains were totally rotted by *pulque* a side trip to Taxco could be worthwhile in terms of the small additional effort involved. Then one way or another he had to return to Key West, talk with Pollock, learn what he could about Marisa's death. McDairmid lived in Virginia, and Peyton James was at Townsend, according to Palmer Syce's addresses.

And Dobbs was around Washington.

Church chimes sounded in the distance as he fell asleep.

Morgan left the spirit shop carrying a bottle of Chivas and one of red Bordeaux, Mouton-Rothschild '53. As he walked along the narrow, cobbled street he felt that he was being followed. After a few yards he paused at a shop window whose angled pane gave him a glimpse of the street behind, and he saw a man stop and light a stubby bulldog pipe. Morgan strolled on, and the other man resumed walking.

When Morgan reached St. Mark's college he turned in through the stone posterns and walked to the entrance of a lecture hall. At the top of the steps he opened the door but stepped aside behind an entrance column and peered through a narrow opening at the space between the posterns. The pipe-smoker was there. Halted, he looked around, came a few yards into the precincts and stopped again. He took out his pipe, grimaced, scanned the quadrangle, gazed for a moment at the door of the lecture hall, then walked to a stone bench, sat down, and unfolded his newspaper. When the man's eyes dropped to the paper, Morgan eased into shrubbery that ran the length of the hall and left the area, reaching Syce's lodgings without seeing the man again.

The entry was fragrant with the aroma of roasting meat as Syce welcomed him and received Morgan's two bottles with exclamations of pleasure and surprise. Carefully Syce decanted wine from the bottle to give the lees a chance to settle before they drank. Then he opened the Chivas and made two highballs.

In the study, Morgan said, "How closely do your employers check on you, Palmer?"

Syce put down his highball slowly. "During my first year here my mail arrived somewhat slowly and I had reason to believe that my phone was listened to from time to time. But since then" . . . he shrugged . . . "I've had no reason to think I'm being watched."

"Were you ever followed?"

"I don't think so." He leaned forward slightly. "May I ask the reason for your interest?"

"I was followed into St. Mark's, and it occurred to me that I might have been noticed leaving here earlier."

Syce went over to the window, pushed the blind slightly to one side and gazed out. Releasing the blind he turned back to Morgan. "Couple of students in the quad, that's all."

"The fellow who tailed me was a tweedy type, perfectly ordinary except for the fact that he *was* following me."

"Odd."

"Exactly." He got up and motioned Syce out of the study. When the door closed behind them, Morgan said in a low voice, "Has your study ever been checked for bugs?"

"Before I moved in it was. Since then, no."

"Then let's assume we were overheard this afternoon and talk somewhere else."

Syce nodded. "It would be prudent." He looked at his watch. "The prints should be delivered within the next hour or so. We'll examine them upstairs to be on the side of caution."

The kitchen door opened and the housekeeper came out, wiping hands on her apron. "Dinner's set, sir. Will you carve the joint?"

"I'll carve," Syce told her, and showed Morgan into his small dining room.

There was a sideboard with an array of cut-glass bowls and decanters. The table was set with fresh linen and gleaming silver. Beside Syce's place was a steaming leg of lamb on a carving board, china bowls of potatoes and Brussels sprouts. Good, wholesome British food, Morgan thought as he sat down. The housekeeper poured wine.

Morgan said, "Where does Dobbs come from?"

"The Mid-West. From one of those big state universities. I believe he had a degree in management or administration or something unrelated to his eventual work. He worked at State for a couple of years, not in the Foreign Service but on the permanent Support staff, and then, somehow, he transferred over to the Agency." Syce helped himself to more sprouts. "We weren't being terribly selective during the Korean period, you know."

"Did Dobbs ever study abroad? Do much traveling outside the country?"

"My guess is he did not. I never viewed him as a leadership type, though he showed some gifts as a paper-handler." He cut a slice of lamb and forked it onto Morgan's plate.

"Does he have children?"

"Three, I think: two sons and a daughter. My wife and I dined there twice. He lived in McLean, you know, nice brick Colonial house. His wife has a law degree but I'm not sure she practices. If she does, it's probably the real-estate sort of thing like so many Agency wives." He refilled their wine glasses. "Good vintage, David; your thoughtfulness is appreciated."

"Dobbs have any intimates?"

"Not that I know of. That way he was never identified with any of the cliques and so was never under any obligations of friendship when some of his associates began to sink. Bob Dobbs could just keep going. And did. Now, of course, he has strong Congressional and Administration support; I regard him as immovable for many years."

Morgan nodded.

"I assume you've been considering him as the prime mover behind your involvement in Roger's death?"

"The evidence . . . if it's even that . . . is entirely circumstantial. Somewhere between three and six people at a minimum could have known the details concerning Hargrave's redefection. If they weren't responsible for Hargrave's murder it has to be the Soviets who were. And they could have learned what was planned either by getting into the communication channel between Roger and the Agency, or by intercepting and reading the cryptographic messages. Tell me: In the period between Hargrave's defection and your departure from the Agency were we getting any unusually high-grade intelligence from a Kremlin source?"

"Yes, but we had several agents in place over there. If you're trying to establish whether Hargrave was one of them, all I can say is that it's possible. Only a few people would have been involved in launching Roger as an agent, and not much would have been in writing. The Director at the time would have had to authorize it, probably with a few sentences on a sheet of paper, and Roger's name would never have appeared. So. . . ."

"Launching Roger," Morgan interrupted. "Aside from the Director, who? Would Ten Eyck have been one of them? Peyton James?"

Syce considered. Then he said, "*If* Roger was launched—and we don't know that he was—either Broom Ten Eyck or Peyton had sufficient seniority and field skills to be involved. And they could handle Russian." He eyed Morgan. "You're going to push on, aren't you?"

"I don't have a choice."

The older man sighed. "I suppose not. But as I was starting to say before your interjection, unless someone now steps forth to assert

Hargrave's good works, I view authenticating him as a practical impossibility. He'll go down in history as a defector who was killed by an Agency man when he tried to return."

"Ah," said Morgan, "but will history tell *why?*"

Syce grunted. "We both know better than that, David." He drank from his wineglass. "Still, I'm concerned about the man who followed you to St. Mark's. When I have an opportunity, I'll make tactful inquiries, but it's not something I'd want to query Six about this evening."

"Or MI-5," Morgan suggested.

"Equally. And I'm worried about the possibility my study has been bugged. If Six did it, that's understandable, they're my employers. But if it wasn't done by any sector of the British Intelligence establishment. . . ."

Morgan said, "The Soviets have a continuing interest in you, Palmer. You know more about their espionage apparatus than anyone currently with the Agency, and the fact that Six picked you up and installed you here would be mighty interesting to them. If I were on the KGB side I'd think a bug and phone tap would be worthwhile, for a few months at least."

Syce stroked the side of his cheek. "I've been lax, I'm afraid. I'll have the place swept. The fact is the KGB can operate here almost as easily as British Intelligence. Special Branch is busy with terrorists. They don't have enough personnel to cover the resident Soviets as well."

"Much less their legal travelers."

"Unfortunately." He laid down his knife and fork and looked intently at Morgan. "Until you showed up, the thought would never have occurred to me, but do you think it's paranoid of me to suggest that the Agency might have installed a bug?"

"Hell, it's as likely as anything else. We could poke around your study, take things apart and make like security klutzes, but that would only warn whoever's at the listening end of the possible bug. So let's stay out of the study; you can still use it for reading and normal purposes until it's swept."

The housekeeper cleared their dinner dishes, brought in saucers of bread pudding and a coffee tray, and said, "I'll be goin' now, Mr. Syce. Just leave things an' I'll clear up in the mornin'. Have a good evening, gentlemen."

"Good night, Anna," Syce said. "Don't miss your bus, now."

Morgan thanked her. They heard the service door closing and Syce said, "She's a good woman, David. Don't know how I'd manage without her."

Morgan's mind flashed to Marisa and his throat tightened.

Syce said, "Those prints should be coming any time now." He filled their coffee cups.

"David, not to sound lugubrious or apprehensive, but considering the violence that's occurred in your wake, shouldn't you reduce your experiences to writing and file it away in some totally secure place against the possibility that you might personally need the record? Or so that someone else could utilize it to . . . carry on?"

"I should," Morgan said, "but things happened too quickly. Where would you suggest I store such a document?"

"Why not mail the narrative to your lawyer with instructions to keep the inner envelope sealed until you either call for it or die?"

Morgan grunted. "I had a lawyer . . . of sorts. If I sent him such a communication and later I'm charged with being a fugitive in a capital offense. . . ? I think he'd run it to the nearest FBI office."

"You could leave it with me."

"Thanks, Palmer, I'll give it some thought. The last thing I want is to jeopardize others. And the fact that I was followed this evening speaks for itself."

In a kindly voice Syce said, "Don't be too hard on yourself, David. It's not as though you had an organization whose resources you could command: You've got a good mind and some horrible experiences to motivate you. Believe me, something will fall into place. I'm older than you by a generation, and I'll confess that when I was younger and active every day with operational matters there came times when, having done everything I could in a particular matter, I simply sat back and waited. No one told me to, it was personal adaptation to circumstances. Then, more often than not, in some unsuspected quarter, something would happen and it would turn out to be the break I'd been waiting for." He rubbed the side of his jaw. "A penetration case I'd worked on for nearly three years. It ended in a blank wall. Then we got a signal from Oslo, a Soviet walk-in. I remembered his name on the far fringes of the case, flew to Oslo, and handled all interrogation. That was it. He told me what I needed to know without his ever realizing its importance. It's happened repeatedly, David, so don't. . . ."

The doorbell rang.

"Ah," said Syce, rising, "that must be the messenger." He removed his glasses, polished the lenses on his napkin, and replaced them. "Back in a moment." He opened the dining room door and closed it behind him. Morgan could hear him crossing the adjoining room. The door to the waiting room opened and closed. Syce's footsteps fading on the entry carpet as he neared the front door. Morgan lifted his cup and drained it, thinking that Syce must have spent a lot of time showing Anna how to make proper American-style coffee.

The wall clock struck the quarter hour. The front door closed so quietly Morgan could hardly hear it. Perhaps Roger's material would supply the answers he needed and he would have to travel no farther. What Palmer had said about the unexpected gave Morgan hope that the riddle was about to be solved. Or would Hargrave's writings warn of a Soviet preemptive nuclear attack on Chinese industrial centers? That would be great for the U.S., Morgan thought, but it won't help me. Such a report—if it could be verified—would tend to indicate that Hargrave had been telling the truth. Richard Sorge, the GRU's penetration of the Nazi embassy in Tokyo, warned Stalin the Germans were about to attack, and Stalin ignored the warning. And it cost Sorge his life, Morgan reflected. Suppose Hargrave's message was on the same grand scale? Who would believe and act upon it? Would anyone care if the Chinese and Soviets fell upon each other?

The silence of the house bothered him. Was Syce in his study, already translating the Russian writing? Too involved to include his guest?

Morgan frowned, got up and opened the dining room door. He crossed the small living room and went out to the waiting room. It was dark, the outside door closed. "Palmer!" he called, then felt ridiculous. Probably his host had gone up to the bathroom. He was turning away when he saw something glinting in the hallway. Bending over, Morgan saw a flash of light on Syce's glasses. They lay askew across his nose; his body was spread-eagled on the carpet.

"Palmer!" Morgan said loudly, and touched the dimly-seen cheek. Syce's eyes were open. Morgan pressed the carotid artery but there was no pulse.

Slowly he stood up. Palmer Syce was dead.

144

THIRTEEN

On finding Palmer dead he had made the quick assumption that his friend died of natural causes; heart attack or cerebral hemorrhage. But as he made a superficial examination of the body Morgan noticed the odor of peach blossoms and drew away coughing. He opened a side window to clear the air and waited before returning to Syce. The light of a match showed Syce's face and lips a reddish, unnatural color that contrasted with the grayish pallor of his neck. Some sort of prussic compound would do that, Morgan knew, and the odor suggested it. Palmer Syce has been murdered.

On hands and knees he groped and felt for the expected envelope, then realized the absurdity of his search. No MI-6 messenger would have handed Palmer the developed films and then killed him. The murderer must have arrived before the messenger, which meant the prints were yet to come.

Morgan dragged Palmer's body into the study and arranged it peacefully on the sofa, glasses in place, one hand on his chest, the other just touching the rug. He turned off all lights, except one table lamp in the living room, then waited alone in the darkness for the prints to arrive.

As he began his vigil, a glass of cognac in his hand, Morgan considered trying to remove evidence of his having been there, but realized the effort would be futile: Anna knew his name because he had given it to her at one o'clock. And she could describe Morgan accurately. He confronted the realization that he would "be sought for questioning" in the case, accepted the implications, and began trying to plot some countering move.

First he had to retrieve the prints, get them to one of the men on his list who could handle Russian. Moreover, there had to be someone there to receive the messenger; otherwise the alarm would be given before dawn, and by then Morgan planned to be out of the British Isles. His suitcase was at the Mitre; it held money and the Mauser pistol, possessions increasingly essential to his survival.

Palmer Syce is another of my casualties, Morgan told himself. If I hadn't come here today he'd be alive now. He heard the church chimes sound again. Now their sound was elegiac, a threnody for the newly dead. He was at a wake, attending the body of his friend. No, the cognac was working on his brain, his mind was wandering.

His eyes were accommodated to the darkness; they could make out the form of Palmer's face, the open, staring eyes. Morgan turned away, wondering when the messenger would come.

He assumed he had escaped death because the killer did not know Syce had a dinner guest. Syce had been killed because he was in touch with Morgan and was assumed to know about Hargrave and Geneva, and the information was lethal.

They killed Marisa for less reason, he mused, and they still have to kill me.

The doorbell rang. Morgan's muscles stiffened. He downed the cognac and got up. With an effort he opened the study door, went into the hallway, and turned on the outside light. Through the small leaded window he saw an Army motorcyclist, protective helmet, and long black leather gauntlets. In one of them a small beige envelope. It was a young face, lips puckered in a tuneless whistle that penetrated through the heavy door. Morgan unbolted it and said cheerfully, "Ah, been waiting for that."

"Bit late, sir," the cyclist said. "We was short of riders tonight. Just sign here, sir." He offered Morgan a clipboard, indicated the line, and Morgan signed Palmer's name, then took the envelope. "Good evening, sir," the cyclist said and went down the steps toward the quad where the motorcycle was parked under a lamp.

Morgan wiped his damp forehead, bolted the door, and turned off the outside light. He went into the kitchen and found a light over the cutting board. He opened the envelope and shook out the contents: seven prints in all, about three by five.

And the negatives.

With poultry scissors Morgan cut the strip into individual frames and slid them into his billfold. The prints and unexposed negative he tore up and burned in a saucepan, rinsing the ashes down the drain. Then he polished and dried the saucepan and returned it to the overhead rack. The stench of burned chemicals made him cough.

146

Leaving the kitchen he considered returning Syce's body to where it had fallen in death but could not bring himself to disturb the corpse again. He had wanted it out of sight when the messenger arrived, and that had been accomplished. Where the body was found tomorrow seemed unimportant; murder had been done and there was no way to camouflage the fact. Nor did Morgan want to, even though he fully expected to be accused of the deed. And he doubted that the killer would ever be identified . . . if MI-6 or the Yard even troubled to look for anyone beyond the obvious suspect: David Llewellyn Morgan.

He left a small light in the study, the door ajar. He put on hat and coat and went back through the dark kitchen where he unlocked the service door. Very quietly, Morgan opened it and looked around, then went out, closing the door after him. He followed a path that led him around the inside of the college green and to a gate that marked the precincts' limit. From there he made his way back to the hotel, stopped at the desk for his room key, and asked for his bill, explaining that an unexpected call was summoning him away.

"But I'll have to be chargin' ye for the whole night, sir," the clerk told him. Morgan said that was understandable and he was quite willing to pay.

In his room he strapped on the Mauser in its shoulder holster and took half the money from his suitcase lining before folding and packing his clothing into the bag. He was about to leave when a thought struck him. At the writing desk he got out an envelope and addressed it to Broom Ten Eyck at the Spanish address Palmer Syce had given him. He took the seven negatives from his billfold and folded a sheet of writing paper to hold them. Then he inserted the paper into the envelope and sealed it.

At the desk he paid his bill, bought a stamp, and dropped the letter in the lobby mail box, thinking that it should reach Ten Eyck even before he did. And if he failed to reach Spain, then Broom Ten Eyck would know what to do with whatever the negatives contained.

Morgan went outside and began walking toward the train station, not wanting to ask about bus schedules to London. Eventually a London train would come by, and until then he would simply wait at the station.

Nearing the station, he started across an intersection when a black Daimler rounded the curb and cut him off. Morgan swore as the car braked, and a man rolled out of the passenger side. Morgan dropped his suitcase and strode toward him angrily, but the man drew a pistol.

147

"No closer," he said in a guttural accent. "Please get in the rear seat." He gestured with the pistol.

"In," the man repeated. "Quickly. Do as I say." Another man left the car, picked up Morgan's bag and put it in the trunk. Slowly, Morgan opened the rear door and got inside. The man with the pistol slid in beside him. "No violence, Mr. Morgan," the man said. "If you attempt anything you will be hurt. You were returning to London? We will take you there. So, try to enjoy the trip."

Morgan grunted.

"I tell you this: A person of great importance desires to speak with you. It is in your interest to be calm, cooperate." The driver shifted the Daimler into gear and the heavy car rolled down the street, gathering speed.

"Who are you?"

"That is unimportant. What is important is that you will be tonight in London. Tomorrow you will go wherever you want to go."

"I'll bet."

There were three of them, Morgan realized, just like Geneva. This time it seemed likely that the other three men would leave the car, and he would remain inside. The irony made him want to laugh, but he was cold with fear.

The men who had taken him were hard, unemotional professionals, and Morgan appraised his chance of escape at nil. What he had gone through at Syce's lodgings had drained him, left him powerless to resist the will of adversaries who were powerful and omniscient. The realization that they had been toying with him assaulted his sense of self-worth. All his adult life he had been conditioned to resist capture, escape confinement, but now he realized that humble acceptance of prison had castrated him, eliminating even his inherent will to resist, strike back.

The muzzle of the pistol was a steady pressure on his rib cage just opposite the heart. Streetlights like flashing strobes showed Morgan his captor's face: swarthy, like Kistos Aristides Soffit; mustached; deep-set eyes; a short lighter-colored scar on the right cheekbone.

The two men in the front seat were taller than the pistol-holder and both were dark-haired and hatless. The driver wore whipcord livery and the man beside him a short leather jacket over a black turtleneck. Morgan felt the tension of his shoulder-holster straps, but by the time he could peel back topcoat and jacket and grasp the Mauser he would be dead.

Dead as Palmer Syce.

The Daimler was speeding along a highway. Moonlight showed milestones like grave markers. Morgan resigned himself to death.

What device had they used to murder Syce? he wondered. The special pistol that fired a burst of cyanide gas? Cloth impregnated with nerve compound? He had not even heard Palmer fall.

"How about some music?" Morgan suggested. "*Dry Bones*—lots of rhythm and a relevant message."

The car was silent.

"No radio in this luxury job?"

His captor sighed. "Try to relax, Mr. Morgan."

"Yeah. I've played this scene before."

"This time you will not be killing anybody. You are a dangerous man, Mr. Morgan, so we take precautions."

What was the accent? A-minus grammar with no clipped British-isms. Nuances of word selection indicated English as an acquired language.

What difference does it make? The son of a bitch is going to kill me, though probably not in this expensive car, and I should be thinking of something other than his accent. How do they know my name is Morgan? Who the hell are they?

The bug in Syce's study, he answered himself. The existential bug that told all and revealed nothing. Hell, he and Palmer hadn't even looked for it; MI-6 was going to run the sweep, but now Syce wouldn't be able to ask Six to do anything in his behalf. Palmer had no need of Six or Morgan or Anna or the Agency; no one, nothing. Death canceled all needs.

Morgan was satisfied that his captors were not from British Intelligence. The Brits would send 'round a Bobby who, with a polite knock and a tip of his Peeler helmet would *invite* the suspect to step outside, sir, please, this way if you will. . . .

Instinct was reasserting itself. Morgan began estimating his chances of shoving aside the pistol and grappling with his captor, but then the man up front could simply slug or shoot him. Morgan juggled the odds, felt a surge of hatred at these men who were about to end his life.

After a while mist appeared on the windscreen. Noiseless wipers rocked back and forth like slave semaphores outlined occasionally by the headlights of an oncoming car. He sensed that they were moving through populated areas, not into the countryside where killing could take place sans witnesses. The idea pleased him briefly, then he reflected that a thick-walled garage would do just as well. The St.

149

Valentine's Day massacre had immortalized mural murder; the garage had been torn down, its bricks sold by a speculator in sensational novelties.

Morgan could be done away with without a trace, and he conceded that he had paved the way by becoming a nonperson, a chameleon of dissimilar identities. In liquidating him his killers would destroy something that had ceased to exist.

He said, "How much longer?"

"Soon. You will see."

"Who do you work for?"

"Don't be trouble, Mr. Morgan," the man warned, "or I just hit you unconscious and no more trouble. I tell you relax."

"Go to hell!"

"I don't mind names," the man said comfortably, "but maybe I knock your teeth out. You don't like that, eh?"

The Daimler sped along past what he thought was Regent's Park. Or were they on Bayswater Road? He needed Buckingham Palace, Marble Arch, or the British Museum to orient himself in central London, but none of those landmarks had flashed by.

"Sods," he muttered. "Miserable, mercenary sods. Why did you kill Syce?"

"Eh?"

"Why did you kill Palmer Syce?"

"I didn't kill no one."

"Bullshit. You killed Syce tonight and waited for me."

"No," the gunman said doggedly. "Maybe you kill Syce, eh? He your good friend."

"Was."

The gunman frowned. "Syce is dead?"

"You know damn well he is, you murdering bastard." A flame of hatred shot through his body. Might as well die now, he thought, while the adrenalin's flowing, and maybe I can take him with me.

As though sensing his thoughts, the pistol-holder moved into the far corner of the seat, the gun still pointing at Morgan's chest. "Almost there," he muttered. "Relax yourself, Mr. Morgan. Soon it will end."

Morgan laughed thinly. "Without that pistol how long do you think you'd last with me, asshole? I'll give you thirty seconds unarmed. I'd break your kneecaps. So hang tight to the pistol."

150

The taunts registered. The man's cheeks showed pale patches. With effort he controlled himself. Cursed in an unknown tongue, but the pistol never wavered.

Shit, Morgan thought, this bastard's too well trained. I can't provoke him.

The Daimler slowed, swerved, and turned abruptly into a drive. A tall wrought-iron gate opened, and before the car went through it, Morgan glimpsed a decoration surmounting the curving arch: the red-and-gold hammer and sickle device of the Union of Soviet Socialist Republics.

The shock of recognition, of sudden orientation, stunned him. Passively he saw the headlights wash the entrance of the Soviet Embassy, then follow the side of the building to an unlighted entry where the Daimler braked and stopped.

"Out," said the gunman. The front door opened and the rider jerked open Morgan's door. He grabbed Morgan's arm and hauled him onto the paving. Between the two men Morgan walked up the unlighted steps and paused while the door was unlocked. They elbowed him inside.

Half dazed, Morgan let himself be led down a dim corridor, up a flight of carpeted stairs. Another corridor, a hallway covered with thick red carpet, a row of dark, closed doors. At one they halted. The gunman knocked. A voice answered. The gunman opened the door and shoved Morgan into a spacious office suite. There was a single light in the room, a photoflood on a high standard, and it focused on an ornate chair.

From the darkness a voice. "Take off your coat and hat, Mr. Morgan. You will not need them for a while."

Obediently Morgan eased out of his topcoat, removed his hat. Silently they were taken from him. He felt arms circling his chest, patting him down, heard an exclamation. A hand removed the Mauser from its shoulder holster. The body search continued. His billfold was taken away, along with his passport. The whisper of shoes on the carpeting told Morgan they were being carried to the desk behind the spotlight.

"I'm glad you did not try to use your gun, Mr. Morgan," the voice said. "Grigor is a superb marksman."

"I'm pretty good myself," Morgan said with an effort at bravado, "but I didn't get the chance."

"Surprise is a most effective weapon," the voice went on, "and it was employed in your case for two reasons. First, I wanted no violence to your person or to my men. Second, to convince you of my peaceful intentions."

Morgan snorted.

"Be seated, please."

He moved to the center of the room, turned the chair to one side and sat down. Light seared his profile.

Some words in Russian and Morgan heard carpet whispers, the door open and close.

"We are alone now," the voice said. "Of course I have a weapon, as well as yours, by way of precaution. But unless you try to attack me you are in absolutely no danger whatsoever. After we have talked you will be free to leave. Do you understand?"

Morgan's tongue moistened dry lips. "I may understand but I don't believe."

"Believe," the voice said, and the floodlight went out.

As it did a desk lamp went on, and, as though by rheostat control, indirect ceiling lights began to glow.

Seated behind the desk was a man in his late fifties. What Morgan could see of his torso was powerfully built. The coat and vest seemed tailored of dark-blue cheviot. White starched collar, Windsor knot in the regimental tie. Above it a close-trimmed black beard, teeth so white and even they were either capped or full porcelain dentures; slanting cheekbones in a well-fed face, penetrating eyes under thick black brows, and above them a thatch of hair the color of coal.

"Sergei Kozlov!" Morgan sucked a deep breath.

"Sergei Vlasovich Kozlov."

Morgan sat forward. "To be sure. Always the patronymic. Well, Colonel, what's happening?"

"General," Kozlov corrected in a mild voice. "A glass of tea? Whisky?"

"Scotch," Morgan said. "Two cubes, light on the water."

General Kozlov went to a carved cellarette and mixed two drinks. He carried one to Morgan and returned to his desk. Morgan downed half the highball thirstily, suppressed questions jamming his mind, and decided to let Kozlov do the talking.

The Russian lighted a cigarette, exhaled, and leaned back in the thickly-cushioned chair. "I last saw you in Cairo, I believe. The Greek Embassy . . . Queen's birthday celebration, was it not?"

"I'd be impressed by your memory except that you have it all on file." He sipped from his glass.

Kozlov smiled. "True, Mr. Morgan. And since then some unexpected things have happened to both of us. I was promoted in rank and you were imprisoned by your countrymen, but worse things could have happened. As you may recall, I spent twenty-one months at Peshlag . . . a hard-labor camp . . . because I was so indiscreet as to remark in my cups that Nikita was not half the man Stalin was in his prime. But you look well, considering. And you've been busy, too. That is the general area for discussion: your activities these past two weeks or so." He tilted his glass and drank. "I ask that you confide in me, Mr. Morgan: after prison were you reinstated—rehabilitated— by the Agency?"

"No."

"For whom are you working now?"

"No one. Myself."

"Free lance, as it were?"

Morgan shrugged. "Call it what you like, I'm unemployed."

Kozlov tapped ash from his cigarette. "Did unemployment take you to Geneva, Switzerland?"

"That was a one-time job."

"You were the lone survivor."

"As it developed."

"Who were you supposed to kill?"

"No one."

Kozlov snorted. "Yet you killed three men, including Roger Hargrave."

"One man, not Hargrave."

"Come, come, Mr. Morgan, it is our understanding that you were commissioned to destroy Hargrave for motives of revenge, frontier-style justice, eh?"

"Wrong. I was retained to protect him."

The heavy eyebrows lifted. "Who liquidated Hargrave?"

"The man called Soffit . . . *your* man, General."

Kozlov held up a hand and shook his head. "At one time our man, yes. But not in many years. This is what we must clear up, Mr. Morgan, if there is to be any daylight whatever in the episode. It must be thoroughly ventilated. That is why I am here, that is why *you* are here. You see," he said, and got up, "I must persuade you that we share a common interest in the truth."

"Fine," Morgan said. "Now you tell me, General, why your *topolshchiki* murdered Palmer Syce a few hours ago."

"Palmer Syce? *Murdered?*" He walked quickly to Morgan. "I did not know of this."

"I mentioned it to the *nyanki* who brought me here." Morgan finished his drink, rattled cubes in his empty glass.

"But I *knew* Palmer!" General Kozlov exclaimed. "I respected him. Your service should never have discharged him. Such a man is irreplaceable! And he is dead?"

Morgan said nothing.

Kozlov whirled around and paced back and forth. "Who killed him, Morgan?"

"The men who brought me here. Your men."

"*Nyet.* No, they did *not.* It was not ordered. There was no reason to. He was harmless, an old man puttering in his garden, living in the past. . . ."

"Exactly."

The tone of Morgan's voice halted Kozlov. Gazing at Morgan, he said, "You were there?"

"In another room. He answered the door and when he didn't return I went looking for him. I found him dead."

"Natural causes, then." He puffed the cigarette agitatedly.

"It was supposed to *look* like a natural death, General, but the odor of gas was there. No, the visitor killed him and got away. Within an hour your Vopos picked me up. Just coincidence?" He sipped ice-water and stared up at Kozlov. "I don't believe in concidence."

Kozlov snatched the glass from his hand, went rapidly to the cellarette and mixed another highball, brought it back to Morgan. "I swear to you by. . . "

". . . by what?"

". . . by Mother Russia that I had nothing to do with his death."

"Some other section of the KGB, then."

"*Impossible.* Such orders could not be issued without my consent."

"That's comforting to know," Morgan said. "The point is that my friend was murdered. Who else would want to kill him but your Service?"

"The same ones who arranged for Hargrave's liquidation."

"I don't get it: Hargrave fooled you and came over. Your people had him killed."

Kozlov shook his head. "We let him go, Morgan. He was dying;

cancer was all through him. He knew it and wanted to go home to die."

"So you let him."

"He had no secret knowledge to take with him. And years ago he had told us all he knew. He was nothing, I tell you, only a husk. A hollow, dying man."

"Why was he killed?"

"That is the question I ask you, Mr. Morgan. Who arranged it? Surely it was the same persons who sent you to receive him."

"Let's theorize," Morgan said, stretching out his legs. "Hargrave decided to come back, with or without information. Your people learned of his plan but too late to stop him. Letting Hargrave emerge in the West as a fugitive from your system after everything he sacrificed to join you would have been intolerable. So you improvised to prevent it. Soffit was already involved in the defection plan, so you got him to alter it." He got up from the chair. "Tell me it didn't happen."

Kozlov seemed lost in thought. His heavy shoulders slumped. Finally he said, "And this is the story you would tell?"

"That's the story I'd tell."

"*Why?*"

"Because," Morgan lied, "I believe it to be true."

"*Ya nichivo ni ponimayu! Nyet, nyet, nyet!*"

"You speak great English," Morgan said dryly. "Give me the benefit."

"It could not have happened as you say. It is entirely impossible."

"Can you disprove it?"

"Ah! How can you prove it?"

Morgan laughed shortly. "The difference is, General, that I don't have to."

"Don't be so sure of that, Mr. Morgan. The Swiss police believe you murdered all three men. I could deliver you to them tonight and the Soviet Union would gain great credit in world opinion."

"But you won't."

His eyes darted to Morgan, then he walked back to his desk. "That is true. I will not." He picked up Morgan's Mauser, pulled out the magazine and stripped cartridges from it. They scattered on the carpet. Kozlov inserted the magazine and tossed the pistol to Morgan. "A Nazi weapon," he sneered. "Even to touch it fills me with disgust."

Morgan fitted the Mauser into its shoulder holster. "My woman was killed, General," he said tautly. "Her house was bombed while she slept. I want to know who was responsible."

"I don't know. Go to America and find out." He sat at his desk and ran both hands through his hair. "Some persons want to destroy you, Morgan. You must realize that. They even kill people in contact with you. Did you tell Syce about all this?"

"I did."

"And what did he say?"

"That you Soviets are predictable."

"What else?"

"We were going to talk after dinner. But he was killed."

Kozlov's head lifted. "You will be accused."

"Of course."

"You don't care?"

"I care a great deal. But I'm not in a position to do much about it." He glanced around the room. "This is a damned fantasy. I'm in a Soviet Embassy with a senior officer of the KGB and I'm not even in the Agency."

"That," said Kozlov softly, "is why you are here. Now, tell me what Hargrave said to you before he was murdered."

"Well, we once went to school together. He asked me about the old place, told me his wife was well—I'd known her before they married—and that was all we had time for. By then we were in the car with Soffit and the driver. Soffit's general appearance didn't inspire confidences."

"His name," Kozlov said irritably, "was Stepavitch. A rotten, mercenary Serb."

"You sound like Goebbels," Morgan remarked. "Was he subhuman, too?"

Kozlov jerked as though he had been slapped. "We Great Russians have no love for the Serbs." Angrily he stubbed out his cigarette, lighted another. "You have told me *all* that Hargrave spoke to you about? He said nothing of China?"

Morgan shook his head. "He didn't even mention fried rice. General, there was no time to talk. We planned to chat later on the evacuation plane."

Kozlov exhaled a cloud of smoke. "Ah, yes. The plane. Did you *see* the plane, Morgan?"

"No. But it was supposed to be there."

156

"Have you ever thought it might not have been?"

"I've considered the possibility."

"Then I will tell you that no plane was waiting for Hargrave and you. What do you say to that?"

"I'm not surprised."

"Does it not shake your faith in your sponsors?"

"I had very little to begin with," Morgan told him. "How much faith do you have in yours?"

Kozlov grimaced, looked around the room and put one finger to his lips. Morgan understood Kozlov's silence. The general did not want to spend additional winters in Siberia. What Kozlov said was, "I have full faith in my superiors, Mr. Morgan, though I can understand your cynicism. Still, you are to be congratulated on avoiding that aspect of the Hargrave conspiracy which was to have left you dead. How did it happen? Were you alerted in some way?"

"Soffit asked me if I was armed."

"A fatal mistake . . . for him. And my *nyanki* . . . as you term them . . . should have relieved you of that Nazi pistol long before you entered this room."

"Nobody cares any more; hard to find skilled labor."

"I absolutely agree. Now, you are quite sure that Roger Hargrave said nothing to you about his apprehension over China?"

"Nothing."

"Did he entrust you with information in any form?"

"I was just the conducting officer," Morgan said, "and temporary at that. If he had anything it seems logical he would have withheld it until debriefing."

"You mean interrogation."

"Perhaps. I wasn't to have been involved in that sequence."

"No. Because you were to have been killed." Kozlov rose from his desk again and went over to the mahogany bar. "Much as I enjoy the West I have never truly relished scotch whisky. I am going to take a little vodka and I invite you to do the same."

"Scotch is fine," Morgan said, "and I'll nurse what I have."

He watched General Kozlov pour vodka into a small tumbler, sniff the liquor, and swallow a healthy jolt. Kozlov wiped his mouth. "Are you hungry, Morgan?"

"No."

"If you don't mind I will have something to eat." He picked up the telephone, pressed buttons, and spoke rapidly. When he finished ordering, Morgan said, "How did you know where to find me, General?"

"I am afraid you must forgive me for not answering. That will have to remain an operational secret."

"Nothing so crass as a bug or phone tap?"

"Please, it is not a matter for discussion."

Morgan smiled. "British Intelligence may decide not to have me charged with Palmer's death, General. Not much political mileage in that. But what *would* be profitable is a charge that Syce was murdered by the Russians. With me they'd have to establish a motive, but everyone knows you kill people all the time."

Kozlov grunted. "Whatever the truth of that I predict that the British will not suggest KGB responsibility. But if they should be so misled we will simply arrest one of their men in Moscow and hold him in Lubiyanka until the British change their mind."

"And apologize."

Kozlov smiled. "So realistic for a Westerner, Mr. Morgan, but you understand the Soviet point of view." He drank more of the vodka and licked his lips. "You know your new Director, Robert Dobbs? What do you think of him?"

"Well, he's not *my* Director, General. I've known him slightly and I think he's an asshole."

Kozlov laughed. "Such candor. Enviable."

"Constitutional free speech. What do you think of *your* Chairman, General? In the Agency we evaluated him as a horse's ass."

Kozlov looked frightened. His expression begged Morgan for prudence and tact. "My Chief is a Hero of the Soviet Union," he said loudly. "A great and wise man."

"Sure," Morgan said, and finished his drink. Its analgesic effect had relaxed him, helped him deal with Kozlov who must, by reason of his promotion, have become head of the KGB's First Chief Directorate, where before he had only headed the Seventh Department. As Minister of the Soviet Embassy Kozlov had been clandestine counselor to the government that suppressed the coup Morgan had helped stage. From that episode they had known each other, though Kozlov had not brought the subject up. Besides, Morgan reflected, the general had gone on to greater accomplishments and could afford the indulgence of not gloating over a regional victory.

"Anything else?" Morgan said.

Kozlov's eyebrows lowered. "What do you mean?"

"I mean we've been drinking and talking, exchanging frank views as professionals do, and now I'd like to get back to what I was doing before your storm troopers dragged me here."

"Storm troopers? No, no, Mr. Morgan, I cannot allow that term."

"Well, the Russian equivalent, then."

"I won't hear them insulted. Well, I am willing that you leave, Mr. Morgan, on condition that you understand my country did not liquidate Mr. Hargrave. He was a good friend of ours, in fact I knew him as a working associate. We agreed to his departure for compassionate reasons, though I doubt that your country would do the same. The point is: Do you understand the situation?"

"I understand part of it, General. But why is this important to you? Why should you care what I think?"

"For two obvious reasons, Mr. Morgan. You have motives for revenge, do you not? I do not want you hunting down innocent Soviet citizens, but what you do otherwise is your own affair. Second, in the likely event that you are apprehended and brought to trial for these supposed murders, I do not want you proclaiming the guilt of the Soviet Union." He put down his vodka glass and walked to Morgan. "In America you are known as a man of great principle. An accusation by you, however baseless, would be believed by many persons. And just now my country does not want that sort of thing."

"Shall I tell you why?"

Kozlov looked at him sharply. "By all means do so."

"It's because your country is scared shitless of the Chinese."

Kozlov said nothing.

Morgan smiled. "The Oriental protégés grew up. They're big, powerful boys now. Brezhnev went ape when we resumed relations with them, signed the trade treaty. You have nightmares over the possibility of a Sino-American front against the Soviet Union."

Kozlov wiped his mouth. "That this is matter of concern is no state secret. In fact, from my personal point of view I would far prefer to join forces with your Agency and work in common against the Chinese enemy than work alone against the combined forces of the Agency and the Chinese. Of course," he said and his eyes lifted significantly, "that is only my personal preference. May I ask yours?"

"I have none."

Sourly, Kozlov said, "You are not complimentary, Morgan."

"I don't have to be. I'm not here on a PR binge. Just since nightfall

Palmer Syce—my friend—was liquidated. You deny complicity, so who did it, and why? Don't suggest the Chinese or Arab terrorists, Palmer didn't represent a threat to them."

"Do you know what he was working on for the British?"

"Not really."

"Then I suggest you find out before you eliminate the Chinese or the Arabs."

Morgan grunted. "That's a safe suggestion; one I can't possibly carry out. Before you suggest the Agency, tell me why I wasn't killed, too."

Kozlov shrugged. "The killer must not have known you were nearby."

Morgan shook his head. "I was tailed to Palmer's house this evening so I think there's a connection between that and his murder. Has to be."

"Perhaps, but things concur not necessarily in logical order."

Wearily, Morgan waved a hand. "All right, General, so you didn't order Palmer killed and the Soviets don't know anything about it. Let's say Irish Nationalists were responsible and get on to other things."

"But are you not convinced."

"Sure I'm convinced. Anna the housekeeper killed him for reasons of her own. Come on, General, let's not waste time."

"Listen, Morgan," Kozlov said heavily, "I tell you the truth about Syce. I had no responsibility. Is that clear?"

"Perfectly clear. I have your statement, General, but it would be far easier to accept if you made a show of good faith."

"Good faith?" He frowned. "What do you mean?"

"I mean a convincer. Something to impress me with your sincerity."

"Such as?"

"Release Alexandra Hargrave, send her out of the Soviet Union along with her children. I can't think of anything that would be more beneficial to the Soviet Union in terms of world opinion."

Kozlov gaped at him. There was a knock on the door and a maid entered with a napkin-covered tray. Ignoring Morgan she went to the desk and set down the tray. She removed the napkin and almost at once Morgan could smell the aroma of beet soup. There was a teapot and a plate of black-bread sandwiches. The maid went out, closed the door, and Kozlov sat down. He stared at the food, deep in thought.

Morgan said, "Especially since she's a widow."

"Silence!" Kozlov roared, "I have to think. Yes, it is a good idea, a fine idea, Morgan. But what I cannot understand, and what infuriates me at this moment: *Why did I not think of it myself?* A week ago I should have done it!" He cused in Russian. "Of course! Let the widow affirm that we did not slay her husband! Let *her* tell the story of his approaching death, his wish to be buried in his homeland!" He looked up and sighed. "Your mind is so much like mine. I could use you, you know, employ you better than your own countrymen, Morgan. You don't hold that coup against me?"

"Not personally. You'll let her go, then. It's agreed?"

He hung a napkin from the top of his vest, poured tea into a thick glass, stirred. "I agree to present the idea to my superiors, Morgan. I am willing to do that. It is my idea, after all, is it not?"

"Entirely."

"You will want to see her?"

"In time. Right now she probably believes I killed Roger."

"The children may not want to come, you know. In America their father is considered a traitor. And they have been brought up as enthusiastic Soviet citizens. Is it necessary they leave, too?"

"They shouldn't be forced. So perhaps Alexandra could be allowed to visit them whenever she wants."

"Better and better. A mother's love. . . ." He bit into a sandwich ferociously. "Everyone can understand that," he managed through his full and moving mouth.

"Now that I've helped you," Morgan said, "I'd like your help, General. Just in a minor way, you understand."

"Oh? How minor?"

"Transportation."

"Where are you going?"

"To Spain."

"Why?"

"I have to get out of England," Morgan said. "By tomorrow they'll be looking for me, so I have to leave tonight."

Kozlov put down his tea and swallowed. He belched. "What is it you want?"

"A car to London Airport."

"What else?"

"Nothing," Morgan said. "Absolutely nothing." He bent over and picked up the Mauser cartridges, put them in his jacket pocket.

"You are a lot of trouble, Morgan," General Kozlov said, swilling tea around his mouth. "In the Yemen I once thought of killing you. If I had, you wouldn't be in trouble now."

"That's an interesting idea, and it expands into a great argument for birth control: Avoid trouble, don't be born."

Kozlov tore a big chunk from his sandwich and chewed moodily. Finally he said, "Where are you going in Spain?"

"Wherever it's safe."

"You speak Spanish?"

"Some."

"I don't like Spaniards. The anarchists killed my older brother in their civil war."

"They eat a lot of lamb and mutton," Morgan said conversationally. "Not much beef. Cook everything in olive oil."

"*Pah!*"

"Exactly." He looked at his wristwatch. "I'd like to leave, General Kozlov."

The general reached for the telephone, pressed several buttons, and spoke in Russian. Presently the door opened and Morgan's escorts appeared. Gesturing with his knife, Kozlov said, "So Morgan can understand, I speak in English: Take him to London Airport. He is leaving on a plane."

"Yes, General Kozlov," they said in unison.

Morgan said, "If you've finished inspecting my suitcase, let's repack it before we leave."

A gesture of Kozlov's knife reinforced the suggestion.

Morgan said, "There was money in the suitcase, General. Quite a lot of money. I hope it's still there."

Kozlov glared at his men. "It will be there, *tovarischki. Da?*"

"*Da. Da!*" they chorused.

"*Idity skarevo!*" Kozlov yelled, and the two men hurried out of the office.

"*Spasibo*," Morgan said. "I appreciate your courtesy, General, and I'll be watching the papers."

"For what?"

"Headlines telling me Alexandra Hargrave has come home."

"Oh, that." He rotated his knife impatiently. "Very soon, Morgan. Very soon. Have a good trip. *Dosvidaniya.*"

"*Dosvidaniya.*"

Morgan left the office and in the corridor found the turtleneck-sweatered man, who escorted him down the back stairway and into

162

the Daimler. Morgan's bag was on the rear seat. He sat alone, chauffeur and turtleneck up front, privacy glass drawn. Grigor the gunman did not join the party. Smoothly the big sedan rolled through the embassy gates. When Morgan saw them close behind him he felt less insecure.

The whole episode with Kozlov had been a charade, Morgan knew, a con job from start to finish. The pregnant question, though, was who had out-conned who?

Brook Ten Eyck should be able to analyze the meeting's significance, for in the years when Broom ranged high in the Agency his special field had been Soviet deception ops. Moreover, he had known Roger Hargrave, and Syce had named Ten Eyck as an officer who could have known about or even prepared Roger's launching as a double agent. At the least, Broom Ten Eyck could translate Roger's documents and appraise their worth. At the most, he might know and be willing to tell who Dormouse was.

FOURTEEN

THE balcony of Broom Ten Eyck's condominium overlooked the Nerja beaches and that narrow portion of the western Mediterranean known as the Alboran Sea. Across it lay the shores of Morocco. West of Nerja, over thirty miles of coastal road, was Malaga. For three days Morgan had been at the condo, sleeping late and sunning himself on the balcony. At Morgan's urging Ten Eyck had flown to Paris to get a new passport for him from Claude Frechette and, while there, to pick up anything for Chipman at Post Restante. Morgan expected him back today.

The late spring sun had toasted Morgan's body deep brown; a barber had bleached and silvered his hair. Ten Eyck had photographed the transformation and taken the picture for Frechette's use in another passport. Once Morgan had that, he would be able to travel again.

Ten Eyck and his wife, Morgan learned, kept an apartment above Madrid's Plaza Mayor, and it was there that Margaret stayed. Ten Eyck's local living arrangements included an attractive Spanish widow in her forties named Juanita. For appearances' sake, she had a house on the hillside behind the condominium. During Morgan's stay she was occupying it, though looking in on Morgan every day.

London papers were flown daily to Malaga, and shortly after Morgan's arrival they headlined Syce's murder, naming Morgan as the scholar's last known visitor. A day later Morgan saw his photograph in the *Guardian* along with a Scotland Yard statement that he was being sought for questioning.

What could I tell them, he wondered. Nothing of any use. Even the description of his tweedy surveillant would fit a dozen British men strolling the Oxford lanes that fatal evening. So just when the Cointrin killings faded from the Geneva press, he was again a fugitive, and he thought of the impact on his son and daughter. And Ghislaine Percival.

She seemed remote to him now, far away and half-forgotten despite the attraction that had flared between them. Morgan raised up on his elbows and looked through the railing at the beach six stories below. He could see pastel bath houses, candy-striped canvas *cabañas,* and a good many sunworshipers sleeping or idly strolling on the light-gold sand. Sun-bras and bikinis were reasonably modest, though far less so than under Franco rule; but no topless bathing as permitted by the French at St. Tro'. Not yet.

A volleyball game was in progress, and he could hear occasional shouts from players as they punched the ball over the net. From a beach café drifted the strumming of a flamenco guitar, and Morgan reflected that he was in Andalucia with its strident gypsy music and sensuous dance.

Among the young women on the beach, he thought, there would be one or two as attractive as Jill if he cared to seek them out. In Paris he had seen no one but Jill, and as a result had come to view her as uniquely capable of affection. No, on the Costa del Sol, relaxed and at ease, rested and unafraid, Morgan mused that their Paris situation had been artificial; much had taken place in too short a time. In any case, he thought, it's unlikely we'll meet again, and I'm sorry I gave her so much dangerous information that could threaten us both.

He wiped perspiration from his face and turned over on the sun lounge cushions. There was *paella* in the oven, brought by Juanita earlier in the day, and he would lunch on it after a while with fresh bread and a couple of glasses of cold Etiqueta Blanca. Away from cities, his needs were few. As in Key West, he mused, and thought inevitably of Marisa.

The pain was there, the ache of remembrance, much as he tried to stifle it. When his mind was inactive, his body physically disengaged, the memories came back, washing the recesses of his mind in a strong, irresistible tide. There would be time for mourning later on when all this was behind him, if that time ever came. But now surviving was paramount in his mind, for only by surviving could he learn what lay behind the murders. He thought again of Syce's homily on unexpected happenings, how it had been proved by Kozlov's sudden intervention.

For now he was in sanctuary, enjoying respite from fear and movement, violent confrontations. Ten Eyck had grasped the situa-

166

tion from Morgan's summary and signed on for the ride. Now he was running necessary errands, and after his return they would get down to the work at hand: analyzing Hargrave's written pages.

Morgan congratulated himself on having mailed the negatives to Broom; otherwise they would have been found by Kozlov, and the strange meeting might have been quite different.

As it was, Morgan thought, all Kozlov knows is that I've flown to Spain. He'll have me searched for in Madrid if he wants me again, but he's finished with me for the present. He made his point, convinced me of his innocence.

He thinks.

Morgan smiled. As Ten Eyck had immediately understood, the covert purpose of the meeting was interrogation. Kozlov needed to know if Hargrave had had time enough to hand over papers or convey a verbal message before the killer struck.

I think I convinced him, Morgan told himself, and General Kozlov isn't open to easy arguments. But he believes me. Whether he'll let Alexandra go remains to be seen, but it's probable he'll try. I had to corner him into agreement without his realizing what I was doing. But, hell, Morgan reflected, like Sergei Vlasovich I had a little training, too.

He was beginning to think of eating when he heard a key in the front door lock. He wrapped a towel around his waist in case it was Juanita again, but through the doorway came Broom Ten Eyck carrying a travel bag.

Ten Eyck was a big man: six-three, with bearlike shoulders and rust-colored hair graying at the temples. A full, red beard camouflaged the pocks of German shrapnel, and the habitual set of his mouth was fierce and challenging. It was Broom's deep, brown eyes, though, that secretaries found irresistible, and at stations abroad as at home, Ten Eyck had gained a reputation as an inveterate bedder of young, attractive females. At Cornell he had rowed varsity crew and become a shot-putter of Olympic caliber, but war had canceled out the coming games and Broom qualified for paratroops instead. Now in his early sixties, Ten Eyck was an exuberant, physical man who jogged, lifted weights, and watched his calories.

"*David!*" he roared, hurling his bag on a sofa, "I'm back from friggin' France and I need a goddam drink of whiskey. Wine's ruined me kidneys." He strode out to the balcony and gripped Morgan's hand. "Russkys blow you away yet? Been screwin' my girl?"

"Not yet." They grinned at each other.

"But you had it in mind, you whoremonger. Damn if I didn't get back just in time." He patted his unruly thatch of hair. "Nub-horns just startin' to grow, damn if they ain't!" He whirled around and made for the balcony bar, grabbed a whisky bottle, and pulled the cork with his teeth. Half-filling a tumbler he plopped ice into it, drank noisily, and emitted a loud sigh. "I'm gonna make it, David. I'll see sunset today. Hey, where's your drink?"

Morgan got a bottle of Spanish chablis from the refrigerator and poured a glass.

Broom wiped his wet whiskers. "Cheers." He lifted his glass. "Bloody war an' a sickly season. Hail the Union Jack."

They drank together. Broom licked his lips and said, "I got the swag, kid. *Tout le grisbi,* as they say. I even stopped at your lodge and gave your hound some vittles. Quite a place you got there, David," he said wickedly, "but you're not so sinful like me. I'd have that fancy place stuffed with hot-and-cold running whores, constant orgy, y'all come . . . but I respected its sanctity an' didn't utilize for disreputable purposes." He drank thirstily and tossed used ice off the balcony. "Know what Margaret called me? An old *pre*-vert, that's what. Well, I got mad as hell. Told her I wasn't no way *old*." He laughed uproariously over what Morgan could well imagine had been an actual marital exchange.

Ten Eyck's affected boorishness, Morgan had learned years ago, was designed to camouflage an extraordinarily disciplined mind, distracting observers from a painful shyness that derived from his excessive size and shambling, uncoordinated movements as a boy.

"Damn airlines," Ten Eyck said grouchily, "nothin' to choose between Iberia and BEA, both wretched. Load you with drinks to divert customers from the miserable food. Take me own C-rations next time. Juanita been here today?"

Morgan told him of the *paella* and Ten Eyck said, "You chow down, I'll take a shower an' we'll get to work, hey? Poor Palmer— papers full of it. Brits want you bad."

Lunch over, Ten Eyck stacked Morgan's few dishes and cleared the table. On it he spread prints of the negatives Morgan had mailed him from Oxford, then took a dark blue passport from his travel bag and tossed it to Morgan. It was American, and the name Ten Eyck had chosen for Frechette's alteration was Daniel Thomas Dougherty. Morgan signed it and stared at his photograph with newly-silver hair.

"The old Silver Fox himself," Ten Eyck remarked. "Mother

168

wouldn't know you." He placed a letter before Morgan. It was from Florida, Morgan saw, addressed to Charles Chipman, Post Restante, Paris. In it was a three-by-five card containing a post office box number and a zip code. Below it was written: *Please write. I love you.* Morgan tore the card in half and fitted the address portion into his billfold, wondering if he would ever use it.

"All right," Ten Eyck said, and took a seat across from Morgan. For a while he read the Russian script, and then he said, "Writer wants someone to know the Soviets are planning a preemptive strike on the Chinese. There's to be a border incident in the vicinity of Zaisan arranged to make it appear that the Chinese crossed in regimental strength and killed numerous Soviet border guards and back-up troops. The Soviets will escalate this incident," he picked up another sheet, "and appeal to the UN Security Council. Whether the Chinese apologize or not, the Soviets are going to make this *casus belli* and hit Chinese rocket centers with nukes, take out some smaller cities, and threaten Shanghai and Peking unless the Chinese come to the bargaining table. If India objects," he scanned another print, "they'll take out Delhi. If the U.S. acts belligerent St. Louis is scheduled to go. How about *that?*" He gazed at Morgan. "The East St. Louis Toodle-oo." Ten Eyck leaned back and yawned. "If Hargrave hadn't been carrying this, I'd say it was toilet paper, readily available from any intelligence fabricator in Stockholm, Istanbul, or Hong Kong. Alternatively, it could be deception material, David, Chinese disinformation stuff. Except that Hargrave was working for the Soviets."

"*Was* he?"

"According to all circumstantial evidence. Oh sure, it would be nice to think ol' Roger was one of ours, planted on the Soviets years ago through a phony defection, but I think he just plain went over, for reasons we'll never know. Maybe his wife—widow—will talk about it, but I don't think she'll ever be heard from, despite what Kozlov said. Besides, she'd have an interest in rehabilitating Hargrave, *post mortem*. She'll tell the tale most calculated to make a hero out of him, give her a dignified, possibly profitable, old age. Tell me I'm crazy."

Morgan gestured at the photo prints. "Any timing suggested?"

"No. I imagine Hargrave was going to supply that as part of the *quid pro quo*. Actually, neither of us knows who wrote this. It's flowing Cyrillic script. Maybe Roger developed that much writing facility, maybe not. So all we have is some documents no one can authenticate or disprove."

"Would it be worthwhile to pass them along to the Agency?"

Ten Eyck shook his head. "No way. There's one thing you ought to know, though. Not long after Hargrave went over to the Soviets a medium-level KGB officer walked in on us at Djakarta. He said that before he left Moscow he'd actually seen Hargrave, and that Roger was working in the First Section. The defector said Hargrave's supervisor was Colonel Sergei Kozlov. At the time there was no reason to disbelieve him."

"Was there ever?"

Ten Eyck shrugged. "Not really. You said you'd asked Syce about high-quality intelligence, from a supposedly internal Kremlin-level source, starting to show up after Roger defected. I'd have to side with Palmer, say we had some things going that checked out over the years. But I wasn't looking at sources, you know. I was looking for deception in the product itself, and the methodology is different."

Morgan fingered the nearest print. "Did you ever come across a source slugged 'Dormouse'?"

Ten Eyck nodded. "Once. Only once, and through error. Apparently a reports typist put it in the Source Description part of the report heading and shouldn't have. That report was recalled the same day and I never saw the slug again. Why?"

"Hargrave told me he was Dormouse, told me never to forget it."

Ten Eyck's eyebrows lifted. "You didn't mention that, young feller."

"I was covering an awful lot, Broom, and Kozlov was more fully in my mind. But when you said Kozlov had been Hargrave's case officer, the Dormouse mention came back. Adds up, doesn't it?"

"Does and doesn't. Dormouse could have been assigned as an agent identity word *before* Hargrave defected. If so, Roger could have been aware of it and dropped it on you to enhance the build up stuff he was usin'."

Morgan gestured at the handwritten prints. "Hargrave said these were 'indispensable,' but it doesn't seem they are."

"Indispensable *to whom*?" Ten Eyck said dryly. "Not to the Agency unless the stuff contains some sort of internal code. And why would it? Obviously he wasn't expecting to be killed. Hargrave was expecting to be flown to CONUS with you. No, it has to be that if the material is authentic, he planned to elaborate verbally when he was debriefed. Maybe he'd have done so during the flight. But according to Kozlov there was never going to be any flight. Of course we don't have to believe Kozlov, either." One hand raked through his disheveled hair.

"None of this tells us why you and he were slated for killing or who made the arrangements. I need a drink." He got up, slopped whisky into a glass. "Only a few things are clear, David. Once Hargrave began the process of coming home a decision was made somewhere, by someone, to kill him. Now it has to be that this decision was made either by the people he was leaving, the Soviets, or the people into whose hands he was going, the Americans. From what Hargrave said to you it's apparent he was expecting to see you at the Geneva airport. We don't know that he actually insisted you be his escort as a precondition to returning, but I gather he was reassured by your presence. You were the Judas Goat, having been set up very craftily to perform that function *and* to take the blame for his death." He walked around the table, fingers scrabbling at his beard.

"You were perfect for the role, David. Dead, you couldn't tell what had actually occurred, couldn't pass along anything of significance Hargrave might have had time to tell you. Kozlov asked you about that, of course. And, dead, you couldn't protest whatever was said to be your motive for killing him. You were widely known as a man who'd gone to prison rather than betray the Agency. You and Hargrave were old school chums, and he'd become your Agency sponsor. Prison broke you, embittered you, and you found a chance to destroy this man who *had* betrayed the Agency and a lot else. Shit, man, it was super pluperfect! Only you fucked 'em up, through sheer, friggin' chance an' they've been killin' right an' left ever since."

"Worried?"

He made an idiotic face. "*Me* worry? *Hah!*"

"Do you see Dobbs behind it?"

"Rapid Robert? He couldn't find his prick with a flashlight. No, the worst I ever saw in him was an adjustable conscience." He shook his head. "Dobbs has no background for it. In the big war he was some general's dog-robber, doubt he ever heard a shot fired in anger. When the lesser conflicts came around he was safely embedded in the bureaucracy. Killing wasn't in his work experience. And for the Director to issue lethal orders would involve making others witting of his crimes, so I think we have to let him off the hook. Your alternate thought, though, that someone very close to the Director, operating almost at his level, could have done it is a more appealing idea even though many of the same negatives prevail." He found his drink and downed it. "The Soviets are the obvious conspirators, David, so why not accept the obvious?"

"Because Kozlov could have killed me and he didn't."

"Kozlov ain't the entire KGB."

Morgan grunted. "Don't spin me the old fantasy of a power struggle in the Kremlin or the Committee for State Security with one side pro-American and the other anti-. Too many man-years have been wasted in that debate."

Ten Eyck gestured at the strewn photo prints. "So there's a Chinese factor, for better or worse. Dobbs told you Hargrave was concerned about the very subject his papers covered. Is it unreasonable to suppose the subject is controversial in the Supreme Presidium? My guess is that for the first time in decades the Soviets are deeply worried over questions of war and peace. America by itself doesn't worry them any more, they've written us off for some time as a threat to Socialist inevitability. There hasn't been even a faint stirring in Eastern Europe for years—hell, we ratified Soviet control over it with the Helsinki accords—so if they're agitated it has to be over China." He began using his hands. "The Chinese are totally unpredictable in Soviet eyes. Their quarrels over questions of Marxist dicta are fundamental. Who's the Propagator of the Faith? Moscow or Peking? Then the zigs and zags of Chinese internal politics: liberalization one year, sanguinary suppression the next; Mao's clique hunted like rabid rats; the Shanghai Communique, Teng's visit; the elimination of Taiwan as an obstacle to Western rapprochement; the threat of modernization which would make China an industrial rival to the Soviet Union if allowed to proceed. Oh, the Politburo's got plenty to worry about on its China borders, and this stuff of Hargrave's could be an accurate account of what the Soviets are planning to do under the title of Historical Necessity. But there's nobody available to verify what Hargrave passed to you. Too bad he didn't live a little longer."

"Too bad, indeed."

"Listen, you don't want to subjectify all this stuff that's been happening. I know your girl's been killed, Palmer, too, and you've done a little killing yourself. You probably itch to do more. But you want to get this revenge shit out of your mind and stay objective, take the big view, like the people who've been doing it to you. They've had you runnin' your ass off, David, an' if you don't pull up short, make some strategic plans, they'll sure as hell nail you. And that I don't want to see." He sat across from Morgan and gazed at him. "Let's run down the positives: You're safe now here. You've got a new passport, a different appearance, you can do what you damn well want. You've had a few days' rest and it's made a world of difference. You haven't got the shakes any more so you must be sleepin' better'n you were when you showed up on the threshold t'other day. You've survived a good deal, but then you're supposed to be able to. It's not like you was some silly-arsed civilian who didn't know how to handle himself, right?"

"Right."

"And what's happened to your original persecutors? Been keepin' track o' them? I have. Ol' Senator McComb's convicted of influence peddlin' and sentenced to five years in the Crossbar Cafe. Eckhardt? Two years for sodomy with one of the Senate pages. Senator Nicoll and his protégé Ambassador Hapgood? One censured for selling an ambassadorship, Hapgood kicked out for buyin' it. That don't give you a feelin' of satisfaction, David? Bullshit, it don't! 'Course, they damn near gutted the Agency while they was ridin' high, but things come 'round, y'know, even off. All it takes is time. Restores me faith in the motherland. So the fellers who're out to get you should be feelin' a good deal more desperate than you've a reason to. An' I don't need to tell you that a desperate man is in no condition to figure where his best interest lies. He reacts reflexively, not from considered good sense. Now, you showed good sense comin' here for a breather an' I toss in the advice for free. Since you're in prime condition again I think you oughta stroll down to the beach, pick out a Swede cutie, an' get laid. Meanwhile, I'm gonna report in to Juanita an' see what she has in mind. Toward sundown we'll have some drinks here, then go down into town an' gnaw some prawns, guzzle the local wine an' beer."

"Sounds good," Morgan said and watched Ten Eyck leave the flat. He locked the door, poured a large glass of wine, and went out to the balcony where he sipped and watched the action on the beach below. When the wine was finished, he stretched out on the chaise lounge and closed his eyes against the sun.

He was following the river bank with Donnie, poking sticks in muskrat holes, their boots sinking into the sucking mud at the edge of the swirling water, dark and laden as coffee dregs. For a week the Farmington had overflowed its banks. Now the spring flood was receding, leaving a soggy litter of roots and branches to be climbed over as the two boys helped each other in their slow progress along the shoreline. Donnie was smaller, a year younger than Morgan, but he had a sheath knife on his belt, with a small carborundum stone to edge the blade when it dulled from hacking bark and branches. There was afternoon sun on their backs. Beside them the current ran strong and silent, whorls forming above some sunken obstacle, and they were talking about girls and birthday parties when they reached the elbow in the river called the Suckhole. The water was high and the racing current formed a vortex where it backed and changed direction, and they climbed the bank to toss small branches into the whirlpool to see them vanish instantly, reappearing twenty yards downstream.

For a while they peeled thumb-thick branches with Donnie's knife, chopped them into short sections, and tried to outthrow each other, heaving their sticks across the Suckhole. The white sticks stayed visible a few inches under the moving water before they were drawn downward, and from the bank they could see them spewed up beyond the bend. Morgan got two across, one sticking in the mud, the other lying half-covered; then Donnie gathered the rest in one hand, spun around like a discus thrower, and flung them over the river. But he slipped in the muddy underfooting, the edge of the bank gave way, and with a scream Donnie pitched into the water. He hit on his back and Morgan saw his terrified face, the heavy brown corduroy jacket, the muddy sole of one boot before the dark current closed over.

With a yell Morgan pulled off his jacket and jumped off the bank, landing in mud to his boot tops. Frantically he waded into the current waiting for Donnie to float up, peering at the sucking flow, hoping, praying, for his playmate to emerge. But the torrent was undisturbed except for its little whorls, and Morgan waded downstream to where the sticks surfaced, waited, then went back and plunged into the chilling water, reaching downward with blind hands, groping until his lungs were bursting, surfacing for air and diving again, never reaching the silted bottom, being turned and tumbled by the current until at length he drew himself vomiting and exhausted up on the shore and sat, face buried in his arms, while he wept.

When strength returned he began to stumble toward the nearest farmhouse over plowed fields, boots sinking deep in the clinging earth, and finally a woman in a calico apron came out on the back porch, heard his anguished cries, the words that burst from his throat, threw a blanket around him, and telephoned for help.

It seemed hours that he sat there, teeth chattering, crying uncontrollably, until a policeman came and told the woman they had found Donnie's body anchored near the bottom by a sunken tree whose branches had snagged his jacket. Then the ride home in the police car, his mother's shocked expression when he told her what had happened.

Later, the newspaper story of Donnie's death, the whispers of schoolmates, hinting he could have saved Donnie if he'd really tried. The funeral home, the tired, pallid face in the coffin, the weeping of Donnie's family at the graveside, and the surging, choking grief he knew would never end.

For years he never went near the Suckhole, and when one day he found himself beside it the water was low, easily moving between mud ridges, leaf-laden branches bending over it, the summer sun glinting on water so clear he could see crayfish scuttling on the bottom. He stared at the placid scene remembering the horror of a long-ago spring day, tears welling in his eyes, and turned away never to return.

But now he was hooked to the bottom, struggling blindly, mouth and nostrils filling with mud, coughing, drawing water with each attempt to breathe as he drowned the way Donnie had, and he yelled and beat at the tree trunk until the hand of a rescuer gripped his shoulder. When he opened his eyes water dropped away and he saw a bearded face and knew that he was safe as Ten Eyck said, "Wake up, David, you having a nightmare? You're okay, nothing's wrong."

The sun was low, the air chill. Remembering the dead face of Palmer Syce, Morgan sat up shivering, saw Juanita staring at him from the doorway. He was panting, breath whistling between his teeth. His forehead was wet.

"A bad dream," he said, and got unsteadily up. The beach was almost deserted. From a café a voice lifted high and raggedly in *cante hondo,* the hoarse gypsy wail of love and death and betrayal. Staccato heels on a wine table, a guitar rushing to a frenzied climax helped bring him back to the reality of the moment. He wet his lips and said huskily, "I'll be all right now. Thanks for waking me."

Juanita eyed him curiously as he passed her going into the bedroom, and while he was in the cold shower Ten Eyck brought him a glass of whisky and told him to take his time, they'd be drinking on the balcony watching the sun set. In Spain there was no hurry. Just take it easy, David, take your time.

Even later when they were in a beach-side café eating spiced prawns and drinking beer the dream clung to him. He could almost feel gooey mud between his fingers and wondered if it were some kind of omen that now, so many years later, he had relived the first death he had known.

175

Toward midnight, as Ten Eyck was leaving for Juanita's house, Morgan said, "I'm going to Paris tomorrow, probably head for Berlin."

"Figure you have to see Capella, eh?"

Morgan nodded. "Syce recommended it, and Art may be able to make some sense of what happened in Geneva, particularly in light of Kozlov's denials."

"Yeah, fuckin' bizarre. Well, go if you must but you're welcome here."

"I know, and I'm grateful for your help."

"Hell, I'm glad you gave me a piece of the action. I've been thinking about those prints, and maybe something ought to be done with the info. I've got a classmate who's on the Foreign Relations Committee. Mind if I send them to him?"

"Wouldn't he just send them over to the Agency for comment? They'd know the report came from Roger through me and you'd be involved. I don't think it's a great idea."

"Well, I'll stash them away for now."

"Sure." I still have the originals, Morgan thought.

"Have a good trip, David. Give Art my best. Tell him I'll drop in one day. And don't let the bastards grind you down." He grinned, shuffled away, put his heavy arm around Juanita's shoulder and guided her through the doorway. Before Morgan turned in he took clothing from the closet and began to pack his bag. He wanted to make the morning flight from Malaga.

FIFTEEN

WITH a change of planes at Madrid's Barajas airport, Morgan reached Paris in early afternoon. From the airport he telephoned Colonel Arnaud who recognized Morgan's voice. "*Tiens, tiens, cher ami!* I assumed you had dropped out of sight. The papers have been full of your name."

"I know. The Oxford murder."

"Lamentably. When will I see you?"

"It would be safer if we didn't meet."

"Agreed. Then I will tell you that I have some addresses for you, nothing more. Do you have writing paper?"

Morgan got out the list Palmer Syce had prepared and checked the addresses as Arnaud gave them over the phone.

Morgan thanked Arnaud and said, "I'm leaving Paris at once."

The colonel said, "I implore you to let me know if I can be of further assistance. You should know that although the Swiss police have not proclaimed your name, that does not signify it is not known to them. So perhaps you should return to America where, it is my feeling, the roots of your situation may be found."

"I plan to," Morgan said, "but not until I've exhausted every contact over here."

"*Bonne chance,*" said Arnaud emotionally, "and do not forget your old collaborator."

When Morgan entered his apartment the maid was giving it a perfunctory dusting. He unpacked and handed her his laundry, glad that she seemed not to notice his silvered hair.

While she washed and ironed his linen, pressed his suits, Morgan showered and changed. Then he went to the desk and began a letter to

Jill Percival. In it he wrote that because of unforeseen circumstances he was breaking off contact and would try to get in touch again after his name was cleared.

He read the letter again, abruptly tore it up, and analyzed what it was he really wanted to say. In simple terms he felt that he had no right to draw her into the vortex of danger around him, and so he wanted to put things on the back burner indefinitely. Marisa was dead and Morgan could not bear to lose Jill to his murderous enemies.

His next and final draft told her so in less dramatic terms, here and there an affectionate touch that he hoped would dilute the letter's impact, for he had no wish to hurt Jill or lessen her regard for him.

Sealing the letter, he addressed the envelope and decided to mail it from the airport when he left for Berlin.

When the maid went out to walk the Yorkshire, Morgan removed his currency from the bookshelf cache. In Germany he would convert some into Deutschmarks, a currency almost as strong as Swiss francs and welcome everywhere.

Next he wrote a letter to his son, asking Bill to believe him innocent of any crimes despite publicity to the contrary, and to destroy the letter after reading. He addressed the envelope hoping there was no cover on Bill's mail.

After the maid left, Morgan had a sandwich and a glass of beer, slept until dusk, repacked his bag, and took a taxi to the airport.

The Lufthansa Boeing 737 reached Tempelhof at 8:15, and by 9 Morgan was unpacking in a room at the Ambassador Hotel on Bayreuther Strasse, a short walk from the Kurfurstendamm where Capella's discotheque was located.

It had been six years since Morgan had visited Berlin. The last time was to help bring an agent through the Bornholmerstrasse crossing point, and he had stayed less than a week. Even then there had been talk of uniting Berlin with West Germany, but now he felt the status quo would be eternal; a divided city in Europe's Red Sea.

He ate dinner in the hotel grill: oysters, venison chops, and German-fried potatoes, with a half bottle of Bavarian red wine. Then in hat and topcoat he crossed Wittenbergplatz and walked to the Ku'damm. The broad street's garish lights struck his eyes with a physical impact; flashing neon signs advertised night clubs and go-go joints; luxury shop windows were more tastefully lighted. Whores and homosexuals strolled the sidewalk, groups collected outside night clubs under the stark illumination of lightoliers. Individually and as a crowd, Morgan thought, they would have been apt subjects for the savage drawings of George Grosz. But who was there now to caricature the decadence of liberated Germany?

He found Il Piccolo in the middle of the block, strobe lights flashing across the entrance that was fronted by an overcoated doorman in a feathered Piemontese hat. The girl who checked Morgan's coat and hat relieved him of a five-mark entrance fee and indicated heavy curtains through which filtered the beat of disco music.

Most of the tiny tables were empty, their occupants flailing and bucking on the dance floor. A crowded bar ran the length of the room, and overhead a large mirrored drum turned slowly giving off flashes of varicolored lights. Toward the far end was a raised, glass-faced record booth, turntable and electronic gadgets supervised by a darkly-handsome youth in open-throat silk shirt hung with medallions on a heavy chain.

Just like the States, Morgan thought, and let the waiter show him to a table large enough for the red dial telephone whose function was to make possible unobtrusive contact between tables. Morgan ordered a glass of Niersteiner and, when the waiter brought it, gave him a note for Herr Capella.

After his heavy dinner, the light German wine cleansed and refreshed his palate, and when his phone rang he answered it, expecting Art's voice. Instead, it was a customer at a distant table asking if he cared to dance. She lifted her arm for identification, a plump-faced woman in a jet-black wig with huge uplifted breasts. Morgan thanked her for the invitation but explained that he was expecting a companion. "Maybe if you fren' don't *kommen*," she said, "you see Trudi later, eh?"

"Maybe," Morgan nodded and replaced the telephone. It rang again and this time he heard Capella say, "Dave, what the hell you doing here? I'm sending a waiter for you. It's quieter in the office."

"That's a blessing." Morgan heard Capella chuckle, and then beside him a waiter bowed briefly before leading him around the disco's perimeter and through a soundproofed door near the record booth.

The office was thickly carpeted, its walls hung with bad Italian paintings. There was a bar with marble figures on it, and a desk of dark wood ornately carved. Art Capella came from around the desk, a heavy-set man with balding hair, dressed in flared slacks and an open-throat shirt. The gold neck chain held an object that looked like a gold turnip but was a good-luck horn.

"My enemies know where to find me," Capella said, giving Morgan a crushing hug, "but I wasn't so sure about my friends. Dave, from what I read you're in trouble, but then I don't believe anything in the papers. Let's have a Strega."

At the bar he poured two small glasses of the golden liqueur and gave one to Morgan.

"*Ein prosit, amico.*" He sipped and gestured Morgan to a velvet-covered chair. "I like that silvery hair, kid. Hell, I'd never have spotted you in a crowd. You on the run?"

Morgan nodded. "The British want me for killing Palmer—which I didn't do—and the Swiss want me, only they don't know my name."

"For those Geneva killings? Hell they don't. Story in *Die Welt* this evening. What's it all about? Had dinner?"

"At the hotel."

"Too bad, I'd feed you some pasta you'd never forget. But have a little antipasto, anyway. It's dinner time for me." He pressed a button on his desk and presently a waiter wheeled in a service cart. Capella tucked a large napkin into his shirt collar and watched while the waiter set the table and opened a bottle of wine. "Try this prosciutto melon." He forked a section onto a plate and the waiter carried it to Morgan. The waiter left the office and Capella said, "If Dobbs could see us now!"

Morgan laughed.

"You're the Agency's black sheep again. Yesterday a fellow from the Base stopped by to ask me if you'd tried to contact me. Said you were armed and dangerous, a killer." Capella grinned, forking antipasto into his mouth. "You don't look like a mad-dog killer to me. Didn't whack Palmer, did you?"

Morgan drew his chair near Capella and, as he was becoming accustomed to doing, told the former Agency official what had happened to him, eliminating Jill Percival from the narration since she was no longer involved. Art Capella listened without interruption, eating each course in turn and refilling their wine glasses.

"Kozlov's a mean bastard," Capella said. "I'm surprised he didn't cut off your balls and give them to you for lunch. General, is he? Well, that was to be expected. He knows where so many decapitated bodies are buried that they have to keep him friendly and motivated." He sipped wine thoughtfully. "I'm surprised Kozlov admitted knowing anything about Stepavitch."

"Wrote him off as a mercenary."

"Any idea how Kozlov found out you were at Syce's place?"

"Anna, the housekeeper, is one possibility, and there's always the old reliable bug and phone tap. Around midday Palmer made a call to his British contact; if the Soviets overheard it, that would explain my later tail, the goons who picked me up and took me to Kozlov. But it doesn't explain why Palmer had to be killed."

"No. And it's not as though he'd fallen into disfavor with the British—our suave cousins don't execute employees like the KGB."

"Kozlov's goons knew my name."

"Well, so did the housekeeper." He inhaled and let air out slowly. "Let's reconstruct: A phone tap tells the Soviets some unusual documents have reached Syce via a traveling friend. Anna identifies that friend as you. The KGB operator says, Holy Stalin, can't have old Syce exploiting what he's getting from Morgan, so let's do two things: kill Syce as a preemptive measure, and grab Morgan for an interrogation of sorts."

"But why wasn't I killed?"

"Because you're useful *alive,* baby. Everyone's busy looking for you as Hargrave's killer. Don't you see? If you're simply dumped in an alley, the Soviets lose an asset. Eventually they'll put out a terminal contract on you, but only when they figure your being dead suits them better than letting you run around. Which means you're far from secure."

Morgan grunted. "Art, I figured that out the second I saw that silencer pointing at me. Kozlov doesn't work by the book. Unlike most of his group he's unpredictable."

"Ten Eyck says Kozlov was reputed to be Hargrave's handler, but Kozlov didn't mention the association, did he? That tells us something, Dave. Let's suppose Hargrave and Kozlov *did* work closely together in Moscow after Roger went over. Kozlov went on to other duties and so, apparently, did Hargrave. But Hargrave might well have learned something about Kozlov that would make shutting him up permanently seem like a good idea. Can't you see the KGB tapping into whatever communication system Hargrave initiated with the Agency, but not moving fast enough to keep him from leaving Vienna? So Kozlov would order the next best thing, an assassination at Geneva via Stepavitch."

"But Stepavitch saw me two days before Roger arrived. On your theory, if Stepavitch was working for Kozlov, the general also knew Hargrave was getting out and could have stopped him in Vienna."

Capella sighed. "That puts Stepavitch working for two sponsors:

yours to begin with, then Kozlov just before Roger flew in. To Stepavitch it wouldn't have made any difference who he worked for at any given moment, or who paid him. My guess is he was going to collect twice: once for meeting Hargrave and once for killing him on Kozlov's orders."

"Kozlov, or one of his associates."

"Amounts to the same: Hargrave's killed and you nearly were." He shook his head. "Peel away the complications and the operation looks like another screwed-up Agency job, or don't you read it that way?"

"It doesn't explain why Marisa had to be murdered."

"I don't see what Kozlov would gain from killing your girlfriend, if he even knew about her. Syce was a different matter . . . a precautionary death. Dave, have you considered trying to contact Dobbs? His sending you out to Geneva started the whole thing."

"Oh, I've considered it; hell, I'm eager to talk to him, but I'm here and he's well-insulated over there."

Capella's eyes narrowed. "I could probably arrange a telecon through Berlin Base."

"I'd be pinpointed. You, too. No, I'm not ready to let Brother Dobbs know where I am till I know more."

Capella smiled thinly. "Wonder if I'm on anyone's hit list? I hope not, Dave. I've got a good thing going here; it was wolf meat until this disco craze began, but I renovated early and now my only problem is whether to keep my swag in Zurich or invest it in the Federal Republic. I've got a nice chalet in the mountains not far from Garmisch—my wife's there now—and I'm here in Berlin, counting the cash and minding the store. It's been a good life these last few years, Dave, and a hell of a lot better one than I could predict when Dobbs pink-slipped me. Things have quieted down. Hell, I remember when the boys began burrowing the Tunnel, tapping into Soviet lines. A hundred typists couldn't keep up with the product, Dave, and nobody wanted to listen to people like Syce who thought the Soviets might know what was going on—as events proved they did, thanks to moles in MI-6. Ten Eyck damn near broke his larynx yelling warnings about deception material, but no one wanted to listen; and finally the Soviets tired of the sport and filled in the tunnel with a blast at the Agency and the U.S., and from then on even dogs wouldn't sniff our shit around Berlin." He grunted. "Not long afterward your friend and mine, Roger Hargrave, the Agency's fair-haired boy, slid over to the other side. Security and the CI creeps kept asking why in the world did

Roger do it? Hell, I think he was too damned embarrassed to continue his career with the Third Best Intelligence Service in the World. Y'know, Dave," he paused, fingering his wine glass, "Roger could have been Director if he'd stayed around."

"But he didn't."

"No, and that changed a lot of things. We got defensive from then on. Who'd he finger? What op would be spoiled next? You were in the field, you know what it was like."

"Only too well."

"I remember the feeling; like you'd had one nut cut off and were hoping you wouldn't lose the other. We hit bottom morale-wise, until Senator McComb started his TV investigation, and *that* became the all-time low." He shrugged. "We saw you go down the drain and some of us felt it was unjust but if the Director wasn't protecting you, what could the rest of us do?"

Morgan said, "Did you ever heard the code-word 'Dormouse'?"

"Not that I remember. Whose code-word was it?"

"Supposedly ours. Next question: Do you think there's a reasonable chance Roger was working for us in Moscow?"

Capella's lips made a sucking sound. He got up, took a cigar from a humidor and lighted it. "Quite a concept," he said after a while. Very faintly disco rhythm penetrated the office wall. Capella looked down at the cigar's glowing tip. "It's hard to imagine anyone bright enough to conceive the idea and carry it off."

"Roger Hargrave."

Capella nodded slowly. "Yes, he could have done it if anyone could, done the whole thing by himself. Maybe no one but the Director knew. It wouldn't have taken big money, a support staff or heavy communications, but oh, Jesus, what guts it would have taken! A real, authentic singleton operation? The Director dies—as he did on the tennis court—and no one left in the Agency knows about Hargrave. Dormouse? Who's Dormouse? Nobody gives a shit who the source is, and the stuff keeps rolling in year after year, no money involved, no payments to be made. Until, finally, Dormouse/Hargrave finds he's dying and wants to come home, be buried in his homeland. Buy the scenario?"

"It's plausible."

"Dave, his death tends to verify it. Suppose Hargrave sent out a message saying 'Dormouse wants to come home to die' through his usual reporting channel which could have been, let's say, microdot.

Then he makes contact with a reliable Westerner to whom he says, 'I'm dying of cancer and I want to come home.' Whoever reads both messages would realize, if he hadn't before, that Hargrave was Dormouse and Dormouse was a trusted, reliable, American penetration of the Soviet Union. Ergo: Hargrave was an American agent all along, his defection only pretense."

"I'd like to think that," Morgan said slowly, "but it's a long jump between reasonable theory and actuality."

"So was the atom bomb when Einstein scribbled $E = Mc^2$. Now, look at it from the point of view of the Soviet penetration guy in the Agency if Dobbs's suggestion to you is to be believed: He can't take a chance that Hargrave may be able to identify him. In fact, according to Dobbs, Roger was going to, right? So this unknown sets things up for Kozlov to take executive action against Hargrave. *Not* in the East where the Soviets would be automatically blamed, but in the West where, low and behold, the unrepentant David Morgan exacts vengeance on the traitor!" He spun around. "I love it! It's thick and meaty and full of nourishment. Damn it, Dave, it *has* to be that way. Nothing else makes sense!"

I wonder if I'll ever know, Morgan thought.

"I can't recall another case where the KGB and an element of the Agency cooperated in destroying a man," Capella said. "But that's what it looks like to me. And but for you they'd have gotten away with it, everyone dead, incident closed. Back to business as usual. Only it happened that you survived."

"Yeah. I keep feeling that if I stop or give up I'll stop surviving."

"Sensible. Stay scared and live longer. That was my slogan."

Morgan got up. "You said a man from the Base warned you about me. Are you in active contact with Berlin Base?"

"Hardly active. Something comes my way, I pass it along. Hell, the Agency got rid of me but I'm still an American."

As Morgan smoked and drank coffee, Art excused himself to check the activity outside.

Five minutes later, he came back in rubbing his hands. "The cash registers are wearing out. Need to borrow some Deutschmarks—no strings?"

"I collected from Stepavitch, remember? But if you can give me DMs for francs and dollars I'd be spared a trip to the bank."

"Sure."

Morgan handed him a stack of bills, Capella came back in two minutes with an envelope full of Deutschmarks. "I hope you've got more capital than that."

"This is walking-around money."

Capella opened a desk drawer, manipulated something, and Morgan heard a snapping sound. Capella lifted out a tape cassette. "When I heard you were looking for me I thought I'd record our conversation. I've found it useful when pushy types come in to shake me down. Want it?"

"Keep it."

"In a safe place."

He shook hands with Capella. Claiming his hat and coat from the checkroom, he put them on feeling suddenly that he was being watched from somewhere in the crowd. The man at the bar—was he the one who tailed me into St. Mark's? Morgan wondered. I never got a good look at his face; why should I remember him now? Or was it the black-wigged woman, Trudi, who telephoned his table? Was she watching him for reasons that had nothing to do with sex? Under his armpit the Mauser felt reassuring. The long exchange with Art Capella had tautened his nerves, made him think he was being watched when there were no watchers around.

Even so, when he reached the Ku'damm he let his topcoat hang open to make the Mauser easier to reach. But from Il Piccolo to Wittenbergplatz the only danger he was aware of came from two unhealthy-looking whores who whispered an invitation to make a threesome at their flat.

At the hotel desk he got his key and bought a late edition of *Le Monde* flown in from Paris. He folded it under his arm, and when he was in his room he turned on the lights and glanced at the front page. One of the photographs was of a veiled woman and his eyes skipped to the story beneath: Mme. Alexandra Hargrave, widow of the recently-murdered American traitor, Roger Hargrave, had arrived in Switzerland to claim her husband's body for burial.

Slowly Morgan sat down on the edge of the bed.

Kozlov, apparently, had come through.

Restlessly Morgan lay in bed unable to sleep, thoughts whirling through his mind. He had to see Alexandra, tell her how Roger had died, ask what she knew of Roger's defection, warn her of the danger she could be in.

Then he heard clearly the first soft scrapings at his door lock.

SIXTEEN

QUIETLY, Morgan rolled off the bed, reached for the nearby Mauser, and slid off the safety as he moved barefoot, soundlessly, to the hinged edge of the door. The metallic probings continued as the lock-picker's tools entered the keyway, depressing tumbler springs. Morgan saw the lock core begin to turn. Then the doorknob itself. The door opened and a blade of hallway light slashed the dark room, widened as the man entered, his shadow lengthening across the floor. The door closed and a flashlight beam played over the bureau, flicked to the end of the bed, halted at the rolled-back covers. As the intruder began to turn Morgan struck the back of his head with the pistol butt, and the man pitched forward, flashlight clattering across the floor.

Morgan knelt on his back, holding the pistol barrel at the base of his brain, but the precaution was superfluous. The man was unconscious. Morgan recovered the flashlight and, holding its ray on the sprawled body, turned on the bed lamp. Next he jammed a chair under the doorknob in case the intruder had a partner.

He took some deep breaths before going into the bathroom where he splashed icy water on his face. He tore a hand towel into strips and bound the man's wrists behind his back, stuffed a washcloth into his slack jaws, then blindfolded him with another strip of towel. Morgan tied the man's ankles together, then stood up and took stock.

The man was of average build, dressed in a gray suit, blue shirt, and dark tie. His black shoes were polished and judging by the soles and heels, fairly new. He did not look like a burglar, but then a thief working a first-class hotel would hardly dress the part.

Morgan went through his pockets, turning them inside out. The lock-picking kit was there, blue-steel probes and spicules in a flat leather case, and Morgan tossed it onto the bed for possible eventual use. Some change in a trouser pocket, a billfold containing German, Swiss, and Italian banknotes, and a West Berlin driving license in the name of Ernst Peter Dorn. It gave his age as thirty-seven; occupation, salesman. Morgan rolled him over and went through the remaining pockets. In one was a neatly-rolled plastic bag containing a hypodermic syringe loaded with yellowish fluid, protective cap over the needle point. Morgan whistled. Not standard equipment for a B&E man. The back of Dorn's belt yielded a Beretta pistol, and as Morgan patted down the legs he felt something below the right calf.

Morgan pulled up the trouser cuff, exposing an ice pick with a thin wooden handle. The point glistened under the light as though recently sharpened. Morgan whistled again. Herr Dorn was becoming more interesting by the moment. He pulled the pick from the two surgical rubber bands that circled the man's calf, placed it on the bed and searched the final pocket, finding only a used handkerchief.

Rising, Morgan removed the Beretta's magazine. It was fully loaded with 9 mm. cartridges, a ready shell in the chamber. From prison conversations with second-story men Morgan had gained the impression they seldom carried weapons, trusting rather to stealth for success in their ventures. This cat was something else. The hypodermic *could* signify drug addiction, but Morgan felt it did not. Pulling up Dorn's coatsleeves he looked for needle tracks but found none, and the realization grew that Dorn had come to murder him rather than simply rob.

Morgan reached for the phone directory and called Il Piccolo. Getting Art to the phone was difficult, Morgan having to breach barriers of language and hostility, but finally he heard Capella's voice and said, "Art, I know it's after two but I could use that company you offered."

"You horny bastard! All right, I'll send along a companion. What was that room number again?"

"Seven-fourteen." He had told Capella earlier where he was staying but not the number of his room. "I don't want a disposal problem," he went on in what he hoped Art understood as open code. "Out and gone by dawn, okay?"

"I hear you. This'll take no longer than fifteen minutes to deliver." The line went dead.

Morgan knelt by Dorn's head, pulled down the blindfold and parted one eyelid. The pupil was dilated. He shined the flashlight into it: no change. A well-concussed subject, he told himself, replacing the blindfold and feeling the wrist pulse. Slow, very slow. Herr Dorn would be out for quite a while.

Only Dorn could answer the question as to whether he was a murderer or just a murderous burglar, and Morgan doubted that he would. So it was only prudent to assume the worst: that his enemies had spotted him and arranged for his death. But who had known he was in Berlin at the Ambassador?

Art Capella.

Was Art, for Christ's sake, working for the other side? It was a chilling thought, yet Morgan could not discard it. Meanwhile, to linger on in Berlin without an overpowering motive would be foolhardy.

He shaved rapidly without nicking his face, dressed, and piled clothing into his open bag. On the bed sheet he left the hypodermic and the ice pick, extracted the Beretta's bullets and added it to the other exhibits. Then Morgan unlocked the hall door, removed the chair wedge, turned out the bed lamp, and sat in the darkness, flashlight in his left hand, Mauser in the other, and waited.

After a while he heard a cautious knock, Art's voice. "Dave? You okay?"

"Come in."

The door opened and he saw Capella outlined against the hall illuminating. The flashlight ray hit his face and he halted. "What the hell?"

"Take it easy," Morgan ran the light beam over Art's body. Hands empty, no visible weapon. "Light switch by the door," Morgan said. "Close the door, lock it, and turn on the light."

"Sure, Dave. Little shook up, aren't you?"

"You'll see why."

The door closed, locked. The ceiling light went on. Art Capella stood blinking at him, then his gaze lowered to the prone, bound man. "You weren't kidding. What's going on?"

Morgan set the flashlight on the floor, slid the Mauser into his right coat pocket but kept his hand on it. "Some items on the bed. Look them over and tell me what they mean."

Capella went to the bed, picked up the ice pick and grunted. He dropped it and held the hypodermic to the light. "Most dope's color-less in solution," he remarked, then lifted the Beretta. "Nice little piece." He weighed it in his hand, tossed it into the air, and Morgan's arm went taut. If Art was an enemy he would try to use the Beretta.

The blue-black pistol dropped into Capella's hand, then onto the bed. Morgan took his hand from his pocket and got up. Handing Dorn's billfold to Art he said, "This doesn't tell much. Know him?"

Capella eyed the photo on the driving license before pulling aside Dorn's blindfold. Half-kneeling he studied the slack face. "Never saw him before, Dave. Have you?"

Morgan shook his head.

"He's got enough equipment for a Brazilian death squad." Capella replaced the blindfold and stood up. "Heavy stuff. Who the hell sent him?"

"Maybe the Base staked you out, recognized me when I got there."

"I wouldn't like to think that."

"What's the alternative?"

Capella drew in a deep breath. "I don't know—unless you have old enemies in Berlin."

"It's the new ones that worry me." He looked down at Ernst Peter Dorn. "What do we do with him?"

"What do you want done?"

"I'd like to stick that syringe in his butt and empty it. Maybe it's only a tranquilizer, but instinct tells me it's lethal. Like the ice pick. The average hood doesn't carry a pick strapped to his leg. Nor a Beretta in his belt. This one's a killer, Art, and he came to kill me."

"No question about it." Capella scratched his balding skull. "Well, two things: We have to get him out of here, and you need to grab the first flight from Tempelhof, regardless of where it goes."

Morgan nodded. He closed his suitcase and locked it.

"I'll call a couple of guys who owe me," Capella said. "They'll drop this Dorn in the Grunewald; with luck he could survive, but I don't much care. I'll see that his wallet, syringe, and pistol get to the cops—they might be looking for him. As to how you leave here without being tailed, my BMW's parked out back. It's green." He gave Morgan the keys. "Leave it at Tempelhof and I'll have it retrieved. Don't stop to pay your bill, I'll do that. Sorry this happened, but maybe some day we'll find out what it means."

Morgan picked up his suitcase, remembered something, and pointed to *Le Monde* on the carpet beside the bed. "Read it while you're waiting," he said. "Alexandra Hargrave's in Geneva."

Capella shook his head. "Don't go there, David. It's too risky. Let things settle down. Now, get going."

Morgan left the room and found the service elevator at the end of the corridor. He rode it to the basement and left the hotel through an

190

emergency exit. The green BMW's engine started on the first try.

Heading southeast he drove carefully through Nollendorf Platz, picked up Bülowstrasse on the far side and turned finally onto the broad highway that led to Tempelhof.

In the airport terminal he checked the Departures board, went to the Sabena counter and bought a ticket to Brussels. An hour-and-a-half to wait. Morgan bought a London tabloid, took it into the men's room, locked himself into a booth, and read it until the PA system announced his flight.

Not more than a dozen passengers were ahead of him as he joined the line at the boarding gate. He was handing his ticket to the attendant when he heard an announcement in English: "There is a message for Mr. Morgan at the Pan American ticket counter. An urgent message for Mr. D. Morgan at the Pan American ticket counter. Thank you." The announcer went into German as Morgan forced himself to smile absently at the attendant. "Nonsmoking, please," he said, his throat constricted by sudden fear. He waited for seat assignment and moved up the ramp, walking stiffly, afraid to look around, mind racing to the realization that watchers would be scanning for reaction among the waiting passengers. Of course, Dorn's sponsors could have put out a blind announcement, not knowing where he was or what name he was traveling under; all they knew was that Dorn was missing, suspected their man had failed.

Morgan bent forward slightly to let his hat clear the frame of the cabin door, and when he turned to go down the aisle a red-cheeked stewardess took his coat and hat and pointed out his seat.

He buried his face in the paper until the door closed, and then as the tractor drew the nose away he breathed deeply in relief. The phony announcement confirmed that Dorn was a killer on assignment. Somehow Morgan's every move was known. Coincidence was possible but not sequentially. His personal security needed drastic tightening.

The Sabena 737 rose swiftly from the tarmac, and below Morgan could see gray, smoky Berlin, the Wall like a child's crayon scrawl on a monotone map. Early traffic edged along the Ku'damm, Grunewald lake glinted metallically, and Morgan thought that Dorn might be greeting dawn from its bordering forest. Teltow Canal was a band of dull pewter that disappeared under clouds as the jet soared and turned to the northwest as though fleeing the rising sun.

Soon he was served hot croissants with Danish butter, eggs, and

Holland ham. Morgan ate slowly, reflectively, and then drowsed on a pillow until the locking wheels jarred him awake.

Without leaving Brussels airport he bought a Sabena ticket to Mexico City and rented a transient room where he slept until mid-afternoon. Refreshed, he boarded the big 707 and watched a French movie until the plane landed at Madrid. Other Mexico-bound passengers got out to stretch their legs in the passenger lounge, but Morgan stayed aboard while the plane fueled and reprovisioned for the transatlantic flight.

Airborne, he watched the jet flames that outlined the trailing edge of the wing, giving it the appearance of a knife cutting smoothly through dark and bulbous clouds. There was little more he could have accomplished in Europe, he reflected, even if Ernst Peter Dorn had not appeared. He was wiser now, more knowledgeable as a result of seeing Broom and Capella.

There were still a few men he had to pump, like Emerson Forey and above all, the Director. Dobbs has a lot of explaining to do, he told himself. He may feel secure in his fortress, but that's because he doesn't know I'm on my way.

And when he finds out, I wonder what he'll do?

SEVENTEEN

H<small>E</small> slept through the night, and after breakfast heard the captain announce they were crossing the coast north of Veracruz. Dry yellow flatland wrinkled into foothills, then swelled into mountains as the plane neared the high central valley.

Clearing Customs, Morgan emerged into a clamor of souvenir vendors, *mariachis,* and disputatious taxi drivers, all eager for tourist money. He converted a thousand DMs into pesos at the exchange window, then asked a taxi driver to take him to the old Del Prado hotel on Avenida Juarez. He was familiar with the central zone, and the hotel was big enough to provide the anonymity he desired. The Del Prado was always filled with American travelers, a favorite of tour groups.

In his room overlooking the Alameda, Morgan unpacked and changed into informal clothing, which meant jacket and shirt with no tie. At the tour desk he bought tickets for an air-conditioned bus trip to Cuernavaca and Taxco. The bus filled rapidly with plump dowagers and exhausted-looking husbands. Morgan reflected that the somewhat thin air could be troublesome to some of these people.

When the tour guide began her monologue, most of the passengers listened intently, but Morgan sank back into his seat and lowered his hat brim, wishing he could suddenly materialize at Emerson Forey's door without having to undergo the guide's spiel.

South of the city there was a brief stop at the roadside *mirador* for what was predictably described as a breathtaking view. Many of the passengers dismounted for the photo opportunity then reboarded for the run to La Cima, at nearly ten thousand feet the highest point in the region. From there the highway slanted downward, and half an hour later the bus entered Cuernavaca. Dutifully the tourists trudged around the cathedral and the Franciscan convent.

193

An hour later and the bus turned down a winding road that led to Taxco's small central plaza, around which were clustered the ateliers of silversmiths and workers in semiprecious stone. The guide led the troop toward the church of Santa Prisca over steep, cobbled streets too narrow for the bus to navigate; Morgan asked directions to Calle del Artista and found it not far away.

Número 49 was an old house constructed of boulders and cement. The wooden door was painted blue, peeling along grain lines; pink window shutters hung askew. Along the side of the house goldenrod towered above weeds in what must once have been a garden patch. A breeze stirred the heliotropes languidly.

From the front of the house Morgan could look out across the valley that had been gorged and tunneled and plundered for silver; tailings from the ancient mines were still visible. Atop the distant rim perched the Hotel de la Borda, surrounded by yellow adobe wall.

Morgan rang the bell and waited. No sound from inside the house. He rang again, then pounded the door. "Emerson! Emerson Forey. Wake up, get with it!"

From a bedroom window a snarl and a curse. A shutter creaked open and a deeply-lined face with a scraggly white beard peered down. Morgan removed his hat and sunglasses, looked up at the old man.

Recognition widened the bloodshot eyes. Forey's mouth opened. "I know you," he shouted. "Hold on. I'll be down."

Morgan wiped his forehead. Sun was warming the mountain air. Under his jacket the Mauser holster was damp with sweat.

The door opened and Emerson Forey said, "Enter, friend. Excuse the general disarray."

The man who stood before him was stooped and ancient. A roll of flabby skin hung over the drawstring of his pajama bottoms. The skin of his chest was yellowish, as though jaundiced in the recent past. The ribs were countable, the collar bone prominent. Dry, purplish lips moved as the human caricature of the man Morgan had known spoke: "I don't get many callers, David." He shrugged. "No reason I should." He gestured at a sprung sofa. "Sit down and I'll get a drink. How about you?" He trudged off toward the kitchen. Morgan followed and regretted it.

The sink was indescribably filthy; it held a jumble of rusting skillets, caked dishes of fired clay, old jelly glasses, bottles, and cutlery. The counter beside it held rotting vegetables on which the flies were busy. The small table was covered with patterned plastic that was stained and burn-marked. Forey ignored all this and made for a wineskin

194

suspended by a chain from the ceiling. A good-sized pig had once inhabited the skin that was now only partly full of whatever Forey proposed to drink. The near leg was rigged with a large cork. Forey held a tumbler under it and pulled the cork. A stream of cloudy liquid shot into the tumbler, almost overflowing it before Forey replaced the cork and held the tumbler toward light filtering in through the dirty window. His hand, Morgan noticed, was shaking. There were objects floating in the tumbler that could have been raisins.

"*Pulque* comes two ways," Forey observed when he had drunk. "With flies, and without. The strained variety costs more, so I do the straining myself." He picked a fly from his upper lip, plucked three more from the half-empty glass. He flicked the insects at the sink. "Doubtless you don't favor *pulque*—it's an acquired taste—but it's all I have at the moment." His tongue licked a few droplets from his lips and Morgan saw that their color was returning. "Damn that lazy woman! I board her and she's supposed to clean up from time to time. *Tina!*" he bellowed. "Get your butt down here. It's high noon and we got company."

His demand was followed by a flood of Spanish imprecations. Steps dragged down the kitchen stairs. Tina reached ground level and leaned against the door jamb for support, the back of one hand listlessly moving black hair from her forehead. She wore a pink nightgown that had once been trimmed with lace. The parts of it that weren't faded were stained. The hand that was not needed for support scratched her right hip, moved down to the buttock. She murmured with satisfaction, turned her red-veined eyes on Morgan.

"What a pig," Forey said. "Ever see anything worse than that, David?"

"Not in Taxco."

"She's a charity case. Used to work those ex-ee-bee-she-own parlors in Acapulco. Took on burros, donkeys. Christ, she'd a taken on bears if their claws were drawn. Well, something got punctured, she ended up in the Clínica, and when that was over with she limped up here looking for work." He gazed around, spat on the floor. "*Work!* All she does is drink my *pulque*. Hey, Tina, sober up. *Hay que trabajar, mi china. Limpidad todo, pero todito, entiendes?*"

She stared at him vacantly, scratching the other buttock. "*Plata,*" she finally said. "*Dinero para comprar.*"

"Buy *what?*"

"*Comida. Carne, pan . . .*" she looked slowly around, taking inventory. "*Jabón.*"

"What a slut," Forey said thickly. "Since my wife died she's the only companion I've had. And all she does is steal my beverages, wouldn't know the feel of a broom handle unless it was in her dirty twat."

Morgan swallowed. "When did your wife die?"

"Two years ago. Typhoid. Medics couldn't even diagnose it until after Beth was gone. Buried up there. . . ." He gestured vaguely. "Never got over it, David, never will." He lifted the tumbler and drained it. "All right," he said to the Indian woman, "have your *pulque* and get busy. *Si. Toma, luego trabaja y fuerte. Andale.*"

She shuffled barefoot to the sink where she found a glass, poured residue from it and milked the wineskin with practiced hands.

Emerson Forey said, "Now that you've found me and Heidi in our sweet little chalet, what do you think of the set up?"

"I didn't come here to criticize your living arrangements. But what would *you* think if you were me?"

Forey nodded. "Yeah. I got that from my kids until they stopped coming."

"You get good retirement money. You don't have to live like this."

Forey's expression changed. To Morgan he suddenly seemed the saddest man alive. Then Forey straightened his stooped back, tried to smile.

"What you in Mexico for, pardner? On the lam?" He chuckled. "That's my John Wayne act; floors the locals. Always good for a drink."

"Let's cut out the clowning," Morgan said, "go have some grilled meat and a salad."

"Never touch the stuff." Forey took another drink, as if challenging Morgan to stop him.

"I need lunch," Morgan told him. "You'll come with me."

"What for?"

"That's *my* John Wayne act. Because I need to talk with you, and we can't talk here. Let the woman work while we're gone."

"Shit, she'll drain the skin, that's what she'll do."

"I'll buy you another. Goddammit, Em, I've come from Europe to borrow your brains, and I'm going to do it."

"Brains? Pissed away with my kidneys." He started to laugh, but the sound caught in his throat, cracked, became a racking sob. His mouth opened and he began to cry convulsively.

Morgan took the tumbler from his hand and emptied it on the flies in the sink.

196

"Come on," he said, "throw on a shirt and we'll get you a shave. There's a barber down the street." He patted the thin shoulders comfortingly. "I have a retained image of you as a wise and sensitive man, Emerson. Let me see some of it."

The racking sobs stopped, Forey wiped tears away with his palms, and said, "You're a kind man, David."

Forey went slowly up the staircase. Morgan turned to face Tina.

"You've got a good thing going here, *chica,*" he said. "The *señor* is a good man. Don't cheat him and you won't have to go back to the *circo.* You can stay here and learn to live decently. Now, he and I are going out to lunch and when we return I want to see a big improvement in the place. Otherwise, I'll find someone willing to work and take care of him."

"I not understand," she said sullenly, closing her wrapper.

"I'll put it simply. *O trabajo o fuera!*"

She looked at him with slow comprehension. Morgan walked to the wineskin and pulled the cork. *Pulque* shot from the opening, flooding the floor. Tina shrieked, dropped to her knees, and tried to dam the spreading flow. He turned on the water faucet and the clogged sink began to fill. "*Anadale, preciosa. Ten prisa.*"

Rising, the woman swept hair back from her forehead, found a mop, and began working on the floor. She eyed the sink's water level, and when it began to spill over she turned off the faucet, went outside, and wrung out the mop. Morgan laid a twenty-peso note on the table. "*Jabón,*" he said. "*Articulos de limpieza.*" Soap and cleaning equipment.

It might be easier to burn the place down and start again, he thought as he left the kitchen. He stood outside the front door breathing clean air until Forey came out to join him.

The retired expert on Soviet Disinformation Operations was wearing a tattered blue Oxford button-down shirt, a pair of chino trousers too large for his shrunken waist, and woven-leather *huaraches* on his feet. "How do I look?"

"About four-hundred percent better. Now, let's visit the barber."

While Forey was being steamed, lathered, and shaved, Morgan scanned a week-old copy of *Excelsior.* The barber chair tilted upright but Morgan said, "Haircut, too."

"Damn it, David, I. . . ."

"Don't be picturesque."

"Interfering bastard!"

Morgan grinned. "Vacation's over, *Señor* Forey. Time to go to work."

"Work!"

"Yeah. In that vein I told your housekeeper to get busy or she'd be out on her ass."

"Now, *David*. . . ."

"Christ, Em, you've become more of a slob than Laughton in *The Beachcomber*. Establishment cats like me get all shook up when we spot a dropout like you. Brings out the do-good, social welfare instinct so many of us try to suppress."

The barber sprinkled bay rum liberally on Forey's face and hair. Forey winced, muttered, but his expression was of grudging pleasure.

Morgan gave the barber a memorable tip and steered Forey out to the lane. "Name a restaurant."

"Don't know any."

"Then we'll walk until we find one."

"Okay, okay, the Bodegón's a couple of blocks away."

Morgan ordered grilled rib-steaks, fried potatoes, boiled carrots, and tomato salad; coffee for Forey, Tecate pilsen for himself. The older man ate slowly, as though eating were a forgotten duty. "My stomach's shrunk," he complained. "I'm a feeble old man. I can't eat like you."

"Half the steak, then. All the tomatoes *and* all the coffee." Morgan grunted. "I came all the way to Taxco to consult your memory, Emerson, on some weighty matters."

"Consult . . . *me?*"

Morgan nodded. "My life may depend on it. Several people have already died because of what I came to get your advice on. I need you reasonably sober and fed."

Emerson nodded.

"Did you know I testified before the McComb Committee?"

"That Senate investigation? I don't keep up with the news too well down here."

"Actually, I testified only up to a point. Because I wouldn't go all the way I was jailed for contempt of Congress. Eleven months, Emerson."

"My God!"

Morgan glanced around. "We need a place to talk privately."

"There's the Zócalo—town square. I used to go there and sit on a bench. And think. No one bothered me."

"Finish your coffee."

198

Forey emptied the cup. Morgan paid the waiter, and they took a narrow street that led to a small public square. There was a bandstand and a water fountain, flower borders that needed watering, and some unsuccessful shrubs. A couple of campesinos were stretched out under a shady pine, broad sombreros covering their faces, folded serapes under their heads.

Siesta time.

They sat on sparsely grassy ground, backs against the bole of an ancient pine, and Morgan said, "I've been traveling, Em, and some of your old friends send greetings."

"Such as who?"

"Ten Eyck, Art Capella, Palmer Syce."

One finger rubbed his chin. "If you see them again don't tell them how you found me." His hand plucked at Morgan's coatsleeve. "Please."

A jet headed for Acapulco traced a chalky contrail high above them. For Morgan it seemed a moment of exceptional peace and reflection.

Forey turned watery eyes to Morgan. "How are the boys?"

"Art's got a discotheque in West Berlin, Broom has a second life on the Mediterranean. Palmer . . . well, Palmer died when I was in Oxford visiting him."

"I'm sorry, very sorry. Working for Six, wasn't he?"

"Yes. Living comfortably, doing the things he loved to do. He died unexpectedly and without pain."

Forey sighed. "So may it be for all of us. Now, David, the weighty matter you wanted to discuss. What would that be?"

"Roger Hargrave was murdered near Geneva airport. As part of the plot I was to have been killed, too, but I managed to get away and since then I've been running."

"Dear God!"

"A few pieces have fitted together but I still lack information on the key question: Was Hargrave a bona fide defector to the Russians?"

"The alternative being, did the Agency send him over?"

"Yes. And a corollary question: Who arranged to kill Roger when he redefected?"

"Was that what he was doing in Geneva?"

"So I was told."

"How did you come to be involved? I thought you were out of the Agency."

"So I was. But Dobbs commissioned me to escort Hargrave. He

said Roger insisted I be there as one of his conditions. But five minutes after I'd met him, Hargrave was dead, shot by a hired killer."

Forey shook his head. "How can I help?"

Morgan filled him in on his assignment and quickly got to the question he had come to ask. "Did you ever hear the code-word 'Dormouse'?"

Forey swallowed. His lips seemed dry again, color faded. "I don't suppose I could have a drink?"

"Later. Please think, Emerson. Try to remember. *Dormouse.*"

"I remember." Forey looked at Morgan. "You won't tell the others. I mean about the way you found me."

"Of course not, Em."

"You can't imagine the self-loathing I feel at times."

"Dormouse, Em."

"Well, if my memory's right, Dormouse was the slug on stuff that came from someone pretty high up in Moscow. Is that any help?"

"Hargrave told me *he* was Dormouse."

"Lord! Then he must have been ours, his defection planned." Life came into Emerson's expression. "Masterful pulling something like that off."

"Alexandra's arrived in Geneva. According to the papers, she's denouncing me as Roger's murderer."

"What else could she say? She's probably playing a role, David. You should try to speak with her."

"What did you think of Dobbs?"

Forey sighed. "He's just a bureaucrat, David. How the hell did he get up there? Listen, you're not thinking he arranged Roger's . . . and to get you, too?"

"Think."

"I'm thinking, dammit. He'd only do something like that if his neck was at stake. If. . . ."

"Go on."

"If he were the penetration agent he said Hargrave was going to expose. But didn't he brief you? He wouldn't walk on such awfully thin ice if he were the man, would he?"

"He might . . . if he expected me dead in a few days."

"What's happened to us?" Forey stopped. "I should talk. Look at me."

"You wouldn't double-cross your own," Morgan said as if it were a question.

200

"I guess I wouldn't," Forey said. "I've been double-crossing mainly myself. You think I could have a drink now?"

"One," Morgan said. "Come on, I'll buy you one."

As they walked back in the sunshine, Morgan said, "I admired the way you had just the one, Em."

"I knew you wouldn't let me have another."

"Em, I've got to get going. Before I do, is there anything I can do to help you get yourself organized, if that's what you'd like to do?"

"I miss Beth. I need to get away from here."

"Is the house yours?"

"Beth's and mine."

"Where do you keep your money?"

"In my post office box, I guess. Checks come every month. When I need *pulque* I cash one."

"No bank account?"

"Beth had one. My name was on it."

"Then let's get those checks into your bank account, draw some *pesos* for your needs."

At the post office Forey opened his box. It was jammed with letters—and annuity checks, fifteen of them, totaling more than twenty thousand dollars! They went to the bank where Forey deposited fourteen in his almost-forgotten account, cashed one for *pesos*.

Walking back toward Forey's house they passed a bar, and Morgan allowed the older man to buy him a drink and have one himself. The liquor had a remarkable effect on Forey's color, gait, and conversation, improving all of them. Morgan realized that Forey would have to taper off rather than stop all alcohol abruptly.

They went into the house. It was silent. The kitchen was filthy as before, flies covered the drying pulque on the floor. Forey yelled for Tina, then went upstairs to look for her. He came down, shaking his head. "Gone," he sighed.

"Where will she go?"

"God knows, but she's got a little money I gave her. That's a chapter ended, Emerson. Let's find a place you can stay until the house is presentable."

"All right. There's a *pension* up the hill. My kids used to stay there when they visited."

"What about a clean-up team?"

"I can ask at the *pension*."

They walked up to the *pension* "El Buen Retiro," where Morgan negotiated a double room.

It was large and clean, opening onto a cool patio shaded by trees, its walls thickly covered with vines and flowering plants. The flower perfume was a welcome contrast to the stench of Forey's house, and Morgan hoped his friend would come to prefer it.

The *pension* owners were pleasant people who agreed to send handymen and cleaning women to Forey's house when they were not needed at the *pension*. Away from Forey, Morgan said that his friend needed to eat well at the *pension* while tapering off from alcohol.

None was available, Señor Quesada told him, except dinner wine on request. Quesada added that he had known and liked the late Señora Forey, and had been pained at the change in her husband.

That evening Morgan telephoned Forey's elder son in Stockbridge, outlined the situation, and suggested that he or one of his siblings come to Taxco and oversee their father's rehabilitation. James Forey reacted with relief and promised action within a day or so. Meanwhile, he expressed gratitude for what his father's friend had done. "I didn't get your name, sir?"

"Agency restrictions. You know."

"Of course. Well, this is marvelous news. I'll start calling right now."

Emerson Forey, sitting nearby, was crying. "I didn't have the courage," he said. "I was afraid no one cared any more."

"Now you know different. C'mon, time for dinner."

They ate in the patio at a candlelit table: roast pork and rice and plátanos. Morgan allowed Forey two glasses of Rioja for which he was exceedingly grateful. "Never really liked *pulque*," he said. "Don't know why I drank the stuff. But I'll never do it again, David. I may fall off the wagon, but not into *pulque* again."

For dessert they were brought a variety of fresh fruit. Morgan took a slice of cold mango, Forey a dish of strawberries and cream.

During the night Morgan woke, saw the next bed empty and started to get up, afraid Forey had run. Then he saw him standing on the balcony, hands on the railing, looking up at the star-punctured sky.

The next afternoon a telegram arrived from Forey's daughter, Jennie, saying she would arrive in Mexico the following day. Forey, overjoyed, wept briefly and went without protest to buy clothing for himself. They stopped at his house and saw a huge pile of useless household items at the curb. From the garden came the steady swish of a machete toppling weeds and goldenrod. Above, the creak of furniture being moved; from the kitchen the swishing of mops in water pails. Morgan noticed an expression of satisfaction in Forey's face.

Forey said, "I'm so glad Jennie will be here. Where are you off to, David?"

"I need to see a couple of people in the States. McDairmid, Peyton James."

"Is it safe?"

"No. It's a necessity."

"I don't want anything to happen to you." His voice broke, he looked away. "You can't imagine how grateful I am to you, David."

"People have helped me along the way," Morgan said quietly. "I'm only repaying a little."

They turned in before midnight. Morgan set his mental alarm clock, and at five got up, shaved quietly, and left the *pension*. Good-byes would be embarrassing to both of them. He didn't know what would happen to Forey, but he had done what he could.

A little before six Morgan reached the bus stop, and after a while a Tres Estrellas bus blatted up the cobbled hill. It paused long enough to let Morgan board, then resumed its noisy, laboring progress to the capital.

All he had to do now, he reflected, was enter the States without being identified.

EIGHTEEN

Aт the hotel Morgan collected his belongings, paid the two-night bill for his unused bed and took a Transportes del Norte bus for Matamoros and the border. It was a long, dull ride with occasional stops for *tacos* and refried beans: Pachuca, Tamazunchale, Ciudad Victoria, San Fernando, and finally the border town of Matamoros.

He had decided to walk across the border rather than arrive at an American airport where immigration and Customs scrutiny might be more intensive. At the Brownsville entry point his body and suitcase were sniffed by dogs seeking narcotics; Morgan had taken the precaution of wrapping the pistol in aluminum foil, sealing it in a plastic bag, and inserting it into a stuffed toy burro before putting it in his suitcase. It passed undetected.

A taxi took him to the airport where he found a commuter flight leaving for Dallas/Fort Worth. There he changed *pesos* and DMs into dollars and phoned Pollock in Key West.

"It's time you were back in touch," Pollock said. "They got Marisa's killer."

Morgan's hand tightened around the receiver. "When? Tell me."

"He had a partner, another ex-Army demolitions specialist, and after the job Crowly—that's his name, Lon Crowly—shot the partner and dumped the body in a quarry up by Largo. There was a couple of detonating caps in the corpse's pockets, and not far away in some diner's trash can they found some old clothing with caps and crimps in it. Feds traced the clothing through laundry marks an' collared Crowly two days ago. Ain't that great?"

Morgan swallowed. "Where is he?"

"In the lockup here, under heavy protection. I reckon they're working him over. Where are you . . . or shouldn't I ask?"

"Closer than you might think."

"Thinking of coming back?"

"I'm thinking about it. If I get to Marathon by air, can you pick me up by car?"

"Say the word."

"It'll take a while, maybe until tomorrow. I still have to make travel arrangements."

"Whenever. I'll put my wife on notice, okay?"

"Just let her know your whereabouts. Meanwhile, keep track of Crowly, will you?"

"Sure. And I'm eager to see you."

He hung up, palms sweating. Crowly. I'd like to toss a bottle of nitro into his cell, Morgan thought. If he talks I've got a better chance of surviving this thing then I've had since Geneva. He wiped palms on his thighs and went to the information desk where he asked about flights to Tampa and Miami. There was a flight to Miami in six hours, to Tampa in three. It'd be safer to wait in Tampa. He bought a ticket for the flight.

There was time to kill. Long distance information gave him an office and a residence telephone number of Ghislaine Percival. He hesitated before calling, wondering whether he should obey the impulse, finally deciding he ought at least to let her know he was still alive.

The operator who answered Jill's business phone was reluctant to connect him with Ms. Percival until Morgan said he was a Paris business associate and gave his name as Lancaster. Moments later Jill said, "It's good of you to call, Mr. Lancaster. I so much enjoyed our evening at Le Berlioz." Her voice was taut. "How are you?"

"Fine. Just fine. Have you had any trouble?"

"Not in the least. Did you read about that fellow in Key West?"

"I did."

"When can I see you?"

"I'm not sure. Some business to take care of."

"I understand. I read the notice from London, incidentally. More of the same, I gather."

"Exactly."

"So you've been traveling."

"Yes." He was running out of things he could say.

"I was hardly overjoyed at your last letter. You don't believe in pulling punches, do you?"

"I'm sorry."

For a while there was silence. "I don't care if you don't want to see me. I want to see you. Because I won't let it just drift away. If you really want to get rid of me you'll have to say so in person, face to face."

He swallowed. "Are you going to Paris soon?"

"Not unless you want me to. Otherwise I'll be here . . . or at home. Are you in this country?"

"Yes."

"Near?"

"No."

"Coming this way?"

He took a deep breath. "I really only called to let you know I'm okay."

"And getting in deeper all the time, from what I read. I . . . I want a firm commitment from you that you'll see me."

"Agreed, but I don't know when."

"Could you give me an idea? Next month? A week?"

"Probably sooner."

Her voice softened. "That's very good news. Now I have something to hope for."

Calling had been a mistake, he told himself as he left the booth, for her voice and words caused him to feel the same emotions he had first felt for her, and that was bad for him, bad for both of them. Seeing her would be even worse, yet he had promised. . . .

Morgan read a Miami paper while waiting for his flight. A two-inch story datelined Key West confirmed what Pollock had told him: The accused bombing-murderer of Marisa Pardo de la Costa, Lon Crowly, was jailed without bond. A second charge, of murdering his accomplice, identity not yet know, was being readied by the State Attorney's office. There was said to be Federal interest in the crimes but the FBI's resident agent declined comment.

There seemed no possible way he could reach Crowly, force the man to reveal who paid him for the bombing and why. Hoping to mitigate his sentence Crowly might eventually tell what he knew of the assignment, but Morgan doubted he would tell everything.

And I need to know everything.

His flight reached Tampa International at nightfall, too late for one of the few feeder flights into Marathon's limited airport. And the bus route, he learned, led down the West Coast to Naples where it turned inward across the Tamiami Trail, ending in Miami where he could take another bus south to the Keys. Either way, Miami was the junction he had to reach, and so he flew to Miami and rode an airport limousine to the downtown bus terminal. Another wait before boarding the Key West bus that seemed to stop at every crossroad along the Overseas Highway, and it was 1:30 in the morning before he got off with his suitcase at a dark filling station inside the town limits.

In another two hours Pollock's dusty jeep arrived.

"Hardly know you with that white mane," Pollock said as he turned the jeep around and headed south. "You look like you been through some bad times. How'd you get into the country?"

"From Mexico. Walked over at Brownsville."

"Back door's good as any. Room's all ready for you, Dave. Stay as long as you like. Jesus, to think all this started with that little trip we took."

Morgan settled back in the uncomfortable seat, let his chin rest on his upper chest, and fell asleep.

He woke when Pollock slowed for highway construction, then resumed speed over the bridge south of Big Coppitt Key.

His neck was stiff, muscles cramped. He stretched and yawned. The cool sea air was laden with the smell of salt. "I'd like to get the boat," he said, "move it up into Florida Bay somewhere and use it as a base. But even before painting on a new name it has to be checked for booby traps. How long before sunrise?"

Pollock examined his watch. "Less than two hours."

"Got any white paint?"

"Plenty."

"I'll need a face mask and a submersible light."

"No problem. But, listen, Dave, I can do all that while you're catching up on sleep."

"No. I need you topside while I'm below."

They drove into Key West, stopping at Pollock's house while he made coffee and collected gear for Morgan. Then they took the jeep to the Marina. Pollock leaned against his jeep; Morgan went aboard *El Gallo*.

The marina's few lights showed him that windblown spray had caked the glass with salt, dulled the brightwork of his boat. In the cockpit Morgan removed his shoes and very cautiously crawled over the weather decks, shielding the light with his hand, searching for trip wires, timers, anything that might spell danger. Next he unlocked the cabin door and opened it slowly with a boat pole, then shined the light below. On his knees he examined the open steps leading down into the cabin, saw no pressure-sensitive device, crawled down and sat on the middle step while he played the light around the cabin.

Had it been daylight he would never have noticed the thin nylon line that stretched across the cabin no more than a foot above the floor. But against the dark background it glistened in the light like an edge of steel. His breath caught, and he played the beam across the trip line, finding that it was secured to the wood of the starboard bunk by a screw eye. On the port side, the monofilament led up through another screw eye and under the bunk cushion. Morgan went back on deck and motioned to Pollock. He held up one finger, then went below with the boat pole. He used it to pry back the cushion until he could see the explosive device: a spring-activated trigger rigged so that its bolt would slam into a percussion cap and detonate six taped sticks of dynamite when tripped by sudden pressure on the nylon line.

With a knife from his galley Morgan cut the detonator cord, severing it from the percussion cap, laid the dynamite on the cabin deck, and removed the percussion cap from the triggering device. Then he cut the monofilament and went up on deck.

He dropped the cap into the water where its copper shell would corrode into harmlessness. The dynamite he laid in the fish well and placed the trigger spring on his chart panel. Pollock watched in silence.

Morgan motioned him away before slowly lifting one of the flush engine hatches. Kneeling, he explored the cavity with his light and saw a pair of wires leading from the ignition system to a support stanchion just under the wheel. Around it was taped an electric detonator and another six sticks of dynamite. Swearing, Morgan lowered himself, cut the lead wires, and severed the retaining tape. Carrying the dynamite on deck he held up two fingers and saw Pollock shake his head. Morgan placed the dynamite in the starboard fish well.

He explored the galley, the forward stowage space, the head, and the refrigerator before emerging on deck again. To Pollock he said, "Professional work. They figured I'd find one and get blown up by the other."

"All clear now?"

"Toss me the face mask."

He stripped and let himself over the side into the water. It was cool but not chilling. He rinsed the mask's tempered face plate, took the submersible light from Pollock, and forced his body under the hull.

Foot by foot he searched the planking, the propellor struts and rudder, finding clamped to the skeg a streamlined device whose volume was about that of a shoebox. At the blunt forward end was a small propellor designed to turn when the boat was underway. He recognized it as a maritime sabotage item known in the Navy—and the Agency—as a limpet. Powerful magnets held it to the metal skeg, and after a predetermined number of propellor revolutions the limpet would explode. Morgan surfaced for air, held up three fingers and submerged again.

The magnets were too strong to let the limpet be pulled directly away, so he had to shove and slide it inch by inch until the small end was clear of the skeg. He surfaced again, breathed deeply and went down. Now he could lever the limpet off the skeg. Immobilizing its propellor with one hand, he stroked upward and found a resting place on the rung of a pier ladder. Pollock responded to his call, lay flat on the pier, and reached down for the limpet. "That's all," Morgan gasped. "Unless there's one in the fuel tanks."

"Jesus, am I glad I didn't fool with the boat!"

Wearily Morgan pulled himself up the ladder onto the pier. After a few breaths he climbed back aboard his boat and went below to towel himself dry. As he dressed, Pollock joined him and said, "What are you gonna do with all this boom-boom stuff?"

"Over the side when I'm out to sea. Get the paint aboard, will you?"

Pollock stowed a gallon can of white enamel in the fish well, along with a can of black enamel for lettering, and large and small brushes. To the east the sky was lightening; soon it would be streaked with the palette of dawn. The men who booby-trapped his boat had done a thorough job, Morgan reflected. How thorough he would know that night when he put to sea. Were Crowly and company responsible? Or a couple of old hands from the Agency?

He locked the cabin door, left the boat, and joined Pollock in the jeep. "I'm beat," he said. "I need a bed."

"Well, you've done a lot of traveling, and a good night's work."

"While I'm sleeping tomorrow, pick up a couple of Zodiacs for me, will you?"

"Those little inflatable jobs? Sure. What else?"

"Two outboards, ten horse each will be enough. Provision the boat, clean the water tanks, and get fresh water in them. Top off the fuel and oil, too."

210

"Uh . . . all that takes money."

Morgan gestured at his suitcase.

The jeep passed Marisa's boutique, and he remembered the money in her safe. Too dangerous to try to get it now; in any case it was probably gone, claimed by her parents. He had intended it for her after his death. Anyway, money was the least of his problems. As a last resort there was his Geneva account, but to draw on it now would involve running a needless risk.

His mind was dulling. He wanted to call his son, talk with him, but that was hazardous, too. His daughter . . . fatigue was overcoming him.

Pollock led him up the stairway to a rear bedroom. It was small but clean, the mattress welcoming. Morgan drew a bundle of dollars from his suitcase and tossed it to Pollock. "Check me about four, will you? And drop by the jail, too. Pick up the gossip about Crowly."

"Okay. If you wake up and Irma's gone, just raid the refrigerator. We'll have a good meal tonight."

Morgan lay back on the bed, closed his eyes, and heard his host leave and close the door. Briefly he remembered El Tigre, then almost at once he was asleep.

Pollock was shaking his shoulder; sunlight flooded the room. "Wake up, I've got news for you!"

Morgan swung his legs over the side of the bed, blinked at the sunlight. What day was it? What time? "I'm awake," he said finally.

"Crowly's out of jail."

"*What?*"

"Someone posted bond for him: two hundred grand, cash, and he walked out!"

"Where is he?"

"Get some clothes on. He's sitting in my shack waiting for me to fly him to Mexico. You wanted him, you got him."

NINETEEN

Morgan never dressed so fast in his life. Pollock said, "I told Crowly I had to locate my copilot, wouldn't fly to Mérida without him." He grinned.

"Good thinking. Let's go."

As they drove to the airport Pollock said, "I was loading your boat when Irma told me there was a charter call. It was Crowly. He told her he'd duck reporters and photographers and get to the airport, so that's where I met him. I left him sucking on a bottle of Crown Royal and went to get you."

"Who put up his bond?"

"I didn't ask him and he didn't volunteer. One thing, though, you can be damn sure he's scared."

"He's got reason to be. I think his employers got him out."

"To whack him?"

Morgan shrugged. "Easier to do it away from jail. Besides, the Feds could be moving him somewhere else." He turned to Pollock. "I'm going to take him on the boat and sweat him. That's kidnapping. You don't have to go."

"Wouldn't miss it."

"All right. I was planning to have you go with me tonight and get back on a Zodiac by yourself. This just speeds things up." His hand stroked the holstered Mauser under his jacket. "How much daylight left?"

Pollock glanced at his watch. "Under two hours."

Pollock parked the jeep to block the door and they got out. Pollock unlocked the door and went in. Morgan followed.

The office consisted of a ten-by-twelve room and a lavatory. There was a littered desk, two chairs, and an iron cot. On it sat a man with short, black hair. His dark facial skin showed several days' beard. He set the bottle on the floor. "You sure took a lot of time, mister. I wanna get outa here."

"Relax," Pollock said easily. "My copilot was sleeping but I got him up and here he is. Say hello to Bert, Mr. Crowly."

Crowly grunted.

He was short and muscular, Morgan saw, eyes somewhat reddened. Salt water would make them even redder.

Crowly got up. "What're we waitin' for?"

"Cash in advance."

"Okay, okay." His hand thrust into his pants pocket and brought out a roll of bills. "Five hundred?"

"Well, I just found out who you are, Mr. Crowly. Taking you out of the country's a penal offense. For that risk me an' Bert'd need five each."

Crowly swore, but he counted out ten one-hundred dollar bills.

"Let's go. I got no baggage."

Morgan walked around behind him as though heading for the whisky bottle, pulled out the Mauser, and slammed the butt into the back of Crowly's head. Pollock caught him as he fell, lowered the unconscious man to the floor.

"That's better," Morgan said reholstering the automatic. "Now we're getting organized. He'll be a little hard to hide in the jeep, so let's trade cars with Irma." He gestured at the money on the desk. "When she comes you can give her that for safekeeping."

Pollock moved to the telephone while Morgan began tying Crowly's hands and feet with lengths of aircraft tie-down cord. Finished, he went into the lavatory, found a razor, and drenched a towel with water. He soaked Crowly's short hair and began to shave it off. Pollock finished talking with his wife and said, "Hey, what's that for?"

"It'll upset him. And make it harder for him to hide."

"If he lives through the night."

"Right." He worked methodically on the stubborn hair.

Pollock placed the hundred-dollar bills in an envelope. "Irma'll be right over. No point in letting her see this dude, is there?"

"Better if she doesn't. Tell her to forget he ever called."

Pollock picked up the Crown Royal and held it to the light. "He downed six or seven shots but there's some left." He wiped the bottle neck with a handkerchief and drank deeply. "You?"

Morgan took the bottle and drank from it. He finished shaving the

214

skull, noticing a variety of scars on the bare scalp. There was a swollen area where the Mauser butt had struck. Here and there droplets of blood oozed from razor nicks. Morgan poured whisky on the oddly-white scalp, spread it thoroughly with the towel. "Speciality of the house," he said as he rose. "Not every shop provides Crown Royal after shave."

Morgan brought a dirty hand towel from the lavatory, cut it in half lengthwise, doubled each half and used one to blindfold the reeking Crowly, the other to gag him. Gesturing at the far wall he said, "Give me a hand with this piece of shit," and together they dragged Crowly across the floor and dumped him in the corner. Morgan draped a blanket over the prone body and swept up the shocks of cut black hair. "Guess we can pass inspection," he said. "Now, what about the boat?"

"It's ready, Dave. I spent most of the day loading it. Even got gas for the outboards."

"After we're at sea I'm going to unload the tuna tower. With a new name the boat needs a different profile."

A car was nearing the shack. Pollock opened the door and stepped out. Through dirty windows Morgan could see Pollock handing keys and envelope to his wife. They talked for a moment, then she got into the jeep and drove away. Pollock came back in. "Here's your change," he said, and handed Morgan several greenbacks. "You've got enough frozen meat and vegetables for a week or ten days, a bottle each of brandy, rum, and scotch. I consolidated the explosives and filled one ice chest. In it there's a case of Olympia should you get thirsty."

"I expect to. Got a deck of cards?"

"Sure. And I'll beat your ass at gin."

"Hell you will."

They played at the desk until nightfall, hearing Crowly groan occasionally from under the blanket. A plane took off. Minutes later another landed, and by then they could barely see the cards.

"Sixteen bucks!" Pollock hit the desk with his palm, counted out the money and passed it to Morgan. "I'm lucky it's time to go."

"Move the car by the door. We'll start this client on his way."

Working together they dragged Crowly into the rear seat well, covered him with the blanket and closed the doors. From the airport they took back roads to the marina.

The car approached the pier slowly. Most of the boats were empty of owners and hired help. Morgan saw old Pedro trudging away under a waterfront light, a brown paper bag big enough for a pint of rum and a few fish steaks clutched in one hand. I'd like to say hello, Morgan thought, but Pedro might talk about it.

Pollock braked the car, "Things look pretty clear."

"Let's move him."

They wrapped the blanket carefully around Crowly, lifted him onto their shoulders, and walked down the pier. When they reached *El Gallo* they rolled their burden over the transom. It hit the deck with a muffled groan. Suffer, damn you, Morgan thought, and said to Pollock, "Go back to the car. If this blows up when I hit the ignition, only one human being will go with it."

"Dave, I. . . ."

"Beat it!"

Slowly, Pollock walked back toward his car. Morgan inserted the ignition key, hesitated, then punched the starter button.

Nothing happened.

He hit the button again.

Abruptly the engines turned over, caught, burbled, and purred.

Thank God, he thought.

Pollock came back with Morgan's suitcase, freed shore lines, and climbed aboard. Morgan turned the wheel, shoved the throttles ahead, and the boat moved out from the pier, heading for open sea.

Moonlight crossed the body of Lon Crowly. Morgan itched for the business to begin.

TWENTY

For the first time in weeks Morgan felt free. All ties with land were cut, he was on his own again, self-sufficient, self-sustaining. That was pretty much the way things had been before Dobbs's suited messengers arrived.

He wondered if he would ever be able to reassemble his life, get it into some semblance of order so that he could live without being hunted.

Running lights glowed evenly, tachs were synchronized. Only an occasional swell sprayed the bow as the boat sliced into the night. Stars were out, the compass showed a course due south. They had been running an hour, cruising easily with a following sea.

Pollack stood nearby sipping a can of beer. He gestured at Crowly who lay half-covered by the blanket. "Don't look like much, does he?"

To starboard a flying-fish broke the surface of a wave and skittered ahead, its tail making staccato drops of fire in the night fluorescence of the water.

"I hope the sharks are hungry," Morgan said.

"Never seen a time when they weren't." He crumpled the empty can and dropped it into a waste bin. "Figure we gone far enough? I haven't seen lights for twenty minutes." He rubbed his hands together. "Gettin' kinda cold."

Morgan, thinking of Marisa, barely heard him.

"Don't feel like talkin', David? Well, I understand."

"Let's get a radio check on the weather."

Pollack turned on the set, pretuned to the Key West frequency. He wiped salt spray from the dial and listened to the repetitive announcements. After a while he said, "Sounds okay ahead. No big weather comin'."

217

Morgan turned over the wheel to him and went below. From his tool chest he got a crescent wrench, brought it topside and began unbolting the stanchions of the tuna tower. When only gravity held the welded tubular structure in place, Pollock brought the boat broadside to the wind and together they toppled it over the leeward side. Fluorescent foam swirled above it and Morgan shook his head. "There goes four thousand bucks. Took me a long time to pay."

"Feels kinda naked without it." Pollock turned the boat back onto course. Morgan went down into the forward storage space and brought back a reel of braided line, four-hundred-pound test nylon. It was what he used when trolling for sharks on an otherwise dull trip.

Kneeling beside Crowly, Morgan unsnapped his sheath knife and set the edge against Crowly's throat. "I'm going to take out the gag so you can answer questions." Roughly, Morgan tore it off.

Crowly spat at him.

Morgan wiped spittle from his face and drew the knife slowly across Crowly's throat. "Know who I am?"

"*Fuck yourself!*"

Morgan's hand began trembling. "Know who I am?" he said hoarsely.

"I paid you guys, didn't I? What's going on?"

"I'll ask the questions," Morgan told him. "Once more: Know who I am?"

"No."

"I'm the man whose woman you murdered."

From Crowly's throat came a long guttural sigh.

"Who hired you to kill her?"

Crowly hesitated. "I don't know."

Morgan grunted. "You had your chance." He stood up, looped the shark line between Crowly's bound wrists, secured it with a knot to the tie-down cord. He unreeled forty feet of shark line and cut it, tying the free end to a transom cleat.

"Now?" Pollock asked, setting a lanyard to a wheel spoke.

"Now."

Together they lifted Crowly over the transom and dropped him into the wake. A scream ended as his body submerged. They watched the line pay out. It went taut and Crowly emerged in the distance, dragged by his bound arms, breasting the wake waves, turning and twisting like a monstrous bait.

El Gallo turned in a wide circle. What it was towing shrieked and begged. The shaven head glistened in the spotlight . . . when the head could be seen.

"You'll drown him," Pollock warned.

"I don't think he'll talk anyway, and I have to get some satisfaction out of this."

"Suppose he talks?"

"You can take him ashore in one of the Zodiacs and leave him where he can be found. Get home and establish an alibi."

"What about you?"

"Don't worry about me. Cut the engines."

As the boat wallowed, Morgan hauled Crowly toward the stern. "Ready to talk?" he shouted.

Something sounding like *Yah* came from Crowly's mouth.

"I think he wants to cooperate," Pollack said, and helped Morgan bring the waterlogged man aboard. They laid him face down so he could vomit up sea water. His body shook, animal sounds retched from his throat.

"I don't know," said Morgan. "I'm not sure he sincerely wants to save his life. The next few minutes will tell."

"Yeah. While he was hiring me for the getaway flight I got the idea he had this self-image he was a tough guy. *Cojones* like medicine balls. He don't look so tough now, Bert."

"No. He hasn't the brains to be an ideologue working for a cause."

"Just a hit man."

Conversationally, Morgan said, "If I put him in again I'm going to cut a leg vein, let him tough it out with the sharks."

"Think he's an Arab? Arabs are supposed to be plenty tough."

Morgan grunted. "That's where I got the idea. Arabs want to get the truth from a tribesman, they drag him around the desert for a few miles. Man, does that sand wear away the skin! In the Yemen I saw what was left of a plotter: rib cage and a bunch of little curling tubes that used to be veins."

Crowly retched again.

Morgan turned him over on his back. "Ready?"

"Ready," the voice bubbled. "Holy God, no more!"

"Give him a little sauce," Morgan said. "I think the Crown Royal's worn off."

"Seems like." Pollock went below and brought back a small plastic cup of brandy. He propped Crowly against the ice chest and fed him the brandy a little at a time. Crowly gagged, but his body stopped shaking. Pollock took away the cup.

Morgan sat on the deck beside Crowly. Softly he said, "You've had a drink and you've had time to think. Who hired you?"

"I don't know. Wait . . . *wait*," he almost shrieked, "I got a phone call. . . ." He was gasping, trying to breathe regularly, steadying his voice, "just a name and an address in Key West." He swallowed, gasped again. "I didn't even know who he was."

"How much did you get?"

"Ten grand."

"Were you supposed to do the job alone?"

"He didn't say. So I hired Buddy."

"Buddy who?"

"Krasner. Buddy Krasner. We was in Nam together."

"That's the guy you killed?"

"Yeah. He was a stoney, a waste case. He'da talked sooner or later."

"How was the money paid?"

"Half in my mail box before the job. Half after . . . same way."

"How did you make contact?"

"He gave me a phone number."

"What was it?"

"I don't remember."

Morgan laid the blade of the sheath knife against Crowly's right leg, turned it until the point dug in. "I've had it with you. Tell me the number or you'll hit the water, and no tow rope this time."

"Wait, Jesus, *wait!*"

"The number."

"It was Washington, see? Seven-eight-five, then nine-five-one-seven. Yeah, that's right." He repeated it. "I called in after the job was done."

"Sure about it?"

"Yeah, I'm sure."

Finally, Morgan thought, I'm getting somewhere. If it was a working number someone would answer. He had to know who.

"And the rest of your blood money?"

"Like I said . . . in the mail box."

"You're not clear yet," Morgan told him, got up, and walked to the pilot chair. He switched on the ship-to-shore telephone and called the marine operator. He gave his call sign and asked to be connected to

Crowly's number. Within ten seconds he heard a recorded announcement, "The number you called has been disconnected."

Morgan replaced the telephone. "Not good," he said. "Crowly, you've been lying. Goodbye." He began lifting Crowly's struggling feet.

"Wait a minute, Bert," said Pollock. "Maybe he made a mistake. He took a knock on the head; hell, a fellow forgets. Right, Lon?"

"Oh, God," Crowly sobbed, "that was the number, I swear it. I don't know no more. You can cut my guts out and I can't tell you what I don't know. Jesus, be reasonable."

Slowly Morgan lowered his legs. "A couple more questions for you; maybe you can work your way out of this yet. Who paid your bond?"

"I don't know. Probably the guy who hired me for the job. The jailer opened my cell, said two hundred grand, cash, was paid the judge's clerk. He let me out the back way."

"And you called Pollock. Why?"

"Looked up charter service in the phone book. So's I could get to Mexico an' drop out of sight." He was breathing heavily, "Worst fuckin' mistake I ever made."

"No," Morgan said, "that was your second worst mistake. The first was killing my girl. Now, aside from her name was any other name mentioned by your employer?"

"No."

"Think hard."

"Nothing, just this Marisa. We tailed her from the shop to her house. I didn't know someone else was livin' there."

"Not that it would have made a difference," Morgan said thinly. "What do we do about the disconnected number, Crowly? Any ideas?"

"I think he's come clean," Pollock said, good cop again.

"Well, I don't. That dead number could have been prearranged to get Crowly out of a situation like this. I'm going to kick him over the side."

The bomber was weeping. Tears streamed down from the blindfold wetting his wind-dried cheeks. "I told you all I know!"

Morgan gestured Pollock forward, away from Crowly's hearing. "I'd like to kill him, but I can't. Either he's told the truth or he'll die with it untold. I don't know. Dead end, I guess."

"Shit!"

"Yeah. Whoever posted that bond to free him will be looking for him. I don't think he'll survive long. So I'll turn back now, head for the south part of Boca Chica Key. Take the Zodiac and run him ashore, somewhere he has a fairly clear shot at the highway. I want him found. Use the Zodiac to get home or sink it and have Irma pick you up, your choice. You've been home all evening."

"He can describe the inside of my shack."

Morgan nodded. "So he went there, tried to get you to fly him to Mexico. You refused, he went away and you went home. I don't think he'll be lodging any complaints with the authorities."

Pollock chuckled unpleasantly. "His employers got two hundred and ten thousand dollars invested in this shit-ass. Yeah, they'll be wanting to find him. If I was him I'd rather have a bullet in my head than a shark on my ass."

"Give him more brandy, cover him up. I'll figure the course."

The wind was from the northeast, waves slapped the starboard bow. Morgan turned off his running lights. The boat was dark except for the compass glow. After an hour he turned on the radar and spotted channel buoys farther east than he had estimated, so he came to starboard and steadied the course until the shoreline began showing as a low blur. He shut off the radar and through night glasses saw the four-second red flasher marking the eastern edge of Boca Chica Channel. Morgan turned east again and watched the fathometer until *El Gallo* crossed the five-fathom line. From there to the coral edge of the key the depth would be a steady two fathoms. Close enough.

He cut the throttles and let the boat drift while Pollock inflated the Zodiac with its air cylinder. Together they clamped on the outboard and lowered the craft over the side, tethering it astern by a line.

Crowly yelled in fright when they eased him over the stern. His feet touched the inflated boat's bottom duckboards and he collapsed there in fetal position. He was finished, Morgan thought; utterly defeated. It didn't make up for Marisa's death.

Wordlessly he shook hands with Pollock and cast off the tether line when the outboard was running smoothly. Pollock turned the little boat and headed for the island, Morgan watching it fade quickly, marked only by its wake.

Morgan took a deep breath, felt his muscles begin to relax. He was grateful for Pollock's help, grateful he had been aboard with him. Otherwise, Morgan thought, I'd have killed Crowly. I know it, and he knew it too.

Overhead he heard the faint whisper of jet engines, glanced up and saw an aircraft's blinking lights.

Morgan shoved the throttle ahead and turned on his running lights. He had decided to enter Florida Bay through Boca Chica Channel, anchor near West Harbor Key, and spend the night. Two miles west he picked up the channel marker buoys, turned in, and cruised under the highway bridge. Another quarter of an hour put him just west of Harbor Key's dredged channel.

He cut the engines and dropped anchor in three fathoms, turned on the anchor lights. The radio brought him Key West's all-night music station. He felt drained.

The boat rocked gently in the bay's low swell, tugged at its chain, creaked and groaned as it moved with the current. By now Pollock was probably home, and Morgan wondered where Crowly was. He could visualize him stumbling along the highway, bound hands trying to flag down passing cars. But who would stop for him? Only the police.

Tomorrow, he thought, I'll paint out the name, alter the Coast Guard registration, and get back to the mainland again. If anyone could trace back the disconnected number Crowly had yielded it was Hugh McDairmid. Morgan could think of no one else.

Meanwhile, he mused, I'll let my enemies digest what happened to Crowly. He doesn't know my name, couldn't recognize a boat he never saw. But he'll never forget my face.

As long as he lives.

Early in the morning Morgan inflated the other Zodiac and tethered it to the stern. Using it as a platform he painted out *El Gallo* and *Key West* and made breakfast while the white enamel dried. Later, with the smaller brush, he lettered a new name and home port: *Le Cygne* and *Cape May*. He changed the Coast Guard registration number by painting a three into an eight. Superficial camouflage, but he believed it would work for as long as he needed his boat.

With the ship-to-shore phone he reached Jill Percival at her apartment. "Great hours you keep," he said. "It's after nine."

"Well, I'm management, you know. So I can come and go as I please. What's that eerie crackling sound?"

"Static. Got a date tonight?"

"Not unless it's with you. Is . . . is there hope of that?"

"I was thinking of reaching the Palm Beach marina toward sundown. I can phone on arrival, or if you want to meet me look for a boat named the swan in that language which you speak so much better than I."

"I'll definitely be there, waiting on the pier. And I'd love to dine aboard."

"Bring your favorite wine," he said and broke the connection.

Pulling out the chart panel Morgan plotted a course that paralleled the northern side of the Keys, coming out into the Atlantic through the Key Largo channel, then following the coastline north. Under favorable conditions he could arrive on time, but if a head wind sprung up Jill would have a long wait.

He hauled the Zodiac aboard, started the engines and began steering through the maze of mangrove islands and sandbars until he was in relatively unobstructed waters. With the sun two points on his starboard bow, he lashed the wheel and began cleaning his boat.

Morgan swept the cabin rug, shined the drop-leaf dining table, dusted chairs, and aired bed linen before making up his bunk. After swinging the boat back on course he hosed down the superstructure and the cockpit, dipped into the chest for an icy Olympia and drank it, leaning on his mop, feeling the sun burn into his flesh. Once more, life was good; he felt a lust for living that he had almost forgotten.

Off Rock Harbor he took the wheel to pilot through Key Largo Cut. On the Bay side, he pulled alongside the pier to refuel, paid for it in cash, got under way, and steered under the bridge and into the ocean.

Morgan moved well into the Stream's indigo current before setting his northward course. To port he passed charter fishing boats, drift boats laden with tourists, dive boats with divers down, overtook a sluggish tanker, and spotted several freighters farther at sea, plowing the ocean lanes.

Again his mind turned to McDairmid. He had to get Hugh's help in tracing the disconnected number. If McDairmid was willing, he might be able to talk about Dormouse. Two unknowns.

A third: Had Crowly lied?

He remembered the beaten man's utter impotence, his fear-induced hysteria and physical exhaustion, and decided the chances were good that Crowly had told everything he knew.

Morgan got up and took a fathometer reading: The depth ran off the calibrated screen. Plenty deep to jettison explosives.

Opening the chest he tossed the dynamite bundles overboard, lifted out the heavy limpet and taped the propellor motionless before dropping it over the side. Otherwise, current would have revolved the propellor, eventually detonating the limpet mine. And that could tear up an acre of bottom habitat, needlessly kill a lot of fish. The dynamite sticks were inert. In a couple of months they would dissolve harmlessly. So much for the boobytraps designed to destroy him.

Near Miami Beach the Stream veered toward shore, and Morgan could see the high-rise hotels and condominiums along the beach. Offshore a heavy Cigarette was making a speed run, plumed rooster tail reaching high into the sky as it tore along, smashing through waves with its rocketing weight.

At the edge of the Stream, gulls circled and dived into a school of fry. Pelicans attracted by the feeding settled down on the water to gulp voraciously.

A slight breeze was coming off the port bow. Morgan corrected for it and settled back in his chair for the rest of the day's run. He tried to visualize what his life might be like were all his problems resolved but he was unable to frame anything more than a vague and superficial concept. He knew that he would always have to live near or on the water, but not necessarily in the United States. And how he could ever free himself of danger was beyond him unless a truce could be arranged with his enemies. But first he had to identify them, then be in a position to trade off something they wanted in return for peace.

Planes were descending toward Ft. Lauderdale's airport. Port Everglades was distantly visible. Another forty miles to go; two and a half hours. This was the longest run he had ever made.

From under a bunk Morgan got out his shark rifle, an M-1 carbine. Rust spots showed on the bluing so he field-stripped and cleaned it carefully, finishing off with a spray of WD-40 compound before returning it below.

The radar screen showed nothing ahead. He lashed the wheel while he showered and shaved, then took a clean shirt from his suitcase and laid it on the bunk.

When Pompano Beach was abeam he turned on the FM receiver, found background music stations broadcasting from Lauderdale and Boca Raton and switched back and forth between commercials. A gull lit on the gunwale and eyed him curiously, cocking its head, then taking sudden flight and soaring away.

A little before seven he saw the Palm Beach marina lights go on and wondered if Jill had been waiting long.

The dockmaster came out to meet him and Morgan asked for overnight dockage, following the outboard skiff to the indicated slip. He maneuvered in and tied up with the help of a passing crewman, and went below to change. When he came up Jill was sitting on the gunwale. Coming toward him she said, "Took your time, sailor," and handed him a gift-wrapped bottle of wine. "I've been perishing with anticipation." Then she stood on tiptoes and kissed him full on the mouth.

His mind whirled back to Paris, to the way her body molded itself to his at the threshold of her room, and it was the same as before, but now his mouth was as thirsty as hers and he pressed her tightly and said, "I've missed you."

"Not as much as I've missed you." She stood back to examine him in the twilight. "Tanner than I expected—and of course the white hair's a shock though actually it looks well. David Morgan twenty years from now. Am I babbling? Sounds like it. Can't you say *some*thing?"

"It was a long trip," he said, "but that's over now. Shall we have a drink? I neglected to bring champagne."

"Well, what do you usually have at sea?"

He itemized his small assortment and they agreed on scotch and water. While he made the drinks she moved around the cabin, commenting on how comfortable it seemed. Their glasses touched and he said, "Welcome aboard."

"Thanks for having me. Are you hungry?"

"A little."

"Show me what to do."

He pointed out the freezer and refrigerator, demonstrated the butane range, then relaxed in a chair while she made preparations. "You *could* have thawed the steaks, you know, but I suppose you had more important things on your mind."

"Whatever that means."

"If it means anything at all. Oh, David, I'm so much in love with you I don't know what to do and you're no help at all!" Abruptly she began to cry.

He drew her onto his lap.

"Do I mean *any*thing to you?" she said. "Anything at *all?*"

"You mean a great deal." He grinned and kissed her moist cheeks. "Perils of the sea: I bring a cook aboard and suddenly I've got a volunteer mistress."

"*Awful* word."

"Sweetheart, then. Are you prepared to spend the night?"

She kissed him, little purse-mouth pecks around his lips and eyes. "I

226

was planning to seduce you; that's what the wine's for. Are you as passionless as you seem?"

"You'll find out."

She snuggled closer. "You've changed my life, David. I don't think of anything but you. I've become a bitch and a termagant around the office; everyone loathes me." Her face lifted. "But you'll change all that."

"I'll try."

"And I'll cooperate." She rose slowly, hands pressing out wrinkles from her apricot slacks. "Will I *ever* cooperate! I expect you to awaken fires I've never known."

"Speaking of fires, the steaks need warming, too."

"What a coarse, unfeeling person!"

He mixed fresh drinks, set the table. Feeling somewhat ashamed of his mismatched cutlery and plastic plates, he found a candle for the hurricane lamp, lighted it, and saw its soft warm glow improve the scene. Jill nodded approvingly and said, "Next time, flowers."

"Uh-huh. Caviar, too?"

"A dandelion will do." The sleeves of her blouse were rolled up to avoid the steak spatters. A delicious aroma filled the cabin, and soon she served the Delmonicos with *petit-pois* boiled in a butter bag, and fresh-made rice. Morgan opened her wine and poured a sample. "*Bon, mon sommelier,*" Jill said, "you may fill *monsieur's* glass."

Passing behind her chair, Morgan kissed the nape of her neck. Jill said, "I love your *hors d'oeuvres.* They promise a substantial entrée."

They dined, making small talk, discovering each other, free from the need to go elsewhere at a fixed time. As he looked at her he thought that he wanted to be with her every evening for the rest of his life.

Together they did the dishes and then went out into the cockpit, sitting side by side, sipping cognac in the calm night.

Water lapped the hull, lights sparkled across the harbor, conversation from a nearby yacht drifted indistinctly through the still air. Morgan could not remember when last he had known a moment of such perfect peace.

He tilted her chin, kissed her cheeks and mouth until their tongues played together. "I want you, Jill," he whispered. "I need you."

"I want *you*, David."

He took her hand and led her down into the cabin, locked the door and turned out the lights. They undressed by the glow of the candle and he saw that her body was perfectly formed. She gave him her breasts to kiss, clasping his head tightly, until in the bunk she welcomed him, shuddering as he entered, no longer a girl but a woman exuberantly sharing with her mate, clasping and twining, moving to his rhythm until at last they lay spent, all tension drained away. He took her hand and kissed it drowsily, stayed awake until her breathing subsided into deep and placid sleep.

In his dream Jill was tied to a chair in a room with Kozlov and Ernst Dorn. They wanted information about him that she couldn't supply. Morgan watched helplessly as the torture continued. . . .

He woke, taut with fear. It was only a nightmare, but he realized that none of it was impossible.

Because of him, Jill, too, was in danger.

TWENTY-ONE

Morgan was preparing breakfast when Jill woke. Naked, she glided around him, kissed his bare shoulders, and hugged him from behind. "I'm your woman now," she told him. "Nothing you can do about it."

"Nothing I want to do about it." He turned the sizzling country ham and in a moment heard the shower go on. While Jill was drying off he made scrambled eggs, beating them thoroughly and adding a splash of cream and two drops of Worchestershire. Frozen orange juice, instant coffee, and toast.

"Hearty eater, aren't you?" she said, slipping into her chair, his discarded shirt around her shoulders.

"I learned to live one meal at a time. Then if you have to skip one it's not so bad."

"And where did you learn that, m'lord?"

"In prison."

"Sometime in the future I want you to tell me about it."

Over breakfast he brought her up to date, ending with trying to get information from Lon Crowly.

"I'm glad you didn't kill him," she said, "but I can understand why you wanted to. Is it ever going to end, David?"

He shrugged. "That's why I've wanted to keep you insulated from it."

She shook her head. "Whatever happens to you from now on affects me. You'll learn I haven't given my love lightly."

He thought of his nightmare. He was crazy to let Jill get involved in his life while someone was hunting him.

He watched her get up and heat more water for their coffee. Morgan went on deck and shielded his eyes against the morning sun.

The marina was active, boats being washed down, provisioned, readied to leave port. Bicycles with baskets of groceries moved up and down the piers.

Jill brought their cups into the cockpit and said, "I could get to love this life very quickly."

On a nearby piling a dark, hook-beaked cormorant was drying its feathers. Pelicans strutted at the far end of the pier near the fish-cleaning trough. Morgan said, "Do you know anything about boat-handling?"

"I took power squadron courses. The boy who was killed in his Corvette had a Bertram, so I learned to make myself useful. And what I don't know you can teach me."

"Is your apartment on the water?"

She nodded. "With dockage for tenants."

"This boat's without a home . . . unless you'll give it one."

"If the master comes with it."

"More or less. I'm going north for a while."

"May I go with you?"

"Not this time. Besides, I want you to have an interval for thinking things over, considering what it will be like to live with a hunted man."

"I've considered for weeks. Last night only confirmed it."

"I'm the least qualified, most unsuitable suitor you'll ever have—the one without a future. But if I can't dissuade you, cast off the lines and let's get the hell under way."

Jill ducked down into the cabin to pull on slacks before jumping onto the pier. Morgan idled the engines while she freed the boat and returned aboard, then moved the boat out of the slip into the sheltered harbor. Beyond the inlet he gave her the wheel and set a course across the Stream.

Later he showed her how to operate and interpret the radar and fathometer, took RDF bearings, and plotted a sample course for Riviera Beach and her apartment's harbor.

When he saw gulls slashing into a school of fleeing baitfish, Morgan rigged a game rod with a feathered spoon, gave pursuit, and shouted instructions to Jill. A famished blue took the spoon and with delighted cries Jill reeled it aboard. By the time Morgan had unhooked the struggling fish the rest were far away.

"Can we eat it?"

"Of course." He killed the bluefish, gutted it, and cut off tail and head. He rinsed it over the side and Jill took it below to wrap and

230

refrigerate. About eight pounds live, Morgan estimated, and it would yield half a dozen succulent steaks.

He showed her the rest of his fishing gear—tackle, reels, line, hooks and lures—and rinsed her rod, reel, and line in fresh water before setting it in a ferrule to dry.

"Who taught you all that?"

"My father." Taking the wheel again he told her of his early life, of hunting and fishing with his father, of his time at Townsend and his schoolboy's admiration for Roger Hargrave.

Jill said, "I was wondering when he'd come up again. I think you're pursuing an illusion."

"No, I'm trying to unravel the past so we can have a future."

In midafternoon Jill prepared bluefish steaks in lemon-butter sauce. After eating he showed her his Dougherty passport and told her about Frechette, the document forger. Jill said, "How can you be sure he didn't tell the police about you?"

"Bad for business. With the Corsicans and terrorists he deals with, it would be fatal. He'd end up in an alley with his throat cut."

"But how come you were spotted so quickly in Berlin? Someone had to know the name you were traveling under, where you were going. Only Ten Eyck knew that."

"I could have been recognized," he said lamely.

"You don't really believe that."

"No," he admitted, "I don't. But why would Ten Eyck sell me out?"

"There's always money."

"I can't think of Broom as a mercenary."

"Does he have a personal fortune?"

"Not that I know of." He shrugged. "And he's maintaining three separate establishments."

"Which could be pretty expensive."

"Very." He took a deep breath. "Or he could have betrayed me for motives that go far back in time. But I'll say this: While I was staying there, Ten Eyck put on a marvelous show. He really convinced me."

"Only because your guard was down."

Morgan's eyes scanned the horizon. Smoke from a tanker's stacks dirtied a portion of the sky.

She said, "You're like the British, trusting old school ties, assuming everyone's a gentleman. That's how Hargrave managed to get away, isn't it? His background was impeccable and so he was trusted. Can't you look at Ten Eyck in the same light? You shouldn't trust a man just because he was forced out of the Agency. You can't assume a bond of loyalty because of that."

"Maybe you're right."

"Even Colonel Arnaud. . . . Didn't you tell him far too much?"

"I guess I did," he acknowledged. "My only excuse is that I was still disoriented, so I reached out for anyone who could help me. All right, I'll be more careful in whom I confide. And I'll need to borrow your car."

"Sure," she said, then ran her fingers through his hair. "I'll bleach those roots tonight. Your natural color's starting to show."

"I should be back in a week. If nothing works with McDairmid or James, that'll end things in the States. In Paris I'll close the apartment, remove the papers I left there."

"I could do that for you."

"We'll see."

In her apartment Jill served a late dinner on her balcony overlooking the private harbor and *Le Cygne*'s safe mooring. Her sun-dark skin contrasted with her white sleeveless blouse, the single strand of pearls that dipped between her breasts. Morgan said, "You look ravishing."

"And I'm ready to be ravished—after coffee, of course."

While she was pouring she said, "I can't help thinking ahead, and I've been wondering where, if worse comes to worst, we might go."

"With an extra drum of fuel I think we can reach Mexico from here. The Isthmus is where I want to go. I've fished for tarpon in that big lagoon by Carmen. Campeche's the nearest point of comparative civilization. It won't be easy, darling."

"As long as I'm with you I won't mind." She kissed his forehead.

"Sure you want to waste your life with a boat bum?"

"Quite sure. Besides, mine hasn't been all that great a life. So far. Though recently it's been improving."

"You're not afraid of being abandoned in the wilds of Tehuantepec?"

"Lord no . . . I can't even pronounce it. Besides, it's settled: We're going together wherever we go. Incidentally, you haven't mentioned a dowery. I have considerable financial assets. Shall I bring all or part along? Even the Owl and the Pussy Cat took plenty of money."

"Some honey, a five-pound note, and a runcible spoon."

She laughed. "What's a runcible spoon?"

"A curved fork with three tines, one sharp. Like a pickle spoon."

232

"And to think I never knew. I always assumed it was rinse-able."

"So did I, until my English master took the trouble to explain. One of the benefits of a small school like Townsend."

"Back to funding our expedition, master. Shall I liquidate some holdings?"

"We can last for at least a year on what I have. After that I guess we'll have to dip into your dowery."

"Shall I sublet this place?"

"Might as well. But not until I come back. Maybe I'll get lucky and we won't have to hide in Mexico."

"To hear is to obey. But I think I'll let Ginna buy me out. She's offered before, and business is at an all-time high. I'll say I'm going back to Europe to live and she'll understand."

Together they did the dishes and afterward Morgan opened his suitcase and took out currency. He counted a thousand dollars into his billfold and gave the rest to Jill. "That guarantees my return."

"But it's so much. I don't have a safe here."

He took a kitchen knife, turned a stuffed chair on its side, and slit the bottom. He fed the packages into the opening and taped it shut with black electrical tape.

"Ingenious."

"Let's hope." He picked her up and carried her into the bedroom where he dropped her on the bed. Then he undressed Jill except for her string of pearls, and lay down beside her.

"I love you, David," she said quietly. "Please hurry back to me."

The sound of birds on the balcony woke him. Dawn was turning the rim of the ocean light gray. Morgan dressed and closed the bedroom door. He went to the telephone and reached the Northern Virginia operator who supplied a Leesburg listing for Hugh McDairmid under Dawntree Farms.

Morgan dialed it and, after nine rings, a voice said, "Dawntree Farms."

"Western Union," Morgan said. "I have a telegram for Hugh McDairmid."

"Mr. McDairmid's sleeping. May I take the message?"

Morgan hung up. Hugh was in residence; that was all he needed to know.

From the bureau he took Jill's car keys and carried his suitcase down to the parking area. Her car was a dark blue Monte Carlo with under three thousand miles on the speedometer.

He had about a thousand miles of driving ahead of him. If he could do seven hundred today and sleep in North Carolina, he could reach McDairmid's place early tomorrow afternoon.

Morgan headed up US 1, stopping for gas at Vero Beach. Near the filling station a diner was opening for breakfast so he went in and scanned the morning paper while waiting. An inside page carried a short item from Florida City where the county sheriff's office announced finding a man's body in a bay mangrove swamp. There were bullet holes in head and body, and the face had been battered beyond recognition; teeth smashed in an apparent effort to prevent identification. The man's skull had been recently shaved.

He felt suddenly chilled. The waitress brought hot coffee and he gulped it black, hardly tasting. Mechanically he ate breakfast, paid, and walked out. The waitress called, "Hey, you left your paper, mister."

He went to the pay phone inside the filling station, inserted coins and placed a call to Florida City. When a deputy answered, he said, "Listen, that corpse with the shaven head is probably a guy named Crowly."

"Yeah. Hold on, mister, I got to. . . ."

"Just listen. The guy he killed was named Buddy Krasner, an Army pal of his. Remember: Crowly and Krasner. Got it?" He hung up.

Driving west he picked up I-95 and kept pace with heavy northbound rigs equipped with CBs and fuzz-busters.

As he drove, his mind dwelled on the fact that Marisa's murderers were both dead; one killed by his partner, and Lon Crowly killed by? By whoever bailed him out of jail. They found him quickly, Morgan thought.

Better him than me.

That night he slept in a cheap motel near Fayetteville. The clerk wrote his license number on the registration card so Morgan signed as G. J. Percival, adding Jill's address.

He was up early and on the road again. It was nearing two o'clock when Morgan reached Dawntree Farms. White fencing bordered the country road, and beyond it he could see a substantial herd of Black Angus. The blacktop entrance road to the residence building divided the pasturage, and to the right a dozen saddle horses grazed.

The house seemed to have been constructed in three separate phases: fieldstone, Colonial brick, then clapboard as sections were added on. Out-buildings, barns, and stables, looked well maintained.

234

The house itself dominated a rise that was partly screened by oaks and majestic spruce.

Morgan guided the Monte Carlo onto a graveled parking area and got out. As he stood gazing at the house an amplified voice said, "State your business."

"It's with Hugh McDairmid."

"Your name?"

"I'll tell the lord of the manor." He began walking toward the steps.

"I *am* the lord of the manor," the voice boomed, "and you don't look familiar to me."

Morgan halted. "Take a good look, Hugh, and you'll realize why I'm not advertising my identity. Normally my hair's another color."

"So it is, so it is. Good lord, come in, man!"

Morgan went up the steps and the door was flung open. Standing with the aid of an aluminum cane was the Agency's original computer genius, thinner than Morgan remembered and stooped, but with the same thick glasses and hawklike nose. Across the top of his head only a few strands of hair remained. He was wearing a rough wool cardigan, gray flannels, and bedroom slippers. To Morgan he seemed an old, sick man.

They shook hands, Morgan closed the door and followed McDairmid into a large, well-lighted study whose walls were lined with books. There was a table of technical magazines, and near it a remote computer console. "Sit down, sit down," McDairmid said. "Coffee? Whisky?"

"Coffee, Hugh."

"Drink only tea myself." He spoke into an intercom and ordered. Then to Morgan he said, "Is it true you killed old Palmer?"

"No."

"Do you know who did?"

He shook his head.

McDairmid sat in an adjustable chair, fondled the handle of his cane. "Strange things have been happening this season, David. Roger Hargrave reappears in Geneva only to be assassinated. Palmer Syce, theoretically secure at St. Mark's, is murdered. Out of nowhere you appear at my doorstep. Is there a connection? Tell me."

"It will take a while," Morgan said. "I'll have to impose on your time and patience."

"I have a great deal of time, David, and I'll muster what patience I can, but I haven't grown more tolerant with age."

"Are we more or less alone?"

"My wife's at a meeting of her church committee. So if you have designs on my life you may take it without interference." There was a harmonic of fear in his voice.

Morgan gazed at him, "I believe you'll feel differently after you've heard me out."

A man servant came into the study carrying a silver serving tray. As he poured coffee, Morgan said, "Dawntree Farms is quite a spread, Hugh."

The elder man nodded: "Now, in my waning days, when I least have need of it, I have all the money one could hope for."

"Ever regret leaving?"

McDairmid accepted a teacup from the servant. "For a time, yes, but the desire for public service faded. Today, who would want to be a part of the Agency? Not I. Certainly not you."

The servant left the study and closed the door. McDairmid said, "We're quite alone now, and I want to be entirely frank with you. If I feel you should be turned over to the authorities I will so tell you, though I'll delay notification until you have, say, a four-hour start. Palmer Syce was one of my dearest friends, and his death affects me deeply. I don't know whether you killed him or not. You say you didn't. Obviously you had compelling reasons for coming here, I would judge, so I'm prepared to listen."

"If you have a tape-recording system here, I'd welcome your turning it on."

"It *is* on," said McDairmid.

"Are you in touch with Robert Dobbs?"

"Indirectly."

"What does that mean?"

"I may decide to tell you . . . later."

"All right. I asked because this began with Dobbs."

Morgan told him the story, refilling his coffee cup until the silver pot was empty. McDairmid interrupted occasionally to query a point and, when Morgan finished, rose unsteadily and moved to a window. After a while he said, "What is it you want from me?"

"Surely you know."

McDairmid turned. "You want to know if Roger really defected, whether Roger Hargrave was Dormouse, our Kremlin source."

Morgan nodded.

McDairmid moved to his desk and sat down. "Before I attempt to answer that I want to clear the air between us. First, I am convinced that you did not murder Palmer, and I think you are a brave man. Whether you will long survive is questionable, but I admire your perseverance. Dobbs's role in all this is incomprehensible. Either he is a moron or an extraordinarily clever and complex manipulator. Kozlov is beyond me since I had no personal experience of the KGB—your evaluation would be far more significant than mine. The attempt on you in Berlin raises grave doubts about your cover and the reliability of Broom Ten Eyck. Now, repeat the telephone number this Crowly gave you."

"Seven-five-eight, nine-one-five-seven."

McDairmid wrote it down, then dialed. Presently he replaced the receiver and nodded. "Disconnected. Very well, I am confident I can determine its previous location. It may take a day or so, and you can telephone me from wherever you happen to be. This inquiry I will have to make in person. As you can see I am somewhat limited in my ability to get about, the unfortunate result of riding to hounds at age seventy. Now, you asked if I was in touch with Dobbs and I responded 'indirectly.' That was imprecise. I am in touch with the Agency itself." He rose from his desk and approached a flush door in the paneled wall. "Come with me." He pressed a button and the door opened, revealing a small elevator cage. McDairmid got in beside Morgan, the door closed, and the elevator began moving downward. After fifteen or twenty feet it stopped, the facing wall opened and McDairmid led the way into a large, windowless room whose four walls were banked with computer equipment. Large reels of tape turned slowly; panels of miniature lights blinked erratically.

"You must never mention the existence of this installation, David. It was established ten years ago as a standby retrieval system for the Agency. However, I added one or two refinements on my own initiative about which the Agency knows nothing. Not Dobbs or even the President knows I have access to the Agency's computerized information. I oversaw the transition from paper files to computerization and I did a thorough job. Every piece of paper in the Agency at that time was transferred to memory banks. Later, when I was approached about this secret installation, I agreed and oversaw it. Then, privately, I linked it to the Agency's master system. What you see here is both a remote terminal and a system that duplicates everything entered into Agency banks."

"Why did you do that?"

"It relates back to your contretemps with the McComb Committee.

237

Its members and investigators were granted access to all Agency files, and shortly afterward it was brought to my attention by one of my protégés that a certain investigator was systematically eliminating all negative references to the senator for whom he worked. So, although the Agency's central memory bank may be plundered by subpoena or Executive Order, these will not. You see, David, I am opposed to the rewriting of history, and I have done what I could in the classified world to ensure that it does not occur. Like Palmer, but in a more comprehensive way, I regard myself as a guardian of recondite knowledge. I suppose all this surprises you."

"Profoundly. It also means you have a long-range view of the country. Otherwise you wouldn't have done all this."

"Quite so. And since I have we can now make a private inquiry relative to Dormouse." He seated himself at a console, tapped away, and sat back. Letters began to appear on the fluorescent screen. Morgan stood behind him reading silently while McDairmid read aloud: "SOVIET RUSSIA SENSITIVE SOURCE: CUMULATIVE REPORT TOTAL: 128. SOURCE EVALUATION: B-2."

"Ask the date of the last Dormouse report," Morgan suggested.

McDairmid punched the query and the screen began flashing a single word: BARRIER.

"I was afraid of that," McDairmid muttered. "The information's been blocked. You should have come here a month ago."

"A month ago I wouldn't have needed to come here."

"Ah. Well, I created the system. Let's see if I can defeat it."

TWENTY-TWO

Morgan said, "Since my ignorance of computer matters is monumental, can you tell me in simple terms what you have to do?"

"Think of it as forcing a detour, or a bypass—a heart bypass, for example—to get around an obstacle." McDairmid was up now, leafing intently through a thick printout volume on a nearby table. Impatiently he closed it, yanked another from the rack. "Circuitry," he growled. "I demand that this creature obey its master. I *order* it to." Abruptly he closed the volume and returned to the console. "It's humanoid, David, don't think it isn't, but it still must obey." Rapidly he reprogrammed and sat back to watch the screen. On it appeared the sentence: DORMOUSE IS DEAD.

"Not what I asked, dammit!" He altered the program once more and now the screen displayed an answer: DIRECTOR AND MERIWETHER CONTROL ALL DORMOUSE INFORMATION.

"Ah," said McDairmid, and turned to Morgan. "Do you know who Meriwether is?"

"No."

"Why, Peyton James, of course. Obvious, isn't it? Peyton controlled all Counter-Espionage Operations. Now, back to our original query." He asked the date of the last Dormouse report, and the screen responded: CONSULT DIRECTOR OR MERIWETHER.

"Which means," McDairmid said, "that we'll get nothing more from it. You're back to human sources again."

"Because the computer is stubborn?"

"Because it can't repeat what it was never given. Dormouse information was never entrusted to the system, that's what it means."

"But you said every scrap of Agency paper was converted into your system."

Leaning back, he looked up at Morgan. "David, we did not go into the Director's personal files, and that's obviously where Dormouse material was kept."

"And remains."

"Except for Peyton's recollections." He blinked, removed his glasses and slowly polished the lenses. "Are you going to tap him?"

"I'd like to try."

"Ah . . . well, want me to pave the way with a call?"

Morgan shook his head. "It might be better if he weren't expecting me. You had your doubts about me, Hugh, but you heard me out. Peyton James might take radical action. No, I'll just ease in on him, see how he takes it. After all, I'm an Old Boy. Entitled to call informally on the Head, wouldn't you say?"

"I accept your judgment," McDairmid said. "But whatever you discuss with him, you must never mention this room."

"My oath." They got into the elevator.

As they stepped out, Morgan was glad to be free of the air-conditioning below. In contrast, McDairmid's study seemed almost humid.

"If you'll stay for dinner," McDairmid said, "we'll be delighted to have your company. And we have an adequate guest room if you care to spend the night."

"I'm grateful, Hugh, but I think it would be just as well if your wife didn't know of my visit."

"Perhaps you're right. Her sense of civic responsibility is more developed than mine. I wish I could have been of greater help to you."

"Well, you pointed me toward Peyton. That's a great deal."

"I hope it will be useful." He stretched back on his sectional lounge. He seemed drowsy, as though he were slipping into a postponed nap. "Our remaining business: the telephone number. Call me in two days."

"I will."

"Goodbye, David. I wish you success."

Morgan drove away from Dawntree Farms and its secret room, gained the Beltway around Washington, and struck north again on I-95.

After Baltimore he decided to leave the Interstate near White Plains and cut over through Danbury toward the Connecticut Valley, head north from Waterbury and stay overnight in a tourist home at Thomaston, say, or Terryville. Then after breakfast a short drive to Townsend where he had first known Roger Hargrave.

It could be, he mused, that there the circle would close.

240

The morning was bright. East of Bristol the fields along Route 6 were emerald green. Like Shannon from the air, he remembered, and felt once more the uncertainty and apprehension when his father had driven him to Townsend that first morning so long ago. He had been barely fourteen and afraid of being bullied by older, larger boys. When his father drove away leaving him alone with his unfamiliar roommate he remembered tears welling in his eyes. The first fight had come two nights later; bruises, bloody noses, yanked hair, and teeth-marks on their wrists. But after he had proved his willingness to fight, the upperclassmen left him alone and no resentment remained, only a consuming desire to excel.

The road from the village to the school was narrow, turtle-backed and lined with ancient oaks. The entrance posterns were topped by decorative wrought-iron that formed the name of the school and, below it, the date: 1789. From there the road meandered past the playing fields: soccer, football, and lacrosse. An arrow pointed down a trail to the trout stream, and Morgan remembered dragging boulders from its freshets to help rebuild the ice-damaged dam, reforming the broad pond where there was canoeing and fishing in spring and fall. The indoor hockey rink stood in a nearby clearing, silent now, but Morgan could recall the scrape of skates, the whap of pucks against the wooden sides, the cheers and excitement of the crowd . . . enthusiastic parents, pretty dates. . . . All so long ago.

The road curved through the pines until he could see the old brick water tower, and beyond it the massive fieldstone quadrangle. Near it, the refectory so closely modeled on Magdalen's great dining-hall.

He glimpsed the theater, the chapel, the gym and science buildings, then the headmaster's house tucked off to one side. Like the other buildings it was constructed of heavy local stone, roofed with slate, covered with greening ivy. By custom, each new boy took tea there, served by the Head and his wife, while his manners and conversational abilities were quietly appraised.

Bells chimed. First period was ending. He drove into the visitors parking area near the central administration building, and through the quad entrance saw Townsend boys burdened with books, crossing on the walks. Some wore quilted, down-lined jackets over their tweed coats, button-down shirts and repp or paisley ties. In his day, flannel slacks had been *de rigeur* by custom and edict; now the young scholars seemed to be wearing cords and desert boots. As he got out of the Monte Carlo he saw a friendly scuffle break out among three younger boys and felt his throat tighten. He had wanted Bill to come here, but

241

his son's heart was set on one of the service academies, and so he had taken the military school route.

He went through the Gothic archway, right over foot-smoothed slabs into the cool dimness of the entrance. To the receptionist, he said, "I'd like to see Mr. James. I'm an old friend."

"Oh." She fidgeted with chain-hung glasses. "The Head isn't here right now. But if you're an old friend, why don't you go over to his house? It's . . ." she began to point, but Morgan said, "I know the way. Thank you."

He returned through the archway as chimes sounded the beginning of second period. Odd that Peyton wasn't in his office yet. Perhaps he'd been banqueting in Hartford or New York and needed to sleep in.

Rather than move the Monte Carlo, Morgan walked along the west side of the quad and glimpsed his fourth form room set under the eaves, leaded panes glinting in the morning sun. So much for nostalgia, he thought; more than thirty years since I studied up there, hunched over my desk reading about Tarquinius the Proud, *septimus rex Romanae*. Life turned out far differently than I could ever conceive.

As he came around the quad, Morgan could see the Head's house, inhabited now by Peyton James. (. . . *of which one part is inhabited by Belgae*. . . .) Peyton had been at Townsend at least a decade ahead of Hargrave. They must not have known each other until Roger entered the Agency, after which they were probably in frequent touch. And if the computer readout was correct, James had launched Dormouse, controlled his activities in the Soviet Union.

The grounds around the house were well kept; early flowers poking through the tilled borders, rosebushes trimmed and budding. Peyton would keep the gardeners busy, sacking the greenhouse regularly for shrubs and potted plants.

Morgan went up the slab walk and rang the doorbell. After a time the door opened and a thin, white-haired woman said, "Yes? May I help you?"

"I'm looking for Mr. James."

"I'm Mrs. James. If you're a parent, the dean. . . ."

"No, I have personal business with your husband. I . . . you see, we were in the Agency together."

Fear flickered in her eyes and Morgan said quickly, "It's just a friendly call, ma'am. I was nearby, and I thought I'd just stop in."

She wet her lips. "What is your name?"

"He'll remember Meriwether, I'm sure."

The door closed. Morgan leaned against the jamb and waited. He thought he heard raised voices, but the sounds could have come from the quad. Mrs. James impressed him as meek to the point of being cowed. Morgan wondered why.

The door opened. Mrs. James said, "Please come in."

Morgan followed her into a neat, well-decorated living room. She gave him a hesitant, awkward smile and disappeared. Morgan sat down.

Since Morgan's last visit to the room the furniture had been changed, the old massive pieces replaced by Chippendale and petit-point. The remembered atmosphere of sherry and tobacco smoke purged to near sterility. Voices above, and presently heavy footsteps on the stair treads. Peyton James came into the room.

He was a large man, almost as tall as Ten Eyck, the bridge of his nose flattened, hair crisply curling in the Roman mode. He wore a Harris tweed suit, striped button-down shirt, and a small bow tie. Halting, he stared at Morgan, said "Meriwether, is it?" and came closer. "Morgan! My God, what are you doing here?"

"I've been traveling," Morgan said without rising. "Picking up things here and there."

"You were supposed to be in Europe."

"Why Europe?"

"That's where you killed Palmer—Oxford it was."

"So you think I killed him. Why would I want to do that?"

"God knows." He swallowed, sat down.

"You didn't expect me and you're not pleased to see me. Shabby welcome for an Old Boy."

James looked down at his knees, brushed an invisible piece of lint from his trousers. "You're a wanted man, Morgan. I can't harbor you from the authorities. It would be bad for me. You'll have to leave."

"Because of Roger? Did I kill him, too?"

"I . . . well, did you?"

"That's how the legend goes. But I was only present at the scene; that's been my misfortune lately. What do you say to that?"

"I don't understand, Morgan. Why are you so . . . hostile?"

Morgan's hands opened and closed. "Aren't you surprised I know about Meriwether?"

James attempted a short laugh. "My Agency pseudo? I supposed you remembered."

Morgan shook his head. "It was *one* of your old pseudonyms and it was barred information. At my level, in the field, I never had access to it. But the Director knew, of course."

James's eyes flickered. "Yes, the Director knew."

"Which Director? Dobbs?"

Half-impatiently James said, "I don't know what Dobbs knows about anything."

"But he knows about Dormouse, doesn't he? Tell me about Dormouse, Peyton. He seems to be the root of all my troubles."

The headmaster was recovering his composure. "I'm pressed for time . . . in the middle of a big endowment drive . . . meetings." He glanced at his watch. "I don't mean to be inhospitable. Truth is my wife hasn't been well, not at all well. I'm concerned about her health. So many things coming together. . . . I lead a quiet sort of life now, well away from the mainstream, and I'm not equipped to handle the unexpected."

"You have my sympathy. I've survived a month of unexpected events, most of them unpleasant, some fairly violent. I saw Hargrave's brains blown out the back of his skull; that was unexpected. I picked up Palmer Syce from the hall floor where he was murdered . . . that was unexpected, too. The girl I was living with was killed by two men both of whom, praise God, are themselves victims of violent deeds. A midnight assassin came into my room . . . but that's all a different world, Peyton, far removed from a headmaster's study. I wouldn't expect you to understand those things, how shocking the really unexpected can be. From here it's the far side of the moon."

Morgan leaned forward. "I'm not going to take a lot of your time, Peyton, because I haven't got a lot of time left. All I want from you is a couple of answers and I'm on my way, neither of us worse off for the encounter." His eyes never left the headmaster, whose fingers moved fitfully. "Your answers are important—I might even say crucial—to my survival. Ever since I was set up in Geneva I've been dodging enemies as implacable as the Furies. I've had to use a rather tired brain, become unaccustomedly resourceful, meet violence with violence. And there's this curious information network that seems to operate among colleagues of your Agency generation, not unlike what I was accustomed to in prison. You're all on similar wavelengths, and I never know whether my arrival is anticipated or not. You, at least, weren't expecting me."

James shook his head.

"I know Roger Hargrave was Dormouse, that you launched and controlled him."

James's eyes narrowed. "How could you know?"

"Roger told me."

"When?"

"Minutes before he was murdered. He demanded I be his escort home so he'd have someone he could confide in. That's why people have been trying to kill me—because they correctly assume I know." He leaned back in his chair. "But why is that so bad, Peyton? I've proved beyond the experience of most Agency types that I can be trusted with secrets. Hell, I went to prison rather than talk. And that, among other reasons, is why Roger trusted me. Why is it so important to someone that the Dormouse identity not be known, even by me? And then there's Kozlov, a general now, Peyton."

"*Kozlov?*" James's face paled. "What about him?"

"We held a most interesting conversation in London. In his embassy, in the KGB *rezidentura*. Kozlov disclaims responsibility for anything and everything. In fact, he suggests that persons high in the Agency are responsible. What do you make of that?"

For a time Peyton James was silent. Finally he said, "I think we should take a walk . . . I prefer the open air. I'll get a rod, tell my wife we're going down to the pond. She's a listener, I wouldn't want her to overhear."

He got up and left the room. Morgan rose and stretched. There was no comfort in the room; it was attractive and clean, but impersonal. Not at all what he remembered. It could have been the lobby of a small country inn.

"Let's go," James said from the doorway. He was wearing a hat flecked with trout flies and a canvas jacket over his tweed coat. He carried waders in one hand, a fly rod in the other. A sheathed fishing knife rode on his hip.

Morgan opened the door for him, closed it after they were both outside the house, and glimpsed movement behind one of the upstairs panes. James's wife? He wondered.

Together they strolled toward the woods, taking the dirt path shortcut to the pond that lay down the hillside. Classes were in session, no one visible on campus. Except for Mrs. James, Morgan thought, no one knew they were together.

"Good fishing this year," James remarked, swishing his rod energetically. "We still stock annually. What were you doing in Key West?"

"A little subsistence fishing; ate some, sold the rest. After prison there wasn't much for me to go back to. I . . . I took what I could get."

"Life," James said, "can be very unfair."

I've heard that before, thought Morgan.

"You ought to be able to get all this cleared up," James continued, "and lead a more appropriate sort of life."

"I'd like nothing better. That's why I've come to you, Peyton. You're the Grand Master, after all. Colleagues along the way have been enormously helpful in enabling me to piece things together; a couple of facts from you and the puzzle will be solved."

They were going down a narrow ravine, pebbles and damp earth sliding underfoot, making it difficult to remain upright.

"There's the foresters cabin up there." James gestured to the high bank beyond the pond. "Rebuilt since your time, though. Kids got the chimney too hot one winter, soot caught fire and burned the place down. So, the class rebuilt it. Larger and better, too. I have a lot of faith in young people, David. I might have been cynical once, but in this job I've learned to respect today's youth. They're capable of so much. . . ."

Morgan thought of his daughter. Shelley had proved herself capable of causing sorrow and anguish; he wondered if she would ever be capable of anything more.

". . . believe how bright they are," James was saying. "For every one we take we have to turn away eleven. And doomsayers wonder about the future of private secondary schools."

Taken from a recent speech, Morgan thought, as James reached the flat side of the pond. The headmaster plucked a fly from his hat and bent it on the tapered line.

Morgan said, "Did you know Hargrave was coming back?"

"No." He swished the line back and forth, stripping it from the reel.

"When you sent him to the Soviets, made it appear that he was defecting, how long was he supposed to stay?"

"There was no time limit. Roger, you see, appeared to be abnormally motivated. We assumed he'd return in five or so years, but it didn't happen."

"Why not?"

The line was whipping back and forth overhead, adding to its length. Finally James made the cast, the line snaked out, the dry fly settled near the far shore of the pond.

"Why not?" Morgan repeated as James concentrated on the fly.

246

"Because. . . . Well, David," the line was retrieved rapidly, "the sorry truth is that Dormouse went sour." The reel whirred, the surface of the pond rippled gently.

"How?"

James examined the fly, shook water from it, and exchanged it for one with barred hackles. "I don't know how. Dormouse was my operation and I detected it going sour in less than two years. Dormouse was sending back information that more and more became weighted with deception material. It was my responsibility to evaluate it, and that was my evaluation."

"You thought he was doubled?"

"Not at first." He began stripping line from the reel, preparing another cast. "I thought he was being *fed* deception material, that he was sending it to us in good faith."

"And later?"

"I did a rather dangerous thing, David. I met him in the Soviet Union—in the Hermitage, as a matter of fact—and made my feelings known. Roger made it a personal thing; accused me of shortsightedness, incompetence. Said I wasn't the proper person to evaluate his reports. I regret to say that we parted on a rather bitter note. That was the last time I saw him."

"So you concluded that he'd been doubled."

The fly lit two-thirds of the way across the pond. The woods were still except for the sound of water gushing over the spillway at the downstream edge of the pond.

"I concluded," said Peyton James, "that he had truly defected, that he was theirs from the beginning. That must shock you—it did me—but you came here for answers, did you not? And I'm telling you things that hardly anyone knows."

"Yes, I'm shocked, but I'm also grateful for your confidences. Do you mind telling me how you concluded he hadn't been doubled?"

"Built into the communication system were innocuous things that could be added to warn me he was in trouble, not to believe what he was sending. I never received such signals. So it had to be that Hargrave was determined to make me believe the Dormouse information was valid when in many cases it was demonstrably false."

"Wasn't that a fool's game; to keep sending back noncredible reports? How could that benefit him . . . or Kozlov, if Kozlov was his controller?"

"That's just the point, isn't it? Roger was *their* loyal and faithful servant, not ours."

A trout rose to take the fly. James tensed, but the lure was spat out, refused.

Morgan rubbed the side of his face. "And nothing to the contrary ever materialized?"

"No." The headmaster retrieved his line and said, "Too late in the day. This is best done at dawn and dusk." Removing the trout fly he returned it to the brim of his hat. "Until his death Roger Hargrave was one of theirs. Why else would he try to report the Soviets preparing to strike China unless it was to gain for the Soviets a guarantee that we would either not intervene at all or grant their fervent hope that we side with them against the Yellow Peril?" He laughed gruffly. "Preposterous."

Morgan swallowed, throat suddenly tight. "Preposterous."

Peyton James was looking up at the treetops. "Doves," he said, "first this season. Good rural harbingers, you know." He picked up his unused waders. "Shall we go back?"

"One final thing, Peyton. Why was Roger killed?"

"To avoid embarrassment, I assume."

"Whose embarrassment?"

"The Soviets'."

"Wouldn't ours have been as great?"

"Possibly, possibly. A returned defector is a very delicate piece of veal. You remember Dr. Otto John? What were the West Germans to do with him when he returned? What would the British do with their MI-6 laddies should they come back?" He shook his head, began climbing up the ravine ahead of Morgan. "My opinion is that Kozlov had him killed, not our people."

"That doesn't simplify my problem, does it? I mean, Kozlov could have killed me in Oxford or London, but he didn't. Why the later attempts?"

"You mean Berlin? That's a good place to dispose of people. You're a well-known former spy, and Berlin has an earned reputation as a place where espionage scores are settled, does it not? Kozlov wasn't going to liquidate you on his doorstep, after all. In England the KGB people under diplomatic cover can get away with a good deal, but the British do balk at outright murder."

"I know," Morgan said wryly, "they want me for Palmer's." *How did he know it was Berlin?*

Up ahead of him James was panting. "I've an idea. You say Dobbs got you into this. Why not recontact him, tell him to get the British off your back? He could do that, in fact he should."

"Wonder why I never thought of that?"

"Call from my place if you like."

"Well, thanks for the suggestion. I'll want to think it over a bit. You know, if I'm wrong the mistake could be fatal."

James was standing at the top. "Come, you must be exaggerating. In America who's going to harm you? Not like Europe, you know." His manner had become open and avuncular, face genial. Morgan could see why he had been chosen Head. No harm in America? he thought. No bombs, no dynamite booby traps, no GI limpet on the skeg. Oh, no. Innocence at play.

Together they walked back toward the school. On the left was the old graveyard that had first been used when Townsend was only a room attached to the founder's church. Some of the stones were slanting; they always did in the spring when the soil was moist from rain.

Morgan gestured at the graveyard. "Where was Roger buried?"

"Litchfield, the family plot. There'll be a small item on it in the next alumni magazine. Not planning to visit his grave, are you?"

"No, this is my last stop before Canada. Unless, of course, I get a sympathetic ear from the Director. That would change everything."

"Of course it would."

For a few moments they walked in silence. Then Morgan said, "There's another reason I ought to talk with Dobbs, should have mentioned it earlier."

"And what is that?"

"Perhaps the most important thing Hargrave told me."

"Oh?"

"The name of a Soviet agent *within* the Agency."

"My God! Who?"

"Peyton, I can't burden you with knowledge as sensitive as that. The revelation stunned me. If I were to name him, you wouldn't believe it."

Disappointed, James said, "Yes, you must inform Dobbs. Think of the implications to our security."

"I've been thinking of them ever since Roger was killed."

Chimes again from the bell tower. James said, "Duty calls, I'm afraid. Chairman of the development fund's lunching with me today;

we've fallen a bit short on subscription giving, and I'm looking to him to make up the deficit. Otherwise you'd be welcome to stay any amount of time."

"You've been more than accommodating, Peyton. Do you remember if Mrs. Hargrave was at the interment?"

"Roger's widow? What was her name. . . . ? Adrian? Anita? Can't think." He shook his head disgustedly. "I *may* have known but I really can't remember." He glanced at Morgan. "Is it in some way important?"

"I wondered if his wife and children would be staying in Russia."

"Very likely. Naught for them here, is there?" He chuckled. "Well, the luck of the road t'ye, as the Irish say. When all this clears up and settles down, why not come back for a real stay at the school? Bring rod or shotgun."

"I might just do that," Morgan said, shook hands with Headmaster James and watched him walk off toward his house, fly rod flexing jauntily.

Morgan took the other lane, reaching his car as chimes sounded and third period got under way.

He guided the Monte Carlo back along the winding route, past playing fields and meadows he hardly saw.

That Peyton James was a liar was clear enough. The question was: Had he lied about important things? He was not a careful liar, though, for he had mentioned details about Morgan's life and travels that he had no reason to know unless he was being kept apprised of developments.

First: He should not have known that Morgan had been living in Key West;

Second: Morgan had not specified Berlin as the site of an attempt on his life. Yet James knew.

Third: Hargrave's China report should have been known only to the translator, Broom Ten Eyck, but James appeared totally familiar with the contents. How? Broom was already suspect for the Berlin incident. James's parroting details of the report Broom had translated aloud for Morgan at Nerja meant Ten Eyck had passed the report along.

To someone.

Morgan took the road toward Hartford, wanting to get off rural byways where the car's Florida plate might attract unwelcome notice. The pond area would have been ideal if James had decided to kill and dispose of him. Morgan, realizing the potential of such a setting, had not challenged James's lies or queried his detailed knowledge. He had fabricated the Canada destination, while letting the headmaster think he might confer with Dobbs.

Dobbs, yes, but not gullibly.

There were other things to do.

Starting tonight.

III

There were gentlemen and there
were seamen in the navy of Charles II.
But the seamen were not gentlemen,
and the gentlemen were not seamen.

Macaulay
History of England

TWENTY-THREE

IT was a pale, gibbous moon, occluded by passing clouds, but it yielded enough light to outline the narrow path as Morgan made his way down from the road through the woods.

In Hartford he had bought a dark jogging suit and running shoes, a ski-mask to conceal his face and hair. At Sears he bought a sheath-knife, a flashlight, a short pry-bar, and a utility belt to hold them around his waist, freeing his gloved hands for other things.

Before midnight he had driven his car into a field half a mile from the school, maneuvering it behind thick bracken. When he got out to change clothing, pheasants cawed protestingly and whirred away. He hoped he was not treading on their nests.

Now he was within the school's broad boundaries, breathing easily despite the prolonged walk. Peyton James's short morning climb had brought him up panting at the top of the ravine, and Morgan reflected that fly fishing provided insufficient exercise for a man of the head-master's build and age.

After a while the woods thinned and Morgan could see clearing ahead. On it stood the foresters cabin, its shingled roof silhouetted against the oval pond. Morgan knelt at the edge of the clearing and looked around. The cool night air was still, nothing stirred. Moon-light glinted briefly from the placid surface of the pond. As yesterday, the only sound was that of water gushing over the bouldered dam.

His watch showed 12:42, and he remembered the watchman's rounds as on the even hours. Old Tim, long dead by now, had caught him late one Saturday night when Morgan was trying to climb back into his dorm. Instead of reporting him, Tim had given him a brief lecture on abiding by the rules, ending with a kick to the rump before unlocking the ground-floor entry.

The school was larger now and the guard force probably bigger. Still, the routine should be the same.

He got up and moved across the clearing to the cabin door. It was locked, as he expected, so he tried each window in turn, finding one left open by last weekend's student campers.

Morgan went in through the window, closed and secured it, then unlocked the front door. Moonlight through the skylight showed a huge fireplace and a dozen wooden bunks that were replacements since his time. New, too, were the tanned cowhides strewn across the otherwise bare flooring, bunkhouse style. Morgan went to a bunk positioned between windows and shadowed, lay down on the mattress, and stretched out. The wool mask made his face itch, so he pulled it off.

Morgan was tired. Dissembling with the headmaster had been the greatest strain, keeping track of James's careless errors while framing his own replies to calm the older man's suspicions. By now Dobbs would have been notified of the visit, alerted to Morgan's Canadian plans.

Will they be looking for me on the Northway tonight?

For an hour he dozed, sleeping in brief stretches, and then he came fully awake. It was a few minutes before two and time to go. A shaft of moonlight made the cabin glow.

Morgan stretched his muscles, then went out the front door, leaving it unlocked in case he decided to return.

He crossed the moonlit clearing and took the path toward the school. By now only the guards should be awake, making their two o'clock rounds. He passed the graveyard where the Reverend Micah Townsend lay, dead of typhoid at the age of fifty-three, dying as Napoleon left Elba to light the torch of Empire once again.

Leaving the narrow road, Morgan found cover near the Quad and listened. He heard the jingling of keys on the watchman's chain. Light flared across an upper rank of windows, then all was dark and silent as the watchman moved away.

From beside a clump of birch Morgan surveyed Peyton's house. The windows were dark. He had not noticed a guard dog on his morning visit, but he would soon find out. Moonlight silvered the roofing slates, made the tall antenna glow. Now was the time.

He darted to the rear of the house and moved along the side until he reached the kitchen door. Turning the knob he pulled, but the door was bolted. He pressed upward on the nearby window and found its pivot latch set.

Sliding the pry-bar under the window he levered it on the ledge, adding weight slowly until he heard the latch screws tear loose. He paused and listened: no dog, no human footsteps. He raised the window and crawled in.

Again he listened, closed the window and unlocked the kitchen door before going into the dining room.

He covered the ground floor a room at a time, found Mrs. James sleeping peacefully in a bedroom that held oxygen equipment, a collection of medical magazines, and a padded rocking chair. Apparently her health was even poorer than her husband had suggested.

Holding the stair railing Morgan moved toward the upper floor, putting his weight on the steps' forward risers to minimize creaking, going slowly, carefully, until he reached the carpeted hall.

The master bedroom was at the front and it spanned the width of the house. In a four-poster bed lay Peyton James asleep, and Morgan decided to search the other rooms before waking the headmaster. Next door was a boy's room, walls hung with college pennants and blow-up posters, the single bed carefully made but empty. Adjoining was a girl's room, primly decorated. Its lace-trimmed bed was empty, too.

He passed by bathrooms, paused at the attic door and decided against ascending. That could be done later.

Next came the guest room. He opened the door slowly. A bar of moonlight showed rumpled bed covers outlining a sleeping figure. Morgan closed the door behind him, approached the bed, and shined his light for an instant on the sleeping face.

In profile, hair fanned out on the pillows, was Alexandra Hargrave.

TWENTY-FOUR

HIS hand gripped the flashlight. Breath caught in his throat.
Alex.

And James pretended he couldn't remember her name.

That was why they had gone to the pond; to avoid Morgan meeting her by chance. Was that also why Mrs. James had seemed so fearful?

In sleep Alex's face was relaxed, almost youthful again, none of the photographed strain apparent.

For whose sake was James so intent on keeping them apart?

Gradually Morgan's breathing returned to normal. A kaleidoscope of questions flashed through his mind. How long had she been here? What had she been told about Morgan? And why was she here at all?

Morgan pulled off the ski-mask, got a towel from the bathroom and knelt beside her bed. Before he pressed the roped towel to her mouth he remembered their love-making so long ago, the sweetness of her lips and breasts, the comfort of her thighs. . . . "*Alex,*" he whispered. "*Alex,*" and gagged her.

Arms flailing, legs kicking, she fought him, but he kept whispering her name, then his, and finally she lay back, fully awake, breath whistling through her nostrils. "It's David," he said. "David Morgan. I didn't kill Roger. I have to talk with you. Please don't make a sound."

Cautiously he lifted the cumbersome towel, saying, "Don't call for Peyton, he's not your friend."

Silently she sat up, drawing her nightgown together, staring at him with frightened eyes. "Your hair," she whispered, "all white. I wouldn't have known you. Oh, David, Peyton said you were hiding in Europe."

"I was here yesterday morning. Did he tell you that?"

"No."

Rising, he sat on the edge of the bed, took her hand. "We must talk," he said. "Why are you here?"

"At the funeral, Peyton invited me to stay while I sorted things out."

"Is he debriefing you?"

"Yes."

"For what reason?"

"He was Roger's case officer—you knew that."

"Only recently." He took a deep breath. "Where are your children?"

"In Moscow. They weren't permitted to come." Her lips trembled. "They didn't want to come, anyway; they view their father as a traitor to Russia who deserved to be killed." She began to cry. Morgan drew her face onto his shoulder, stroked her hair until the spasms ended. Alexandra dried her eyes. "I'm so confused. I thought Roger would be free, that we would join him and live happily ever after. Instead, ever since he left Vienna it's been a nightmare. *Horrible*." She shuddered.

"I know," he said, "because I've shared it."

"He said you killed another man . . . in England. Someone else from the Agency."

"Palmer Syce. I had no reason to end his life, and I didn't. I respected him." He shook his head. "Get dressed and I'll take you where we can talk."

Her face showed apprehension. "Where, David?"

"The cabin by the pond. I was there earlier, it's empty. The boys only use it on weekends." When she did not move, he said, "Don't be afraid, Alex. We have to talk . . . for *both* our lives."

"You . . . you promise not to harm me?"

"I swear it. My God, we were lovers."

"Yes. But lovers can hurt each other." Slowly she pushed aside the covers. Morgan rose and drew her to her feet. "No lights," he warned.

"Turn your back."

He heard her moving behind him, and in a few moments she took his hand. "Tiptoes?"

"Exactly."

She was holding her moccasins as he led her up the corridor to the staircase, and they descended in single file. She followed him into the kitchen and through the doorway to the moon-bathed yard. The time was 2:30, the watchmen would be back from their rounds.

Until they reached the cover of the woods they did not speak. Then her first words were, "Why did you come tonight?"

"Instinct more than anything. While I was talking with Peyton he pretended he couldn't remember your name, denied knowing where

260

you were. My arrival shocked him to the point of hostility, and I began to sense an odd atmosphere about the house, a feeling of emotions, events suppressed . . . like the shadow-wife. How can I express it? Disjointed. Things were off-key. So I came back."

"Lord, how you frightened me!"

She was wearing jeans and a short fur jacket. Her soft moccasins were silent on the trail. Morgan pointed out the cabin, and at the clearing edge they halted long enough to listen and glance around. Clouds covered the moon as they dashed for the doorway, and when they were inside, Morgan shut the door. Alexandra said, "Was Roger ever here?"

"No. A fire destroyed the original cabin but this one is much the same; the fireplace survived."

A lighter flared at the end of her cigarette. She walked to one of the log chairs and sat down. "I have to go back to Russia," she said, "because of the children. I hate everything about it, but it's their home. It's almost all they've ever known. This . . ." she looked around ". . . is the imperialist world they hate passionately. But they are my children. The boy Michael looks so much like Roger. . . ." Her voice wavered, trailed off. She blotted her eyes on a furred sleeve. Finally she said, "We had so *much* together—truly we loved each other. And it broke my heart when we learned of his cancer. Did . . . did he tell you?"

"It was evident he was very sick, but we had only a few minutes together, we couldn't cover a lifetime." He looked up at the pale skylight. "I was to have been killed, too."

Her hand touched his.

"I'm talking out of sequence, Alex, and your right to the full story is greater than anyone's."

She nodded wordlessly, and he began.

The telling took long. At times Alexandra interjected questions and Morgan patiently explained.

After he finished she got up and walked over to the fireplace, tossed a dead cigarette into it and lighted another.

"I had no idea," she said slowly, "no idea at all. I've been so out of things." Tears showed in her eyes. "Nothing turned out right, the way it was supposed to. Oh, *David*." She cried, quietly at first, then racked by sobs. This time she sought the comfort of his arms.

After a while she dried her eyes. "I'll be all right, David. This is not the time for me to break down."

He said, "Roger told me he was Dormouse, said everything would

261

be explained in time. That's what I want you to do, Alex, explain and authenticate." Abruptly he shrugged. "It doesn't really make any difference now, does it? Roger's dead, your children alienated."

"Roger was murdered before he could clear his name."

"And Peyton's been urging you to keep quiet."

She nodded. "He said other men's lives depended on my silence."

He grunted. "That's probably true, but what kind of men? *His* kind . . . his and Dobbs's. It's their lives and reputations he wants to preserve. And I've stirred him up. The last thing I told him yesterday morning was that Roger had revealed the identity of a high-level Soviet penetration of the Agency. Roger didn't, but James can't be sure."

"*Is* there such a penetration of the Agency?"

"It seems so, but I have no evidence. I feel like a player going in and out of a game he doesn't understand. Perhaps you've had dreams like that."

"One of mine has me entering a room of people who alternately ignore me, then make fun of me in a language I can't comprehend. That runs very close to my actual experience in Russia. In another dream I'm naked on a crowded beach where everyone else is fully dressed because the weather is quite cold. And, of course, it's usually cold in Russia." She sat down and sighed. "It was Peyton who made the proposal to Roger that he appear to defect to the Russians, then gain their confidence. Peyton said it would take about two years. Roger was to reveal certain operations in order to validate himself. Then he was to give them deception material while reporting valid intelligence back to Peyton. After five years, he promised, we could come home. Five years. . . ." She shook her head. "I remember how desperate we felt after eight years had gone by. Yet we continued to believe there must be good reasons to keep us there even though the importance of Roger's jobs was diminishing year by year."

"Did Roger and Peyton ever meet in the Soviet Union?"

She shook her head. "He would have told me if that had happened. Roger once suggested a meeting in Leningrad—at the Hermitage— but the only time he went there I was with him and no contact was made."

"James told me he'd met Roger at the Hermitage, so that was another lie. Alex, he also told me the operation went sour because Roger had been cooperating with the KGB all the way."

"An absolute *lie*! Colonel Kozlov, for some reason, lost confidence in Roger. Kozlov never said so, but Roger began to be shunted aside. His access to reportable intelligence was diminishing and we began to live with the fear of discovery."

"I think you *were* discovered, but Kozlov couldn't denounce Roger; it would have meant his own head. So he handled things cleverly. In London he had me brought to his embassy and we talked half the night—incidentally, he's a general now—while he attempted to persuade me he wasn't behind Roger's murder. I told Kozlov I'd believe him if he let you come to the West. And he did."

Her face was wooden. "It was a void," she said with effort.

"What?"

"Leaving Stockholm was like dropping into a void. Then Kozlov was there, helpful, attentive. At first." She looked up at Morgan. "Are you sure the man who brought you in was Kozlov?"

"Yes."

"He has look-alikes, you know, at least two of them."

"It was Kozlov." Something was sidetracking her thoughts. "I knew him in the Mid-East," Morgan told her. "We were antagonists at close remove. Why?"

"Because he let you go without harming you. His veneer is superficial. Beneath it is callous cruelty. I know."

"Well, that night he was like an old school chum. Believe me it was a pleasant surprise."

"I don't think I understand."

"Because," said Morgan, "he saw me as more useful alive and on the run. Oh, he took a calculated risk because he knew I knew at least something of the Dormouse episode. His gamble was that I didn't know enough to talk about it credibly, that I had no proof. So I'm free and you're here because it was in his interest to allow it. Now let's go back to why Roger was chosen for the mission."

"Yes."

Morgan took a deep breath. "Others beside Roger had the requisite skills and intelligence to be a double agent targeted against the Soviets. Why Roger? Because Roger also had the qualifications to become Director. Dulles hand-picked him out of Oxford, remember, and Roger's own abilities moved him up the ladder at an early age. That, unfortunately, didn't sit well with the Founding Fathers who realized the Agency was ripe for professional leadership from within. Until Roger outstripped his seniors they thought they had the plum in hand." He studied her immobile face. "Sending Roger to Russia as a defector effectively ended his candidacy, so he was conned into doing it, accepting the risks and allowing his name to be blackened with treason. It was a noble, selfless thing he did, but the reasons pressed on him were ignoble. He was betrayed. His return—and yours—was blocked. I don't believe there was any intention of retrieving him, ever."

Her body shuddered.

"When I was able to cull Agency files for Dormouse references all that could be forced was the number of his reports; a hundred and twenty-eight, Alex. Further details, questions, were referred to the Director and or Meriwether. Well, the Director who approved the Dormouse project was fired in the wake of Roger's apparent defection and then he died. Meriwether turned out to be Peyton James, and he hasn't shown himself anxious to talk."

"Why should I?" came a voice from the doorway, and when they turned they saw Peyton James standing there, fully dressed, a shooting vest with rows of 12-gauge shells and his tweed jacket, a shotgun in the crook of his arm. The headmaster, out early for a round of trap, should anyone see him.

"You were doing brilliantly, Morgan. Fascinating recital, but no master can allow a student to outshine him, now can he? No, stay there, the two of you. Alexandra, my dear, I'm truly sorry that Morgan came back to discuss the past with you. It was better buried than tilled again by Morgan. And you, sir, I truly hoped you were going to Canada, but I couldn't quite believe you would fall in with my suggestion so readily, and so my sleep tonight was troubled . . . and restless. David, you were quite valuable as a fugitive, you kept the spotlight focused on yourself and away from the Agency. . . ."

". . . and its sins."

"Of commission and omission. And our tedious, parochial, internal rivalries. But you tired of fleeing. You determined to turn and fight. That was a mistake, David."

Morgan glanced at Alexandra. "I don't want any harm to come to her. Surely she's suffered enough at your hands."

James walked into the cabin and took a stance, feet apart, on one of the tanned hides that covered the bare floor. He was erect, imposing; the headmaster suddenly taking charge of an unruly situation. "To suffer is the destiny of some," he intoned. "I've been truly fond of you, Alexandra, and I admired Roger enormously. But there are imperatives to be considered when dealing with the destiny of nations."

"Whatever that means," Morgan said.

264

"It means that compassionate inclinations must, from time to time, be suppressed," James said with a touch of anger. "That wasn't taught you at the Farm, but those of us who founded the Farm and the Agency around it know these simple truths. I learned in the war what it was to sacrifice a man, a team, even a city. Churchill let Coventry be destroyed in preference to revealing British access to German codes. I learned, too, from Gehlen—that man of polished cynicism—what sometimes must be done in order to survive. You, Morgan, have managed to survive. Surely you know how marvelously focused one's mind can become when simple survival is the issue."

Morgan nodded. "I managed without sacrificing others."

"You too would become ruthless in time. Consider how you've changed since the days of your naiveté; reflect on your future . . . what it might have been had you survived this time."

Alexandra said, "You're going to kill him?"

"Indeed I am."

Morgan heard her swift intake of breath. She said, "And me, aren't you, Peyton?"

"Very likely, though I may have to consult concerning details. You would have been useful. But for Morgan you would have been allowed to return to Moscow, there to live out your life in peace. Now, David, don't become incautious; I shoot trap three times a week with excellent results. I could hardly miss you at this range."

"Stay calm, Peyton. Your heart won't stand the strain."

"You noticed, eh? Lamentably, the result of sedentary living. You led me on, David, let me think you were unsuspicious. After you were gone, I realized how unwise I had been. It occurred to me that you had detected my errors. Tell me which one you noticed first."

"You said Roger's reporting was worthless. You didn't know I learned Dormouse was rated a B-2 source. I waited for other inconsistencies."

"Ah, well, I haven't had the challenge of a mind like yours for quite a time. Roger, too." He turned to Alexandra. "He was more than a match for me, though it took him a very long while to perceive the truth."

"He never did," Alexandra said quietly. "He believed in you. Always."

"Then he was too gullible to be Director," James declared. "I thought he would soon realize the situation and join Kozlov out of rage, for vengeance. But he never did?"

"No, Peyton," said Morgan, "he was loyal to the end—and optimistic, too. All he wanted in repayment for all those years was to clear his name."

James said, "Had I disposed of you yesterday Alexandra's safety would not be imperiled."

"Nor would your own," said Morgan. "I've been framed as a fugitive, so the law might have let you get away with disposing of me. But Alexandra is something else again. She's a guest in your home, your wife knows about her. And before coming here I took the precaution of letting someone know, someone who knows about Dormouse and you, someone in a position to ask hard questions, and he won't let Alexandra's disappearance pass unnoticed. You'll be asked about that, too, Headmaster . . . role model for the boys of Townsend. You think you're still a manipulator of minds and events, but you lived on the daring of others, men who were your betters by far."

James stiffened, the cords in his neck stood out. "Shut up."

"You could easily have gone to Moscow. You'd have loved the flattery, the dacha, the apartment, the chauffered car. That's what you wanted from the Agency but it was not to be had, not while men like Hargrave stood in your way. So you schemed and ended up being manipulated by a mediocrity like Dobbs. God, it must gnaw your entrails to see him in the Director's chair you'd reserved for yourself!"

"Stop! Shut up, damn you!" The shotgun barrels moved menacingly.

"The lesson you should have learned from Gehlen was to get out while you still have something the other side can use."

"*No more!*" The shotgun barrels wavered.

Suddenly Morgan fell flat on the floor and jerked the hide from under James's feet. The headmaster fell backward as Alexandra screamed.

On his knees, Morgan scrambled to the fallen man who was half-turning, trying to rise and point the shotgun at Morgan, who yelled, "*Stay down, Alex*," and twisted the shotgun from James's grip. He tossed the weapon aside, fitted his forearm under James's chin, and bore down crushingly against the windpipe.

The headmaster's booted heels pounded the bare wood floor as he struggled to get from under Morgan. Veins in his forehead stood out. His straining eyes were ghastly white. Relentlessly, Morgan forced his forearm harder against the throat while James's hands clawed at his head, trying to pry Morgan off, his body bucking convulsively.

266

Morgan hugged the headmaster in a desperate embrace and gradually the convulsions slackened, the arms fell away, and James lay still.

Morgan rolled aside and picked up the shotgun.

In a thin voice, Alexandra said, "Is he dead?"

Morgan stared down at Peyton James. From the darkness came Alexandra's muffled sobs.

Morgan's body was trembling from effort and emotion. Holding the shotgun in his left hand he knelt and touched James's neck artery. No pulse.

Rising slowly, he stared at Alexandra.

"I wanted him alive. I wanted him tried for his crimes, imprisoned for the rest of his rotten life." He glanced down at the headmaster.

Alexandra found her way to the edge of a bunk and sat down.

Morgan said, "Peyton was responsible for the years of hell you and Roger were forced to live through. Remember that. And I have one less enemy."

Alexandra said nothing.

Setting aside the shotgun, Morgan bent over, crossed James's hands, and pulled the body up and onto his back in the fireman's carry. Staggering under the headmaster's heavy frame, he went slowly out of the cabin and through bracken, down to the edge of the pond. Turning, he released James's wrists; the body dropped into the water with a noisy splash. Morgan toed it into deeper water where it floated face down and slowly disappeared. Bubbles erupted on the surface, then the pond was calm again.

Morgan retrieved the shotgun from the cabin and dropped it into the lake near where he had last seen James's body. Then he joined Alexandra at the doorway. White-faced she said, "Tell me . . . what to do."

"Go back to the house and bed. In the morning, do whatever you've been doing. Let Peyton's wife miss him, start the search, but let it all come as a surprise to you. Be concerned, anxious, but don't over-do it."

"And . . . afterward?"

He shook his head. "I can't tell you what to do with your life from now on. I know you're torn between this country and your children, but the decision has to be yours." He took her arm and guided her across the clearing to where the path began.

There she stopped and turned to him. "You won't help me decide, David?"

"I can't."

She looked away from him. "And what will happen to you?"

"I wish I knew. But you'll be safe as long as you say nothing. Confide in no one, not even your children, least of all anyone from the Agency. If you go back to Moscow you'll be under Kozlov's protection. If you stay here . . . well, there'd be no protection at all."

"But you're going to keep on, aren't you?"

"Yes. I should have forced Peyton to cooperate yesterday. Tonight, I was too busy trying to save our lives to think of making him give me more answers." He paused. "Even so, I may have enough. And we're alive."

She was silent for a while, and then her low voice said, "I might be more grateful if I cared about living." Her eyes searched his face. "Do you?"

"I care a great deal. You will, too, when you see your children again."

"I'll always remember what you've done for me . . . and for Roger."

He drew her to him, kissed her forehead. Her arms went around his shoulders, then dropped away.

Morgan glanced at his watch: nearly four o'clock. "The watchmen will be starting rounds again. I think you should be going."

She nodded, then in a quiet voice said, "David, do you ever think of that night on the water? Over all the years have you remembered?"

"You know I have."

"Did. . . ." She smiled briefly. "It's foolish of me, a middle-aged woman, I know, but I've always wondered. . . ."

"What?"

"If you loved me then . . . even a little."

"Of course I did." He kissed her temple. "Alex, it broke my heart when you went away. Would you have cared?"

"Not then, I'm afraid. But now, yes, I care, David. It means a great deal that you did. I can warm my memories with that."

They parted then, Morgan watching her figure disappear as she hastened through the woods. And when she was gone he turned and gazed at the cabin, listening for sounds of any kind. As before there was only the burbling of water over the spillway.

The moon was cleansed of clouds. Its light helped him find his way through the woods, across the field, and back to where he had left the car.

He pulled off his running gear and changed back into street clothes and leather shoes. Straightening, he stretched, saw the gliding moon, and breathed deeply. He felt tired but strangely energized.

At the far end of the field a pheasant clucked and cawed. Beyond the tree line the sky was just beginning to lighten.

Morgan got into the car and started the engine.

Now, at last, he knew what he had to do.

TWENTY-FIVE

IT was close to noon when Morgan parked the Monte Carlo at the Philadelphia airport. After leaving Townsend he had phoned Jill and asked her to join him; her flight was due in fourteen minutes.

Inside the airport he positioned himself at a telephone near the Eastern arrival gate and called Hugh McDairmid in Leesburg. When McDairmid came to the phone Morgan said, "Any luck on the disconnected number?"

"Oh. You. I wondered if you'd call. Yes, I'm glad to report that I was partly successful: no name, but an address. In Washington. Out Connecticut near the District line. Surprised?"

"Not really, were you?"

"Only somewhat." He gave the street number to Morgan who wrote it down. "Anything else I can do?"

"Not now, thanks."

"I do hope you'll visit again. I hate unfinished business."

"Thanks again, Hugh."

"More than welcome. Goodbye."

Morgan leaned against the wall by the phone, tired from the long drive. Suddenly he spotted Jill in the line of passengers: pale blue slacks, white wool turtleneck with a teardrop-pattern scarf. He took her overnight bag as he kissed her. "I've missed you."

"I'm glad you had me come." They walked toward the exit. "Is everything all right, David? You look tired."

"It's been thirty hours since I slept."

"Mmmmm. I want you refreshed and vigorous." Her fingers clenched his tightly.

"I'll sleep while you drive."

"Are we going somewhere?"

"Washington."

Outside now, Morgan guided her toward her car. When she saw it she said, "Looks sort of dirty, mud on the wheels. Have you been abusing my bird?"

"It was in a field. I'll tell you about that on the way."

He unlocked the trunk, put her bag beside his. Jill got behind the wheel, adjusted the seat. "I thought we were going to relax for a while. Instead you've put me to work."

He closed his eyes.

"How do we get from here to wherever we're going?"

"Take 76 to I-95. Follow it south."

"Aren't you going to tell me about the past three days?"

"Sleep now, talk later."

The clangor of urban traffic eased into the steady hum of the Interstate and Morgan felt himself sinking into sleep.

South of Baltimore he woke. The car was being gassed but Jill was not beside him. As he forced himself awake he saw her coming from the restaurant with a plastic cup of coffee. "Hel-*lo*," she said. "If you're hungry I can run back for a sandwich."

"Coffee's fine." He took it from her, sipped from the hot, steaming cup while she got behind the wheel.

"I love watching you while you sleep."

"Do I snore?"

"Occasionally, but I don't mind."

"Maybe I need a curettage."

She laughed. "I didn't think they did that to the nose."

"Well, they do." He moved his head slowly. "I feel half-stupefied. Never had worse coffee, either."

"Sorry, there wasn't much choice."

Sitting back he blinked; the afternoon sun was blinding. "Like panned oysters, Blue Crabs?"

"Love 'em."

"I'll take you to the best seafood place around. Great coffee, too, and it's on the way."

"Ummm, just thinking of it makes me hungry. Ready to talk, master?"

He brought her up to date, ending with his discovery of Alexandra Hargrave and their cabin encounter with the headmaster.

When he finished he crumpled his empty cup and dropped it into the waste container. Jill said, "What will Alexandra do now?"

"Go back to Moscow, I guess. What else can she do?"

"It's so tragic, so sad, David. Bodies and ruined lives all over the landscape." She shook her head. "Even now you don't have a clear idea who's responsible."

"Nothing that would hold up in court. But, hell, it would never get to court. It's too unbelievable."

"And even Ten Eyck betrayed you. That must make you bitter."

"Take the Beltway and we'll peel off after a while."

"To check on the address?"

"To feed you . . . first."

At Crisfield's in Silver Spring they sat at the long seafood bar, drank draft beer, and ate a dozen oysters apiece, freshly shucked by a weathered barman with gnarled hands. Jill said, "Is it true what they say about oysters and the male libido?"

"Absolutely."

"Have another dozen. Or two."

The next dozen were sautéed and served with the best french fries Morgan had ever eaten. Jill said, "I'm glad you brought me here."

"I'm glad you could come."

Replete, they returned to the car and Morgan got behind the wheel. He drove south on Connecticut Avenue into the District; south of Chevy Chase Circle he began to read street numbers, finding the one he sought not far from the office of Shelley's orthodontist.

An arcade ran through the building, a Szechuan restaurant on one side. "How about casing the joint, partner?"

"Glad to. Only, what am I looking for?"

"Use your imagination. I'll drive around the block."

When he returned she was waiting at the curb. "Ten offices," she said, "of which only one seems uninhabited, and I heard clicking sounds inside."

"What's the name on the door?"

"DelMar Personnel."

"I like the sound of it," he said. "Meet me on the other side of the block. I won't be long."

As she drove away he went into the arcade and took the stairway to the second floor. It was an old building; dust on the window ledges, door glass smudged. DelMar Personnel was halfway along the balcony. Morgan inspected the door frame for burglar alarm tapes and wires. Though he saw none he knew there could be a contact-breaker mounted atop the inside frame. The lock was a Schlage. He knocked briskly on the translucent panel: No response. Just the quiet, unobtrusive sound of clicks that reminded him of a miniature electric railway.

The adjacent door opened and an old man looked out. "Wastin' your time, son," he said. "Those folks ain't never there. Must come and go at night."

"Thanks," Morgan said, "but I have an appointment, so I'll just wait around until someone comes. Okay?"

"Suit yourself." He closed the door.

Morgan got out the lock-picking kit he had taken from Dorn in Berlin. Carefully he inserted the blue spring pry, then the companion tool with its spiculed tip, clawed it past the tumblers, and applied pressure to the thin steel bar. The cylinder turned and the bolt returned to its housing. The door was open.

Pocketing his tools, Morgan went into the office.

There was a desk and a spindle railing. Beyond it, an assortment of automatic communications equipment. The clicking sounds came from contacts traversing grids as connections were made and broken without a switchboard operator. Large tape reels turned slowly. This was a bookie station, used to relay incoming calls to anonymous destinations. So this was the room where Lon Crowly's call had been received and relayed to another location.

He studied the door frame for evidence of an alarm system. There were no magnetic contacts. That was understandable; the operators would not want police coming to the installation in case of a break-in. The equipment was too massive to be hauled away, too specialized to interest the average burglar, and damage could always be repaired. He had seen what he came to see, found what he had set out to find.

Closing the door quietly, Morgan went back the way he had come. Two white-coated Chinese waiters were smoking outside the kitchen door, relaxing before the dinner rush.

He walked around the block and got into the car beside Jill. As she started up, she said, "Did I pick the right place?"

"You did. It's a special phone installation to reroute calls."

"The Agency, then."

"Well, the KGB didn't haul all that gear up there. Jill, pull into the library parking area, and do a little research."

"Am I doing this for love or money?"

"For love. Xerox the entries for Robert Dobbs in *Who's Who* and the Green Book."

"What's that?"

273

"The Washington social listing. Dobbs is in it ex officio."

She was gone less than ten minutes, returning with two sheets of Xerox paper. Morgan glanced at them, folded them into an inside pocket. "Now let's find an inn for the night."

"I was afraid you'd forgotten."

They registered at a small residential hotel within easy walking distance of the University Club and the Hilton. Their suite was large and well-appointed.

Before unpacking, Morgan phoned room service for a bottle of Taittinger, which arrived while Jill was in the shower. Morgan twirled it in the ice bucket, polished their glasses, then let the champagne chill while he studied the Xeroxed pages. Dobbs's son was Robert, Jr., married, and living in Colorado. Two daughters, Nancy and Prudence, the latter a student at Sidwell Friends, Nancy at American University. Night classes? he wondered, opened the champagne and filled both glasses. He carried one to Jill who took it through the shower curtain and called, "What a delicious surprise. Cheers."

Later they made love with the haste and urgency of lovers too-long parted. Outside it was dusk, the sound of traffic diminished to a whisper. His eyes compared his rough, muscular body with hers, so marvelously smooth.

"That was wonderful," Jill said. "Keep plying me with champagne and I'll never want to leave."

He refilled their glasses, bringing the bottle to their bedside, and when they had drunk she curled against his body, head on his arm.

"You're truly beautiful," he said. "Each time we're together I feel I should offer a prayer."

"Then you'll keep me around a while?" She nuzzled the hollow of his throat.

"Indefinitely."

Afterward he phoned the university registrar's office and asked to leave a message for Miss Nancy Dobbs.

"Her first class meets at eight, sir. Perhaps you could still reach her at home."

"They said she was en route to the university."

"Well, Assyrian Culture doesn't begin until eight o'clock, but I could take a message for her."

"On second thought, since there's time, I'll meet her at class. What was the room?"

"Wesley Hall, two-fourteen."

274

"Much obliged." He hung up and Jill said, "What was all that about?"

"I'm going to kidnap her."

"*David!*"

"It's Dobbs's turn, Jill. He won't play unless I force him to. So I need leverage. Nancy will do." He touched the side of her face. "I need your help."

They had a late dinner in the Hilton's Polynesian restaurant with its huge clay firepots, bamboo and wicker furnishings, exotic menu. Morgan chose it for anonymity; the place was filled with vacationers and conventioneers with their families.

"My thought," said Morgan as he toasted a terimaki bit in the alcohol flame, "is simply to get Nancy out of the way so I can deal with her father." He fed Jill the tangy morsel on a bamboo sliver, began cooking one for himself. "In other words, the illusion of kidnapping . . . but I can't do it without you."

She shrugged. "I don't mind burning a bridge or two. What's your plan?"

"You contact her outside class, pose as a journalist interested in doing a piece on her: What it's like to be the Director's daughter; has it affected her life? How? What are her plans, her interests?"

"Ummmm. Yes, I think I could do it. Go on." Deftly she removed the sliver from his fingers. "These *are* delicious!"

"You'll have to improvise after you've sized her up, but it occurred to me that you might say you're doing it for one of the naughtier magazines so she won't rush to tell Dad."

"Name a naughty magazine," Jill challenged.

"Create one she's never heard of . . . with a suggestive title: *Ovid,* say."

"How about . . . *T & A?*"

"Well, well, not as sheltered as I thought. You get the idea. But if she's really straight, name a respectable journal. If Nancy says she has to consult the Agency's PR man, tell her that's out, you won't put up with censorship. Make her feel apologetic . . . and cooperative. Take her out to dinner, then to your motel room for a long interview. Use a tape recorder, camera, secretarial notebook, anything to lend authenticity."

"I didn't know I had a motel room."

"Out of town journalists always do."

"What if she asks for my credentials?"

"You tell me the answer to that one."

"All right. I'm a higher-level person than a street-type crime reporter who might need to flash something to get through fire and police lines."

"Right. Keep her on the defensive at all times. The only problem is you're beautiful. I suspect she's not, so for empathy wear something tacky."

"It occurs to me that Nancy may have been interviewed before."

"Check the periodical literature guide in a library. If she has, that would give you an opening: you want to update, ask the questions that weren't asked before, set the record straight."

"You have *all* the answers. I never really had a chance against you, did I?"

"About the same chance Nancy Dobbs has with you."

The next night Jill made contact with the Director's elder daughter. "It's going to be even easier than we thought," she reported to Morgan. "Nancy is about five-eleven in her stocking feet. Her figure is, well, skinny, and unlikely to improve. See for yourself." She handed him a Polaroid. Stringy hair, muddy complexion, legs like matchsticks. The girl's eager smile showed a retainer wire across her upper teeth. Poor Nancy, Morgan thought.

Jill said, "But on the positive side, she's a nice girl. I mean, if forced to I could like her. She's pitifully eager, rabbitlike, and no one's ever paid her the slightest attention. I guess that's why she's studying for her Master's."

"So, when's the interview?"

"That's up to you. And as far as she knows her father has no plans to leave town." Jill stroked her mousy wig.

"How about tomorrow night after classes?"

"Fine. I'll give her supper at that place you pointed out toward Baltimore—Queen's Contrivance?"

"King's," he corrected. "Rent a car and get a motel room out near Rockville. Did Nancy say anything about clearing with the Agency?"

"No. You'd hardly believe her one request: that she not be required to pose for a centerfold."

"That's *all?*"

"That's all. And I promised."

"Make your plans, then," he told her, "and I'll make mine."

TWENTY-SIX

Inside Wesley Hall classroom lights burned bright. Outside, the campus was dark, shadowed except for the steps where Jill Percival waited, floppy hat over her wig, leather tote bag across one shoulder.

She felt tense, uncertain she could accomplish the charade. Class should be ending shortly, her watch gave it a few minutes more. A couple came out of the library, arms linked, and passed on. In the near distance a watchman paused under a campus light to fill his pipe. Traffic rumbled around the Circle.

Then from above, from behind the lighted windows, Jill heard the scraping of chairs, the rising hum of voices. Across the street, bells sounded in the great church steeple. Class was over.

The doors opened, students came down the steps in ones and twos; some gathered in small groups. The outward flow of bodies engulfed them.

Jill went up two steps to stand directly under the light, eyes scanning the moving faces until she saw Nancy Dobbs coming through the doors, and their eyes met almost at once. Nancy waved and Jill stepped down to greet her.

Nancy's hair was stringily unkempt, but her cheeks were glowing. "I hope you haven't been waiting long, Francesca?"

"Just a few moments. Let's take my car—it's just over there. I'll bring you back." Jill linked her arm with Nancy's and drew her toward the Visitors parking area where she had left her rental Grand Prix.

"What a perfectly *beautiful* car," Nancy said. "Mine . . . well you should just *see* my old thing." She had to bend over quite far to get in the passenger door. "Just as soon as I have a job I'll get a new one, believe *me*."

"I rented this one," Jill told her. "Expense account, you know. *And* dinner." She turned onto Massachusetts Avenue. "I'm hungry. Hope you are."

"Famished."

"It'll take us half an hour, but it will be worth it."

"Shall we get . . . started?" Nancy asked.

"Oh, I think not. I'd much rather get an overall impression of you through normal conversation and dining. I've found it best not to *force* these things. We have lots of time, after all. After dinner we'll go to my place and really get down to business. You won't mind if I tape record, will you? For the sake of strict accuracy, of course."

Nancy nodded. "This is quite an adventure for me, Francesca. You see, no one ever interviewed me before."

"Then I've got a scoop, haven't I? Did you tell your father?"

"I promised not to, didn't I? I mean, it's really none of his business. He's being interviewed all the time and he never asks my opinion about *any*thing, so why should I confide in him about this?"

"Right!" Jill said with heartfelt approval. "Now you've touched on something I want to be sure to cover later on."

"And what's that?"

"Why, what it's like to be the daughter of a famous and important man; whether it's different than having a father who is, well, commonplace. The Washington scene is supposed to be *filled* with the broken families of dominating males. Of course, we don't have to go into your entire family scene, Nancy, unless you'd like to."

"I *want* to," she said rebelliously. "I want to speak for myself for once, not have father speaking for me." She put her hand on Jill's wrist. "*I'm* a person, too."

Jill nodded. "That's the point I want to make, Nancy. This is going to be one of my very *best* interviews!"

The Chinese restaurant was doing an enviable business, Morgan saw, as he entered the arcade and went up the creaky stairs. Only one of the offices was lighted; a denture manufactory at the far end of the floor.

He thought of Hargrave's China papers and what their true value might be. Ten Eyck had dismissed them as worthless, but Broom had special reasons for deprecating the information.

From his coat pocket Morgan took the lock-picking kit and selected his tools. In quickly, door closed and bolted, he pulled down the window blind and turned on the overhead light.

278

Relays clicked softly and irregularly, tape reels silently turned. Morgan went behind the thick electronic panels and found a lineman's trouble phone with small alligator clips at the end of its dangling wire. With it he could use any of the lines that fed out of the relay panels, and he estimated that there were more than a hundred pairs. Only a dozen or so were inactive. From them he would select one. It would have been a lot easier using a pay phone, but this call could take a bit of time and Dobbs's people would have a hell of a time tracing it. He'd love to see the expression on Dobbs's face when they finally told him the call had come from their own relay center!

He checked his watch. By now Jill should be driving north with Nancy Dobbs, keeping her beyond her father's reach for the night. Add the time for their dinner, the "interview," driving time from the motel to American University and from there to the Dobbs home in McLean, and Morgan could count on having from four to five hours in which to work.

More, he hoped, than he would need.

It had taken Hugh McDairmid a day to come up with the unlisted number of Dobbs's private residential phone.

In midafternoon Morgan had driven out to Leesburg to make further arrangements with the laird of Dawntree Farms, timing the drive both ways while traffic was off-hour slack. The average was twenty-three minutes.

With a pen light Morgan examined the unused pairs on the exposed back of the panel; none was numbered. He selected a set at random, tested with a copper penny, and saw tiny sparks against the darkness of the interior. The line was live. He clamped an alligator clip on each terminal and dialed Information. When the operator responded Morgan cut her off. Live, indeed.

He pulled over a chair and sat down. Taking a deep breath he began methodically to review his mental check list. Finally, satisfied everything was covered, he dialed the number of Robert Dobbs's phone.

A woman's voice, soft. "Yes?"

"Bob, please."

"Oh, well, I. . . ."

"Honey, this is important or I wouldn't be calling this number, right? Hop it."

"Yes, of course." Intimidated, semiapologetic. "May I say who's calling?"

"Well, if you have to say anything at all, tell him it's Roger. And I haven't got a lot of time."

Presently Dobbs's voice. "Who is this anyway?"

"It's that fellow you sent off to Geneva all innocent and unwitting. Remember?"

Sound of an indrawn breath. "Yes . . . I . . . yes, of course I remember. Where are you? Why haven't you contacted me before?"

"Because I've been busy staying alive. That problem's solved—temporarily, at least—so during the lull I thought I'd get in touch with my employer. You *were* my employer, Bob; are you still?"

"Certainly. Look, I *have* to know what happened in Geneva. So. . . ."

"And you will. But in return I'll need some confidences, too: What happened in Oxford, for instance? And Berlin? I need to know about Ten Eyck, also, not to mention the headmaster." He found himself gripping the receiver as though it were the throat of an enemy.

"Yes," said the Director. "Well, let's meet tomorrow . . . wherever you'd like."

"Alone? Like Atlanta?"

"Really alone this time."

"I'm all for it," Morgan said, "in fact I insist on it. That's why I called. Only it'll have to be tonight, Bob, and on my terms. You see, I've got Nancy."

Morgan let his words sink in, then looked at his watch. "I'll give you half an hour to verify. Her Toyota's in student parking at American, but she isn't. When I call back be ready to drive, Bob, alone. Don't call a meeting or alert your troops. Your one chance of keeping her alive is to do as I tell you, without variation."

Over the line came a gasp, a muffled whimper. Elvira Dobbs listening on an extension.

"Listen, honey," Morgan said roughly, "if you love Nancy you'll have your husband do as I say. Nothing tricky, nothing cute. I've had too much of that from Bob. Persuade him."

"I . . . I will," she choked.

"Splendid. Your half hour starts now." He broke the connection and unclamped the alligator clips. He hung the handset on its bracket and shoved the chair back to where it had been. Next, Morgan turned out the light and rolled up the window shade. The black lettering *Del Mar Personnel* stood out in reverse.

Unbolting the door, Morgan polished the knob and listened before stepping out onto the balcony. At the far end the dental laboratory light was still on. From below came spurts of conversation as a group left the restaurant. He closed the door very quietly and went down to the street.

"These snails are just delicious," said Nancy Dobbs as she removed another from its shell. "I've only had *escargots* once before, Miss Licht." She smiled nervously over her pronunciation.

"A good garlic-butter sauce can cover a world of culinary abuse, Nancy. Remember that when you're cooking for two." She savored a snail on her two-tined fork. "And what's with the 'Miss Licht'? I thought we were Nancy and Francesca."

"I'm sorry, I didn't mean . . . it's just that you're a very unusual person—sophisticated, traveled, mature—and I'm . . . well, whatever I am, I'm not that." She leaned slightly forward. "But I'd *like* to be."

The announcement did not surprise Jill. "Your father is well-traveled. I've seen photos of him getting on and off Air Force One with the President or the Secretary of State."

Nancy's upper lip twitched. "Unfortunately, those trips never included any of *us*, not even Mother. Though Father did give us autographed photographs of the President."

"That's something, isn't it? A souvenir."

One waiter removed their dimpled plates while another refilled their wine glasses. Nancy lifted hers and smiled. "Francesca, I hope we'll be friends long after the interview is published."

"That," said Jill lifting her glass, "will be entirely up to you."

As he drove south toward the Potomac River, David Morgan reflected that from now on the course of his life was changed unalterably. The Potomac was his Rubicon, there was no turning back.

Roger Hargrave had faced such a moment when he left Stockholm for the Soviet Union, and from then on his life was never again the same. How useless, his widow had said; how wasted those years, their hopes, had been. DORMOUSE INFORMATION BARRED, the cathode screen announced. REFER TO DIRECTOR OR MERIWETHER.

So much for Roger's long years of danger. DORMOUSE IS DEAD. Somewhere, sometime, the scales had to balance.

His mission was a confrontation postponed too long; facing his executioner at last.

Nothing could bring Roger back to life, or Palmer, or Marisa. For the rest of his life they would be only memories, blending gradually into the background of his mind like shadows of a summer dusk. Jill blunted the edge of sorrow, but he would never forget the proud, dark-eyed Marisa who had restored his life and dignity.

The Cabin John bridge took him into Virginia and he turned right, driving through darkness past the Agency's fenced precincts, glancing

281

briefly at the glimmering lights beyond the wooded barrier, and he thought of the coincidence that brought him near the place he had once honored in word and deed.

Never again was his loyalty to be commanded or bought.

Cut your losses, he thought; don't linger or dwell on what is unredeemable.

Hardly any traffic on the highway; he was making better time than his test average. Good. A few additional minutes would help him.

Leaving Fairfax County a sign read, and just beyond it: *Entering Loudon County.* Board fences, whitewashed and stark in the moonlight. Fences of stacked chestnut rails, cattle staring stupidly at his headlights. He wondered if Jill was having difficulty with Dobbs's daughter. He looked at the dashboard clock. By now they should be driving toward Rockville and the motel. Ms. Francesca Licht and guest.

Somewhere behind him lay the general area of Dobbs's home, and Morgan wondered if the Director had summoned his Security Chief or the FBI . . . or both. It was Morgan's calculation that he would not, and half an hour was insufficient time to contact and bring in mercenaries. No, Dobbs would estimate that his only chance of survival lay in playing by Morgan's rules. At this point the Director could not risk Morgan's seizure by the law; that would give his adversary a forum, a chance to talk to interested ears. The only way Dobbs wanted him was dead.

At the outskirts of Leesburg Morgan pulled into a dark filling station that had an outside pay phone. He called McDairmid and said, "I'm on my way."

"Everything's ready here," McDairmid responded and hung up.

Morgan consulted his watch. In a few minutes Dobbs's exploratory half-hour would end. He sat in the Monte Carlo watching the radiant digits change. Above, the moon was cold and remote, bathing the countryside in soft, dim light. After a while Morgan went to the phone and dialed the private number of Robert Dobbs.

Alexandra Hargrave boarded the Pan American jet and was shown by a stewardess to the window seat she had chosen.

JFK was busy, baggage tractors moving around the tarmac like articulated caterpillars, jumbo jets being towed toward the flight line. Overhead the Dopplered *whoosh* of a 707 landing, a line of aircraft waiting for takeoff, lights impatiently twinkling.

"Would you care for a drink now?"

282

Alex looked up. "Why, yes, I think so." She was unaccustomed to ordering American drinks.

"Martini, Manhattan, a Bloody Mary . . . ?"

"A martini, please."

"Straight up, or on the rocks?"

"I . . . no ice in it."

"Straight up, then." The stewardess checked her order card. "We'll be serving dinner after we're airborne, with a choice of wine."

"That sounds tempting. Thank you." She was, in fact, hungry, having eaten only skimpily the past few days. Helping care for Mrs. James, prostrated by the discovery of her husband's body, had occupied most of her time. She had attended chapel services for the headmaster, the irony of her presence troubling her through every moment.

Today Peyton James had been buried, her second funeral in a month, and she was emotionally drained, living precariously on nerve, burdened by secrets never to be revealed.

As the plane drew outward in a long crescent she saw the terminal lights strong and steady, forming a vast and gleaming expanse that her children would criticize as conspicuous capitalist consumption. The way things turned out it was better they had stayed behind. Here there would have been nothing for them but impenetrable confusion.

Her throat tightened as she thought of Roger, brave, determined, so beautiful in life. She brushed tears away as the stewardess delivered her chilled martini.

She sipped slowly, pleased by the almost-forgotten sensory pleasure, the welcoming reaction of her taste buds to the clean, dry flavor.

Cabin lights dimmed as the jet surged forward, and she felt an accompanying release of spirit as it lifted off and gained the smoothness of the air.

Alexandra Hargrave leaned over for a last glimpse of Manhattan, crosshatched with lights, wispy clouds near the Trade Center towers. She would never again, she knew, meet anyone under the Biltmore clock, have cocktails in the Oak Room, dine at Twenty-One, or dance at the Pierre. All were part of a past that could never be disinterred, a way of life that years ago—without her realizing it—had ceased to exist.

She thought of David Morgan; he was so like Roger and she wished him peace and happiness wherever he was. Roger, she thought, would be proud of his protégé.

The aircraft entered a layer of clouds that blurred and then blotted out the land mass. Now they were over the Atlantic, flying the Great Circle route that lay invisibly across the northern ocean.

Toward home.

Jill and Nancy sat in facing chairs, tape recorder on the coffee table between them, cassette turning as they talked. After only a few minutes Jill began running out of questions, so she encouraged Nancy to tell about her loveless childhood, which Nancy was doing in a flat voice tinged with a resentment she was trying to control.

David should be in Leesburg by now, Jill thought with a glance at her wristwatch. If the schedule was holding, if all the details flowed together to the focal point. She prayed nothing would go wrong. Like Nancy insisting on calling home.

This is just a sideshow, she told herself, but without it nothing else can happen. So I have to keep it going.

When Nancy's voice trailed away, Jill sat forward and said, "Can you tell me about some of the world figures you've met through your father? Has he entertained them at your home?"

"Oh, I've never really been in on that sort of thing. Father goes to banquets and embassies, sometimes he takes my mother, but not us, not me." Her tone was rancorous. "To put it plainly, my father lives in a different world from the rest of us, and. . . ."

"Perfect!" Jill exclaimed. "Now please develop that theme. It goes back to what we were discussing earlier. The possibilities are fascinating. More coffee?"

"Please. Francesca, you're so thoughtful, so understanding. You know, I just might go on to journalism."

Jill refilled their cups. "With your father's connections you should be able to find employment very quickly." This was going to be a long, incredibly long, night.

"But, you see, I wouldn't want to do anything through my father." Her lips drew together. "It's terribly important for me to do things for myself, be my own person, you understand."

"Completely. So, what *are* your aspirations, Nancy?"

Jill sat back, sipping coffee occasionally as her unwitting captive talked.

Jill ached to have these hours behind her, be rid of the wig, the ill-fitting clothing, the celery-stalk who sat there pouring out her childish heart.

She longed to be with Morgan.

284

". . . suppose I might call home, Francesca?" The girl's words came as a shock. Focusing, she said, "What on earth for?" Heart pounding.

"To . . . well, to let my mother know I'll be coming home late."

"Good lord, you're twenty-two; surely you don't report hourly to your parents?"

"No," said Nancy uncomfortably, "but. . . ."

"Besides, we've established a fantastic mood; you're evoking things so *well* I wouldn't want to risk breaking it. Now, go on with what you were saying . . . about liking to play baseball with the boys. . . ."

Danger, for the moment, was over.

But Nancy might be more insistent about calling home. What then? The door was locked, and Jill realized that she could probably jerk the phone cord from the wall before Nancy finished dialing.

Still, it would be far better if there were no violence to mar the illusion of an interview. David's plan was filled with risk. And Jill did not want to be the one to make it fail.

"Do you think Dobbs will play?"

McDairmid shrugged. "Maybe. What's your feeling?"

"I think he will . . . to a point. Because he hasn't much choice. But on the contrary assumption we've gone to considerable trouble."

"Which is always the best approach."

They were by the whitewashed fence that enclosed the east pasture in front of McDairmid's house. Inside the fence, a yard off the ground, ran a cattle wire whose amperage McDairmid had increased enough to stun whatever touched it. On its western side the pasture was bordered by the private blacktop that led from the county access road to the house. Windows were dark except for McDairmid's study where slivers of orange light showed on either side of the lowered shade. McDairmid's wife was asleep; the servant had retired two hours ago. Cattle were in their stalls, out of the way for the night. Morgan wanted no false alarms.

He looked at his wristwatch, wondering if Jill was still with Dobbs's daughter. If Nancy insisted on leaving early Jill was to telephone McDairmid before leaving the motel. By now, though, Dobbs should be nearing Leesburg, out of touch, isolated from everything but his thoughts.

Dobbs is not liking this, Morgan mused. He's never done anything on his own that took personal courage. He'll be uncertain, confused. During their last conversation Dobbs's voice had been sullen with the overtones of defeat. The Director had accepted Morgan's instructions, repeated them dully, swearing that he had alerted no one, that he would come alone.

Still, Morgan thought, Dobbs is crafty. And he'll be desperate because he knows this could be the end of the game.

"I make it another three to four minutes, David." McDairmid looked up from his watch to the yellow-silver moon. He was half-sitting on a shooting stick. At the border of his road was a golf cart modified for his needs. It enabled him to cover all but the wooded sections of his land, running quietly so as not to disturb his herds.

Morgan said, "I never intended to involve you this much, Hugh. I don't know how it's all going to turn out, but I'm grateful."

McDairmid snorted. "Don't thank me, I'm thanking you for the opportunity to help. Any decent organization deals with its own bad 'uns, right?"

"Right. But I didn't know you had such strong feelings against Dobbs."

"Call it the loathing of a creator for a destroyer. Oh, yes, I feel strongly about the Director."

Hearing the tone of his voice the chestnut gelding nickered and pawed the gravel. The thoroughbred was tied to a nearby post, saddled and ready. McDairmid called, "Now, now, Starbright. Good boy. Easy." To Morgan he said, "Give him some sugar," and passed Morgan a handful of cubes. Morgan went over, stroked the horse's neck and let him take two sugars from his open palm.

"What a beauty," Morgan said. "How many hands?"

"Close to seventeen. I couldn't bring myself to put him away. . . ."

"Then he was the one?"

"Balked at a wall . . . probably partly my fault." He gazed down at his thin legs. "But . . . maybe I'll ride again one day. I'd like to. He needs riding. . . ." Abruptly he looked away. "Strange, the love one feels for an animal."

They heard the sound of the engine first, then they glimpsed car lights coming up the county road. "Duty stations," McDairmid said. He folded the seat of his shooting stick, and, gripping it as a cane, limped over to his electric vehicle. With a rising hum it moved away.

Morgan touched the Mauser holstered under his left armpit, took the Model 10 Ingram submachine gun he had gotten from emergency stores under McDairmid's house and slung it across his back. Its box magazine held thirty .38 rounds, and there was a thick cylindrical

286

sound suppressor screwed onto the neck of the weapon's short barrel. A narrow canvas strap across Morgan's chest held it out of the way.

The lone car followed the road along the fencing at the pasture's north side, lights drilling through the night. Morgan unhitched Starbright's reins, gripped them in his left hand and fitted his left foot into the stirrup. Then he levered up and into the saddle, finding the other stirrup with his toe. Starbright stood steady while Morgan stroked the side of his neck.

The car turned into the mouth of the estate road. It came smoothly along the blacktop and when it was halfway to the house it stopped. Lights and engine went off.

"Stay where you are," boomed McDairmid's voice through the bullhorn.

His electric wagon whined down the shoulder turf toward the entrance. There McDairmid would strew tetrahedral spikes across the road, sealing it from other vehicles.

Morgan rose in the stirrups and looked across the pasture in the direction from which the car had come. No following cars, none with lights on at least.

He heard the quiet hum of McDairmid's vehicle, then his amplified voice: "Get out, close the door, and walk to the fence."

The car door opened, ceiling light went on, and before the door closed, Morgan saw the figure of Robert Dobbs. In darkness again it left the roadside and moved across the shoulder to the white fence.

"Climb the fence," McDairmid ordered. "Walk to the center of the field."

Morgan watched Dobbs climb the fence into the pasture and pause before stepping carefully over the cattle wire. Moonlight showed his progress to the approximate center of the pasture. Again McDairmid spoke: "Take off your clothing."

The electric wagon was coming toward Morgan now. Dobbs's frame twisted as he began to undress. McDairmid headed for the switchbox that would send current through the wire when he closed the knife switch. "In you go," he called to Morgan who turned the gelding toward the open gate and guided him through a narrow gap in the cattle wire. He was in the pasture now, where Dobbs was pulling off his trousers.

Close to Dobbs a floodlight went on. The Director jerked as though from physical impact, shielded his eyes and got out of his undershirt.

Then he stood exposed to the light, naked but for his jockey shorts, shivering in the cool air.

Morgan approached from behind the floodlight, Mauser in hand. A dozen feet from the Director he reined in Starbright and spoke. "If there's any doubt in your mind about Nancy, take a look at this." Into the lighted area he tossed a photo Jill had taken of the girl. Dobbs picked it up. He stared at it and his shoulders slumped.

"I believe you," he said unevenly. "What do you want from me?"

TWENTY-SEVEN

"How circumstances change," said Morgan. "A few weeks ago you wanted me to perform a small technical service. Afterward you wanted my life. In candor, sir, staying alive hasn't been easy. The notorious turncoat Roger Hargrave wanted to return home to deliver a final warning to his countrymen, then die on his native soil. Why did you thwart his small ambition?"

Looking up, shading his eyes against the glare, the Director said hoarsely, "What do you want of me?"

"I'll ask the questions, sir, and. . . ."

Dobbs interrupted. "Are you going to kill me?"

"Do you deserve better than Peyton James?"

"Oh my God. Then it was *you* who killed him!"

Under Morgan's weight Starbright shifted uneasily. "Peyton's dead," Morgan said, "but years ago he destroyed himself. No more questions, sir. It's time for answering."

"*Please.* Is Nancy—my daughter—alive?"

"Does that mean you feel emotions as human beings do? Where was that humane sensitivity when Palmer Syce was being snuffed out?" Morgan pulled hard on the reins and Starbright reared, menacing Dobbs with his hooves. The Director stepped back. Morgan let the gelding settle down before he spoke again. "Why was Palmer killed?"

"I . . . I don't know."

"Think of your daughter," Morgan warned. "Are you going to sacrifice her to your games?"

Dobbs lowered his arms. "You'll spare Nancy? You swear it?"

"If you tell the truth."

The light was bothering Dobbs's eyes. He blinked and said, "You took the Dormouse documents to Palmer, that meant you'd told him everything. Even if you were apprehended, Palmer still had all your knowledge." He swallowed, "I . . . we . . . couldn't let him live."

"As simple as that, and I blamed Kozlov all along." Morgan shook his head. "How did you even know I'd seen Syce?"

"He called London Station to ask if you were dangerous."

"What was he told?"

"That headquarters would be queried."

"Was Broom expecting me?" Morgan asked.

"He was warned you might go there."

"And Ten Eyck let Berlin know I was coming."

. The Director nodded. "You had no friends," he said defiantly. "It was Arnaud who told us where you were, who you planned to see."

"Hardly a surprise," Morgan said, "but he didn't try to kill me. That was left to your Berlin agent, Dorn."

"No, that's not so. You were only to be captured and held."

"Another lie. I saw his equipment."

"He . . . to protect himself," Dobbs said weakly. "Killing would have exceeded his instructions. You were to be held until it was . . . convenient to produce you."

Morgan grunted. "Without the rabbit the hounds would have nothing to chase?"

The Director looked up earnestly. "Believe me, there was nothing personal in it."

"Nothing *personal*? That makes it all right? You forget the woman I loved—Marisa—was killed by your men just because you thought I'd confided in her!"

"No . . . I . . . that was a mistake, an error," he pleaded.

"Not true. Before Lon was killed he told me his target was the girl, not me, sir. *I* was in Geneva where I was supposed to be killed by Stepavitch. Sent there by you to be murdered and blamed for Roger's death. And from your point of view I had to be silenced because, as you anticipated, Hargrave revealed things to me: the sham of his defection; his identity as Dormouse; his China preoccupation. Bottled up in the Soviet Union, Roger was harmless and safe, but when he demanded to come home, unknowingly he triggered his own assassination. By that simple act—*think of it!* The very men who dispatched him long years ago, used him, blackened his name for a higher cause, now wanted him dead."

"I never learned about Dormouse until I became Director," Dobbs cried. "Like you I thought Hargrave defected."

"But when you found otherwise you discovered Peyton held the key, and learned why Dormouse couldn't be permitted to return. Over the years the Agency treated Roger with criminal indifference, even exposed him to Kozlov, hoping the KGB would liquidate him and eliminate your problem. When Kozlov refrained in order to protect himself, you had no opportunity until Roger flew to Geneva. Alive he was a time bomb menacing you. Dead, he was no threat. So you and Peyton—to protect yourselves—had him killed."

"You . . . you can't prove that."

"Do I have to? I'm here," he thrust the Mauser into the rim of light, "and you're down there. You dealt with Kozlov, treated with the enemy. Conspired with the KGB to dispose of one of our own men, then had him murdered. And Palmer Syce."

"Meriwether said it was the only thing to do. He helped me."

"*Helped* you? He *manipulated* you, sir." Morgan sighted along the barrel at Dobbs's naked chest. Only a few hairs between the flat pectorals and they were mostly gray. "Peyton's interest in silencing Roger was even greater than yours." He paused. "And I know why."

Dobbs stared at the Mauser, looked slowly away.

Morgan said, "A man like you must always analyze where his interests lie, sir, and you almost always did. But once you failed. You saw a coincidence of interest with Meriwether, but it was an illusion."

"I . . . well, I came to realize that."

"But you never understood Meriwether's real motives, because he was even more clever than you. Peyton James launched Roger and betrayed him. Ten Eyck became an ally because he was one of the older boys who foresaw Hargrave as Director and resented it. Roger was too brilliant, too young; he didn't have the seniority they did. Am I right?"

Dobbs looked up, his face ghastly gray in the light. "I . . . I came to believe that was their motive."

"And Peyton's other motive?"

"I don't understand."

"Think back," Morgan said. "You told me Hargrave planned to reveal a KGB penetration in the Agency, remember?"

"Yes, but . . . that was only to interest you more. I . . ."

"You fool. Peyton James *was* that penetration. Kozlov knew it. He put on a charade with me to find out what I'd say, determine if Roger had ever found out. But Roger couldn't tell me because he was killed. And I had no way of knowing, even suspecting Peyton, until I learned who Meriwether was. McDairmid forced his name out of the memory bank." He took a deep breath. "An imperfect world, sir. Someone neglected to eliminate that reference in the Dormouse tape."

Dobbs stared at him. One hand lifted, then dropped to his thigh.

"I think Peyton James was recruited while he was working with General Gehlen," Morgan said. "God knows, that whole Pullach operation was riddled with Soviet spies, so why not Peyton, too? For the Soviets, James was in a perfect position to relay information on German holdings and American operations. He was a stellar agent: above suspicion and with a controlling hand on our counter-espionage. My God, what damage he must have done! And when James went into retirement he kept open his channels to the Agency . . . and you. So when Roger's final anguished pleas to return arrived, you turned to the Dormouse case officer for advice. And Peyton informed the KGB." His mouth was sour with hatred.

"What else could I do? I wasn't one of you. I had to turn to someone who would know what to do." His voice was high-pitched, defensive. His body shook uncontrollably.

"Get dressed," Morgan told him.

"No. Don't kill me. Please, I beg you."

"Cover yourself," Morgan ordered. "You sicken me."

Heavily, the Director went to the pile of clothing. As he donned it, Morgan watched carefully for the dragging weight of a weapon, saw nothing suspicious, but kept Dobbs covered with his pistol. "It's no riddle why you became Director," he said. "For some you were malleable. For others you were a compromise figure, the one man no one could really object to because you'd never done anything that even a McComb could find objectionable. Your image was that of a cautious man who loved order. Yet what did you ever sacrifice to establish it in the world? The overwhelming irony is that only through taking risks can order be maintained. You don't know *who* you are. You don't even know *what* you are, sir. So I'll tell you: You're a murderer by remote control. You're a conspirator, a traitor, and. . . ."

"You've killed, too," Dobbs cried wildly. "You're a criminal, a fugitive." His eyes were large. "Murderer!" His mouth moved oddly. "*Jailbird!*" he shrieked. Morgan fired. The bullet slammed the ground at Dobbs's feet.

"Don't tempt me," Morgan said, fighting to control the gelding with reins and knees.

"I wasn't the only one in the Agency." Dobbs's voice rose. "I'll tell you everything if you'll let me live!"

"There's nothing I don't know," Morgan told him. "You have

292

nothing to trade, sir. The country's been shamed enough, and because of you and James and others like you the Agency's become a dirty word. Worse, it's a useless appendage on the body politic. No wonder Kozlov and his masters can afford charitable gestures."

Morgan breathed deeply, smelling the scent of powder from the Mauser's muzzle.

"Which brings me," Morgan continued, "to the information Hargrave called indispensible but which Ten Eyck pissed all over. Do you know why Roger and his information had to be destroyed, sir? Because your friends in the Agency and the administration think common cause should be made with Russia against China. They took sides long years ago. James with his special interest in Soviet survival couldn't permit Soviet plans to destroy China to become known. Roger believed this country should know. Hargrave was not a partisan of China *or* the Soviet Union, his loyalty was to this country. He didn't want to see us drawn into a false situation, involving us in nuclear war. Had he lived he might have suggested that we should be neutral in their conflict . . . for once defining our national interest with consummate care. I think that would have been Hargrave's position, sir, and for what it's worth, it's mine. But the chance is lost, isn't it? For who can give a dead man credibility?"

"*I* can," screeched Dobbs. "If you let me live, I'll tell the President. He'll listen to me, I'll persuade him. Let me, Morgan."

Morgan stared at him. If Dobbs did that it would vindicate much of what Hargrave died for.

He said, "Convince me I could trust you."

Dobbs's mouth was working, lips opening and closing, a tic pulling the corner of one eye. "You'll come with me. You'll go to the President with me. Then you'll. . . ."

The sound of the shot made the gelding rear in terror. The impact in the center of his chest knocked Dobbs backward. With outstretched arms he dropped on the floodlight, dead, as the bulb burst and there was sudden, total darkness around the body. Morgan fought Starbright to keep the horse from bolting, forcing his head down, turning him in a narrow circle until he was under control. His heels dug into the gelding's flanks and he galloped toward the gate.

Near the hitching post, Morgan saw McDairmid in his wagon. There was a rifle across his thighs.

Dismounting, Morgan walked to McDairmid. The gelding followed.

Sharply, Morgan said, "Damn you, what the hell did you do that for?" He stared warily at the rifle, wondering if McDairmid would now turn it on him. "Dobbs could have led us to the President."

But McDairmid laid the rifle aside and said calmly, "Don't be naive. He'd have never let you get near the President. I was your senior by many years. I helped found the Agency and it treated me well. Dobbs perverted its processes, and yes, I hated him. So I claimed the prerogative of execution."

Morgan looked up at the moon. It was lower now, haloed by mist. He still felt stunned by McDairmid's unexpected action.

"Don't forget, David, the privilege of liquidating Peyton fell to you."

"That was chance, not design."

"Besides," McDairmid continued, "considering everything Dobbs was offering you, I was afraid you might weaken and let him live."

"I was thinking of it," Morgan conceded, "but only to learn more."

"Well," said McDairmid, "I couldn't be sure." He started the electric motor. "I'll sweep spikes if you'll remove the body."

"Someone has to," Morgan said dryly. "Can't have you involved."

"Wouldn't do, would it? I suggest you use his car. And Starbright should be stabled for the night."

"Oh, I'll take care of things," Morgan said, "but there's still Broom Ten Eyck."

"Indeed. I thought you might plan a visit to Spain."

Morgan shook his head slowly.

"He'll try to kill you, you know," McDairmid said.

"I know. Wherever I go he'll be behind me."

"Until he's dead you'll have no peace."

"I have no contacts left in Europe," Morgan said. "No place to hide and plan. Ten Eyck knows my apartment, my documentation, everything. If I were to go back I wouldn't survive, especially not in Spain. It's Ten Eyck's turf." Leaning back he stretched. God, he was tired!

"Then you must go away, David. Disappear."

McDairmid touched controls and the little wagon turned and hummed away. Morgan took sugar from his pocket and fed it to the gelding. He leaned against the hitching post until the wagon came back. McDairmid switched off its motor. "I liked the way you were handling things, David, so I waited until you'd put it all together for Dobbs. Not much of a man at the end, was he?"

"Never was," Morgan agreed, "but the night's biggest surprise was you."

"Because you never knew me well. I've killed before without

294

regrets. Do you think what happened bothers me?" He eased himself from the wagon, moved slowly to the switchbox, and cut the current to the cattle wire.

"Goodbye, Hugh."

"Goodbye."

Without looking back, Morgan got into the Monte Carlo and drove it into the pasture, thinking that by now Jill should have left the girl near the university and be on her way back to the hotel. In a few hours he should be able to join her. He stopped the car beside Dobbs's body and opened the trunk. With difficulty he lifted the still-limp body and fitted it into the trunk. Then he drove to Dobbs's car and stopped to look it over.

The keys were in the lock, so he used them to open the trunk. Interior light showed a small metal box tucked away in an upper recess. From one end of the box extended a short antenna wire. It was a radio beacon transmitting a position signal.

Morgan stared at it, fear piercing his mind like a blade. Followers could have the place surrounded. They could take him at will.

Morgan swore.

Overconfident, he had neglected to search the car, yet the beacon could have been anticipated. Dobbs's cunning was not likely to fail him when his life was at stake. Perhaps in death Dobbs would have the final victory.

He wrenched the box loose and hurled it to the ground, then closed the trunk to shut off the inside light. Too late, he thought, for precautions, when they've seen everything that happened. Through night scopes they must be watching me.

Yet, he thought, I can't just try to get away and leave Hugh with a body to explain. He looked around, peering at the moonlit road. No cars, no visible men. Perhaps I've got time to start disposal. If they've set up a road block I'll try to crash it and get through.

He got behind the wheel and was about to start the engine when he hesitated.

Why hadn't the security people closed in? Plenty of time to track the beacon's signal before Dobbs was killed. And if they were nearby the shot should have brought them running.

Why not?

He got out and picked up the bent metal box. The lid was partly off, showing the wiring, the powerful nickel-alloy battery. He pulled the cell from its connectors and felt corrosion wetness on his hand. His tongue touched both terminals but there was no shock. The battery was dead, corrosion long advanced. Someone had neglected to check the beacon. Powerless, it had sent no signals at all.

What irony, he thought in relief, and tossed the beacon into the shrubbery. In what's left of Dobbs's Agency, no one gives a damn.

Still shaken, Morgan got back into the car and drove away. Two miles down the county road he turned into a narrow lane and hauled Dobbs's body from the trunk. He laid it face down on the narrow shoulder, arranging the stiffening arms above the dead man's head as he had fallen in death. Then he drove back to Dawntree Farms where he rode Starbright to the stable and unsaddled the gelding before shutting him in a box stall for the night. He left the stable with a length of heavy nylon rope which he hitched around the bumper of Dobbs's car, joining it to the Monte Carlo. Then he towed it to the county road and slowly back toward Washington. When he saw a wide shoulder he stopped and severed the tow rope. After wiping the trunk lid he started the engine and left it running to exhaust the tank. That would explain Dobbs leaving the car and walking toward some distant farmhouse for assistance, surprising a deer-jacker on the way. . . .

Still, he thought, as he got behind the wheel of the Monte Carlo, Elvira Dobbs knew her husband was going to meet David Morgan. Would she implicate him or would she let matters take their course? She lacked corroboration, for Nancy could tell only a wild, incredible tale.

He drove without lights, then turned them on to detour around the town of Leesburg. Dormant as it was someone might glimpse a car with Florida plates and remember.

Palmer Syce had said to count on the unexpected happening, and tonight it had: with McDairmid ending Dobbs's life for cause he judged sufficient.

Who would succeed? Morgan could not recall the name of Dobbs's deputy. Some faceless military figure, anonymous and uninspiring. But it made no difference really, none at all. The next Director, whoever he was, would serve the country better.

Soon he saw the Potomac glinting under the waning moon, the pale glow of Washington beyond. It was an effort to follow the road's white boundary lines, keep wheels on the highway.

For Jill, he thought, explanations could wait. He would tell her of the night's outcome, but to go into it deeper . . . make sense from all that happened . . . would take time.

After they found refuge.

TWENTY-EIGHT

In Ft. Lauderdale Morgan sold his rechristened boat for cash to a bearded young Latino whose lack of interest in ship's papers and deeds of transfer suggested that he planned to use it for one fast hash run from the Bahamas and nothing more. With the money Morgan and Jill bought a thirty-nine-foot sloop-rigged motor sailer on which, they decided, they could be comfortable for quite a while. The fiberglass hull was sea kindly and maneuverable, and the diesel engine had been recently overhauled.

Uncertain that it would do any good, Morgan wrote out a summary of the intelligence Roger Hargrave had brought from the Soviet Union, reconstructing the documents he had left taped under the table in his Paris apartment. He considered sending the summary to the Attorney General but decided against it: anonymous information never leaves a lawyer's hands. Instead, he mailed the envelope to the Senate majority leader, feeling that Hargrave's warning would have the best chance of being disseminated outside the Executive Branch. At the very least, copies would reach the Senate Intelligence Committee and perhaps leak from there to the news media. A remote chance, but he could think of no other way to keep Roger's legacy from being wasted.

After shakedown and provisioning they sailed the boat—named *Pendragon* by now—southwest across the Gulf to Progreso, the port of Mérida in the Yucatan. The voyage was pleasant and relaxing with long starlit nights and bright days, only one of which brought a spell of bad weather. Shared watches and shipboard chores developed a new and stronger rapport between them, and they wore clothing only in the night's coolness, exposing their browning bodies daily to the unclouded sun. Morgan let his beard grow and saw his artificially white hair yellow from salt and sun, darken at the roots.

Jill went ashore at the port and returned with dye to match the color of Morgan's beard. Port people were incurious about them, and for two days they ate well and luxuriated in freshwater showers and a king-size bed at the port's small hotel.

While shopping, Jill found a Miami paper that was more than a week old, but she bought it because of a lead story from the White House: the President had appointed a new Agency Director, a former ambassador who was a longtime political crony. Confirmation hearings were expected within a month. The article referred to the violent and mysterious death of the previous Director three weeks ago and mentioned speculation over possible Soviet responsibility. The President, according to the article's last sentence, had eulogized the assassinated Director as a victim of the never-ending Silent War.

With a sense of relief Jill tore out the story and put it in her purse for Morgan. So far, at least, David had not been accused of the crime.

From the pier she suddenly saw him stretched out as if he were dead, a book fallen from his hands. In panic, she looked right and left, saw nobody, hurried down the pier boards, her heels clattering.

The sound woke him. As he sat up, Jill stopped in relief. He waved, smiled, and reaching out for her shopping bag, steadied her hand as she came aboard.

"For a second I thought you were dead," she said.

"Not yet," he laughed. "You'd better stop having nightmares in the daytime."

Jill showed him the newspaper story. Morgan read it, then set it aside. "So much for Dobbs," he said finally. "But that's not the end."

"Ten Eyck?"

He nodded. "Are you ready to disappear?"

They sailed down the west coast of the Yucatan peninsula as far as Campeche, where they put in for shopping at the pharmacy and marine supply store. The next morning they put out to sea, resuming their search for a quiet, undisturbed bay with a sliver of sandy beach. After four days they found one south of Champotón, the jungle reaching close to the water's edge, the sand like scattered gold. Water from a spring trickled down a narrow channel in the sand, and near its source Morgan dug a collecting well that he lined with wooden staves where the water, shaded by fronds, stayed cool and sweet.

There were wild plantains and guavas, mangoes, palm-hearts, and small tart lemons to flavor the snapper and grouper he easily caught handlining beside his boat. And a hundred yards into the jungle a family of *jabali* yielded an occasional young pig to Morgan's marksmanship, pork they roasted on the beach in a stone-lined pit covered with kelp and palm fronds, washing it down with spring-cooled wine.

After Morgan taught Jill to use the scuba gear they began taking the Zodiac to an offshore reef, diving below into the quiet green world of coral fans and rainbow-colored fish.

Their days and nights settled into an uneventful routine of living and sharing all things together, and Morgan realized that he had never known such complete happiness in all his life.

After two months they sailed back to Campeche for a day of shopping and reprovisioning. They went on their errands separately, and when Jill came back to the boat she said, "It seems someone's been making inquiries."

"Who said so?"

"The woman who runs the drugstore . . . she's very friendly. She told me a man in hunting clothes had been asking about an American couple with a boat."

"What did he look like?"

"She said he was tall—*un grandote* was the phrase—and he spoke Castilian Spanish. He said he was a friend of ours."

"Go on."

"So of course she said she remembered such a couple and gave him our description. He seemed satisfied and went away."

"What about his face?"

Her eyebrows drew together. "His face?"

"Yes, his features. He had a face, didn't he?"

"I'm sorry, darling. Yes, he was unshaven, but . . ."

"Did he have a beard?" Morgan pressed. "What color?"

"I . . . I'm afraid I didn't ask." She took his hand. "What's the matter?"

"Ten Eyck. I didn't go for him so he was forced to come after me."

Jill's face turned away. "These months . . . so perfect, David. I let myself be lulled." When her eyes turned back he was staring at her. Quickly she said, "We can't go back to the cove. Surely it . . ."

Morgan was shaking his head. "Not how I see it at all. God knows how he picked up our trail, but Broom's off his own turf so he's at a disadvantage." Morgan's hands balled into fists, opened and closed.

"We're going back then . . . and wait?"

"*I'm* going."

"Meaning . . . ?"

"That you stay here. The hotel's not bad, and . . ."

"You don't know me very well." Firmly her fingers laced his. "Four eyes are better than two, four ears. . . . Whatever is done we'll do together."

He drew her to him, kissed her forehead, fondled her hair. "Even the rabbit is known to turn and fight his pursuers," Morgan said quietly. "And I've been fleeing far too long." He kissed her cheek. "Broom knows a good deal about killing, but so do I. And we have the advantage of knowing he's around."

"You're right," she said, forcing a smile. "It has to end."

His fingers ruffled her hair. "I'm going back to town," he said. "Some things to buy."

"I'll get the boat ready."

"I won't be long."

At the hardware store Morgan bought several reels of lightweight, green, monofilament fishing line, and stopped at the drygoods emporium for other items. Then they cast off and sailed from the harbor, back to their beach and bay.

Morgan took the monofilament reels ashore and went into the jungle. Fifty yards in he began setting the outer perimeter trip line, running it knee high through leaves and branches, forming an arc that ended at the beach. He set two shorter concentric trip lines ten yards apart, bringing all three together at one end and tying them to a tree. The far ends he gathered together and tied, pulling the trip lines taut before leading a single monofilament along the pier and onto his boat. Jill drew it through a porthole and tied it to a skillet balanced on a ledge.

Morgan came in carrying a coconut. Jill nodded and helped him arrange his other purchases. As light failed they had an evening drink on the seaward side of the deck. Then they went below to make dinner.

The next day the hunter came.

TWENTY-NINE

H<small>E</small> sat on a knoll in the jungle sixty yards from the wheel of the motor sailer, watching through field glasses, a large unshaven man in lightweight camouflage wearing an old Afrika Korps cap on his head. Beside him on its canvas case lay his rifle. Areas of bluing were worn away from the rub of travel, and light filtering down through the branches and lianas of the jungle roof glinted dully on its smooth perfection. It was a Mannlicher-Schoenauer .380 whose dented walnut stock had a cheek-piece and a high comb to lay the face in line with the Kahles 4-power scope.

He could see the crudely-built pier that led from the crescent beach to the deeper water where the *Pendragon* was moored and anchored fore and aft. He was not a seaman, but all that he saw suggested care and foresight and efficiency, qualities he prided in himself. There was laundry on a line and the way it lifted in the breeze told him what windage to correct for.

The rifle's magazine lay apart from the weapon and he looked down at it, seeing two of the 180-grain soft-nose bullets it contained. Yesterday morning the magazine had been full, but one of the cartridges had been expended on the Indian guide who led the jaguar-hunter into the jungle and told him where the white boat bobbed inshore. The guide's body was buried in a grave too deep for buzzards but shallow enough for access by jungle cats.

The hunter saw the inflated rubber boat tethered astern by a snubbing line. It rolled in a shallow swell exposing the blades of the outboard motor.

The young woman, he knew, was somewhere below in the cabin. Wrapped in a sheet, the man was sleeping on the far side of the deck. Breeze lifted a corner of the sheet, stirred the sleeping figure's hair.

The first shot, he decided, would bring the woman on the deck. The next shot would get her.

He slid the magazine in place, hand-fed a single cartridge into the chamber. The bolt closed with the smooth precision of oiled metals meeting. Now he raised the rifle and, in sitting position, elbow on left thigh, sighted through the scope until the sheeted body was in its field. The head was too small to target. Crosshairs found the middle spine.

Sweat dribbled down his face, salting his eyes, stinging raw mosquito bites. He lowered the rifle to wipe them clear, then raised it and sighted carefully again.

The trigger-pull was smooth. The rifle bucked and its muzzle-roar reverberated through the jungle.

The slug slammed into the sheeted form, shoving it slightly. He waited for blood to stain the sheet, ready to fire again, but the form lay motionless.

Suddenly something flicked over his head, looped around his throat, cut deeply in. Against his spine a powerful knee bowed his body forward. Dropping the rifle, he tried to twist sideways as his fingers clawed the wire garrote, nails digging into his own flesh while the savage strand sank deeper. His legs thrashed, torso lurching from side to side as colors flooded his vision. Blood-red, gray. His hands tried to grip the sawing wire behind his head, but strength was fading. His head swiveled to one side and his bulging eyes rolled upward.

The last thing he saw was the face of his enemy.

From behind, Morgan sustained his pull on the wooden handles of the biting wire. After the body was completely slack Morgan released the garrote and tossed it away. The body toppled over and a fecal stench arose.

Morgan did not need to remove the hunter's cap to recognize Broom Ten Eyck's stubbled, pockmarked face. Blood oozed from the dead man's lacerated throat.

"We were the finalists, Broom," he said, "the last contenders. And now there's only me."

Morgan got out the hunter's sheath knife and carried it into the jungle, slashing the monofilament triplines. Ten Eyck had passed the outer one without tripping the alarm, but the second line, snagged, lay slack. An hour after dawn the skillet had been jerked down. Its clatter woke them and Morgan slipped silently over the boat's far side, swimming underwater to the cover of branches that overhung the shore.

From there he had entered the jungle and trailed the moving man.

Morgan shoved Ten Eyck's rifle into dense undergrowth and hurried down to the beach. From the end of the pier he hailed Jill, who came on deck, pistol in hand. "Is he . . .?" she called, and he nodded. "Start getting our things together."

When he reached the cabin she hugged him tightly. "Ten Eyck?" she whispered.

"Himself. Thank God for the warning."

"I was so afraid he'd hear you, David."

"He was too intent on the boat, on killing me. He had a marksman's skills, but not a hunter's instincts."

Jill cracked eggs into a skillet and Morgan went up on deck. He unsheeted the bunched pillows that formed the simulated figure. Ten Eyck's target. A coconut fringed with boar hair rolled away. There was a gouge in the deck where the rifle bullet had entered. Morgan carried the pillows below for further use.

After breakfast they loaded the Zodiac with canned food, water, and weapons. Before starting the outboard, Jill said, "I hate sacrificing our boat."

"There isn't any choice. They have to think us dead."

"I know, but *Pendragon*'s meant so much to me."

Morgan untied the snubbing line. "I'll join you behind the point, so stay there. This won't be pleasant."

Nodding, she started the engine and steered away. Morgan went back to the knoll where Ten Eyck's body lay. Already insects were gathering on throat and eyes. Small lizards scurried away. The sight of the corpse filled him with revulsion, but he dragged it down to the beach, along the pier, and onto the deck. Then he returned and cleared the site where Broom Ten Eyck had waited. There must be nothing inconsistent with the scene he was setting below.

With a knife he cut off Ten Eyck's clothing and boots, leaving only the soiled undershorts. Morgan worked as quickly as he could.

He secured a scuba tank to the naked back, adjusting shoulder straps for proper fit, then drew a heavy weight belt around the dead man's hips. After fitting a face mask around Ten Eyck's head, Morgan dragged the body to the gunwale and levered it over the side. Turning in the water, it sank, regulator and pressure gauge hoses twisting like wild tendrils.

For the rest of his life, he brooded, water would signify death:

Donnie and the Suckhole; Peyton James, the pond. And now Ten Eyck consigned to the sea.

The surface calmed and Morgan could see the body below. It lay face down on the sand, bright yellow air tank clearly visible.

But something was lacking.

He reviewed the scene, then tossed a pair of black flippers over the side. They sank, too, coming to rest not far from the body. Current moved Ten Eyck's hair, the loose ends of his webbed strapping. Small fish were gathering around the neck. By nightfall, crabs and eels would have made progress on the body. After the current or a scavenger carried away the skull with its identifying teeth no one would be able to say the skeletal leavings were not from the body of David Morgan.

And that was his hope. Ten Eyck's death would enable him to live. He tossed the hunter's boots and clothing into the cabin, turned on the stove's butane jets without lighting them, then set one of the pillows afire. He glanced around the cabin a final time, went up the companionway, and closed the cabin doors. Gas would fill the cabin and find the licking flames.

Morgan left the boat and walked down to the beach, following the shoreline around to where Jill was waiting.

He waded out and got into the Zodiac. When the explosion came it was deafening as a bomb at close range.

Steering past the mouth of the bay, he saw the burning vessel nearly torn apart, listing and straining against its mooring lines, sheets of flame climbing the masts, spurting through dark diesel smoke that blotted out the superstructure. Morgan watched the bow go down, and turned toward open sea.

Windblown spray flecked their faces. Waves broken by the boat's blunt bow drenched and cleansed their bodies. Morning sun warmed them as the boat bore south.

In a few hours they would reach a village down the coast, and there begin their journey to another, perhaps safer, place.

THE END